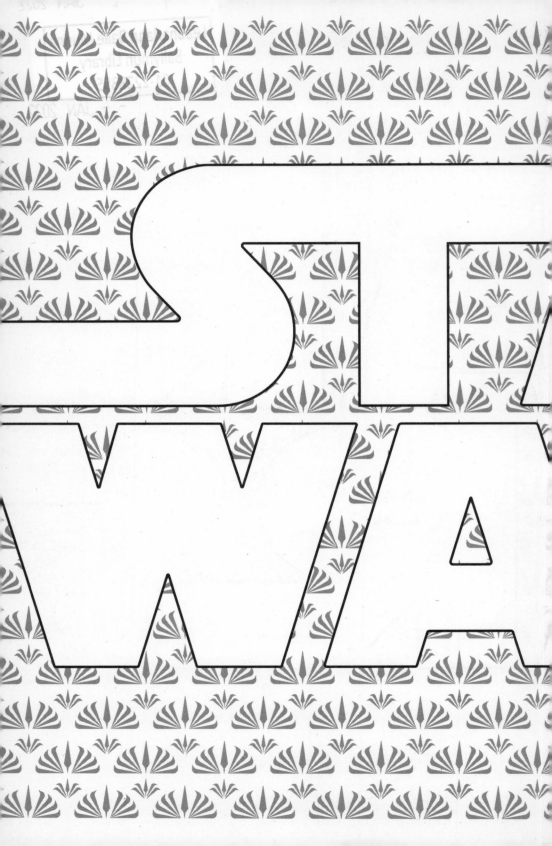

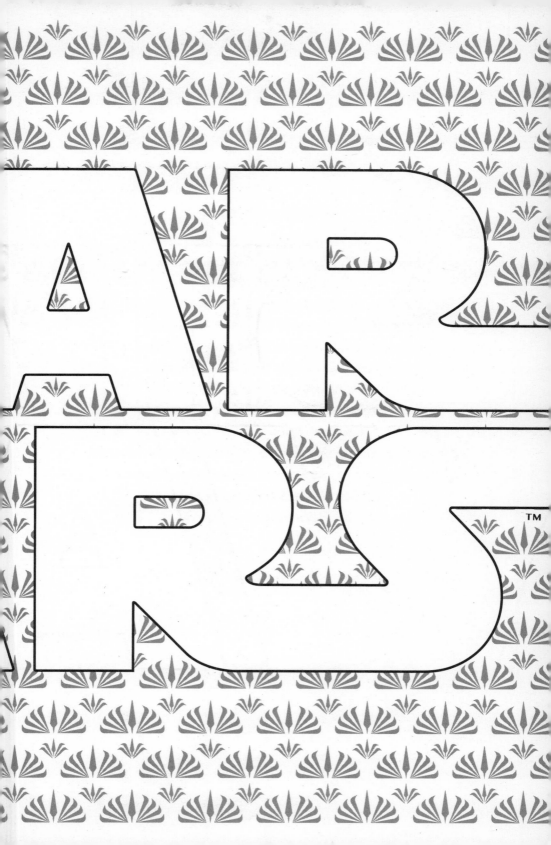

BY CAVAN SCOTT

Star Wars: The High Republic: The Rising Storm
Star Wars: The High Republic: The Great Jedi Rescue
Star Wars: Dooku: Jedi Lost
Star Wars: Life Day Treasury (with George Mann)
Star Wars: Adventures in Wild Space—The Escape
Star Wars: Adventures in Wild Space—The Snare
Star Wars: Adventures in Wild Space—The Heist
Star Wars: Adventures in Wild Space—The Cold
Star Wars: Choose Your Destiny—A Han & Chewie Adventure
Star Wars: Choose Your Destiny—A Luke & Leia Adventure
Star Wars: Choose Your Destiny—An Obi-Wan & Anakin Adventure
Star Wars: Choose Your Destiny—A Poe & Finn Adventure
Sherlock Holmes: The Patchwork Devil
Sherlock Holmes: Cry of the Innocents

THE RISING STORM

THE RISING STORM

Cavan Scott

1 3 5 7 9 10 8 6 4 2

Del Rey
20 Vauxhall Bridge Road
London SW1V 2SA

Del Rey is part of the Penguin Random House group of companies whose
addresses can be found at global.penguinrandomhouse.com.

Penguin
Random House
UK

First published in the United States by Penguin Random House in 2021
This edition published in the UK by Del Rey in 2021

www.penguin.co.uk

A CIP catalogue record for this book is available from the British Library.

Hardback ISBN 9781529101898
Trade paperback ISBN 9781529101904

Printed and bound in Great Britain by Clays Ltd, Elcograf S.p.A.

The authorised representative in the EEA is Penguin Random House Ireland,
Morrison Chambers, 32 Nassau Street, Dublin D02 YH68

Penguin Random House is committed to a sustainable future
for our business, our readers and our planet. This book is made
from Forest Stewardship Council® certified paper.

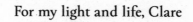

For my light and life, Clare

THE STAR WARS NOVELS TIMELINE

THE HIGH REPUBLIC

Light of the Jedi
The Rising Storm

Dooku: Jedi Lost
Master and Apprentice

I THE PHANTOM MENACE

II ATTACK OF THE CLONES

Thrawn Ascendancy: Chaos Rising
Thrawn Ascendancy: Greater Good
Dark Disciple: A Clone Wars Novel

III REVENGE OF THE SITH

Catalyst: A Rogue One Novel
Lords of the Sith
Tarkin

SOLO

Thrawn
A New Dawn: A Rebels Novel
Thrawn: Alliances
Thrawn: Treason

ROGUE ONE

IV A NEW HOPE

Battlefront II: Inferno Squad
Heir to the Jedi
Doctor Aphra
Battlefront: Twilight Company

V THE EMPIRE STRIKES BACK

VI RETURN OF THE JEDI

The Alphabet Squadron Trilogy
The Aftermath Trilogy
Last Shot

Bloodline
Phasma
Canto Bight

VII THE FORCE AWAKENS

VIII THE LAST JEDI

Resistance Reborn
Galaxy's Edge: Black Spire

IX THE RISE OF SKYWALKER

A long time ago, in a galaxy far, far away. . . .

THE RISING STORM

The galaxy celebrates. With the dark days of the hyperspace disaster behind them, Chancellor Lina Soh pushes ahead with the latest of her GREAT WORKS. The Republic Fair will be her finest hour, a celebration of peace, unity, and hope on the frontier world of Valo.

But an insatiable horror appears on the horizon. One by one, planets fall as the carnivorous DRENGIR consume all life in their path. As Jedi Master AVAR KRISS leads the battle against this terror, Nihil forces gather in secret for the next stage of MARCHION RO's diabolical plan.

Only the noble JEDI KNIGHTS stand in Ro's way, but even the protectors of light and life are not prepared for the terrible darkness that lies ahead. . . .

Prologue

Ashla, moon of Tython

The screams had never left Elzar Mann. Many months had passed since Starlight Beacon's dedication ceremony, since he had stood alongside his fellow Jedi. Since he had stood alongside Avar Kriss.

The eyes of the galaxy had been upon them in their temple finery, that damned collar itching as he'd listened to the speeches and platitudes, first from Chancellor Lina Soh, leader of the Galactic Republic, and then from Avar. *His* Avar. The Hero of Hetzal.

The Beacon was their promise to the galaxy, Avar had said. It was their covenant. He could still hear her words.

Whenever you feel alone . . . whenever darkness closes in . . . know that the Force is with you. Know that we *are with you . . . For light and life.*

For light and life.

But that hadn't stopped the darkness from closing in later that day. A wave of pain and suffering, a vision of the future too terrible to comprehend. He had staggered, grabbing hold of a rail, blood gushing from his nose as the pressure in his head threatened to split his skull in two.

What he had seen had haunted him ever since. It had consumed him.

Jedi dying one by one, picked off by a twisting, unfathomable cloud. Stellan. Avar. Everyone he had ever known in the past and everyone he would meet in days to come. Faces both familiar and strange torn apart.

And the screams.

The screams were the worst.

He had made it through the rest of the evening in a daze, going through the motions, not quite present, the echo of what he had seen . . . what he had heard . . . burned onto his mind's eye. There had been mistakes, a few too many glasses of Kattadan rosé at the reception, Avar asking for that dance she'd mentioned, Elzar leaning in a little too eagerly, a little too publicly.

He could still feel her hand on his chest, pushing him back.

"El. What are you doing?"

They had argued, privately, his head still spinning.

"We're not Padawans anymore."

It had been months since he saw her again, and when he did, the atmosphere was as frosty as a dawn on Vandor. Avar had changed toward him. She was more distant. Preoccupied with her new duties as marshal of Starlight Beacon.

Or maybe he was the one who was preoccupied. Elzar had meditated on the vision day and night since the dedication. He should have gone to Avar, to apologize and ask for her guidance, or if not her, then Stellan Gios, his oldest friend, but Stellan had duties of his own. He was a Council member now, responsible for guiding the Order as a whole. He would not have time. Besides, asking for help was hardly Elzar's style. Elzar Mann was the one who solved problems, not posed them. He found solutions. Answers. New ways of getting the job done. So, Elzar did what he had always done: He tried to solve the problem alone.

First he had consulted the Archives in the Great Temple, poring over countless textfiles and holocrons in the collection, even going so far as attempting to decipher the mysteries of the Ga'Garen Codex, the ancient grimoire whose text had confounded linguists for thousands of years.

Even then, sitting in the Archives, under the watchful gaze of the statues of the Lost, Elzar had heard the screams at the back of his mind, seen the faces of the slain in every reflective surface or passing Padawan.

The Codex had brought him here, to Ashla, Tython's primary moon. The ancients had called this stretch of land the Isle of Seclusion, which was exactly what he needed if he was ever going to fully understand what he had seen. He needed solitude; focus. The last straw had been receiving a message from Stellan's old Master, the esteemed Rana Kant, congratulating him on his elevation to Jedi Master. Furthermore, the Council had a posting for him; he was to be marshal of the Jedi outpost on Valo on the edge of the Rseik sector.

Him? A marshal? How could they be so blind? Couldn't they see he wasn't ready? Couldn't they see how troubled he was?

Elzar walked toward the ocean, feeling the warm sand beneath his feet, discarding his outer robes as he approached the water. Yes, this was better. This was where he would finally see the truth. Where he would finally understand. He didn't stop at the shore but strode out purposefully into the waves. Up to his knees. Up to his waist. Soon he was swimming out to sea, stopping only when he could no longer see land. He spun slowly, treading water, surrounded only by the sea and the Force itself.

It was time.

Elzar took a deep breath and pushed himself down beneath the waves, eyes closed, water rushing into his ears, blocking every other sound.

Show me.

Guide *me.*

Give me the answers I seek.

There was nothing. No revelation. No response.

He kicked back up, drawing air into his lungs before plunging back down again.

I am here.

I want to learn.

I need to understand.

Nothing changed.

Where were the answers he'd been promised? Where was the understanding?

He repeated the ritual, breaking for air, plunging back down, letting the ocean swallow him whole. Again, and again, and . . .

It was like hitting an air pocket. All at once he wasn't sinking, he was running, his fellow Jedi at his side as nightmares snapped at their heels. They weren't in water, but in fog. Thick. Acrid. Impenetrable. Nothing made sense. Not the chaos, not the panic.

Not the fear.

He opened his mouth to cry out, seawater rushing in from far away, from a different world, from a different time.

What is this?

Where is this?

Speak to me!

And the Force spoke with such strength that Elzar was thrown into a spin, images flashing past his stinging eyes like purple lightning.

Avar.

Stellan.

A Tholothian . . . Indeera Stokes? No, one of her tendrils was missing, an unfamiliar face contorted in rage.

Bones splintering.

Skin cracking.

Eyes clouded, no longer able to see.

And the screams. The screams were louder than ever. Harsher than ever. And his scream was loudest of all.

Where?

Where?

WHERE?

Elzar's shoulders heaved, seawater spluttering from his lungs. He was back on Ashla's shore, salt drying on his skin, baked by the burning sun. He looked around, eyes still blurry, trying to focus on the golden sands that stretched out to either side of him, wingmaws circling in the sky above, ready to pick the flesh from his bones. But he wasn't dead yet. None of them were.

He pushed himself up and stumbled back toward his Vector, gathering his robes as he went. He needed to get off Ashla. Needed to leave the Core. The Force had spoken. It had already answered his question, if only he had listened.

One name, a planet, where he would finally be able to put things right.

Valo.

Chapter One

The Rystan Badlands

A comet plowed into the ice field, setting off a devastating chain reaction. Asteroids and space rocks bounced off one another like billiard balls. The only difference here was that most of the balls weighed millions of tons and could crush a ship like an egg. Those that weren't completely obliterated by the impacts were reduced to razor-sharp shards that only added to the wave of destruction.

No spacer entered the Rystan Badlands lightly. The ice field was filled with the twisted wreckage of cruisers that had attempted to run the gauntlet of colliding planetoids and failed. On a good day it was a dangerous, idiotic endeavor. On a bad day it was suicide.

Today was a *very* bad day.

The *Squall Spider* bucked as it weaved through the spinning rocks. The craft was small, barely larger than a shuttle, but it was fast and as maneuverable as any of the Jedi's famed Vectors. In fact, anyone watching the strange arachnid-like craft could have been forgiven in thinking that a Jedi sat at the controls. Who else could have negotiated the ever-shifting starscape, weaving left and then right to avoid being pulverized by giant balls of ice? But the being in the pilot's seat couldn't have been further from a Jedi. The Jedi were the defenders of life and light the galaxy over. They lived for others, never for themselves, maintaining peace and harmony wherever they roamed. In short, they were heroes.

Udi Dis, on the other hand, had been born a Talortai but now only identified as a Nihil. As broad as he was tall, the avian had dedicated his life to piracy and plunder, taking what he wanted and decimating whatever was left. It wasn't a noble life, but it was the only one he knew, and it had given him a place in the universe that had repeatedly spat in his face.

The only thing Dis had in common with the Jedi was his connection to the Force. Many Talortai were sensitive to the energy field that bound the universe together, but few of his species ever made use of it, the cowards. They said it wasn't their right, that to do so was somehow immoral. Dis had never understood why. If you were lucky enough to have abilities, shouldn't you use them, hone them to gain an advantage over those who didn't? This was why the majority of Talortai were doomed to remain where they were, scratching out a meager existence on Talor while he was out here in the stars. Sure, he had been let down many times, sometimes by others, most often by himself, but the Force had never betrayed him, not once. Life would have been better if he hadn't gotten himself addicted to reedug, but for now he was sober and had never felt so alive.

Dis clutched the controls with clawed hands, his muscled arms bunching as he slewed the *Spider* sharply to starboard, skillfully avoiding the debris that, with a lesser pilot at the helm, would have killed everyone on board. But Dis knew the badlands like the back of his feathered hand, even though he had never flown them before. All Talortai had an innate sense of direction, feeling the vibrations of the cosmos in their bones, but Dis's navigational skills were off the chart. Thanks to his talents, he could feel the location of every asteroid in the field. He didn't need maps or even a navidroid. All he needed was the Force.

Behind him, the door to the *Spider*'s cockpit slid open, stale air gushing from the planet-hopper's cramped corridors. Dis didn't turn to see who it was. There was no need. He heard the scrape of the boots on the deck plates, felt the swish of the cloak through the air, Dis's feathers ruffling in response to the presence of the man he had pledged to serve for the rest of his life.

Marchion Ro.

The Eye of the Nihil.

Had he been surprised when Ro approached him about this mission? Of course he had. He had no idea the Eye even knew his name, let alone what he could do in the pilot's seat. Dis had spent the last few years serving on the Cloudship of a saw-mouthed Crocin who went by the name of Scarspike, a thug who spent more time abusing his crew than planning raids. And it showed. Dis had killed Scarspike after a botched attack on Serenno's funeral moon. They had lost three Nihil that day, but Scarspike had lost more, Dis opening his scrawny throat with a slash of a wingblade. Dis had no idea if the Cloud's slaughter had first brought him to the Eye's attention. Maybe, maybe not. All Dis knew was that he suddenly found himself elevated beyond the Strikes and the Clouds and all the Nihil's ranks to join Ro's personal retinue. His aggrandizement didn't go unnoticed. The Nihil had a strict hierarchy. You started as a lowly Strike, working your way up to Cloud and eventually to Storm. The Nihil horde was organized into three Tempests, each commanded by a Tempest Runner. There was Pan Eyta, a towering Dowutin with ideas above his station, the cold and efficient Twi'lek Lourna Dee, and the latest appointment, a scheming Talpini known as Zeetar. It was fair to say that the Talpini's promotion had put Pan's squashed nose out of joint. Dis's sudden promotion had only rankled him further. Pan and Dis had almost come to blows, the Dowutin claiming that Ro was undermining the Nihil's Rule of Three. Unlike the Tempest Runners, the Eye was supposed to have no crew of his own. Yes, he had the casting vote when making plans, and yes, he provided the navigational Paths that the Nihil used to avoid Republic entanglement (well, most of the time, at least). Dis suspected that if it weren't for the Paths, Pan would have sent Ro spinning out of an air lock long ago, but the navigational aids were too valuable. They gave the Nihil the edge, so Eyta's concerns fell on deaf ears. Dis was welcomed aboard Ro's vast flagship, the *Gaze Electric,* which was largely maintained by a crew of silent droids, its many chambers empty, like a palace with no occupants. It was here, in Ro's inner sanctum, that Dis had learned they were heading to Rystan on a private mission—not that they could have taken the *Gaze,* of course. The ship rarely left the Nihil's base on Grizal, and even then split itself into a smaller secondary craft that left the bulk of the *Gaze* behind, but even that would be too cumbersome to make it through the ice field in one piece. They needed something smaller. They needed the *Squall Spider.*

"How long until we clear the badlands?" Ro asked, resting a gauntleted palm on the back of Dis's seat.

"Just a few minutes, my . . ."

Dis swiveled in his chair to face his leader. "I still don't know what I should call you. My Eye? *Sir?*"

Ro's thin lips curled at the obvious distaste in Dis's voice, his dark eyes glinting in the red light that streamed in through the viewport.

"You can call me . . . Marchion."

Dis's chest swelled. He had never been one for the chain of command, which was probably why he had stayed a Strike for so long; that and the fact he'd spent most of the last decade in a reedug stupor. But now look at him, on first-name terms with Ro himself. No one called the Eye Marchion, not even Pan.

"I still think it would've been easier to use a Path," Dis said, finally bringing the *Spider* out of the ice field to slingshot around Rystan's weak star.

Ro walked over to the vacant gunner's station to recover his mask, which had remained on the console ever since they had left the Great Hall.

"But then I wouldn't have seen a master at work," the Eye replied, wiping the mask's frosted visor with his sleeve. "You're every bit as impressive as your heritage suggested you would be, especially now that you're free from your . . . affliction."

Yeah, he was free all right. Ro had made Dis throw what little remained of his stash into a trash compactor back on board the *Gaze*. His mind was clear for the first time in years, his connection to the Force stronger than ever. There was no way he could have made it through the ice field when he was on reed. He owed Ro so much.

"And to think we had a Force-user in our midst all these years . . ." Ro continued, checking the filters of his mask. "Scarspike was a fool. I'm glad he's dead."

You're not the only one, Dis thought, but kept the thought to himself as the *Spider* dropped into Rystan's thin atmosphere.

"Have you ever been to a tidally locked world?" Ro asked.

Dis shook his head.

"They're fascinating," the Eye told him. "One face constantly angled toward the sun, its surface little more than charred desert."

"While the other's a frozen wilderness," Dis said, the blasted terrain not inspiring much confidence. "So where do we land?"

Ro pointed at a band of barely habitable land that ran between the two extremes. "There."

"Is there a spaceport?"

"Not exactly."

Ro directed them to a patch of barren ground, clumps of rollweed tumbling across the wasteland.

"Are you *sure* this is the place?" Dis asked as the landing gear deployed. "There's nothing here."

Ro merely smiled as he slipped his mask over his head. "Oh, you'll be surprised . . ."

Chapter Two

The Cyclor Shipyards

Not long ago, Padawan Bell Zettifar would have been excited by the sight that stretched out beneath him. He was standing on an observation platform in the largest hangar he had ever experienced, just part of the vast shipyards that orbited Cyclor, a relatively small green-and-brown planet in the Mid Rim. Below, gleaming bright in the hangar's floodlights, was the vision in polished durasteel known as the *Innovator.* The starship, now hours from launch, was a technological marvel. Over 300 meters long and bristling with the latest scientific and medical equipment, the *Innovator* was quite simply the most sophisticated research vessel ever built, a fact its designer—the famed Aqualish engineer Vam Targes—had told Bell himself when he had arrived at the shipyards.

"It runs on a network of no fewer than forty-two intellex-grade droid processors, don't you know?" Targes had informed him as they strode through the ship's vast operations center on a whirlwind tour, the engineer's vocoder whirring excitedly as it translated Vam's native Aqualish to Basic.

"That's very . . . impressive," Bell had offered, only to be told in no uncertain terms that it was considerably more than that. It was outstanding!

"The entire network is supported by a multi-motion framework of my own design, one that rivals the Jedi Archives on Coruscant, if I do say so myself."

Bell didn't know if that was true, but he hadn't wanted to contradict the engineer. This was Vam's moment, after all, or rather it would be when the *Innovator* arrived on Valo in a couple of days. The ship was to be a showpiece at the upcoming Republic Fair, the latest of Chancellor Lina Soh's Great Works. Soon millions of festival-goers would be marveling at Targes's achievement, and if they were anything like Bell, they would be dazzled. The *Innovator* boasted state-of-the-art cybernetic workshops alongside multiple bioengineering labs, analysis stations, research facilities, and a medical library second only to the Docha Institute on Dunnak.

But as extraordinary as the craft undoubtedly was, it was still nothing compared with the beings who had constructed the ship rivet by rivet. The Cyclorrians were a wonder, unlike anything Bell had seen before. Insectoid in nature, they stood about a meter in height with large bulbous heads dominated by a pair of large compound eyes, much like the heat-flies that had buzzed through the halls of the Jedi outpost on Elphrona where Bell had received most of his training. He watched as they swarmed across the glistening hull, completing final checks, each Cyclorrian working in unison with their teammates without seeming to utter a single word. It was incredible. Each seemed to know exactly what job needed doing instinctively, none of them getting under one another's feet, each perfectly complementing the next. And the enthusiasm for their work was infectious. In the twenty-four hours since he had arrived, Bell hadn't seen a single Cyclorrian complain, despite Targes's reputation as a strict taskmaster. The insectoids just kept on working, hour after hour, antennae twitching happily as they buzzed from one task to the next. You couldn't help but smile in their presence. It was exactly what Bell needed, especially now.

Beside him, Ember stirred. The charhound had been sitting patiently at his feet, Bell's constant companion since they had left Elphrona. The dog had started life as a stray that had been adopted by the Elphronian Jedi, becoming something of a mascot at first and a loyal friend ever since. When Bell had left Elphrona, Ember had simply hopped into his Vector, her intention of staying by his side clear. She had been there ever since, his guardian and confidante. Now she was on her feet, looking expectantly at the door of the observation platform as it swished open to allow Indeera Stokes entry. The aging Jedi laughed as Ember bounded over, jumping up onto the Tholothian's legs to be rewarded by a tickle beneath the orange-flecked chin.

"Yes, yes," Indeera said. "I'm pleased to see you, too. Now down you get. That's it. Good girl. Good girl."

Ember obeyed, trotting back over to Bell where he had remained at the edge of the platform. Bell looked down at her and smiled, the charhound's excited tail thwacking against his boots.

"I'm sure she likes you more than she does me," he commented as Indeera joined him.

"I think we both know that's a lie," she said, joining him to gaze down at the majestic craft below. She leaned against the railing, shaking her head at the spectacle of the Cyclorrians hard at work. "Stars above, it takes your breath away, doesn't it?"

"Indeed it does, Master. The *Innovator* is as impressive as those who constructed it."

As always, Bell felt a pang as he addressed Indeera by her title. It was true, the Tholothian was his teacher now, having agreed to take on his training after his previous Master, Loden Greatstorm, had been lost defending settlers against the Nihil nearly a year ago. Their last conversation played regularly through his mind, Loden at the controls of his Vector.

"I'm not your Master anymore, Bell. You're a Jedi Knight."
"Not until the Council declares it, and I want you there when it happens."

Now that would never be. Loden had told him that he would see Bell soon and had never come back from the attack. No one knew what had happened when Loden had abandoned his Vector . . . *their* Vector . . . to save the Blythe family from the Nihil. The Vector had been reduced to atoms by a Nihil cannon, and Loden, well, he was just gone. Indeera constantly reminded Bell that Loden's final wishes had been for his Padawan to be Knighted, but Bell knew he wasn't ready. How could he be, when he felt so empty inside, like something was missing?

"Bell?"

He swallowed, suddenly aware that Indeera was studying him. His new teacher, no matter how weird that felt. And it shouldn't. He'd known her for years, even fought by her side, and respected her more than any Jedi alive, which, of course, was the problem. Loden Greatstorm wasn't coming back, that much had become blatantly clear, but no matter how much Bell admired Indeera, she could never replace the noble Twi'lek.

Bell offered a weak smile. "I was just thinking about how excited the crowd will be at the Republic Fair, seeing the *Innovator* for the first time."

"They will. And what about you?"

"What about me?"

"Are you looking forward to Valo?"

He shifted uncomfortably, careful not to kick Ember who was nuzzling against his legs, her pelt warm through his synthleather boots. "It will be good to see Mikkel and Nib. And Burry, too, of course." That was all true. He'd come to think of all three as friends, especially the Wookiee Burryaga, whom he had gotten to know after serving together at Hetzal.

"Of course," Indeera parroted, still regarding him with those warm eyes. "There will be much to experience together." She looked back at the ship. "Loden would have loved it. He would have loved this."

A lump formed in Bell's throat as Indeera continued. "I can imagine him standing here with us, watching the Cyclorrians work, appreciating their skill."

Bell's voice cracked as he tried to control his emotions. "And what do you think he would say? If he were here?"

The Tholothian pursed her lips. "I think he would compliment you on the shine of your holster buckle, tell you to smile more often, and point out that if you're *ever* going to master a lateral roll you're going to have to log at least two more hours a day in your Vector."

A grin broke out on Bell's face, despite himself. The last part of the sentence was pure Indeera, who always seemed happier in the sky than on her feet.

"He would also remind you how a Jedi faces the death of those they love," she continued, and Bell's smile immediately dropped away. "Because Jedi *can* love, Bell. We're not droids, nor should we ever be. We are living creatures rich in the Force, with everything that brings. Joy, affection, and, yes, grief. Experiencing such emotions is part of life. It is light."

"But—"

"But while we experience such emotions, we should never let them rule us. A Jedi is the master of their emotions, never a slave. You miss what you might have shared with Loden if he were here. That is natural. I miss him, too. And so we acknowledge that hurt. We understand it, even embrace it, but eventually . . ."

"We let it go," Bell said, looking back at the *Innovator* so Indeera couldn't see the tears she must have known were in his eyes.

The Tholothian reached out, placing a comforting hand on Bell's forearm. "I didn't say it was easy. Just like a lateral roll."

That made him smile again, as did the slight squeeze she gave him before turning back toward the ship. "Besides, no one is ever really gone. No matter what happens, Loden will be with you, now and forever. He is a part of all of us now."

Again the tears pricked his eyes. "Through the Force."

"Through the Force," she agreed. "You believe that, don't you?"

He nodded, hoping that she was fooled while knowing full well that she wasn't. "Yes. Of course I do."

"I'm glad to hear it," she said, not sounding convinced. "Now, unless there's anything else . . ."

"We should get off this platform and actually do something with the day," he said, keen to bring the conversation to an end.

Indeera's comlink beeped before she could respond.

"Maybe the Force agrees with you, my not-so-young Padawan." Indeera fished the comlink from beneath her tan-colored jacket and activated the channel.

"Stokes here."

"This is Stellan Gios," a voice crackled over the link, the Jedi Master's usually rich tones rendered tinny by the vast distance between them. While Starlight Beacon had improved communications on the frontier, the comm network was still stretched to breaking point, even here in the Mid Rim. Chancellor Soh had promised a complete line of Beacons stretching from the Core to the farthest reaches of the Republic, but until that pledge became a reality, they would have to cope with bouts of static that frequently drowned out communications.

"Apologies, but can you repeat that?" Indeera was forced to say as the rest of Master Gios's greeting distorted beyond recognition.

"Of course," he complied. "I was just checking on your progress for my report to the Council. Will the *Innovator* be ready to launch on time?"

"Ahead of schedule," Bell cut in, before blushing as he realized he had spoken when the question was directed at his Master. Indeera made a show of rolling her eyes, although the smile on her lips told him he wasn't in trouble. For all her wisdom, she wasn't one to stand on ceremony.

"I'm glad to hear it . . . Padawan Zettifar, isn't it?"

Bell nodded even though Stellan couldn't see him. "Yes, Master Gios. The Cyclorrians are a marvel, as is the *Innovator.*"

"Then I look forward to seeing it for myself, and to finally meeting you, of course. Nib Assek has been singing your praises."

Bell's blush deepened. "She is with you?"

"On our way to Valo, yes. She's looking forward to seeing you again."

"She is too kind," he stammered, not knowing what to do with himself.

"And my Padawan is too modest, even for a Jedi," Indeera cut in. "The Force has blessed him, as you will see for yourself, old friend."

Bell's eyebrows shot up. He had no idea that Indeera knew Gios, let alone that they were as close as her tone suggested.

"I don't doubt it," Stellan said. "Until Valo, then. I hear the pickled cushnip is to die for."

"Better than we ate on Theros Major? I'll be the judge of that."

Stellan chuckled on the other end of the line. "Why am I not surprised? Now, if you'll excuse me, I have an appointment with a cam droid."

It was Indeera's turn to laugh. "Well, if you will get yourself promoted to the High Council . . . People will be asking for your autograph next."

"I'll send them your way instead. Gios out."

"What's he like?" Bell asked as Stokes slipped the comlink back beneath her soft leather jacket.

"Stellan? One of the finest Jedi I've ever known. We met on Caragon-Viner, long before I went to Elphrona. He's younger than me, of course, but—"

Indeera paused, her white tendrils shifting slightly on her shoulders. Bell didn't have to ask why. He had felt it, too, a cooling in the Force, its flame dimming just for a moment, before burning brighter than before.

"Something's wrong," he stated simply, Ember jumping up as the atmosphere between the two Jedi shifted, her hackles raised.

"That's an understatement," Indeera agreed, already making for the platform's doors. "Inform the *Innovator* we're on our way."

Chapter Three

Safrifa

Will you help us?

Ty Yorrick had lost count of the times she had heard those words, usually delivered with a side order of pleading eyes and, more often than not, missing limbs. You had to be desperate to approach someone like Ty.

The swamp farmers of Safrifa were desperate.

They had found her repairing her ship on the edge of the bog fields, preparing to leave after a successful extraction operation where she had liberated the son of the local marsh-lord from a rival clan. There had been blood and screaming. Always blood and screaming. Some of the gore still caked her armor while the screams would linger when she finally fell into her cot that evening, even after taking keekon root to help her sleep. In all honesty she didn't mind the screams. They had been her companion for the best part of a decade, the one constant in her ever-changing life.

The novian ore she had received for the kid's safe return would come in handy. Her ship needed parts, and parts meant money. She knew an armorer on Keldooine who would take the novian off her hands, smelting it down to forge saw blades. Maybe she'd buy one herself. Less money for the ship, but her arsenal had been depleted after that botched job on Alzoc III. Kriffing Hoopaloo, stealing half her stash. Other mercs would have tracked down the traitorous parrot and ripped the smarmy beak clear from his face, but Ty wasn't any other merc. Bad things happened and you dealt with it. There was no point wasting time or effort on battles you didn't need to have, especially if no one was paying you.

She had sensed the swamp farmers long before she heard them slosh through the bog. Sensed and assessed. They were no threat to merc or beast. No threat to anyone. Most Safrifans were scrawny little creatures with skin the color of stagnant water and hair that hung like pondweed in front of large oval eyes. They were industrious, though. Ingenious, too. Ty had trudged through one of their floating beds— a long, narrow plot of thick soil raised from the marshwater by mud and decaying vegetation to stop the roots of their kru-kru crops becoming waterlogged. The farm had stretched on for kilometers, each plot framed by willow trestles and surrounded by a network of narrow canals. At first glance, you would be forgiven for thinking that nothing could be grown here, but the Safrifans had proved otherwise. Resourceful and resilient. Ty liked that. Admired it even. And now they were here, waiting patiently to speak with her. It could only mean one thing.

"Nice ship," the warbling voice commented in broken Basic. "What it name?"

"Doesn't have one," Ty replied in their native tongue, not turning around from her work. The damn stabilizer was hanging on by a thread.

"You speak our language?" the farmer asked, surprised.

"Enough to get by." She was lucky like that. It had always been the same. Ty picked up most languages quickly, a useful talent in her profession. Sometimes she let people know, at other times she kept quiet and listened. She had nothing to fear from these two, even as they dithered behind her, not knowing what to say now that their small talk had failed. She hadn't been lying, though. Her ship, a battered YT-750 freighter, didn't have a name, only a registry number logged in the Republic records. Several numbers actually, depending on the job or employer. She didn't see the point of giving anything a name—ship, weapon, or even the two droids that assisted her on missions, a sarcastic admin unit and an admittedly useful astromech. Like the ship, they were tools, nothing more. Why form attachments to something that could never be attached to you? Maybe it was a throwback to her training. Maybe not. Ty just thought it was common sense.

"What do you want?" She needed this conversation over. She had places to go, parts to buy.

"We have novian. Not much. But enough."

"Enough for what?"

Instead of answering, the farmers offered a simple statement: "It is killing our children."

Ty stopped working, the all-kit tool dropping down from the exposed stabilizer core.

"What is?" she asked, an air of resignation in her voice.

"A monster. A bad one."

Was there any other kind?

"How long has it been happening?"

"Three weeks. We have laid traps but it smashed them. It wrecks our plots, ruins the crops."

"How many?"

"Crops?"

"How many children?"

"Does it matter?"

Correct answer.

Finally she turned, taking in the pathetic sight in front of her. They were little more than walking skeletons, skin stretched over prominent bones. The taller of the two, relatively speaking, lifted a leather pouch. "We have novian," he repeated, his companion hunched behind him, leaning heavily on a staff.

Not much novian if the size of the bag was anything to go by. Hardly worth her time.

It is killing our children.

"Where?"

"In the Sorcan Swamp, three days' hike from here. One, if you have a skimmer."

"Do you have a skimmer?"

"No."

He looked at her and she looked at him. His companion looked at the marshwater. Exhausted. Without hope or expectation.

Back in the day, she would have used a set of Verazeen stones to make the decision, telling herself that she was leaving things to chance. To the will of the universe. One side of the stones was etched with moon symbols, the other suns. The process was simple enough. Throw them at the ground, decide whether you were banking on more suns or moons, and let fate guide your way. She'd been taking more of an active role recently, choosing her own path instead of relying on the stones, and right now she knew that the job wasn't worth it. She should get back in the ship and blast off for Keldooine. It was the sensible thing to do. Logical, even.

He needed to say the words.

"Will you help us?"

And there they were.

Chapter Four

Rystan

Cold had never worried Udi Dis. He had never experienced it growing up, but that had been so long ago now, the tropics of Talor little more than a distant memory. There had been so many worlds since then, so many routes plotted and sold. His father would have been ashamed of the life his son had led, but what else was new. None of this stopped Dis's breath catching as the *Spider*'s ramp thudded down on the dusty ground. The cold was intense even here in Rystan's habitable band, but Dis couldn't let it show. He wouldn't. He strode down the ramp wearing a fur-lined cloak and mask to protect his eyes from the wind, the metal clattering beneath his clawed feet, ignoring the chill that sliced through his feathers like a vibroknife.

"There he is," croaked a voice as Ro himself exited the craft. Dis dropped into a defensive position, his grip on his wingblades tightening, the curved weapons the only possession he still had from home. A bundle of furs was rushing toward them, leading a trio of large creatures that looked like escapees from a bio-splicer's nightmare, a hideous mix that was part blurrg and part bantha. Not for the first time, Dis wished his affinity for the Force, the kinesthesia that allowed him to navigate the stars with such precision, extended to the Jedi's fabled premonition, a sense of danger before it struck. For all he knew, those thick pelts hid a disintegrator or laser-flail.

He flinched as Ro's hand settled on his shoulder.

"At ease, soldier. That's our contact."

Soldier. It had been a long time since Dis had been a soldier. It had been a long time since Dis had been anything. Long before he found the Nihil.

Ro strode past him, stepping off the ramp as the newcomer threw her arms wide.

"Marchion, Marchion, Marchion," she wheezed with familial joy. "You have come back to us. Finally. You have returned to the Path."

"Kufa," Ro responded, but he made no attempt to return the embrace that the old woman so obviously desired. Instead she let her arms fall to her swaddled sides once more, content to grin at the man who had unleashed a reign of terror on the Outer Rim. "It is good to see you, Cousin."

Another surprise. Was this crone, with her leathery skin and toothless smile, a relative of the Eye himself? Dis knew little about Ro's past, save for the fact that he had inherited the title of Eye from his father, Asgar. Beyond that, no one knew much about Ro's lineage, or even his species with their slate-gray skin and pitch-black eyes. And yet there was something in the face of this woman—with its strange tattoos so similar to lightning bolts of the Nihil—that was familiar, even if Ro looked like he could snap her like a barium reed.

"We have missed you," the woman said, gazing up at the Eye. "When we received your message, the Elder barely believed it . . ." She trailed off, lifting a shaking finger to his mask. Ro allowed her to touch it, another first as far as Dis knew. "Although I would rather see your face. It's been so long."

Ro guided her hand back down, holding it warmly in his hands. "Later. When we are in the Shrine."

That, at least, seemed to placate her for the time. "Yes. Yes, the Shrine. Although the temperature will be worse, not better."

"I can well believe it."

"But it will be worth it . . . to look upon the Leveler. To feel its nullifying peace."

"As our ancestor did, long ago."

"As we were taught. All of us."

Tears shone in the old woman's dark eyes. Dis wondered if they would freeze.

"You have truly come back from the darkness."

Ro released her hand.

"You will take us, then?"

Kufa's gaze shifted to Dis, as if seeing him for the first time. "And who would you bring to the fields of Golamaran? Who would you bring to the Shrine?"

"This is Udi Dis," Ro told her, raising a hand in Dis's direction. "A . . . a friend."

Dis liked that. Not a bodyguard. Not even just a pilot. A friend.

The old crone's eyes bored into him.

"He is . . . what?"

Dis wanted to yell that he was freezing.

"He is Talortai," Ro answered for him. "A species strong in the Force."

Her eyes flicked back to her cousin's masked face.

"The Force?"

This time Dis spoke up. "I am a navigator. A pathfinder."

She chuckled, obviously amused by his choice of words. "Are you now? Well, whatever you are, whatever you can do, you are welcome." Again she glanced up at Ro. "As were the credits that came before you. Such generosity."

"I knew the journey here would be difficult for you," Ro said. "Do you still have that old rust bucket?"

"The *Open Hand*? Yes, yes I do. Half devoured by rust-weevils, but she still flies, although not to the Shrine." She patted the hide of one of the shaggy beasts that waited patiently beside her. "The slarga will get us where no transport will fly. They are strong." She glanced back at Ro. "They have to be, where we're going."

The ride to the cave entrance was long and arduous. Thankfully the first part of the journey had been taken by hoversled, the slarga snorting at the back of the speeder that coughed and spluttered as it traversed the Golamaran ice flats. The landscape was barren, a frozen waste stretching out into darkness in all directions. Out here, in the tundra, Dis was grateful for the thick pelts that Kufa had supplied. The stink of stale sweat clung to the matted fibers, but they kept the wind from freezing his bones as Ro perched up front with his cousin.

Before long, Kufa announced they must go the rest of the way on slarga-back. They swayed into the gloom, the light from the hoversled diminishing as its droid pilot sped away as fast as its struggling repulsorlift would allow. The dark was almost absolute and yet their ponderous caravan continued in silence, any sound swallowed up by the howling gale that threatened to pluck them from their mounts. Somehow the slarga knew where they were going, thick heads held down against the wind, wide feet crunching into the snow.

Dis reached out with his senses, satisfied that Ro was still in front of him and trusting that the old woman knew where she was going. He had to stay alert. There was no knowing what terrors hunted the ice flats, if any life could survive such temperatures in the first place. But if it could, it would be hungry and the slarga would make for a good meal, as would they, even old Kufa whom Dis imagined was little more than skin and bone beneath all those furs.

After an hour that seemed like a day, Dis's mount lurched to a halt, and for a second he wondered if it had succumbed to the cold and was ready to collapse onto its flat brutish face. He heard boots crunch into the snow ahead. Ro had dismounted and was helping the old woman down from the lead slarga. Dis followed suit, grateful for the glow rod that Kufa ignited, waving it northeast of their current position. They battled against the wind, the light from Kufa's glow rod blinking on and off as snow sheeted between them. Soon Dis couldn't sense the slarga they had left huddled together, let alone see them. There was nothing but snow and ice and wind and noise. His body ached, his wingblades heavy from where he had hefted them on his back, every step a trial in itself. Time lost all meaning, and Dis feared on more than one occasion that his senses had abandoned him. Which way was north? Which was south? Was Ro even still ahead of him? He called out, but couldn't even hear his own voice let alone if the Eye had replied.

Then suddenly he stopped, his senses returned to him. Kufa and Ro had paused, and Dis forced his usually keen eyes to focus through the grime plastering his goggles.

The old woman had led them to a rocky outcrop in the ice, her glow rod illuminating a cleft in the petrified stone, barely wide enough for a monkey-lizard to squeeze through, and yet that was exactly what she was doing, her furs snagging on the rocks. Dis thought she was going to get caught, but she squeezed through the gap like a screerat sliding through a crack half its size. In a second she was gone, and Dis felt a sudden sting of panic that she had taken the glow rod with her, until he realized the illuminator was in Ro's hand. The Eye offered the rod to him, intending to follow his cousin, but Dis shook his head. The old woman seemed to know where she was going, but there was no telling what was waiting for them on the other side of that cleft. Dis wasn't about to let Ro push himself into the arms of a frost-spider. Drawing his wingblades, Dis followed the crone into the unknown.

Chapter Five

The Cyclor Shipyards

Vam Targes's bristled head snapped up from a terminal as Indeera and Bell ran onto the *Innovator*'s spotless flight deck.

"Jedi?"

"There's a problem," Bell blurted out before Indeera could stop him.

Targes's mandibles chattered in concern. "What kind of problem?"

Bell inwardly cursed himself. "We . . . don't know."

"We felt a disturbance in the Force," Indeera cut in to spare the young Jedi's blushes.

"And you can't be more specific?" the Aqualish asked through his vocoder, before correcting himself. "No, of course you can't. The Force is hardly empirical, because that would be, you know, useful."

Both Jedi had gotten used to Vam's nature. The Aqualish meant no disrespect. He was used to absolutes. Components. Equations. The laws of physics. While much of the galaxy trusted the Force, to those of a scientific mind its vagaries must have been intolerable.

The engineer turned to a nearby Cyclorrian at a bank of analysis consoles. "Run a diagnostic sweep."

The insectoid chittered a question in a language that Bell had tried, and failed, to pick up since he had been back in the Mid Rim.

"All systems," Vam snapped in reply. "If the Jedi say something is wrong, then something is wrong, and we need to find it immediately."

The Cyclorrian's skin flushed purple as it went to work. While Bell hadn't mastered their language, he had learned enough about the insectoids to know that the sudden change in color indicated deep stress. He hated causing discomfort to anyone, but the shift in the Force had been so pronounced. He reached out again, visualizing the Force as a raging fire, silently asking Loden to help guide him. As ever, there was no response from his former Master, but there was no mistaking the sudden breeze that fanned the flames he saw in his mind.

"It's not on the ship," he muttered under his breath.

"What was that?" Vam asked.

"The threat doesn't come from within . . ."

"But without," Indeera confirmed as a klaxon wailed.

Ember ran at Bell's feet as they raced to the flight deck's central control table.

"What is it?" Bell asked.

"The hyperspace proximity alarm," Vam replied, his clawed hands flicking switches and adjusting controls. "It's an experimental system I've been perfecting that monitors vibrations in realspace to predict the arrival of craft from hyperspace. I was hoping to present it to Chancellor Soh herself at the fair."

"And?" Bell prompted. "Are there vibrations?"

"There's a siren, isn't there?"

"But where are they coming from?" Indeera asked, ignoring the Aqualish's exasperated tone.

"As I said, I am working to *perfect* the system. It is still in the experimental stage."

"So we don't know," Bell stated flatly, trying to control his frustration.

Vam flashed him a knowing look. "Annoying, isn't it?"

"Point taken."

"Perhaps we can help," Indeera said. "Do you have a range of coordinates?"

"Of.course," Vam said, flicking a switch. A series of numbers scrolled down a screen set into the table.

The Aqualish frowned.

"What's wrong?" Bell asked.

Targes jabbed a button, and they turned to see the space surrounding the shipyards displayed on the main viewscreen. "The data suggests the opening will appear in one of these locations, but no one in their right mind would jump this near a gravitational body. There must be something wrong with the calculation."

As if to prove him wrong—or rather his calculation correct—a ship appeared on the screen, jolting into realspace. It was a junker, patched together from a number of different vessels, although Bell guessed that it had started life as a Corellian deep space cruiser, but no civilian ship would boast such armaments. Turbolasers. Blaster cannons. Torpedo arrays. And even this display of raw strength paled into insignificance against the threat of the three lightning bolts that were slashed across the craft's blunt nose cone. They meant only one thing.

The Nihil.

Indeera was already running, Bell and Ember keeping pace. "Scramble all skywings," she commanded. "And tell me this flying laboratory has weapons."

"We're a *scientific* vessel," Vam shot back. "Besides, it's just one ship."

"The Nihil never come alone," Bell shouted back as he jumped into the waiting turbolift.

"Do they know we're here?"

On the Nihil Cloudship, the seething lump of Gloovan hate known as Sarn Starbreaker eyed the shipyards hungrily.

"Well?" he demanded wetly when no one responded to his question.

A bulb-headed Fluggrian at the comm terminal cocked her head, listening to the device crammed into her tiny ears.

"I'm picking up frenzied chatter on all frequencies. They know all right."

Good, Starbreaker thought. That meant they were scared. He liked it when they were scared. When they were scared they made mistakes.

"Any distress calls?"

"Not any that can get past our jammer."

Starbreaker grinned, his slime-covered face glistening with anticipation. "Perfect. Target the shipyard and fire."

His crew didn't have to ask what weapons. They knew their Cloud well. When Sarn Starbreaker said fire, he meant *all* the weapons. Every single one.

Scarlet beams lanced from the Cloudship's laser banks, followed by a barrage of plasma torpedoes. Explosions bloomed across the hangar's defenses, each prompting an excited gargle from the Cloud. Cyclor's shipyards were full of fresh pickings, but Starbreaker only had piggy little eyes for one prize, the treasure that lay within Hangar Twenty-Two: the pride of the Republic science corps, the *Innovator.* He had enjoyed torturing the security officer who had finally given up the hangar number, but he would enjoy cracking open the *Innovator*'s hull even more. He had no idea what treasures would be found when his raiding party rampaged through its corridors. In fact, he barely cared. He just knew they would be valuable, not to him but to his Tempest. This would be the hit that would finally see Pan Eyta promote him to Storm, with all the glory . . . and *riches* . . . that came with it. Sarn licked his lips, savoring the bitter tang of his own mucus. Yes, this would be *glorious.*

"We have a breach," the Fluggrian reported. Starbreaker didn't know her name, but she answered to *you,* which was good enough for him.

"Then launch the fighters," he growled, flicking a switch on his command chair that sent his voice booming through the Cloudship. "Feed the Storm, my friends. We will feast well tonight."

The *Innovator*'s landing bay bucked as another salvo hit the hangar. The Nihil weren't wasting any time. Bell raced over to his Vector, popping the canopy with a nudge from the Force just as Indeera had shown him. Ember scampered up one of the fighter's bladelike wings, jumping into the backseat as Bell leapt up to land perfectly behind the flight controls.

He glanced over to see that Stokes was already aboard her own Vector and running through her pre-launch sequence, not that the tiny craft needed much in the way of flight checks. Each Vector was a symphony of simplicity, with little if any need for computer equipment or sensors, not when it had a Jedi behind the yoke.

Targes's voice crackled over the comm as the Vector's canopy clicked shut over him.

"They've breached the hangar. Fighters incoming."

Bell was impressed. The Aqualish was keeping himself remarkably calm, all things considered.

"Any word from the Core?"

"We can't get through. All transmissions are being jammed."

"Understood. Stand by."

Bell didn't have to look to see if Indeera was ready. He could sense it. He fired his thrusters, the Vector streaking toward the bay doors. When she had taken over his training, Stokes had insisted that Bell fly a Vector of his own rather than copilot, a decision that suited him well. Unlike the *Nova,* however, he had resisted giving the tiny fighter its own name. It hadn't seemed right. Not after Loden. The Jedi teachings were correct. No attachments. They just got in the way.

Behind him, Ember barked once as they cleared the doors and shot into space.

"You all right back there, girl?" Bell shouted over his shoulder. "Ready to crew the blasters?"

The hound yapped again, drawing a smile from the Jedi. "Good to know you have my back."

He swung around, shifting the Vector to the left to avoid debris that had been blasted clear from the shipyard. Laserfire raked the hangar, sending fresh shrapnel flying in every direction. The hull wouldn't last long, and then there would be nothing to stop the Nihil from reaching the *Innovator.*

No, that wasn't true. There was him.

Smaller fighters had swarmed out of the main Nihil ship, darting toward the shipyard. Bell picked out a ragged-looking hopper barely any larger than the Vector, its stubby wings laden with laser cannons. Bell didn't need a targeting computer or a holosight. He only needed the Force. His thumb brushed the trigger on his flight stick, and the emitters fired, deadly beams finding their target and slicing deep into the Nihil's hull, rupturing the fighter's fuel line. The hopper erupted into starlight.

Behind him, Ember yapped and Bell smiled, pleased with the strike. "The next one's yours, girl."

Indeera Stokes's voice came over the comm, the Vector automatically switching to a Jedi-only channel.

"Careful, Padawan. Do not glory in the death of your enemy. That way leads to the dark side."

Bell felt a sudden flash of resentment, which he instantly fought to quash. Indeera was right. He *had* felt satisfaction at the Nihil's demise, satisfaction that was fueled by the feelings he tried so hard to ignore. Anger. Grief. He still had much to learn.

"Thank you, Master," he said, sending the Vector into a spin to avoid fire from another fighter. "May the Force be with us."

"For light and life," Indeera replied, engaging an enemy of her own.

The fighter was on Bell's tail, the pilot firing indiscriminately, gambling that sooner or later they'd get lucky. Bell kept spinning, creating a moving target that was ten times harder to hit. Any other time, he would bring the Vector up and over, the hunter becoming the hunted in his sights, but this time there was no need.

The Nihil starfighter erupted into silent flame, and Bell swung away, using the Force to switch channels to thank the local defense pilot he'd sensed zeroing in on the Nihil's tail.

"You're welcome," came a synthesized voice in reply. "Do you want to let us handle the fighters while you take on that beast out there?"

Bell glanced to his left as the owner of the voice brought his Z-29 Skyhawk alongside the Vector. The pilot was a Cyclorrian, gloved fingers wrapped around the controls. Bell thanked the Force for the translator unit that was making sense of the insectoid's chirrups and clicks, not to mention the starfighter at its controls. The Z-29 was the latest of a fleet of Skyhawks produced at the shipyard. The Incom Corporation had already signed a number of lucrative deals to supply Skyhawks to worlds throughout the Republic and beyond. You didn't need the Force to sense the pride in the pilot's voice. He knew that this battle, although dangerous, would be a chance to show off the Z-29's speed and maneuverability. The Nihil had made a mistake attacking one of the finest shipbuilders in the Mid Rim, especially with two Jedi present.

Ember barked, and Bell laughed.

"I stand corrected. Two Jedi and a charhound."

He was sure that dog could read his mind sometimes.

"Jedi Zettifar?"

Bell apologized to the waiting pilot, telling him to proceed as he had suggested. The Cyclorrian peeled off with a wave of his antennae, rejoining his swarm-mates in the battle of their lives.

Bell looked around, scanning the space around the hangar. "Master?"

"I'm with you, Padawan," Indeera responded, her Vector appearing at his starboard wing.

"And the Force is with us all."

Bell banked to port, angling away from the stricken hangar. Indeera matched his bearing perfectly, turning with him as they sped toward their new target—the Nihil Cloudship.

Chapter Six

Safrifa

As the monster dragged her ever closer to the stinking wound of its mouth, Ty's only thought was that the crikking thing had more teeth than was strictly necessary.

She should've guessed it was going to be a Drengir. A year ago, she'd never even heard the name before—no one had—but now the damn horrors were everywhere, bursting from the ground on just about every planet along the galactic frontier. When she had first heard one described Ty had sniggered. Sentient plants? Seriously? How in void's name could a plant be a threat? That was before she had seen one face-to-gnarled-face, a hideous mound of writhing branches with spurs of knotted wood. Tales of infestations spread as fast as the monsters themselves, whispered in hushed tones in a thousand watering holes or huddled around campfires. Entire worlds were said to have been lost to the Drengir blight, settlements strangled by their barbed vines and populations consumed. Nothing seemed able to stop them once an infestation had taken root. Even the Hutts were said to have suffered, the teeming metropolises of Nal Hutta all but transformed into seething jungles. Tall tales? Some folk dismissed such reports as nonsense, but as far as Ty was concerned the threat was as real as the creepers that were dragging her ever closer to that snarling maw.

Ty had laid out ground rules for herself when she had started out on this road. That had been one of the first things that Caratoo had taught her, the grizzled old merc imparting wisdom to the newest recruit of his band. "Know where your limits are. Know where to draw the line." Of course, Caratoo's line had involved betraying anyone who trusted him, but the lesson had remained with her, long after the Kerk had made the mistake of turning his back on her. Ty's rules were clear. No attachments. No complications. She hunted only animals, not sentient life-forms, unless of course the sentient life was trying to kill her.

The Drengir was *definitely* trying to kill her.

She pushed back, sending a telekinetic wave against the creature strong enough to break the neck of an acklay or maybe even a roggwart, but not a Drengir. Never a Drengir. Did they even have necks?

This wasn't her first encounter with the monsters. The first had nearly killed her. It had been on Galidraan during a hunt for a batarikan. She'd found the serpent, Drengir roots crammed into the snake's eyes and nasal cavities, its body leached of all nutrients. Unfortunately most of the locals had suffered a similar ghastly fate, the infestation out of control. Ty had barely escaped with her life, although KL-03 had been more concerned that they'd lost yet another commission. Kriffing droid. Next time it could take down the monsters.

If there was a next time.

A Drengir root crept up the side of her face, slithering toward her mouth, thorns scraping across her lips. Oh no. She wasn't going that way.

Ty pushed again. If she couldn't break the Drengir's nonexistent neck, she could at least break these damn feelers. The Drengir roared, its vines stretching beyond the point of no return. Finally they snapped, the Drengir's moundlike body slamming into a tree. Ty yanked the root from her mouth, wincing as the thorns sliced through her bottom lip. Another scar to add to the collection. Another chance to die of toxic shock. Who knew what bacteria lived on those things, or in the marshwater for that matter.

"No escape. The harvest is ours."

The voice raked through her head sharper than any thorn. Now the Drengir was riled, but so was she. They'd tried to do this on Galidraan, to overwhelm her with their poisonous thoughts, images of despair flooding her mind, or entire worlds reaped for the sustenance. That's all she was to them, all anyone was. Food. Meat. Sustenance. Survival.

The Drengir surged forward, sending out creepers to snag trees and branches, anything to drag itself closer. Good. That meant it struggled to move on its own. Ty didn't know much about the Drengir—no one did—but she knew that meant it was young, and young Drengir were still vulnerable. At least, that was the theory.

Ty leapt, higher than it should have been possible for her or any Tholothian to jump. She didn't make it to the canopy of karenga trees, but managed to grab a low-lying bough that stretched from one tree to another. The branch bowed, dropping her perilously close to the Drengir, the creature bellowing in hunger.

"The harvest is ours. The harvest is ours."

Not today.

Hooking her boots around the branch, Ty clambered directly above the creature. Her body ached, and the silver tendrils that hung from her scalp itched, even the phantom one. *Especially* the phantom one, sliced off all those years ago by a Weequay knife. If the missing tip was itching, she really was in trouble.

The branch dropped.

Ty whipped her head around to see that the Drengir had managed to snare the end of the bough and was pulling down sharply. She was caught in the middle, too far from the vine to try to kick it free and not close enough to the trunk to climb higher. The branch groaned, its wet bark starting to splinter. If it broke, there would be nothing to stop her tumbling down into the Drengir's embrace.

Food. Meat. Sustenance. Survival.

She had one chance. Looping both her knees over the branch, she hung facedown toward the monster. It snarled and frothed, grasping back up toward her. Ty closed her eyes and reached down, not with her hands, but with her feelings, with her very spirit. She reached beyond the creature that longed to consume her and beyond the water that pooled beneath its ravenous bulk. She searched through silt and roots, looking for the one thing that could save her, the weapon she had dropped when the Drengir first attacked.

There. There it was, caught beneath a root, right beneath the Drengir's weight. Damn and blast.

A barbed vine looped around her left wrist.

Ty reached out again, this time not searching, but calling.

Beneath the Drengir something shifted, something Ty had owned for a long, long time. From long before Galidraan. Before even Caratoo. She increased the pressure, the muscles in her arms taut. Still it wouldn't come, twitching in the muck, unable to break free.

Another creeper found her right wrist. The Drengir pulled her closer.

Ty visualized her weapon in her mind; its long grip, the vicious spikes that would have so disappointed the old Azumel who taught her to build it. The focusing lens, the emitter, the activation switch.

Purple light flared beneath the Drengir, and Ty pulled up with all her might.

The blade sliced through the root. It was free. Next it sliced through the Drengir itself, splitting that hideous beaklike mouth in two. The Drengir wailed as the two halves of its body came apart like rotten fruit, splashing into the marsh.

Ty's lightsaber found her hand, and the branch broke.

She tumbled down, flipping to land in the middle of the Drengir's remains. She killed her blade, wiping mud from the hilt before slipping it back into its holster. Slowly, she pried the vines from around her wrist, careful not to get scratched. It wasn't over, that she knew from reports she had intercepted back and forth from Starlight Beacon. Cut a Drengir down and it would regenerate. All it needed was one tiny scrap of its former self. But Ty had promised the Safrifans they would be free of the thing and would be good to her word, another old lesson from Caratoo, even if he hadn't believed it himself.

Now came the hard work, hacking the dormant Drengir into strips, hanging them from the branches of the nearest tree, and then waiting for them to dry out enough to catch light. She probably had enough fuel in the microflamer in her belt to start a small bonfire. That would be enough, until every scrap was burned.

The harvest was hers.

The walk back to the marsh-farm took longer than Ty wanted, especially stinking of charred Drengir. She had recorded the blaze on a holo, evidence of the kill now that the body was gone. The farmers were waiting for her, relief on their faces and their meager offering still in its malligator purse. But that's not all that was waiting for her. Ty's hand dropped to her lightsaber when she spotted the spacecraft next to her own ship. A figure swept down its ramp, as tall as the Safrifans were short. Ty recognized the species—a Kuranu with their smooth light-purple skin and large pupil-less eyes. The newcomer was female, wearing a pristine flight suit, a small spherical droid hovering at her elbow. The unit served only one purpose, to deliver an anti-bac solution into the Kuranu's palm whenever required. The species had almost a pathological fear of germs, which explained the look of disgust that she tried to suppress as she took in Ty's swamp-encrusted outfit.

"You are Ty Yorrick," she finally stated, "the so-called Saber for Hire." Her tone was blunt and to the point, as functional as the tight smile she flashed in greeting.

"It depends who's asking."

"My name is Mantessa Chekkat."

Ty glanced over at the small ship. "Looks like you've come a long way."

"I have," Chekkat acknowledged. "Looking for you. I was hoping that you could help me."

And the cycle began again.

Chapter Seven

Beneath the Golamaran ice flats

If the journey from the *Squall Spider* had felt like an eternity encased in a stasis field, the trek through the tunnels beneath the ice plains was unbearable. Every fiber of Dis's body ached, which was a relatively new experience for the pilot. His tarsus muscles burned from trying not to slip on the ice-slick floor, while his neck was stiff from crouching to avoid stalactites. Dis had experienced discomfort in his long life, of course he had, but Talortai were hardy to say the least. They healed quickly, the reasons for their heightened regenerative abilities largely unknown. Maybe it was genetic, maybe it was all thanks to the Force. The elders were purposely ignorant, scared of admitting their own abilities to themselves. Dis had no idea why, but had heard the legends of the great cull, an army descending on dragon-wing to cut through the population with their blazing crimson blades. In another time and place it would have been called putting down the competition, but back then, over four thousand seasons ago, it was nothing short of genocide. The Talortai, once legion, became an endangered species, and stayed that way purposely, rules set in place by the elders. The penalties for nonconformity were severe, as he had learned to his cost.

Dis banished the thoughts of home with a shake of his head. Why was he thinking of Talor with its council of cowards? It was the monotony of the descent, maybe. Yes, that's what it had to be, he told himself as he grasped hold of the walls to stop himself from stumbling into Ro and Kufa.

The old woman had surprised them when they had squeezed into the narrow passage, opening her furs to release a trio of small flying drones, about the size of thermal detonators. Dis had raised his wingblades to cleave them in two before they attacked, but instead the floating spheres blazed with a brilliant light, illuminating the tunnel as clear as day. At least they could now see when they slipped on the ice.

Now his wingblades were back between his shoulders, sacrificed to the need of keeping his hands free to steady himself. His breath frosted in front of his beak, and the furs itched intolerably, but at least the woman had finally lapsed into silence as she led them down, down, down. For the first hour of their descent, the tunnel had echoed to her questions: Were the rumors true? Had Ro really become a pirate? Did he still practice their rituals? Had he heard from other members of their family? The Eye gave nothing away, answering with as few words as possible, even when the crone called him by a name Dis had never heard before.

Were the rumors true? Well, it depended on the rumors.

Yes, he had become a pirate among many, many other things.

No, but the rituals had never left him.

As for the family? He doubted they would welcome him with open arms. Maybe a vibroknife between the ribs?

That Dis understood.

Ro had questions of his own. How many of them were left?

"The faithful?" Kufa barked a bitter laugh. "Not enough. You've seen it out there. Seen *them,* with their golden robes and flashing blades. So *resplendent.* So *glorious.* The guiding light of the galaxy." She gave another snort. "They are guiding us to destruction. The faithful know it, as we knew it on Jedha. As we knew it on Dalna. But the recreants are in the ascendant and the tide can no longer be turned."

That seemed to worry Ro, who clutched his furs around him. "But if you truly believe the war is lost . . ."

"Why do we come here? Why do we return to the Shrine?" She spat, the thick glob of phlegm sliding down a jagged stalagmite like a scumslug. "We don't. The ice caves are empty, the Leveler forgotten. I doubt even the attendants still function. We shall see."

"But you . . ."

"I haven't stepped foot in these tunnels for over a decade." The shame in her voice was evident, and without warning the woman spun around, as sure and steady on her feet as Dis was unbalanced.

"Is that why you are here, Cousin? Do you bring us hope? Will you reopen the Hand? Will you deliver the message?"

Ro shook his head. "It is not my place. I am no prophet."

Kufa searched his mask, eyes narrowed as if she could see through the frosted glass. "Maybe. Maybe not. All the best prophets have been lost at one point or another. That is how they find the Path."

And so they continued, the slope becoming all the more treacherous. The discussion stopped but the unease remained. No, it grew. Intensified. Something Dis had never experienced, not even when he was run out of the nest.

He reached out with the Force, his feathers bristling beneath the pelts. Ro stopped, turning back to him as he slipped the wingblades from his shoulders, holding them ready by his side.

"Udi?"

"We must keep going," Kufa insisted, the light droids keeping pace with her, leaving Ro and Dis in increasing darkness.

The Eye took a step closer.

"What is it?"

Dis stood rigid, ready to act. Ready to defend.

"I don't know," he finally answered. "There's something missing."

Ro leaned in.

"Tell me what you're feeling?"

"I feel nothing," Dis said bluntly. "Our gifts are not like the Jedi."

"You don't receive warnings?"

Dis shook his head. "No, but we sense vibrations."

"That's how you can pilot through meteor storms and comet fields."

"We can tell the movement of things. In flight. In battle. But down here, in the tunnels . . ."

He reached out again.

"There's nothing."

That wasn't true. The low rumble that echoed through the passageway belied the fact that there was definitely something in the shadows, a growl, building to a roar.

The light from the spheres bloomed as Kufa hurried back. "We need to move."

Ro peered into the darkness again. The roar sounded again.

"What is it?"

"Something I thought would still be asleep."

She barged past them, her feet scrabbling as she started to climb the way they had come.

"Wait," Ro said, grabbing her furs. "We're leaving?"

The old woman pulled herself free of his grip. "As swiftly as we can, if we want to live."

"But the Leveler . . ."

"Will still be there when the owner of that roar has passed, but we won't be. We'll be either on the surface or sliding down its gullet."

"What about the faithful?" Ro argued. "What about finding the Path?"

Dis thought she was going to strike him.

"What use is the Path if you are dead? I'm trying to protect you. We can come back, but only when the cobonica has passed."

"And that's what the sound is? A cobonica?"

"What do you think?" She tried to continue on her way, but Ro wouldn't leave her. "Let me go!"

"No."

That was the voice that Dis had heard in the Great Hall the day he joined the Nihil. That was the voice that commanded the Storm.

Ro shrugged off his furs and, kicking them aside, pulled a cylinder from his belt. For a second Dis thought it was the artifact he had seen Ro studying on the *Spider,* until Ro pressed his thumb against the control on the side of the device and a yellow blade slid elegantly from its tip.

A lightsaber. The Eye of the Nihil had a lightsaber.

Ro stood, legs braced and saber burning, and glared into the darkness. The roar turned into a bellow and was joined by a slithering and a scraping, the stone beneath Dis's feet trembling as he took his place by his Eye, fragments of ice falling like snow from the ceiling.

"Ready?" Ro asked, staring straight ahead.

"Ready," Dis confirmed.

But he wasn't. Not for the size of the creature or the speed of the attack. There was no way to truly understand what was launching itself at them, no way to differentiate between the shaggy fur-covered tentacles that shot forward like skim-snakes, each as thick as a Gamorrean's waist and lined with serrated suckers. A limb wrapped around him, the barbed teeth slicing through the pelts, through his feathers. Dis slashed wildly with a wingblade, the keen edge slicing through the flesh beneath the slime-encrusted fur. The cobonica howled in fury, another tentacle whipping, but this time Dis was ready. He had felt it coming. Yes! His senses were back. He could sense every twitch of the creature's muscles, even the flow of the thick, inky blood that pumped through its veins. He could even feel every swing of Ro's lightsaber across the narrow corridor, knowing exactly where they would strike and which limbs would fall.

Which limb would wrap around the Eye's leg.

Dis cried out a warning as the bony suckers sank into Ro's leg. But the Eye didn't scream; instead he twisted, thrusting the point of his laser sword into one of the beast's milky-white eyes. The lens popped and foul-smelling ichor flowed, accompanied by a shriek and a frenzy of flailing limbs that threatened to bring the roof down. Dis continued his assault, slashing with his blades again and again, even as the monster extinguished one of the bulb droids by smashing it against the wall. The sudden flare blinded him, and he tried to duck as his senses warned him of the feeler swinging in like a club. It was no good. He was fast, but not that fast. The tentacle slammed him against the icy wall, his wrist shattering on impact, the wingblade slipping from numb fingers. In a second the tentacle was around him, thrashing him repeatedly against the side of the tunnel. He saw another flash and smelled the tang of burnt flesh. Someone was firing a blaster at the creature. Ro? No. It was Kufa, a rifle in her mittened hands. What else was she hiding beneath those damn furs?

The old woman's act of defiance didn't last long. An arm whipped out, knocking Kufa from her feet and the rifle from her hand. It went off once as it hit the ground, the bolt blackening the ice next to Dis's head. In an instant a tentacle was around her leg, dragging her toward the creature's maw. She grabbed a stalagmite in a vain attempt to anchor herself but the rock snapped in her hand, leaving a dagger that she stabbed into the monster's flesh. It was no good. Dis was caught between the creature's bulk and the tunnel wall, unable to breathe. Ro had vanished, crushed beneath the monster's undulating body, and Kufa would soon feel the embrace of the cobonica's serrated teeth. There would be no coming back for any of them. No regeneration. No renewal.

Dis closed his eyes and welcomed death.

Chapter Eight

The *Coruscant Dawn*

Stellan Gios's lightsaber flared into life, the cross-guard clicking into place. He had barely brought the glowing blue blade up into a salute before the fight was on, his opponent charging in, plasma blazing green. Stellan took a step back, calculating the swing of his rival's attack. It came as he expected, and he blocked the blow easily, feinting back before immediately pushing forward again, putting the white-haired woman on her back foot. She parried, gripping her hilt with two hands, her weight kept forward. Stellan took another step back, using her momentum against her. She stumbled, but not enough for Stellan to disarm her. Good. He liked a challenge. The woman threw herself into a spin, her emerald blade arcing. The light itself would have been enough to dazzle any other opponent, but Stellan wasn't just anyone. He was a Jedi.

Stellan retreated on his line, calculating the exact point where her blade would reach him. He drew his own lightsaber up front, rotating his wrist so their blades clashed, blue pushing green to the side. Again, her momentum worked against her, just as he had predicted, but she used the Force to maintain her balance, sliding her blade under his with a crackle of energy. She drew back sharply, forcing Stellan to give more ground. He would have to be careful. The wall of the chamber was behind him. Another couple of steps and he would be cornered. He could flip up and over, forcing her to turn, but that would break the purity of his line. Instead he allowed her to lunge, blocking the attack and letting his blade slide down hers, the resulting scream of charged plasma like the howl of a hroth-beast. Now Stellan had her. He waited for her containment field to hit the energy of his crossguard and twisted sharply, locking the T-formation around the end of her blade and forcing it down. The tip of her lightsaber burned into the marbled deck in front of her, and the fight was already lost. Stellan brought his elbow back sharply, ready to slice her lightsaber in two.

"Solah!" Jedi Nib Assek barked, yielding before Stellan could disarm her.

"Are you sure?" he asked, eyes full of mischief.

She chuckled. A low, husky sound that always made Stellan smile. Nib sounded as though she smoked twenty cigarras a day, although he knew for a fact that she had never touched any of the filthy things in her life.

"I think we've given them enough of a show haven't we?" Nib said, waiting for him to break his stance.

With a flourish, Stellan disengaged, bringing his weapon back up into the traditional salute. Nib did the same, her blade almost hiding the lopsided smile Stellan knew so well. They held the stance for a second and then retracted their blades.

With a nod of the head, he turned and took a step toward the small audience gathered on the other side of the chamber.

"That was an ancient form of lightsaber combat, developed during a point in our history where lightsaber battles were commonplace. Of course, today such duels are purely ceremonial or used in the training of Padawans."

"That's great. Thank you, Master Gios. We can cut there."

The cam droid that had been floating nearby beeped, its cluster of lenses retracting.

A young woman stepped forward, slipping a sleek datapad into the jacket she wore over a plain cream shirt.

"Are you sure, Ms. Dairo? The differences between the forms are fascinating—"

"And probably more information than the holonet requires, Stellan," Nib reminded him gently, slipping her lightsaber back into its holster. "You'll have to forgive Master Gios," she told the reporter. "He is used to gaggles of adoring younglings that hang on his every word."

Stellan accepted the jibe in the spirit it had been given, smiling at the young woman who had asked to record the duel. "If only that was true. I know of at least two former students who chose to meditate whenever I launched into the intricacies of lightsaber history. It is a particular passion of mine."

Rhil Dairo's eyebrow arched up. "Now, that *is* interesting. I thought the Jedi Code stated there is no passion."

Stellan felt a wave of discomfort roll off the golden-haired Wookiee who was standing at a respectful distance behind the reporter and her cam droid, the same unease Stellan had sensed from the Padawan during the duel with his Master. Burryaga was one of the most empathetic Jedi Stellan had ever encountered, a gift that had saved hundreds of lives during the Great Disaster. However, on this occasion, his concern was misguided. Stellan wasn't embarrassed by Rhil's question. She was only doing her job, after all.

"Indeed it does," Stellan told her. "Strong passions are something we try to control within ourselves, as emotions can cloud our judgment, especially in stressful situations. They can blind us to the truth, and to the leading of the Force. That said, it would be foolish to suggest that a Jedi has no desires or interests. In fact, I would go so far as to say that it would be dangerous, leading only to complacency. Yes, I have a passion for learning and teaching. It is part of who I am. But I am also prepared to set such things aside at a moment's notice. My 'passions' must never be greater than my mission. Does that make sense?"

"Now I wish I'd kept Tee-Nine rolling," Rhil said, glancing up at the bobbing cam droid. "That was *gold.*"

"Don't encourage him," Nib warned playfully. "I doubt your droid has enough storage capacity."

Rhil laughed, flicking her bangs out of the cybernetic implant that was clamped over her right eye, the lens the same color as her droid. "Well, we have enough for now. Thank you."

"You're welcome," Stellan said, realizing he'd been using the hilt of his extinguished lightsaber to punctuate his impromptu lecture. He slipped it back into its holster, checking to see if Master Kant's lightsaber was still in its now customary place on his belt. Yes, it hadn't come loose in the demonstration. He patted it once, noticing that Rhil had spotted the weapon hanging beneath his robe. Stars alive, she *was* good. Maybe he'd explain why he wore it at another time. For now, he had indulged himself long enough.

"We should check in with the chancellor," he said, turning to Nib.

"Excellent," Rhil chimed in, indicating for T-9 to start recording again. The hovering droid's light flicked back on.

"Maybe you shouldn't come with us," Nib said, eyeing the droid with suspicion. "The chancellor may be in session with the Senate."

"In which case we'll stop recording immediately," Rhil assured her. "Or at least kill the sound, choosing an angle where what is being said won't be picked up. GoNet has been given full access while we're aboard the *Coruscant Dawn.* The chancellor herself—"

"The chancellor has said that she wants the coverage of the Republic Fair to be as transparent as possible," Stellan agreed. She was right, of course; Dairo's presence on the *Coruscant Dawn* had been Lina Soh's idea. Stellan applauded such a resolve, although he had made the suggestion that the reporter largely stay with the Jedi contingent while aboard the chancellor's ship. Good intentions or not, Soh still needed to work!

Rhil bit her tongue when Stellan Gios talked over her. She didn't like having other people fight her battles for her, but sometimes an argument wasn't worth having. Instead she let the Jedi guide her out of the training chamber, T-9 bobbing after them.

She still had to pinch herself that she was here; Rhil Dairo, walking through the corridors of the chancellor's personal flagship. She had certainly come a long way from reporting on micro-g basket weaving as a cub reporter on Cordota, or whatever non-story her producer had picked for her that day. Now she was walking shoulder-to-shoulder with Jedi. And not just any Jedi. A member of the High Council, no less.

Rhil liked Stellan. He was a bit stiff, sure . . . a bit earnest and, on days when she wasn't feeling generous, a little too keen on the sound of his own voice, but she could tell that his heart was definitely in the right place. Of course, it didn't hurt that he was a handsome son-of-a-blaster. Oh no, not at all. That chiseled jaw beneath the dashing beard, those blue eyes. And the smile. That smile! That was the real killer, right there. No wonder the Council had decided to make him their poster boy.

Nib Assek couldn't have been any more different. Whereas Stellan was all easy charm and manners, the silver-haired Jedi Knight kept herself at a distance. Stellan explained *everything*, but try as she might, Rhil couldn't get Assek to open up. Not that she didn't like the older woman. When she *did* speak, Assek had a wicked sense of humor, which was largely aimed at Stellan. Rhil got the impression that the two Jedi hadn't known each other long but had already formed a natural working relationship. Even the lightsaber duel had been interesting. Rhil couldn't shake the feeling that Nib had been holding back, not exactly making mistakes on purpose but deferring to the Council member. It was probably just for the cam, but it was certainly interesting.

And then there was Burryaga, Nib's Padawan and possibly the kindest, sweetest soul she had ever met. Sensitivity radiated from the Wookiee like light from a glow lamp. Even now, as they entered the chancellor's office at the very heart of the *Coruscant Dawn,* Burryaga stepped aside to let Rhil and T-9 pass, an act of kindness that didn't go unnoticed by his Master.

"Burry," Nib said softly, keeping her throaty voice down so as not to disturb the chancellor who, as she had suggested, was in session. "Ms. Dairo is supposed to be observing us, which includes you. We're to act as if she is not here."

The Wookiee's head sank slightly, and Rhil's hard reporter heart broke all over again.

"It's okay, big guy," she said, resisting the urge to reach out and pat his long hairy arm. "I appreciate the courtesy. The galaxy could do with a few more Burryagas if you ask me."

"Ain't that the truth," Nib commented, sharing a smile with Rhil. Perhaps that's how she would get through to the Jedi Knight. Through the Padawan.

A glance from Gios told them that they should be quiet. Rhil indicated for them all to continue, sending a command to T-9 via the neural link to kill the sound until she knew how sensitive the chancellor's conversation actually was. Lina Soh was standing in front of a vidwall, the screen split into a grid of feeds displaying various senators from across the Republic. Rhil immediately recognized the noble brow of Senator Noor of Serenno, the main representative for all matters concerning the Outer Rim. Now, there was a man who was all too aware of his own importance, forever plumped up in the thick Carannian furs he insisted on wearing no matter the weather. The next square showed Senator Vaadu of Phindar, his yellow eyes rendered a sickly green in the flickering light. The rest of the wall was taken up by a dark-skinned woman with long red hair—Samera Ra-oon, the Valon tasked with organizing the Republic Fair on her home planet—and a face no one on the frontier could fail to recognize, the Hero of Hetzal herself, Avar Kriss. Master Kriss was the marshal of Starlight Beacon, the famed space station that acted as the center of Republic activity in the Outer Rim. Of all the images, Kriss's was flickering, and Rhil could see stars behind the woman's head, distorted slightly as if behind transparisteel. Was Kriss broadcasting from a starfighter?

At their approach, Norel Quo, Chancellor Soh's primary aide, turned to face them, his Koorivarn eyes widening as he spotted T-9. He started for them, wagging a scaled finger, and Rhil prepared to be ejected from the chamber forthwith. The decision was taken out of all of their hands when the chancellor apologized to her holocommittee and indicated for her aide to stop.

"Norel, it's fine. They can stay."

The aide turned back to her, his ridged brow furrowed. "But Madam Chancellor, the conference—"

"Will continue as planned," Soh insisted, returning her gaze to the screens. "As everyone is aware the administration has afforded full access to GoNet. Of course, all footage gathered will be vetted for security purposes before broadcast, so we can speak freely." She turned back toward Rhil. "This *is* pre-recorded material, I believe."

Rhil nodded. "Yes, Chancellor. We won't be going live until the night of the opening ceremony."

"Excellent. Then join us. You, too, Master Jedi."

Quo stepped back to let Stellan and the others join the chancellor, although it was clear the Koorivar's grip on his datapad had tightened. Stellan and Nib shared welcoming nods with the other person present in the room, Soh's Kalleran deputy, Larep Reza, another rising star in the Senate and the official most likely to replace Soh when the chancellor's term ended. He certainly looked the part, with his striking fins framing a smooth nose-less face, dark stripes fanning out from a pair of eyes that were already older than his years. The cams loved him, as did the political commentators, not to mention the gossip-holos that were as obsessed about his love life as they were about his broad, finely muscled shoulders.

Rhil sent a silent command to T-9, reactivating the droid's quadronic mics. Soh had already returned to the conversation at hand.

"And everything is proceeding according to schedule?" she asked Samera.

"Absolutely. There has been a *slight* issue with the holoprojectors in the *United in Song* exhibit but—"

"I'm not sure that the chancellor needs to concern herself with the specifics, administrator," Quo cut in.

"On the contrary," Soh said. "I want to know *everything.*" She turned her attention back to Samera. "I saw the concept art for the *United in Song* attraction. It looked positively charming."

"Wait until you hear the melody . . ." Samera said with the faintest of smirks. "It's . . . unforgettable to say the least."

"What about the *Innovator*?" Senator Noor asked, obviously keen to keep the meeting on track.

"Almost ready for launch," Stellan informed them. "Jedi Indeera Stokes and her Padawan will be traveling with it, ready for its arrival during the opening ceremony."

Soh beamed at the news. "Excellent. It will be a sight to behold."

As would the chancellor's frock, Rhil thought. Here, on the bridge of her state ship, Soh was wearing a smart but modest trouser suit, the only nod to her famed flamboyance a brooch made of sparkling lucryte. Yet the same gossipvids that spent so much time pairing Larep Reza with every eligible socialite in the thousand systems were working themselves into a frenzy over what outfit Lina Soh would be wearing for the fair's opening. Not only was Soh presiding over the Republic in the period that could easily be described as the galaxy's golden age, she was a gift from the Force for the fashion industry, her elaborate gowns ending up being cloned for every shopping net and star market. On anyone else, such glamour would seem an extravagance, but Soh had the galaxy's heart. She was loved from the Deep Core to the wildest reaches of the frontier. No one since Chancellor Digrenara had done more for the Republic. Rhil had to admit being a little starstruck in her presence, hardly professional, but she hoped understandable. The woman had a pair of targons, for kriff's sake—Matari and Voru, named after the gods of the ancient Coruscanti. Now, what was *that* if not a statement of intent?

"Will there be a security detail?" Senator Vaadu asked.

Stellan frowned. "As I said, Jedi Stokes and Zettifar—"

"Yes, yes, yes," Vaadu interrupted. "But what about Republic Long-beams and Skyhawk interceptors."

"That won't be necessary," Soh tried to reassure him.

It didn't work.

"Not necessary? With the current climate?"

"You mean the Nihil," Soh said, her voice losing just a fraction of its usual sparkle.

"Of course I mean the Nihil. We've all seen the reports. The attacks aren't going away, Chancellor."

"But they are lessening," Stellan pointed out. "We have seen a drop in Nihil activity in the last few months, especially in the systems surrounding Valo. We believe those strike forces still in operation are mere remnants of the main fleet we engaged in the Kur Nebula nearly a year ago."

"But what of the attacks on Quantxi and Salissia?" Vaadu pressed. "Remnants or not, they still pose a threat."

"Not to the fair," Samera said. "We will have a full security contingent, including Longbeams stationed at all major jump points into the system . . ."

"Plus a squadron of Jedi Vectors on Valo itself," Avar Kriss added, speaking for the first time since Rhil and the others had entered the chamber.

"And will you be there, Marshal?" Noor asked.

There was a pause. Only a slight one, but noticeable all the same, before Stellan swooped in to rescue the situation, ever the gallant Jedi

Knight. Was that a flicker of annoyance on Kriss's usually placid features?

"We are reviewing the situation on a daily basis."

Noor harrumphed. "But the Nihil would think twice if the Hero of Hetzal is on Valo—"

Stellan opened his mouth, but this time Kriss got there first.

"I am certainly planning to attend, Senator. However, if the Drengir menace is to be contained . . ."

The mention of the latest crisis to set root in the frontier only heightened the tension in the room. Rhil had seen the reports—most of them still classified. Entire worlds were being overrun by the things. There were numerous theories on how they spread, from barely conceivable ("They've lain dormant beneath the surface of every planet for millennia") to the frankly terrifying ("Their spores grow inside the bodies of unwitting victims"). Either way, there seemed to be no end in sight, although recent accounts suggested that the Jedi had found a way to stem the tide; accounts the Phindian senator was obviously now beginning to doubt.

"You assured the Senate that the Drengir were being dealt with, Chancellor," Vaadu said, his voice laced with concern.

"And they are," Soh told him. "By Marshal Kriss and the brave Jedi of Starlight."

"Among others," Noor muttered darkly.

On the screen, Kriss's expression darkened. "Senator? Is there something that you wish to say?"

"Only that I wondered if the reports are true."

"And what reports are those?"

"That the Jedi of Starlight Beacon have formed an alliance with the Hutt Cartel."

Rhil tried her best to hide her surprise. There had been rumors of a union with the Hutts, known across the galaxy as warlords at best and gangsters at worst, but she hadn't been able to get confirmation.

Avar Kriss's expression didn't waver. "We are working with certain factions of the Hutt Council, yes."

"And you think that's wise?"

"We think it prudent considering the threat posed by the Drengir."

"A threat that at this point has *not* reached Valo," Soh interjected quickly.

"Nor do we expect it to, especially with the leverage afforded to us by our . . . new allies," Kriss added.

Noor was anything but mollified. "The Hutts cannot be trusted."

"In this, we believe they can be," Kriss insisted. "They have as much to lose as the Republic if the Drengir aren't uprooted. Plus, once the current crisis is contained, I believe that we could petition for a new treaty with Nal Hutta . . ."

"With criminals and racketeers, you mean!"

"With *powerful neighbors* whom I truly believe could be influenced to put their considerable resources to good use. This could be a new beginning for the territories around Hutt space, a new era of peace between our peoples."

"Which is the aim of all our efforts," Soh reminded them all, taking control of the conversation once again. "But I feel we are allowing ourselves to be distracted from the matter at hand. This meeting concerns the Republic Fair, a fair that is far from the other troubles we have discussed, troubles that *are* being dealt with."

"I still believe—" Senator Noor began, although the chancellor was quick to avoid a rehashing of his previous points.

"All will be well, Noor. That I can promise you. We have been working with the Jedi every step of the way. A Jedi Master has even been assigned to Valo prior to the completion of their Temple to assure the safety of the planet."

This, at least, seemed to put Noor at ease. "Yes. I know of the Master in question. Elzar Mann."

"A fine Jedi and a trusted friend of this administration," Soh said.

"Master Mann has been in constant contact with both Starlight and the Temple on Coruscant," Kriss assured them.

"And is also working closely with my office," Samera added. "He is very impressive."

Was that a slight flush on the administrator's cheeks? Rhil made a mental note to check that out when they arrived on Valo. It could be an interesting angle to follow.

"Elzar will know immediately if there is a disturbance in the Force," Stellan assured them all.

Senator Vaadu raised a hand on the vidwall. "My apologies, Council Member. I didn't mean to suggest that you haven't made the necessary arrangements. If anything, I am concerned that any incident, no matter how small, will play into the hands of . . . certain agitators in the Senate."

"Tia Toon," Reza said flatly.

"You know he is only looking for an opportunity to push his precious Defense Force Program."

"A program that the Senate has voted down at every possibility," Noor said. "The financial implications alone . . ."

The chancellor raised a hand, silencing the senator.

"Yes, yes, we know the arguments, and you know my position. The program doesn't fit with the philosophy of this administration and the Republic as a whole. But I also understand Senator Vaadu's concerns. Senator Toon will be at the fair . . ."

"Along with representatives of the SoroSuub Corporation," Vaadu added pointedly.

"As is right and proper," the chancellor continued. "But we will not allow him to use it for his own political or financial gain. We have all worked too hard for that." Soh's posture changed, her head rising slightly. "And there is still much work to do. The fair will go ahead, my friends. It must. Not for the spectacle, nor the glory, but for the message it sends to the galaxy as a whole. The Nihil want us to run back to the Core and cower in our beds. They want us to give up on our dreams and ambitions. That will not stand. They have committed terrible crimes but are nothing more than a rabble. Rest assured, I have studied intelligence reports and risk assessments. I have sat through multiple briefings and countless simulations. Every decision I have made is based on fact, not conjecture or fearmongering. As for the Nihil, well . . . we have seen their like time and time again, pirates and agitators, and yes, we will see their like again in the years to come. The difference between us and them is that we are united, while they are disparate; we are many, while they—by their very nature—are few. And, as discussed, we *have* stepped up security measures around Valo and will continue to do so if the attacks, sporadic though they are, endure. But know this; the one thing we will *not* do, that we will *never* do, is live in fear of something that *might* happen with no discernible evidence that it *will* happen. If we did, if we halted our plans even for a second, then the Nihil or the Drengir or anyone else who conspires to disrupt our way of life would win without even firing a shot."

Soh paused, not for applause, but as a sign that the conversation was at an end. That didn't stop Reza from adding a heartfelt "Well said," or for Noor to nod sagely on his holoscreen.

"We have no doubt that everything will run exactly as planned," the senator said, trying to save face following Soh's impromptu speech. "However, we would be neglecting our responsibilities—"

"If you didn't at least question our actions," Soh conceded, with her most diplomatic smile. "I understand, Noor. Really, I do. Nonetheless, there is still much to do . . . If that is all, I thank you for your time and I look forward to seeing you all on Valo."

One by one, the officials made their farewells, their holosquares fizzing off in turn.

"Well, that went well, I thought," Soh said, walking back to her desk, which sat in front of a glistening map of Republic space.

"Except for the mention of Toon and his schemes," Reza added, walking with her. "That damn Sullustan is nothing but a thorn in all our sides."

"He is but one senator," Soh reasoned with her deputy, sitting gracefully behind her desk before reaching down. The deep purr told Rhil that at least one of the chancellor's great cats was behind there, no doubt curled up at Soh's feet. "A senator with little support."

"But for how long? With the political temperature as it is—"

"The temperature is just fine," Soh snapped, weariness entering her voice for the first time. "There are concerns, of course there are. The Outer Rim can be dangerous. We all know that. That is why we have Starlight. And that is why we are having the fair. Yes, it will bring people to the frontier, and yes, it will bring investment: a showcase of everything the Outer Rim has to offer, but also a chance to build new bridges with our galactic neighbors. The Duinuogwuin. The Togrutas."

"The Nihil?" Reza asked. "Whatever Noor says, he is still concerned."

"Which is natural, but we do not need the DFP. Noor knows it, and, in his heart of hearts, Tia Toon knows it as well." She allowed herself a short laugh. "Can you imagine Noor letting a unified security force be established on Serenno? Count Kresto would burst a blood vessel."

Rhil made a note to look into this Toon and his proposed initiative, whatever that might be. She had never heard of him, or the program, although it was clear everyone in the room had experience of whatever controversy surrounded it. She could ask now, but it wasn't her place, especially as Norel Quo was bustling across the chamber, a look of concern etched on his pale features.

Soh looked up, noting her aide's concern.

"What is it, Quo?"

"We've had word from Cyclor, madam," he said.

"From the *Innovator*?" Stellan asked, tensing instantly.

"I'm afraid so," the Koorivar replied. "There's been an attack."

Soh stood up, her targons leaping to their feet beside her. "What?"

Gios already had a comlink in his hand. "Jedi Stokes. Padawan Zettifar. Please report."

There was no response.

Chapter Nine

The Cyclor Shipyards

"Jedi Vectors on an intercept course," the Fluggrian burbled as the Cloudship's tactical computer tracked the incoming signals.

Starbreaker was pleased to note that there was no fear in the Strike's squeaky voice, only excitement. He felt it, too. He rubbed his hand across the scar on his cheek. A Jedi had given him that on Mandrine, their accursed lightsaber burning through the thick layer of mucus that usually protected Gloovans from extreme heat. It had only been a nick, but it had been enough to brand him for life. Pan Eyta had told him he was lucky that the Jedi hadn't taken his head, but Starbreaker didn't feel lucky. The scar was a constant reminder how his raid on Kiapene trading post had been unsuccessful. He had lost a lot of Strikes that day and barely escaped with his Cloudship in one piece. This was a chance to even the score.

Thumbing a cam control on the arm of his chair, he zoomed in on the image of the Vectors on the scope. At least two potential kills. Starbreaker had lost eight Nihil on Mandrine, but even he would have to admit that the majority of them were incompetent rabble. If anything, the Jedi had done him a favor. He had taken more care choosing his

new recruits, and two Jedi skulls were worth more than the slugswabs
he'd lost. Those three lightning bolts were as good as his.

"How many scav droids do we have?" he growled.

"A full complement," the Fluggrian replied.

Five dozen. Excellent. Enough to pick the *Innovator* clean once the
raiding parties were on board, and more than enough to slice through
two Jedi Vectors.

"Launch 'em," he barked.

"How many?"

"All of 'em. Every single one."

Long ago, Loden Greatstorm had led his newly minted Padawan
toward the Elphrona Outpost's main training gallery.

"Today we will practice with training remotes," he had said, and
Bell's heart had sunk. He had only been Loden's apprentice for two
days and had spent most of that time meditating at his Master's request, preparing his mind to learn. Finally he was ready—and for
what? Training remotes? He'd been using remotes ever since he had
first constructed his lightsaber on board the *Crucible,* Professor Huyang
peering over his shoulder. Bell had thought being a Padawan would
bring new challenges, not just repeat the same old lessons.

His frustration had only grown when he felt Loden's amusement
over his Padawan's obvious disappointment. Was Loden *laughing* at
him? Well, he'd show the Twi'lek exactly what he was made of. He'd
slice that damn training remote in half. No, better than that. He'd
crush it like an egg with the Force. The thought had made him smirk,
imagining his new Master's face, the components of the remote tinkling to the floor as he released his grip on the Force.

Then they'd come around the corner, stepping through the ornate
ashstone arch that led to the gallery.

Bell's mouth had dropped open, and his Master's amusement had
grown.

The training remote was waiting for them, ready to duel, but so were more than a hundred identical drones hovering in front of the fifteen-year-old.

"You need to listen," Loden had said. "Not just hear."

"You said training *remotes*," Bell had said, resisting the urge to draw his lightsaber. "Plural."

"That's right."

Bell could sense there was another bombshell on the way.

"You're going to make me wear a blindfold, aren't you?"

In answer, Loden had pulled a long red sash from his robes, which he'd proceeded to wrap not only over Bell's eyes but over his ears as well, robbing him of both sight and sound.

"Jedi must never rely on their senses alone," he had said, his voice muffled by the cloth. "The Force will show the way."

Bell tried to remember Loden's words as he dropped his Vector into a barrel roll, laserfire streaking past the canopy. The Cloudship was too far out of range to return fire, but that would change soon enough. Indeera had told him not to glory in the death of his enemy, but there was no ignoring the sense of anticipation that burned in his belly, the longing to take revenge for Loden up here, where his Master had been lost. In the stars.

He forced himself to breathe.

"There is no emotion," he muttered, still focused on the Nihil craft. "There is peace."

The Jedi Code brought him comfort, keeping his focus on the here and now rather than the pain of the past or the dangerous lure of a vengeance-filled future.

"There is no passion, there is—"

His voice dropped away as a swarm of tiny bronze dots erupted from the Nihil cruiser. They were too small to be ships, each barely the size of Ember, but they were just as deadly.

"Scav droids," he muttered as they streamed toward him, the explosions from the nearby battle reflected against their rust-colored bodies. Bell had seen the results of a scav swarm on Rekelos. They were a relatively new weapon in the Nihil's armory, sent to mob ships or settlements, dismantling machinery with their grasping manipulator arms, the resulting loot stored in large crablike shells ready for pickup. He had never expected them to move so quickly or in such large numbers.

"Hold on," Bell told Ember, gunning the engine as he searched for gaps in the tightly packed throng. "What do you think, girl? Any way to squeeze through?"

Ember whined a response.

"Yeah, I can't see any, either, but that doesn't mean they aren't there. The Force will show the way."

Bell closed his eyes. He reached out, feeling the vibration of every droid's thruster just as he had felt the thrum of the remotes all those years ago. Suddenly he could sense the gaps in their formation, chart a path through their number to get to the Cloudship.

Back in the training gallery, the young Bell had taken up a defensive stance, his lightsaber burning bright. The training remotes had surged forward, and he had broken into a spin, his swirling blade slicing through each and every drone before they could even fire. He hadn't planned the response, but followed the prompting of the Force.

To this day he didn't know who had been more surprised by the tactic, himself or Loden.

"I've never seen anything like it," his Master had admitted. "A lesson for both of us."

And now the Nihil would learn the same lesson.

Bell threw the Vector into a spin, drilling through the scav droids. He plowed forward, his corkscrewing wings smacking the droids aside before they could grab hold of the ship.

Ember didn't whimper, even as Bell used the Force to keep her from bouncing around the cockpit. He was glad he'd brought her with him. Another Jedi might have left the charhound behind on the *Innovator,* but Bell needed her near. He focused on Ember's breathing as they streaked forward, keeping her calm, stopping her from feeling dizzy or panicking as they turned over and over.

No chaos, only harmony. No chaos, only harmony.

One of the last lessons Loden had taught Bell was that true mastery of the Force came not from protecting yourself, but others. As long as Ember was with him, he would keep her safe.

Bell cleared the swarm and, finally leveling his craft, opened his eyes.

That was when the harpoon punched through the front of Bell's Vector and lodged in his belly.

Chapter Ten

The Shrine beneath Golamaran

Death never came. Not for Dis. Not yet.

The cobonica shuddered, a ripple rolling through its massive body. The tentacle that had been mashing him into the icy rock fell away, slapping to the floor. Out of instinct, Dis struck at it, his remaining wingblade cutting deep into its immobile flesh. All the other tentacles were down. He could count seven . . . eight . . . nine lying in a tangled heap. The air stank of adrenaline, sweat, and dark thick blood, the monster's twitching limbs illuminated by the two remaining light spheres, as was the sight of Kufa still stabbing mercilessly with her calcium dagger.

Sluk. Sluk. Sluk.

Dis staggered over to her, telling her to stop, even as black blood splattered against her face. He called her name sharply, and her eyes snapped up to focus on him, the stalagmite sweeping around to bury itself in his flesh.

He stepped back sharply, the point missing him by a hairbreadth. "Hey!"

Her eyes went wide as she realized what she had nearly done. She looked at him and then back at the blubbery, hairy horror lying still before them. She had lost her mittens in the fight, revealing digits that were thin and bony, the knuckles dotted with ritualistic ink that had long since faded.

"Where is he?" she croaked. Dis looked back at the creature, its huge sac of a body at the center of the tangled web of tentacles, sagging like a deflated dirigible. Its eyes stared lifelessly from beneath its coarse mane of thick, twisted hair. Dis found himself searching for the orb Ro had ruptured and felt a ludicrous sense of respect when he found the wound, still dripping gore even in death.

But of Ro himself there was no sign. Had the creature devoured him, or did the Eye lie crushed beneath the body? If so, what had killed the monster? Surely not Kufa's poor excuse for a weapon?

The cobonica bucked, its body jerking. Kufa scuttled back like a rock-weaver; Dis dropped instinctively into a defensive stance as they prepared for round two. The monster wasn't dead.

Was it?

A long golden blade burst from the creature's body like a rocket, hacking at the monster from within. Skin and blubber fell away as Marchion Ro burst from the belly of the beast, lightsaber in hand and helmet streaked with gore.

"Thank the Path," Kufa cackled, throwing the stalagmite aside. "I knew you'd survive."

Dis, on the other hand, could only breathe in awe. "You are . . . incredible."

"I'm a damn fool," Ro replied, killing the blade. "I should never have let us be ambushed, not this close to the prize."

"The prize?" Kufa asked, her old eyes narrowing.

"The Leveler," he said, meeting her gaze before looking back at the alien corpse. "That thing . . ."

"The cobonica."

"Yes. Do they hunt alone?"

She chuckled. "Have you seen the size of it?"

He grunted, pulling off his mask to clean the filters. "Closer than I liked."

"By the Paths," Kufa breathed, staring at Ro's gray face. "That tattoo . . ."

Ro's face softened, the gray skin darkening around the silver markings that were etched into his skin, looking for all the worlds like part of a star map.

"It is nothing."

"We both know that is not true."

"Kufa . . . the creature."

She shook her head. "They are highly territorial. We won't see another for kilometers."

"Then we should continue." He wiped his visor with the corner of his cloak. "How much farther?"

"To the Shrine? Twenty minutes at most. Can't you feel it?"

Ro didn't answer, looking instead to Dis, his dark eyes flicking down to the Talortai's wrist.

"You are injured."

"It is nothing."

"Are you sure about that?"

Dis showed him by flexing the arm that was broken. "The bones are already mending."

"Incredible."

"Not for the Talortai. We heal quick."

"So I see. But what of your other blade?"

"Here it is," Kufa said, recovering the curved weapon by the light of the glow drones. She returned it to him, eyeing a crack that had all but split the blade in two. "Shame you can't repair that as easily as your wrist."

Dis tested the blade's weight, sweeping it through the air. He grunted in displeasure.

"The balance is off?" Ro asked.

"Unfortunately, yes." Dis fought the urge to throw the weapon to the ground. He'd forged that blade a lifetime ago, and now it was ruined.

"Then it's a good job we still have this," Kufa said, plucking her blaster from the tunnel floor.

"Will we need it?" Dis asked, turning back to the Eye. "I thought we were heading to a Shrine."

Ro stepped over a still tentacle and carried on into the shadows without another word.

Dis didn't know what he felt when they finally reached their destination but it certainly wasn't surprise. His stomach turned, his head spinning as if struck. He stumbled, dropping the broken wingblade, and thudded into a wall. Ro was beside him in an instant, holding him up, his legs as weak as a newborn.

"Are you all right?" the Eye asked.

"I think so." Dis opened his eyes and breathed deeply. They had emerged into a vast cavern, the glow drones high above them. Ahead was a frozen lake that Kufa was already scooting over, arms thrown out wide to keep her balance.

Dis steadied himself, breathing heavily. What in Talor's name was wrong with him?

"Can you continue?"

"Of course," he replied, his voice thick. He glanced down to his feet. The fallen wingblade had snapped in two. He left it, trudging after Ro who still had his helmet tucked under his arm. Every step was an effort, even before they reached the ice. Dis couldn't work out what was wrong with him. Surely this wasn't shock delayed from the attack. He had survived worse in his long life. Much worse.

Ahead of them, Kufa dropped to her hands and knees, crawling through an impossibly low gap in the far wall. Dis and Ro followed, Dis fighting back panic when his furs snagged against the rock. He flailed for a moment, unable to breathe, until Ro reached back into the crawl space, pulling him through.

"Can you stand?" the Eye asked.

"I can." Dis used the wall to pull himself up, his body as heavy as his head was light. What was this? A lack of oxygen? That was certainly possible this far underground, but it seemed like something more. His vision was blurred, lights dancing in front of his eyes. It was all he could do not to curl into a ball.

Ro, on the other hand, was striding forward, looking around himself in awe. "This is it," he breathed, voice full of wonder. "The Shrine beneath Golamaran."

They were in another chamber, this one bigger than the last. Kufa was hurrying across the cavern, heading toward a computer terminal built into the rock itself. She pressed a series of controls and illuminator panels activated high among the stalactites, bathing them all in harsh light. The air was still, almost reverent, and Dis was sure that he could smell the faint tang of incense.

Ro was suddenly in front of him, appearing so quickly that Dis almost reacted with his remaining blade. He stepped back, nearly slipping. Why hadn't he sensed Ro's approach?

"This is a sacred place," Ro said, but Dis struggled to focus on the words. Nothing seemed real. The hum of the lights. The creak of Ro's leather. The sun beating down from Talor's eternal sky.

Dis shook his head, trying to clear it. He wasn't on Talor. He was under the ice on a planet far from home where there were monsters with tentacles and hair and teeth and . . .

"You are not worthy."

His head snapped up and he found himself looking at his father. But that wasn't possible. His father was dead.

"You must leave this place," the Talortai said, his face twisted into hate, "and never return."

Dis's legs buckled, his knees hitting frost-covered stone.

"Dis?"

Not his father's voice. Ro's voice. And then another. Thin. Female.

"He is being cleansed," he heard Kufa say. "Such is the Leveler's power."

The entire world was flickering back and forth like a faulty hologram, strobing between the cave and his father's home, back to the day he was exiled from Talor long ago.

"You have brought shame on the family." His father's words again, followed by Ro.

"Would you like to see it?"

"See what?" Dis croaked.

Ro chuckled. "Why we came all this way, of course."

Dis didn't want to see anything. He wanted to screw his eyes tight to stop Ro morphing back and forth into the figure of his father. Had he been drugged? What if there was a toxin in the rock that he'd somehow scraped himself up against, something that had gotten into his blood.

"Get up, witch!" his father yelled at him. "Get out!"

"Well?" Ro again, grabbing Dis's arm, pulling him up. "Do you want to see it or not?"

Dis couldn't respond. Couldn't stop himself from being guided . . . pulled . . . guided across the chamber. He no longer had either of his wingblades. What had happened to them? He pictured one, lying broken in the other cavern, the other slicing his father's throat. No. That hadn't happened, had it? He'd cut Scarspike's throat. The cobonica's throat. Someone's throat.

There was another arch, another doorway. Cavern after cavern. Bones on the floors. Humanoid bones. His bones. No, that was stupid. He wasn't dead. Was he?

"Witch!"

His father's voice echoed around his skull. Skulls on the floor. Skeletons. Bangles on exposed wristbones, rib cages swathed in frozen rags.

Dis felt the cold. He felt the warmth of Talor's sun. He felt his father's wrath, his father's blood, gushing from the wound across his throat, the wound Dis had slashed. He heard the elders, driving him from the nest, calling him a witch over and over, the cries he'd tried to drown in a hundred reed-dens on a hundred planets. That was the past, but it was also now. He was on Talor and he was in the cavern, held up by Ro and Kufa.

Fear squirmed in his belly, and he didn't know why. A Talortai was supposed to be brave, but he wasn't a Talortai . . . not anymore. He was Nihil. The Nihil feared no one. The Nihil *were* feared.

"I can't go on," he wheezed, wanting to be sick, wanting to sink to the floor.

"You must," Kufa urged. "You must see. All will be clear. Look."

He did as he was told. They had led him into a smaller chamber, its walls blackened from centuries of candle soot. Four figures stood in front of them, their backs to the entrance, silent and immobile. Each was covered in a thick rime, long curving blades in their hands.

No, that wasn't right. The blades *were* their hands. They were droids, deactivated long ago, their joints frozen solid, heads bowed in respect, like supplicants.

"Look closer," Ro urged.

Dis took a step forward, breaking free of his companions' grip. There was something in front of the droids, a shadow in the wall.

He slipped, sliding on a patch of black ice, crying out in alarm as he tried to steady himself. The droids' heads snapped up, all four of them at once, frost falling like snow from their servos. They turned in unison, even speaking as one.

"You defile the Shrine."

Ro stepped up beside Dis, taking his arm again, supporting him.

"No. We come here to pay our respects."

Get out.

He flinched, hearing his father's voice once more, but this time there was no condemnation, only fear.

"You are not welcome," the droids replied. "You will die."

"Short and to the point," Ro commented as the droids stepped forward, blades raised. The Eye flexed his arm, ignited his lightsaber as if he'd been born to wield it. "I appreciate that. Are you ready?"

The last question was directed at Dis.

"I thought you . . . you came here to worship?" he croaked.

"The Leveler isn't a god."

"Then what is it?"

"Balance," Kufa replied, the blaster rifle in her hands.

"You said your ancestors brought it here . . ."

The droids took another step. His father pleaded with him to leave, blood spilling from the gash in his throat.

"Shouldn't they know who you are?" Dis asked.

"They're about to find out."

The droids charged, weapons raised. Ro blocked the first attack with his lightsaber, the droid's blade shorn clean in two. It staggered forward under its own momentum only to be reduced to slag with a bolt from Kufa's blaster. The rest of the droids weren't so easy. They moved with a fluidity that he had rarely seen in automatons, parrying with the skill of a Jedi. Dis had no blades of his own. Instead he grabbed the nearest droid's arm, ripping it from its shoulder joint. The other arm came around and Dis ducked, the blade nearly removing his head from his shoulders. He returned the favor, thrusting his stolen blade up into the droid's chin and through its processor. The droid tumbled back. Good. This felt good. It felt better. He was fighting, in the cave, not on Talor. He was in control. The Force would guide him. He would be strong.

Pain erupted from his chest, along with the tip of a blade. He gasped, his scavenged weapon dropping from his fingers. His knees buckled, only the blade keeping him on his feet. The attack had come from behind. He hadn't sensed it. Why hadn't he sensed it?

The droid dissolved in another blast from Kufa's rifle. Dis crumbled to the floor, still stuck like a pig. Something clattered down next to him. The final droid, felled by Ro, its neck severed.

Dis coughed, blood splattering the ice beneath his head.

A face loomed in front of him. His father? Ro? He couldn't tell.

"Udi?" Ro asked. "Are you still with us?"

Dis nodded, although he knew it wouldn't be long. Ro grabbed the droid's blade, ready to pull it out. Dis wanted to shout no, but it was too late. The blade came free, and the blood ran free. This time there would be no healing. This time the wound wouldn't close.

He felt Ro's breath on his face as the Eye leaned close to his ear. "What did you feel? Tell me? What happened to you?"

Dis's throat was full of blood. "I didn't . . ." he spluttered. "I couldn't . . ."

The words wouldn't come.

Ro stood, leaving Dis where he lay. Shadows started to close in as the Eye walked to Kufa, his lightsaber still burning. The old woman was on her knees, gazing up at the thing in the wall.

"So," he said, standing behind her, the two figures blurring in Dis's vision. "The legends are true . . ."

"Did you really think they weren't?"

Ro's voice was full of awe. "Such power . . . even from within the ice."

"Balance will come," she responded, an ancient mantra.

"Balance will come," Ro agreed.

Dis barely heard the Eye's blade slice through the air or Kufa's body slump to the ground.

Ro raised a comlink to his lips. "I have found it. Follow my beacon."

Then there was a beep, repeating over and over. Dis couldn't move. He couldn't think. The Eye of the Nihil walked back toward him, clipping the comm to his belt.

"Thank you," Ro said standing over him. "You have served me well. Served your Eye. You were the proof I needed, with your special gifts. Your work here is done."

Without another word, Ro brought his foot down on Dis's head.

Chapter Eleven

The Cyclor Shipyards

*T*here is no *pain. There is no pain. There is no pain. There is no . . .*

Who was he trying to kid? The pain was all-encompassing, overriding every thought, every instinct. All he could hear was noise: Ember's barking, Indeera yelling over the comm, the pounding of blood in his ears.

But Bell wasn't dead. Why wasn't he dead?

The harpoon had slammed through the bow of the Vector, spearing him to his seat. The tiny craft should have depressurized, but he wasn't being pulled along the blood-slick shaft toward the breach. He forced himself to focus on the projectile. Thick barbs were holding it into place, larger cousins of the hooks that were now lodged inside his guts, but the breach hadn't been completely sealed by the weapon. Bell's vision blurred but he could see cracks in the hull exposing the cockpit to the vacuum.

Still Ember barked. Still Indeera called.

There is no pain. There is no pain.

They were moving. The Vector's thrusters had cut, but the momentum of the ship was shooting them forward, with nothing in the void to slow them down. He looked up through the durasteel canopy. They were on a collision course with the Nihil Cloudship, the cruiser getting closer by the second. The impact would detonate the Vector's power core, but he doubted it would do enough damage to take the enemy out with them, not with that armor plating.

There is no pain. There is no pain.

Bell couldn't move his arms. He reached out with the Force, the way Indeera had shown him, flicking the switch that fired the Vector's retrothrusters. Yes, that worked. They were slowing.

Slowing.

Slowing.

The Vector came to a stop, Bell breathing heavily. He tried to focus on the controls. Hitting the retrothrusters was one thing, but piloting the ship using the Force? That was impossible. Indeera had managed it once, fighting the Nihil over Elphrona, but it had exhausted her. Bell was in too much pain to even attempt such a feat.

He could barely even talk.

The Vector jolted. Bell cried out, fresh pain gripping his belly. They were moving again. Why were they moving?

"Bell?"

Indeera's voice again. She sounded strained, as if she was trying to concentrate, difficult in the midst of a battle.

"I'm here," he managed through gritted teeth.

"Thank the Force. When you didn't reply—Well, never mind that now. They're reeling you in, Bell."

Yes. That's what it was. He could feel the vibration through the harpoon. He caught something. A fragment of a conversation, from the Cloudship, from the Force. A vision of a flight deck, a squat figure in a command chair, crowing about what they had done . . . catching a Jedi on a hook . . .

Reel 'em in, boys. Reel them in.

Could it be real? Probably not, especially in his condition. The Force was mysterious, but there was every chance he was imagining things.

But he wasn't imagining the air in the cockpit or the sound of Ember's worried yelping. There was oxygen. There was pressure. There was the Force.

"Indeera," he wheezed. "You're sealing the breach."

"No . . ." came the response. "The shrapnel I used to patch the hole is sealing the breach."

He tried to focus, seeing twisted metal strips patching the hole around the chain. She had done that, reaching into his cockpit with the Force, nudging the shrapnel into the right place so the vacuum of space did the rest.

"That's . . . that's amazing."

"You can thank the Force later," she said, although Bell could hear the weariness in her voice. Such a feat would have cost her, especially during a battle. But as always, Indeera's thoughts were for others, not herself. "How bad is it?"

Bell looked down at the metal protruding from his stomach.

"Bad."

"You're not finished yet."

"Where are you?"

"Not far, but I'm still dealing with scav droids. Can you shoot the cable?"

He tried to focus on the long cord that tethered him to the Cloudship, the cord that was pulling him in.

"I'll try."

Some chance. Every movement brought fresh agony. The controls might as well have been in another ship for all he could reach them.

"Bell?"

He slumped in his seat, Indeera's voice fading. He just needed to sleep.

Ember barked, Bell's eyes snapping open.

"That's it, girl," he said, not looking around at the scared animal. "Keep barking. Keep me awake."

"Padawan!"

"I'm here."

He drew on the Force, trying to deaden the pain, trying to move. His hands found the flight stick, his numb fingers the trigger. He mashed the button. A laser burst from the Vector's cannons, missing the cable on the first attempt but finding its target on the second.

But they were still moving. The cable was still intact. A laser-resistant metal. The Nihil weren't as primitive as their junkbucket ships would have you believe, but Bell doubted if it would handle two Vectors firing on the same point.

"Indeera," he croaked, his voice weaker than ever. There was no response, or at least he didn't think there was. His ears were buzzing, the sound blocking everything else. "Master—are you there? I need you to fire with me, hit the cable together."

Still no reply. His head lolled forward and he snapped it back up, wincing at the pain. Ember's yelps filled the cockpit, cutting through the ringing in his ears.

"That's it, girl," he gasped. "Keep barking. Bark at the Nihil."

Ember did as she was told, jumping up onto the back of his chair, a paw on his shoulder, warm through his robes. Good. He needed warmth. He had never felt so cold.

"Indeera?"

There was no response. He reached out, searching for her presence. Yes, there she was, in her Vector, unable to reply. She wasn't hurt, not yet, but it was only a matter of time. Scav droids were crawling over her hull, slicing through the plating. Bell could feel them, feel Indeera spinning and diving, trying to dislodge them, all the time concentrating on the cracks in Bell's own fighter. More scav droids joined the assault, slicing, cutting, scrabbling. Indeera was using the Force to keep their ships together, but it was a fight she was doomed to lose.

She couldn't save them. She couldn't save them, and it was all his fault. He had been so sure when he had corkscrewed into the scav droids, so pleased with himself. Bell Zettifar, Padawan. Bell Zettifar, student of the legendary Loden Greatstorm. Bell Zettifar . . . idiot. He was no different from that wet-behind-the-ears apprentice who fantasized that he would teach his Master a lesson by crushing a training remote using the Force alone. Arrogant. Naïve . . . and potentially brilliant.

It couldn't work. Could it? There was no way . . . except if he took the line the Nihil had quite literally thrown him.

Bell grabbed hold of the harpoon, concentrating on the vibrations that rumbled through the woven metal as his Vector was reeled in. He followed them in his mind, out of the Vector, along the cable, into the Nihil cruiser.

"That's it," he said to himself, imagining the cable winding around a huge oiled spindle, hearing the creak, creak, creak of the mechanism. The Vector was almost in range now, but he would only have one shot. He needed to know where to hit, when to hit. He conjured up an image of the walls of the cruiser, of the ceilings. Cables. Power relays. Capacitors. All coming from the same source, at the rear of the ugly brute of a ship. The power core, throbbing, pulsating, transforming fuel into raw energy, powering every stolen weapon, every laser bank, and every ion discharger. A bomb waiting to happen.

A Jedi didn't kill unless there was no other option. A Jedi protected. A Jedi defended. But no matter how well the Cyclorrians were faring against the raiders, this ship would be waiting, ready to launch the next attack and the next and the next. How many ships had it already attacked? How many settlements had it ravaged?

No more.

He focused on the fire of the power core. Felt its heat against his face. The delusion of a dying mind or the leading of the Force? He knew which he believed.

Ember barked, Indeera fought, and Bell pressed down hard on the trigger. He didn't see the lasers lance out, but he saw the result. The Nihil ship exploded in a ball of light, silent in the void, but Bell felt as though he could hear the screams of everyone on board. The lives he had snuffed out to save others. As a youngling Bell had been told this was the burden of every Jedi who took a life, no matter how justified: that every silenced voice would stay with them until the end of their days. He had never believed it until now, but welcomed the truth of it. The voices would be a reminder to always look for another way.

Of course, *always* was a relative term, especially with a harpoon in his gut. Superheated debris struck the Vector, spinning it around. This time he couldn't protect Ember. He could barely protect himself. He caught sight of Indeera's Vector, smothered with scav droids. There was something else, flicking out in front of him. It was the harpoon's cable, severed in the blast. Bell smiled through bloodstained teeth. Indeera had saved him. Now it was time to repay the favor, one last task before the Force took him.

Bell reached out with his senses, nudging the cable as it whip-cracked through space. It sliced through the scav droids, wiping them from Indeera's hull. More would replace them, but he had bought Indeera time to focus. Finally, she could worry about herself.

His eyes closed as the Vector whirled toward the Innovator's hangar.

"That's it, girl," he wheezed at Ember, still scrabbling in the back. "Keep barking . . . Keep . . ."

And Bell Zettifar fell silent.

Chapter Twelve

The *Coruscant Dawn*

The *Coruscant Dawn's* comm board had lit up like a Solstice tree the moment news of the shipyard attack had reached the Core.

Norel Quo had gone into overdrive fielding requests and arranging meetings for Lina Soh, who stood as calm as a Jedi Master as the tempest raged around her. If Stellan had been impressed with the woman before, his admiration had grown by the second in the midst of such a crisis. The tension in the room reached fever pitch within seconds, and yet she remained calm and controlled, at least on the surface. He could sense her true emotions, the concern that knotted her stomach, but they never even remotely approached panic. She sat behind her wroshyr-wood desk and gently stroked the yellow head of one of her targons, listening to every report and piece of advice in turn.

"Do we have word from Cyclor?"

Stellan glanced at Nib, who looked up from the computer terminal she had commandeered the moment the situation became clear, Burry at her side, monitoring news feeds.

The gray-haired Jedi shook her head. "Nothing from Stokes or Zettifar."

Burryaga grunted. Soh looked to Stellan for a translation.

"There is amateur footage of the attack being broadcast from the shipyards."

The chancellor was already up and walking back toward the holowall. "Show me."

With a nod from Stellan, the young Wookiee transmitted the images to the nearest projector droid. Static-blown footage of the assault stretched across the wall, looking as though it was being recorded from the *Innovator* itself. Behind him, Rhil gasped as scav droids streamed through a gaping hole in the hangar's ceiling only to be met by brave Cyclorrians armed with blasters, firing up from the *Innovator*'s hull.

"They've breached the defenses," Larep moaned.

"And are largely being held at bay by the Cyclorrians," Stellan pointed out.

"But where are your Jedi?" Quo asked.

Stellan turned back to Nib and Burry. "Can we see what's going on outside the hangar?"

Nib checked her controls. "Official signals are being jammed. There's no way to access the feeds."

"Then how are we seeing this?" Soh asked, indicating the scrambled image.

Nib shrugged. "The Cyclorrians are some of the most ingenious engineers in the known galaxy. They must have found a way to bypass the Nihil's blockers."

"Then they need to pass the knowledge on to official channels," Reza snapped.

Stellan peered closer at the footage, trying to see what was happening beyond the breach. There were stuttering flashes of light, barely more than a cluster of pixels. Where were Indeera and Bell? The Cyclorrians were putting up a fine defense, space-suited insectoids even tackling scav droids on the surface of the *Innovator*, fighting hand-to-manipulator-arm to save the pride of Soh's fleet, but they were ship-builders, not soldiers.

"What is the nearest Temple Outpost to Cyclor?" he asked out loud.

Burryaga responded in Shyriiwook.

"Derra? I see. So the marshal is . . ."

"Tera Sinube," Nib provided.

Stellan tapped the comlink sewn into the sleeve of his robes. "This is Council Member Gios. Patch me through to Master Sinube on Derra."

There was a click and then a young voice responded promptly.

"This is Master Sinube."

Stellan had met Sinube at his investiture and had been impressed with the Cosian, who had risen swiftly up the ranks in recent years.

"Master Sinube, there has been an incident on Cyclor, or rather above it."

"At the shipyards, yes, we know."

"We have lost contact with the Jedi assigned to the *Innovator* . . ."

He didn't have to finish the sentence. "I have dispatched a team to offer assistance. A squadron of Vectors led by Jedi Engle."

Stellan raised his eyebrows. Porter Engle, the so-called Blade of Bardotta. The Ikkrukki was a legend, some three hundred years old. He had served the Order for centuries but in his twilight years had taken a posting on Elphrona as outpost cook of all things. He'd obviously been reassigned from Elphrona, since the Nihil raid that had seen Bell lose his Master. Two Jedi both from the same outpost, now reunited above the skies of Cyclor, if Bell lived, of course. Still, if Engle was already on his way, the Padawan's odds of survival had increased.

"Communications seem to be down, although some of the Cyclor-rians seem to be bypassing the block."

"I'll have my Jedi look into it."

"Keep me informed."

"Of course," the Cosian replied. "May the Force be with us all."

Stellan killed the transmission and turned to see the chancellor conversing with a number of officials on the holowall, including Pra-Tre Veter, one of the three Grand Masters of the Jedi High Council.

The horned Tarnab acknowledged Stellan's arrival. "Master Gios."

"Grand Master," Stellan responded. "Master Sinube of the Derra Outpost has dispatched reinforcements, a drift of Vectors led by Porter Engle."

"The Force will be with them," the Grand Master said. "And what of Stokes and the boy?"

Stellan glanced at the raw footage from the shipyards. "Still no word."

Veter's snout flared at the news. "May the Force deliver them from peril."

"In all honesty, Grand Master, I am more concerned about the shipyard."

Stellan glanced at the owner of the heavily accented voice. It belonged to a tan-skinned Sullustan whom Stellan knew all too well, as did every member of the Jedi Council—Tia Toon, the senator who had caused such consternation in Lina Soh's earlier meeting and who seemed ready to cause trouble now that he had joined the conversation.

"Tia . . ." the chancellor began, only to be shut down.

"Yes, yes. I know what you are about to say. Our thoughts are with those caught in the middle of the attack, but we must also consider the financial implications of this act."

"Senator!"

"I'm only saying what everyone is thinking. Sullust has invested heavily in Cyclor."

"As has much of the galaxy," Chancellor Soh pointed out. "The shipyards are second only to Corellia."

"And yet they have been defended by what? Two Jedi?"

Soh spoke before Stellan could step in. "As you have just heard, reinforcements have been sent."

"Yes," the Sullustan spat. "*Jedi* reinforcements. Again, we are relying on the Jedi to protect us."

This time Stellan *had* to speak. "As is our duty, Senator. The Jedi have pledged—"

"We know about the Jedi's covenant, Council Member," the Sullustan snapped, his jowls wobbling furiously. "Marshal Kriss's vow has been playing on loop for months on every holonet channel from Muunilinst to Tarabba. But powerful as the Jedi are, it is foolish to place all of our lives in their hands. Unfair even. The DFP proposes—"

Now it was Soh's turn to interrupt. "Yes, Senator Toon, I am fully aware of your proposition, but this is neither the time nor indeed the place to discuss the Defense Force Program."

Toon's dark eyes widened. "Not the time? Chancellor Soh, need I remind you that Cyclor is not a frontier world. The Nihil have struck in the heart of the Mid Rim. Where next? Ubrikkia? Gizer? *Coruscant?* The Jedi are many, but they are also finite. This crisis shows—"

"This crisis will pass." Lina Soh's voice was like durasteel. "Just as Hetzal passed."

That was a mistake. "Passed? Tell that to the victims of the Emergences. Or the billions who have found themselves at the mercy of these pirates."

"Billions we have helped. Billions who have been rehomed. Even Hetzal is stronger than ever before, the Rooted Moon—"

"Reseeded with specially engineered crops that will grow at twice the speed of traditional kavam," Toon interrupted, completing her sentence. "Yes, yes, I have seen the holoreels. The Jedi's legacy protected above all."

"Our manufacture of *bacta* protected."

"Be that as it may, the Great Disaster should have been a wake-up call, and yet what happened? Valuable credits that could have been used to establish a proper defense against the Nihil plowed into the folly of the Republic Fair."

Now Soh's voice rose. "The Republic Fair will be a sign of solidarity. Of strength."

Toon snorted. "The Spirit of Unity. Yes, we've seen the posters,

Chancellor, but all the propaganda in the galaxy won't distract from the fact that the fair is a dangerous extravagance that should have been canceled the moment the *Legacy Run* was destroyed. All that time . . . all that money . . . frittered away on, on frippery and ostentation! The Republic Fair is a dangerous vanity project that puts the lives of our citizens in jeopardy. The Senate knows it and so do you, Madam Chancellor."

"That is enough!" Larep Reza's shout cut through the Sullustan's argument, shocking the senator into silence. "The chancellor is right. How dare you politicize this attack for your own gain."

Soh raised a hand, but the damage was already done.

"My own gain?" Toon spluttered. "I think only of the people, throughout the Republic, who live in fear of a cloud on the horizon every day of their lives. And what of those who believe the *chancellor's* politicizing, who believe the rhetoric, the promises. People who think they are safe, when this attack proves they are anything but, as do the other attacks that have blighted the frontier in recent months. *These* are the people your administration is failing, Madam Chancellor, and these are the people who will see for themselves, mark my words." With that, the Sullustan looked pointedly behind Soh, snorting with obvious derision. "After all, you already have the cams with you."

Stellan turned, knowing full well who the senator was referring to. Rhil Dairo stood at a respectful distance with her ever-present cam droid, observing everything.

"The Senate approved GoNet's presence," Soh argued, prompting another snort of derision from the Sullustan.

"I know. I was one of those who voted to allow it, in the vain hope that the galaxy would see the truth, but somehow I doubt this footage will make the cut. It hardly fits your narrative, but let it be known that I am more than happy to speak to Ms. Dairo, on the record."

"Master Gios." Nib's urgent voice cut through the argument. "We have word from Cyclor."

At last, Stellan thought, turning to Nib's terminal. "Is it Stokes or Zettifar?"

Nib shook her head sharply. "No. It is Porter Engle and the drift from Derra."

"Put it on speaker," Soh commanded, shooting a look at Tia Toon. "So we can *all* hear."

A press of a button and the Ikkrukki's gruff voice echoed around the chancellor's office.

"Communications are restored," he said, his words edged with static. "The Nihil had dispatched scrambler droids on the edge of the system."

"And the battle?" Grand Master Veter asked.

If the veteran Jedi recognized the Grand Master's voice, it didn't seem to faze him. "The locals have fought valiantly. Most of the Nihil raiders have been taken out along with the scav droids."

The sound of laserfire played over the speakers, followed by a grunt from Engle.

"Porter?" Stellan asked.

"Apologies, Master Gios. The stragglers are a scrappy bunch."

"And the lead ship?"

There was another pause, followed by the screech of static.

"Jedi Engle!"

"I'm here." The Ikkrukki's voice was more distorted than ever. "Although there's no sign of the Cloudship. The Cyclorrians say it was destroyed."

"What of Stokes and . . ." Soh paused, searching for Bell's name.

"Zettifar," Stellan filled in for her.

"Bell? Bell's here?" The Ikkrukki sounded surprised at the revelation. "I haven't seen . . ." His gruff voice trailed off.

"Porter?" Stellan prompted.

"I've found him," came the reply in a tone that chilled Stellan's blood. "And it's not good."

Chapter Thirteen

Beyond

Bell had no idea where he was, but he knew he didn't want to die.

"Is that selfish, Master?" he asked, his voice sounding strange, his words slurred. "Have I failed?"

There was no answer but the sound of Ember barking somewhere near him. Bell smiled. Good dog. She was doing just as he asked. Giving him an anchor.

But an anchor for what? To survive? To carry on?

There was more. More noise. More chaos. Even in the silence of space. Bell could feel it, the Force burning brighter than ever, ready to consume him, ready to transform him from . . . what? What did the teachings say? He struggled to remember. Sitting on the cold slabs of Elphrona Outpost. Listening to the Masters. Not even a Padawan yet. Just a youngling being led into a wider world.

"Transform you the Force will, from this crude matter to the light. Become luminous you will. Become energy. The energy of all living things, from the cinderhawks in the air, yes, to the charhounds howling in the night. From the Force you came. To the Force, you'll return."

Is that what was happening? Was he returning to the Force? He could certainly hear them, the cinderhawks calling high above and the charhounds . . . a charhound barking . . .

Ember.

His anchor.

Good dog.

He was back in the Vector, unable to move. People were dying all around him, out in space. Friends. Enemies. People he had never known. Would never know. Because, like it or not, the flames were getting closer by the minute.

"Transform you, the Force will."

"No . . ."

The word escaped his dry lips. He didn't want to go. Not yet. He had more to give. To the Jedi. To the light. He had only just begun.

There were explosions through the flames. Screams. Anguish. Victory. The barking of a charhound. Good dog. Good dog.

But he couldn't see anything. The flames were too bright. They were licking around him now. Purifying him. Cleansing him. Was it too late? Was this death? So many thoughts, so many memories, the past and the present crashing together as one.

Sitting on the outpost floor, listening to the visiting Master. Seeing a crystal in a cave. Feeling its warmth. Knowing it was his. Knowing it had called for him.

Loden choosing him as a Padawan. Walking into a training gallery, full of floating remotes.

Falling. Falling so far. From the *Nova*. From a cliff. Toward the planet. A child in his arms. So scared. So fragile. "It's going to be all right. Going to be all right."

Hearing that Loden hadn't come back. Standing on Starlight, his lightsaber held high above him with the others, Indeera Stokes in Loden's place by his side. Someone was speaking. Another Master. Another speech.

"Whenever you feel alone . . . whenever darkness closes in . . . look up and know

that the Force is with you . . . know that we are with you. This is our promise. This is our covenant. For light and life."

For light and life.

The flames were everywhere now. All-consuming. Blocking everything out.

And yet he didn't reach out. He couldn't. What if he didn't like what he saw?

"Bell?"

"Master?"

"We've got you, Bell."

It was a woman's voice, a voice he should know, but he couldn't think, not anymore, not with the flames and the memories and the fear. Should he be afraid?

The Vector was moving. Bell coughed and moaned, but that was good, wasn't it? That meant he was alive. Ember was barking, barking so loud, louder than the flames as they were guided through the debris, through the remnants of the Nihil fighter, to the *Innovator,* to safety.

Hands grabbed him. Three-fingered Cyclorrian hands. Human hands. The hands of Indeera. Yes, that was her name. And the hands of another. Gray skin. Long beard. Missing eye. Porter? Porter Engle. What was *he* doing here?

"Stand back."

That was Engle, all right, light bursting from his lightsaber, slicing down through the harpoon, cutting Bell free.

And they were running, running . . . Bell laid out on a gurney, being rushed down one corridor and another, guided by Indeera, by Porter, by people he didn't know, would never know.

"Ember?"

"She's here, boy. She needs you. Stay with her."

Yes. Good dog. Always by his side. Down the corridors. Into the infirmary. Tanks up ahead, full of . . . what did they call it? He couldn't remember. It wasn't important. The flames were calling. The Force was calling.

"That's it. Get him up. Carefully . . . *Carefully!*"

So many voices now. Some shouting. Some calm. Some in pain. So much pain. He just wanted the pain to stop.

And he was falling, not into the fire but into a tank, the liquid cool against his skin, the flames retreating, the voices muffled . . .

Ember muffled, but still there, on the other side of the glass, waiting for him, tail wagging, tongue hanging from her mouth.

His anchor.

Bell needed an anchor, now more than ever. He couldn't speak, a breather strapped tight across his face, drugs pumping into his veins. He couldn't say a word, but that didn't matter, because he had nothing to say.

He'd seen the flames. Seen the Force. And it had left him colder than ever before.

Chapter Fourteen

Lonisa City, Valo

"Elzar, there's been an incident..."

Samera Ra-oon bustled into the operations room, her green eyes growing wide as she spotted Stellan Gios's holoform projected on the far wall by a hovering cam droid. She raised a hand, mouthing a silent apology to the Jedi in dark leathers taking the call.

Elzar Mann mouthed that it was fine before turning back to the flickering image of the Council member. Elzar had been friends with Stellan Gios his entire life. Stellan, Avar, and Elzar. Three Padawans, three Masters, and yet kindred spirits. Always seeking one another out the moment they returned from missions, so different and yet so alike. One bound by tradition, one by duty, and the other... well... Elzar knew his faults. He was always driven to push the boundaries and try new things... things that usually ended with all three getting in trouble. Together. Always together.

"It wasn't him, it was me."

"No, it was me."

"It was all *of us."*

Now Stellan looked tired. Older. The weight of the galaxy on his shoulders. It was probably just the transition from outpost marshal to Council member. If any of them could cope with such a heady elevation, it was him. He *deserved* it. Yes. Yes, of course he did.

"And the *Innovator*?" Elzar asked, dragging himself back to Stellan's update on the situation on Cyclor.

"Safe," Stellan confirmed. "The Cyclorrians fought off the remaining Nihil, aided by Engle's drift. The boarding parties never made it aboard."

"And the Padawan injured in the raid? What was his name?"

"Bell Zettifar. He's on the ship, being patched up. It was a near thing by all accounts. A harpoon in the gut."

Elzar sucked in air through his teeth. "Lucky the *Innovator* was there. The finest medlabs in the Republic."

"Luck had nothing to do with it. The Force provided."

Soh's budget provided, Elzar thought, but didn't say it. State-of-the-art equipment. More bacta than any other ship in the Mid Rim. Bell was probably floating in a tank of the shiny new gunk, knitting together as the *Innovator* prepared for its maiden cruise.

"Are they still on schedule?"

"For launch? Just about. Vam Targes is conducting minor repairs on the hull, but it shouldn't hold things up. The chancellor is keen for the *Innovator* to arrive on time."

Elzar shared a knowing look with Samera, who was standing patiently to the side, both hands gripping a datapad. Of course Soh was keen. Nothing must disrupt the fair. Samera looked away, trying to suppress the playful and highly contagious smile that Elzar felt spreading across his own face.

Stellan's holographic brow creased. "Is someone there?"

"Um, yes." Elzar forced his attention back to the face of his old friend. "Coordinator Ra-oon." He indicated for Samera to step forward, noting how her back straightened as she came into view, slipping instantly into business mode.

"Council Member Gios," she acknowledged. "I didn't mean to interrupt."

Stellan waved the concern away. "There's no need to apologize." Elzar felt Samera bristle slightly. She wasn't apologizing, merely stating the fact. After all, this was *her* operations room at *her* fair. Typical Stellan. "You've heard about the attack on the shipyards, of course."

"Of course," Samera repeated. "We have stepped up our security measures accordingly."

"Not that anyone expects the Nihil to strike here," Elzar added.

Stellan raised his eyebrows. "Before today no one expected the Nihil to strike so deeply into the Mid Rim. The Senate is obviously concerned."

"And the Council?"

"Cautious. Grand Master Veter has assigned more Jedi. Porter Engle's drift will accompany the *Innovator* to Valo and stay until after the opening ceremony."

"And we will be pleased to have them," Samera cut in. "Is Jedi Engle a Master?"

Stellan's eyes sparkled. "Several times over."

Samera looked confused, glancing at Elzar and then back at Stellan. "Is that even a thing?"

This time it was Stellan's turn to issue an apology. "I was being flippant."

"Let's just say that Engle has been around for a *long* time," Elzar told her.

"Not that you should remind him," Stellan added. "He is one of the most respected Jedi in the Order, his name mentioned in the same breath as Masters Brisbane, Maota, and Yoda."

"Excellent." Samera glanced down at her datapad, scrolling through a list of names. "Then maybe we can assign him to the chancellor's party? A special liaison for Regasa Yovet."

"The Togruta head of state?"

Samera looked back up at Stellan. "The attack on Cyclor has spooked the Togruta ambassador. He's threatening to advise that the regasa no longer come to Valo."

"That . . . would not be optimal."

Elzar stopped himself from shaking his head. Since when had Stellan started using words like *optimal*? Elzar had hoped that he would be a good influence on the Council, not the other way around. He was starting to sound like Council Member Rosason. Worse than that. He was starting to sound like a politician.

"Engle might not be the best choice," Stellan continued, his brow knotted. "He has a tendency to be . . . terse."

"That's one way of putting it," Elzar muttered, hoping Stellan couldn't hear him. Engle was a lot of things, but a diplomat wasn't one of them.

"Let me give this some thought," Stellan said. "I'll talk with the chancellor. See what she would like to do."

"What about Avar?" Elzar chipped in, maybe a little too quickly. He could feel Samera's eyes on him and ran through various micromeditations to stop himself from blushing. The suggestion was valid. Since Hetzal, Avar Kriss was one of the best-known Jedi on the frontier, maybe in the entire Order. And she was marshal of Starlight, for stars' sake. Surely the Togrutas would see her being assigned to the regasa as an honor of the highest class.

"It's a good suggestion." Stellan stroked his neat beard, another new habit he'd picked up in recent months. "Can you leave it with me, co-ordinator?"

"Of course," Samera replied politely.

"I will get back to you as soon as possible so you can put the ambassador's mind at rest."

Good luck with that, Elzar thought as Stellan turned his attention back to him.

"I will see you soon, Elzar."

Elzar couldn't help but smile at the thought. It had been too long since the three of them were together, probably not since the dedication ceremony on Starlight. Not since . . . Elzar's mood darkened as he remembered the vision that had swept over him after Avar had dropped her bombshell about staying aboard the Beacon.

"Elzar?"

His smile became forced, but Elzar pushed on through. Besides, his first reaction had been the most honest. He *was* looking forward to them all being here. Mann, Kriss, and Gios. The three firebrands. That's what Quarry had called them before they were Knighted. His old Master hadn't been far from the truth.

"I'm looking forward to it, Stellan. Valo out."

He killed the transmission and the buzz of the holotransmission disappeared, along with Stellan's face.

Samera blew out. "I've met a lot of Jedi, but boy, is he intense."

Elzar dismissed the projector droid. "He just likes things done in a certain way. I know Stellan can appear . . ."

"Haughty?" Samera suggested.

"Standoffish," he suggested. "But he really isn't, when you get to know him. He just wants everything to be perfect. Everything is black or white for Stellan."

Samera raised an impish eyebrow. "I thought that was the case for Jedi the universe over?"

He chuckled. "You know what I mean."

"Maybe I do." Their eyes locked just a moment longer than was probably decent, before she broke the gaze and looked across at a map of the fair on the wall opposite them.

"Still," Samera continued, "you can see why he's all over the holonet. Whatever his faults, he's definitely easy on the eye."

She looked back down at her 'pad, trying to hide her smirk.

Elzar placed his hands on his hips, feeling the leather of his belt beneath his fingers. "Should I be jealous?"

She turned away, not looking up from the notes she was scrolling through. "Of course not. Doesn't envy lead to the dark side?"

She was teasing him, and he couldn't help but like it. "Among other things. What was the situation?"

"Hmm?"

"When you came in. You said there was a situation."

"Oh. More of the same, I'm afraid. Ambassador Tiss is—"

"Getting his head-tails in a twist?"

"Like you wouldn't believe. He's asked for a three-fold security sweep of the regasa's suite—manual, droid, and Jedi."

"Jedi?"

"The presence of the Order is the only reason they've agreed to let Queen Yovet visit the fair." Again, she flashed him a lopsided grin. "Don't let it go to your head."

Elzar put on his best Stellan voice: "That, my dear coordinator, is not the Jedi way."

The grin grew wider, revealing a perfect set of white teeth. "I'm glad to hear it, Master Jedi. Anything else just wouldn't be proper."

The sun was shining bright as they stepped out onto Administration Plaza. Elzar looked up, enjoying the warmth on his face, and watched wispy clouds scudding across a sky as blue as an Ankarres sapphire. It was true what they said: Valo was a paradise, its capital city—Lonisa— nestled next to an inland lake so large it might as well be an ocean. Crystal-clear water on one side, forest-lined mountains on the other, and air as pure as Elzar had ever smelled, even on Naboo where he had first served as a Jedi Knight, taking a much-prized position at the Gallo Temple.

No wonder the Senate had chosen Lonisa for the first Republic Fair in generations, a slice of heaven in the Outer Rim, now the focal point for the festivities, celebrating the Republic in all its infinite glory. Science. Innovation. The arts. The cuisine. Its streets were bustling as they headed toward the sumptuous hotel where the Togruta delegation would be staying. They could've taken a speeder, but Samera liked to walk whenever possible, just one of the qualities Elzar had come to appreciate. She was exceptionally good at her job, always managing to keep her cool when everyone else was running around like a headless lemock. He'd felt the connection from the moment he'd arrived on Valo. The playful smiles. The gentle jibes. It felt good, the tonic Elzar had needed since the dedication.

Since his vision.

If anything, their newfound friendship only cemented that he had been right to follow the leading of the Force on the moon of Ashla. This felt right, all of it. He'd spent the last few weeks walking the streets and touring the fair park, reaching out with the Force, looking for any hint of danger. All the time, the vision was there in the back of his mind, but it diminished slightly with every passing day as if his very presence on Valo was counteracting the evil he'd foreseen. He didn't understand why, but he didn't have to. The Force wasn't some kind of technical manual, laying out every step of a plan. It was something you interpreted, something you felt, and Elzar felt more at peace than he had for years. Even the thought of becoming Valo's Jedi marshal didn't fill him with dread. Not long ago, the thought of being shackled to one planet would have made his head throb, but now that he was here, all that had changed. How much of that was to do with Samera? There was certainly an easiness between them that rivaled his friendship with Stellan or even Avar, an easy comfort that he liked almost as much as Samera's laugh. She laughed often and loud, especially in Elzar's presence, and he did, too. More than he had in years.

He glanced over at her, admiring her long red hair, which she'd gathered into a high plait. She was talking through her latest conversation with the Togruta ambassador, but he wasn't listening, not really. Instead his eyes dropped down to the long line of her neck before flicking back up. She spotted him looking and he glanced away, pretending to look up at the giant sky-islands that floated above the lake. Each was designed to replicate the environment and landscape of a key planet in the Republic. It was one of the fair's main attractions, a way for visitors to explore just some of the Republic's rich diversity in one place.

"Have you been to Onderon?" Samera asked suddenly.

"The planet?"

She nodded toward the floating platform. "No, the island."

He shook his head. "Not yet. I visited the slopes on the Rhinnal island though."

"Did you ski?"

"No. I wanted to see the environmental controls. To maintain that much snow in this heat . . ."

"Yes, yes, it's a marvel of enviro-engineering, but you *have* to try the turbo-ski run. Perhaps I can show you after the opening ceremony."

"Will you have time, with the fair in full swing?"

"I'll make time."

She caught his eye, and this time he didn't look away.

"So, what's on Onderon?" he finally said, breaking the moment.

"Jungle safaris."

"Without the wildlife, I hope."

She gave another tinkling laugh that made his heart jump. "We don't want our visitors eaten. There are birds, though, high in the canopy, and a few Izizian monkeys, but nothing that can kill you where you stand, although if it's wildlife you're after I hear there is a hragscythe in the city zoo."

"Perhaps we can go see it after our ski trip."

Samera's lips drew back. "Maybe we can." She looked up at the array of repulsor platforms. "I still can't believe we pulled it off. Forty-two islands, all ready to open on time. They said it couldn't be done."

"*They* hadn't met *you*." He leaned in close. "Don't let it go to your head."

"Oh, I certainly will," she replied. "It's the Valon way."

Their eyes locked for a moment and all of a sudden there wasn't anyone else on the street. Another vision flashed across Elzar's mind, one infinitely preferable to the darkness he'd experienced on Starlight. He saw himself, years from now, the dark hair he'd been growing out now shot with gray, the marshal of a successful outpost, dining with a respected local official with emerald eyes and a graceful neck.

"Look out." A voice broke the spell. Samera gasped as Elzar grabbed her arm, pulling her back from the hoverpod that had almost mowed them down, its trailer stacked high with containers.

"Thank you," Samera said, putting a hand over her beating heart. "I didn't even see that coming."

"Neither did I," he admitted, feeling both a sense of relief that she was okay and a pang of guilt. What had he been thinking? *This* was why he never stayed on one planet for too long. The temptation to linger was too great. That and other things. Soon Jedi would be arriving from all over the galaxy—not to mention Starlight. What would Avar say if she even got an inkling of what he'd just been thinking? Would she be surprised? Probably not, but she'd be disappointed. He needed to concentrate on the job at hand. He was here because this was where the Force wanted him to be. Everything else was a distraction.

"We should get inside," he said abruptly, suddenly all too aware of how close he and Samera were standing. He took a step back, turning to look up at the imposing façade of the Hotel Republica, lavishly refurbished thanks to a grant from the fair committee. All the visiting dignitaries would be staying here, from the chancellor to Regasa Yovet herself. *Remember who you are,* Elzar told himself as they crossed the road, avoiding the steady stream of speeders. Samera, for her part, stepped slightly ahead, marching up the hotel's marbled steps in front of him. She wasn't stupid. She'd noticed his discomfort, seen him stiffen and step away hurriedly, changing the subject. No, she wasn't the stupid one. When would he ever learn?

Elzar followed her toward the turbolift, the doors pinging open to save them from an awkward wait in the lobby. Samera stepped briskly into the car and punched a button.

"The ambassador is waiting for us on the seventeenth floor." Her voice was sharper than before. More professional, maybe even cold.

Good, Elzar thought. That was better. That was how it was supposed to be. Samera was a coordinator, he was a Jedi, and that was the end of it.

Chapter Fifteen

Grizal

Grizal was not what Lourna Dee had expected when she joined the Nihil. She hadn't expected luxury. After all, she'd run away from that. But a forgotten prison complex as far off the star map as you could get without venturing into the Unknown Regions? That was something else.

Surrounded by thick forest, the installation was secure and structurally sound, although paint peeled off the stone-block walls and just about every barred window in the place was cracked. Most wings of the facility were still locked down, and in the few that were now occupied, the Tempests had stuffed or taped the panes to keep out the drafts. Most Nihil had set up homes in the cells in the main two blocks, tiny rooms lining three levels of the atrium, rusty gantries leading to sturdy staircases. For some, such accommodation only brought back memories of periods of incarceration that they had tried very hard to forget, even if the thick durasteel doors could be opened at any time. Camps had sprung up in what Lourna assumed had once been exercise squares, while others stayed on their ships, especially those visiting from other cells across the galaxy. Ro had been insistent. The Nihil needed to do two things. First and foremost, they needed to be quiet. The chaos after the Great Disaster had brought them a lot of attention, which had largely been the point. It had been a line in the sand, a wake-up call for the Republic, but the response from the Jedi, well, that had been something else. Ro had gambled that the so-called keepers of law and order in the galaxy would be taken by surprise by the Nihil's tactics, that they wouldn't be ready for combat, their skills dulled by years of being top of the food chain. The reality had proved somewhat different. The Jedi had proved to be more than a match for the Nihil, and the people . . . the people who should have feared the Nihil instead looked to the Jedi more than ever, still listened to that damn signal broadcast by the Republic's shiny new beacon. They still had hope. So Ro suggested a period of inactivity, to lull the galaxy into a false sense of security. Some might even say he'd ordered it. His influence had definitely grown since the Battle of Kur. So the Nihil didn't so much retreat as lie in wait. There were still a few raids, nothing major, and most of the rackets that funded the Storm were still in operation, under the radar, stockpiling resources. A little blackmail here. Protection money there. One of Pan's Strikes had even managed to swipe a reedug consignment from the Reekrider Cartel before it had reached its destination on Athiss, but nothing that would draw too much attention.

In the meantime, they needed a main base, a citadel that could be both a sanctuary and a fortress if things went further south. Pan Eyta had suggested the Great Hall, built by Ro's father in the heart of No-Space, but that was hardly practical. It was little more than a floating platform, the vacuum of space held back by a force field so it appeared that you were literally dining in the stars. It was impressive but barely defensible, a place to inspire awe but not to withstand the Jedi onslaught that was surely just a matter of time.

The prison complex had been located by Zeetar, the Talpini whom Ro had elevated after Kassav's Tempest had crashed and burned so spectacularly at Kur, taking Kassav with them. Zeet had come from Lourna's own Tempest and was a brilliant engineer responsible for many of the Nihil's latest innovations, from improved Path drives to the scav droids that had made stripping ships so much easier. Yes, the place was a garbage heap, but it was secure, and that was all that Lourna cared about. Like the Great Hall, no one would be able to find the planetoid without the Paths.

Of course, there were drawbacks. Lourna had never seen so much rain, lashing the weather-beaten walls of the complex day and night. Pan Eyta hated it and spent as little time here as possible. That suited her, although she would have liked to be able to keep track of her counterpart, especially after she'd joined Zeetar in relocating her Tempest to the camp. Lourna didn't trust Zeetar, but Lourna didn't trust anyone so that was nothing unusual. However, she did enjoy Pan's face when, on a rare visit to Grizal, the Dowutin lumbered into the work space she had converted to her quarters. He took one look at Zeetar and drew back his lips into a snarl.

"Is this a joke?"

"Do you see anything funny?" Zeetar snapped back.

Lourna did, although she would never let either of them know, remaining as impassive and steely-eyed as possible.

Pan swaggered up to Zeetar, intent on staring straight into the Talpini's beady little eyes. Usually he would have loomed over Zeetar, but things had changed.

"I see a little runt with something to prove," Pan growled. "A little runt getting ideas above his station."

Lourna had smiled when she had seen what Zeetar had done prior to Pan's arrival. The tiny Talpini had constructed a colossal powersuit complete with pneumatic legs that put him head and shoulders over anyone on Grizal. Zeet himself was perched in the protective cage that made up the mech's broad chest, the imposing setup completed by flame rifles on the loadlifter's droid arms and grenade launchers mounted above his head. Now, for the first time, Zeetar was leering *down* at Pan.

"Strange," Zeet sneered, his thin voice as weedy as the powersuit was imposing. "I thought we were all the same. Three Tempest Runners together. Equal in all matters."

"Yeah?" Pan replied, holding his ground as Zeetar clumped forward in an attempt to make Pan step back. "Why don't you jump out of that rig and we'll see just how equal we are."

Zeetar pursed his lips and cocked his large head. "Aww, are you feeling threatened? Poor little Dow-Dow."

Pan swung in hard from the right, only for his massive fist to be caught easily in the powersuit's steel grip. Zeetar squeezed his own hand, his suit mirroring the action thanks to the sensors that snaked up from the control gloves he wore over his stubby hands. There was a sickening crunch of bone and a grunt from Pan, the Dowutin's free hand immediately going for the blaster hanging from his belt.

"Enough!"

Neither Tempest Runner looked at Lourna, but the effect of her voice was instantaneous. The pair froze, glaring into each other's faces.

"Zeetar, release him. Pan, back off."

Now Pan's head snapped around to face her. "Who died and made you Eye?"

"Who made you stupid?" Her gaze turned to Zeetar. "Both of you. Squabbling like new recruits. We are supposed to direct the Storm, especially in Ro's absence."

Zeetar was the first to back down, releasing Pan's fist. "You are right, of course. That was foolish of me. I apologize."

"Damn right it was foolish," Pan snapped, rubbing his bruised knuckles. "And don't think we can't see through your stupid apology."

Zeetar spread his mech's arms, a smirk on his round face. "Just trying to be the bigger man."

Pan snarled, taking a step forward, but Lourna stepped into his path before he could resume the fight.

"Do I have to stop you myself?"

He glared at her, his breath hot against her face. Lourna didn't speak, letting the silence work for her. All the time Lourna considered her options: a headbutt to break his thick nose, a knife in the guts, slipped between the armor plates that were hidden beneath Pan's Saava silk shirt, maybe even a well-directed knee to the groin if she really wanted to humiliate the big oaf. In the end, all she had to do was remain obstinate. Pan's eyes flicked between Zeetar and Lourna before he finally relented with a snort, turning his broad back to her, proof of how much he trusted her, the ignorant fool. How easy would it be to blast a hole between those broad shoulders?

"What's this about?" he grunted, trying to take control of a situation that had rapidly accelerated out of his control. "Why did you call me back to this stinking hole?"

"What do you think?" Zeetar asked. "You messed up, Pan. You messed up badly."

Pan wheeled around angrily. "What did you say?"

"He's talking about Cyclor, Pan," Lourna added, the Dowutin's face darkening at the planet's name.

"What about it?"

Zeetar made a play of scratching his neckbeard, the mech suit copying the motion like a deranged puppet. "Oh let me see. An entire Cloud lost. The sector put on alert. Messages back and forth between the Jedi and the Senate. Tell me, Pan, should we call in the idiot responsible for the attack. What was his name? Sarn Starbungler."

"Starbreaker."

Zeetar snapped his fingers. "Of course, that's it. Oh, but we can't, can we, because now he's star*dust*. That's why we called you here. Because if the idiot in question is dead, why not go straight to the moron at the top."

Pan made to lurch forward but this time Lourna put a firm hand on his chest. He stopped, nostrils flaring. "It wasn't Starbreaker's fault. There were Jedi at the shipyards."

"There are *always* Jedi," Zeetar countered. "What were you thinking, Pan? Ro specifically said—"

Pan threw his thick hands in the air. " 'Ro said . . . Ro said.' Have you heard yourself? Five minutes as a Tempest and you think you know best." This time Lourna didn't stop him when he took a step forward, a thick finger jabbing at Zeetar's face. "Me and Lourna, we've been here since the beginning, more or less. You? You're nothing more than a jumped-up grease-jockey. Maybe I should grant you some slack, because you *obviously* don't know how things work around here, but to be honest I am fed up with the druk that flows from that mouth of yours. We ain't the Republic, Zeetar, and we sure as hell ain't the Jedi. We do what we want when we want, no matter what anyone says, Ro included. He rides the storm that we create. Our Tempests. Our Strikes. Yeah, we owe him for the Paths, but this is bigger than him now. And if he doesn't like it, he should step aside, whatever his spineless lackeys bleat. Spineless lackeys like you."

"Is that right?"

Lourna's words had stopped the fight but hadn't defused the situation. Those three words, spoken from across the chamber, killed everything dead. All three Tempest Runners turned to see the figure standing in the doorway, taking in the long cape, the heavy mask.

The calm fury.

"Ro," Pan grunted, a simple acknowledgment, no attempt to cover what he had been saying, no attempt to backtrack.

"Pan," Ro returned, stepping coolly into the room, the door swishing closed behind him. "It is good to see you on Grizal."

The Eye reached for his mask as he walked, seals hissing as they released. He pulled it from his head in an easy movement, revealing his smooth gray skin and those unnerving eyes that seemed to bore into your soul. Lourna noticed that he had let a light beard grow on his cheeks. That was new, although the look in his eyes was old. Disappointment. Rage.

Ro stopped in front of Pan and held out his helmet, not a challenge but an expectation. Pan tried to keep his head up as he took the helm, reduced to little more than a servant in the blink of an eye. The Dowutin stepped back, cowed, letting Ro pass. The Eye took in Lourna and Zeetar, uttering their names in greeting before stopping to appraise the Talpini's powersuit.

"You've upgraded. Most impressive, wouldn't you say, Pan?" He didn't turn to face the Dowutin when he spoke.

"Yeah," Pan grumbled. "It's great."

"Your mission?" Lourna asked, not to change the subject but only to prolong Pan's humiliation. "Was it a success?"

"Beyond anything I could have wished for."

"And Udi Dis? Did he serve you well?"

He didn't answer, searching her face for a moment before stepping away from the three Tempest Runners, his leather cloak billowing.

"How have things been going here? The work on the Path-jumpers?"

"Proceeding as planned," Zeetar replied eagerly. "We need a field test, but—"

"That will come," Ro promised, turning to Lourna. "And the other cells?"

"Lying low, as per your instructions."

He stopped, seemingly studying the star map Lourna had mounted along the far wall. "Ah, yes, my instructions. Tell me, Pan. Have you been following my instructions? Because we had a firm strategy, didn't we? A plan that everyone bought into. Zeetar. Lourna. *You.* No major strikes for the foreseeable future, nothing that would draw attention to us. Nothing that will prompt a reaction. You abided by that, didn't you Pan? You kept your end of the bargain?"

Pan took a step forward, glaring at the Eye's back. "Ro, listen . . . we need to talk. There needs to be—"

Lourna didn't know what Ro did, whether he clicked a control on his gauntlet or pulled a device from his belt. All she knew was that there was a click and energy crackled from the helmet in Pan's hands, flowing up his thick arms. He toppled like a great oak, his body convulsing.

Ro simply turned and strolled almost nonchalantly back to his tormented lieutenant.

"There needs to be change? Is that what you were going to say, Pan?" The Dowutin couldn't respond, his jaw locked as the energy surged through his body. Ro was standing over him now, a control unit in his hand. "You're right, of course. There does have to be change. Change to the lies that spew from that mouth of yours."

Pan was staring up at him, eyes wide with pain. Somehow, incredibly, the Dowutin managed to hiss through clenched teeth, "Stop . . . this . . ."

"Stop? Like you stopped the raids?" Ro didn't shout. He didn't have to. His voice was low and dangerous above the crackle of searing energy. "Did you think I wouldn't know? That I wouldn't hear? You attacked a major shipyard in the Mid Rim. And for what? A destroyed Cloudship and over sixty Nihil dead. No one escaped your Tempest's raid. No one. It achieved nothing, except placing the Republic on high alert. After everything we have been working toward. Everything *I* have been working toward. You risked it all because you were impatient, because you cannot see beyond your own greed."

He bent down, staring into Pan's pained eyes. "I knew sparing you was a mistake. Kassav would have obeyed orders. Kassav would have done what he was told. You should have been the sacrifice, not him."

Lourna half expected Ro to spit on the Dowutin, to hear the saliva hiss as it rolled down Pan's electrified cheek. She could smell the Tempest Runner's flesh cooking as the energy raged, every muscle bunched beneath his armor. But Ro swept from the room, not even looking back, leaving Pan to literally fry in his own juices. Lourna and Zeetar exchanged confused glances. Were they supposed to follow or to help their counterpart as he shuddered helplessly at their feet? For the first time in months, Lourna didn't know what to do. She had pledged to follow Ro without question, to obey his commands to the letter, but this? Kassav had been a tactical decision, but this was just a fit of pique, a punishment that outweighed the crime. The Tempest Runners were supposed to be able to be autonomous. Pan had gone against Ro's wishes, yes, but he didn't deserve to die. Not yet.

She crouched down, keeping a safe distance from the coruscating energy. There was no way she could pry the helmet from Pan's hands without being burned herself.

She looked up at Zeetar. "Pull it from his hands." The Talpini didn't move. "The energy won't harm your powersuit."

"You don't know that."

"He could die."

"Sounds like Ro wants him dead."

"Yeah," came a strained voice. "And how long before it's your turn?"

They both looked down. It was Pan, his face taut, bloodshot eyeballs looking as though they were about to start steaming.

But he wasn't dead yet.

Pan let out a bestial growl, his clawed fingers digging deeper into the helmet. Metal crunched and sparks flew. Lourna jumped back up as impossibly . . . unbelievably . . . Pan crumpled Ro's helmet as if it were a tin can.

Not so helpless after all.

With one last gigantic effort, the Dowutin ripped the helm in two. The lightning ceased, releasing Pan from its grip. The Tempest Runner breathed out, his muscles shuddering one last time. Lourna moved to help him to his feet, but the hulking alien turned his head so fast she thought he was about to sink his teeth into her fingers.

"Don't touch me."

"I wanted to help you."

"I doubt it was for my benefit."

She took a step back, allowing him to rise painfully to his feet, the two halves of the smashed helmet still in his hands. Steam was rising from his parched skin, burns raw across his wide forehead and cheeks. He swayed slightly on his feet, and to her surprise, this time Zeetar moved, shooting out a mechanical pincer to grab the giant's shoulder, stopping him from slumping to the ground.

Pan didn't pull away, but neither did he offer thanks. He just stood there, breathing heavily, his shoulders hunched and his back arched.

Instead, it was the Talpini who spoke first, a simple question that Lourna should have guessed was coming.

"What did he mean . . . sacrifice?"

Pan licked his cracked lips. "What do you think?"

Zeetar looked at Lourna. She sighed. "Kassav's death was a tactical choice."

"On Ro's part?"

Her silence gave him the answer.

Zeetar's eyes searched both their faces. "But Kassav's entire Tempest . . . everyone died, Lourna."

"To protect the Storm."

"To protect Ro."

"And you *knew*?"

The Dowutin took a step toward Zeetar but this time there was no challenge, no bravado. For the first time since Zeetar had been elevated, Pan was looking at the Talpini as an equal.

"You can't blame her." He glanced back at Lourna. "I don't, because it's not about us. It's about *him.* We do the work. We risk our lives and the lives of our Tempests and he reaps the rewards."

"The entire Storm reaps the rewards," Zeetar replied, although the words had no conviction.

"Really? You know the way it works. Yes, the spoils get spread around, but most work their way up."

"To us," Lourna reminded him.

"And to Ro. And for what? What does he actually do?"

"He provides the Paths."

"Does he?"

Dropping the remains of Ro's helmet, Pan reached into his armored jacket, pulling out a holoprojector.

"I hope this still works," he grunted, fumbling with the controls, his fingers obviously still stiff from his ordeal.

"Let me," Lourna said, holding out a hand.

Pan handed it over, looking her straight in the eye. "You sure you want to see?"

Lourna responded by taking the unit and activating the projectors. A holo of Udi Dis appeared, the Talortai's face frozen mid-conversation.

The Talortai's eyes were wide, frenzied, the pupils reduced to pin-pricks.

Lourna looked back up at her counterpart. "He looks . . ."

"As high as a kitehawk," Pan said.

"I thought he was straightened out."

"He was," Pan admitted. "But once an addict, always an addict, especially when a free sample finds its way to his hand."

Zeetar's eyes narrowed. "Let me guess . . . one of your Strikes took out a reedug shipment?"

Lourna shook her head, everything suddenly making sense. "The Reekriders."

"Just play it," Pan rumbled.

She clicked a button and the image came to life, the sound from the projector tinny but clear.

"You're just jealous," Udi Dis crowed, his voice shrill, a known side effect of the merchandise he'd been foolish enough to sample. "You hate the fact that Ro chose me."

"And why would I be jealous of that?" Pan's voice now. Lourna looked closer and could see a hint of his reflection in Dis's glassy eyes.

"Because I've got to go where you haven't." Dis gestured wildly behind him, his feathered arm sweeping up to point at something off cam. "The *Gaze Electric*. I've seen things you will never see. I know Ro's secrets, everything about him."

Pan uttered a sharp mocking laugh on the recording. "Rubbish. Why would Ro share anything with trash like you?"

"Because he trusts me."

"Pities you more like."

"Yeah? Then how come I know where the Paths come from and you don't? I've seen her."

"Her?" Lourna's question echoed Pan's own response on the holo.

Dis licked his beak, pleased with himself.

"Yeah, her. A woman. She's old. Older than me. Maybe even older than you. And it's all here," Dis tapped his temple in fast succession.

"In her head. She just thinks them up. Sees the universe as it is. She's brilliant. And she's his."

Pan reached over and took the projector from Lourna's hand, cutting off the image. Lourna let him, staring at the space where Dis's holo had been.

"A woman?" Zeetar asked, posing the question that was on Lourna's lips. "What kind of woman?"

Pan slipped the device back into his jacket. "An old one. You heard it yourself."

"Can we trust him?" Lourna asked. "He was addled out of his mind . . ."

"And didn't come back from Ro's mission," Zeetar added.

"Yeah," Pan said, "Funny that. The thing is, why would he lie? Ro won't let us see his precious database. Maybe that's why. Maybe he doesn't want us to know that his entire empire is built on the brain of one ancient crone." He looked at them both, examining their faces. "But think about it. This woman, whoever she is, provides the Paths, and Ro merely throws them our way, scraps from his table. But what if we had the entire meal, what if we could gorge ourselves silly?"

Lourna's mouth was dry. This moment had been coming for a long time. Pan had been strutting around like an Alderaanian peacock for months, and now she knew why. What other intel had he gathered? But one thing was certain: Whatever Pan was planning, they weren't ready, not for this.

The Dowutin snatched up the remains of Ro's helmet and stalked toward the door. "Where are you going?" she called after him, although the answer was obvious.

Pan stopped at the door and looked over his shoulder. "To finish what Ro started. It's time we took what is ours. What do you say, Lourna? Splitting the spoils three ways instead of four? Makes perfect sense to me."

Chapter Sixteen

Lonisa City Zoo, Valo

Elzar stared at the hragscythe and the hragscythe stared back, three sets of eyes to Mann's one. The creature wanted to kill him, of that there was no doubt. There was nothing malevolent about the desire. Hragscythes killed, that was just what they did, hunting through the Onderon jungles, ready to tear their prey to messy, red pieces. One of the deadliest predators in the Japreal system. One of the deadliest predators in the galaxy, full stop. Six eyes, eighteen claws, three heads, and more teeth than a pack of nexus. A natural-born killer to be treated with respect. And yet in just one day this magnificent beast would be gawped at by thousands of festival-goers. There would be younglings pulling faces and tourists taking image scans, parents posing their children in front of the monster safe in the knowledge that the ravenous beast was behind modulating containment fields.

No wonder the hragscythe was glaring. He would glare, too, if he were trapped in an enclosure, no matter how "enriched" the cage might be. Void's Teeth, he would thrash and flail and try to blow the coop apart by pure force of will.

Elzar ran a finger along his collar, the hragscythe's keen eyes following the movement. The morning was already unbearably hot, the sun beating down, unseasonably warm even for a Valon summer from what he could gather. He had meant to walk to the lake before the chancellor's transport touched down, to let the presence of so much water cool him. Maybe he'd even stand near the antigrav fountains that had been activated two days previously in the Arts and Culture zone, the work of a famed water sculptor whose name had escaped him for the moment. Instead, Mann found himself here, in Lonisa City Zoo, strolling among the exhibits. Elzar corrected himself. Not exhibits. Living creatures, plucked from their natural environments and dumped here. He was being uncharitable, of course. The zoo would do great work long after the Republic Fair had closed its doors, conducting valuable conservation and breeding work made possible by a generous grant from the fair committee that had completely renovated the once-tired collection that had stood here for generations. Everywhere he looked, Elzar saw new enclosures and educational booths, ready to inform and entertain, while also pointing guests to the nearest refreshment stalls. It was amazing how quickly the work had been completed, construction droids and Bonbraks still putting the finishing touches on the various paddocks. One of the bat-eared Bonbraks—Valo's other sentient lifeform, tiny and more than a little foulmouthed—had tried to stop him from entering the zoo grounds, chirping at him that they weren't open and to come back later. A quick nudge in the right direction ensured that the Bonbrak had gone about his business, instantly forgetting that he'd seen a Jedi in the first place. Elzar could just imagine what Stellan's reaction would be. The fledgling Council member was always squeamish when it came to influencing another being's thought patterns, but Mann didn't see the problem, especially if it kept everyone happy. The little Bonbrak would go on with his life safe in the knowledge that he had done his job to the best of his ability, keeping unauthorized folk out of the zoo until opening time. Besides, Elzar had clearance to go anywhere, more or less. If anyone else questioned his presence, he would simply say that he was sweeping the area for threats. He closed his eyes and reached out with the Force to make the lie a truth. All was well. The zoo was safe, if you ignored the fact that most of its inhabitants could gore, slash, or chew you to death given half the chance.

When he opened his eyes, the hragscythe had melted back into foliage that hid it from view.

Yeah, you stay in there, Elzar thought. *It would serve all those gawpers right. Let them peer through their image-lenses and complain to the keeper droids that you were nowhere to be seen. You look after yourself.*

The comlink built into his cuff chirped. Elzar sighed as he brought his arm up to his mouth, spotting the time on the chrono next to the communications device. He was already late.

"Jedi Mann?" Samera's voice was clipped, professional, and there was no mistaking the use of his title. Maybe she had people with her. Maybe not.

Elzar had already turned and was striding toward the nearest exit. "I'm on my way."

"Understood."

The comm cut off. Yeah, Elzar understood, too. The message had been received loud and clear.

The chancellor's shuttle was already touching down as Elzar pulled into the landing bay on the speeder bike he had picked up from the Temple. He hopped off the saddle and resisted the urge to jog over to join Samera and the welcoming committee. The coordinator turned to acknowledge his presence without even one word of greeting as he hurried to take his place. At any other time he would have said that she looked stunning in her smart trouser suit, her hair pinned high, but if her frosty reception didn't give him reason enough to pause then the presence of the members of the fair committee certainly did, especially the infuriating Captain Idrax Snat. The humorless Neimoidian headed up the Valo Security Force and, in Elzar's not-so-humble opinion, should never have reached such a lofty position. Elzar had spent most of his dealings with Snat fighting the urge not to plunge his lightsaber through his own hand. He had never met someone so convinced of his own importance and yet so incapable of doing his job. Elzar had no idea how the captain had risen to his ridiculously high rank, but at least he seemed to have the sense to surround himself with VSF agents who actually knew what they were doing. Elzar knew Samera felt the same way about Snat … Samera whose long neck was still far too diverting. Thankfully the whine of the chancellor's boarding ramp banished most if not all thoughts that were unworthy of a Jedi. Elzar adjusted his robes as all eyes turned to the open hatch. Chancellor Lina Soh did not disappoint as she emerged from the shuttle, wearing a gown of shimmering silver, her ever-present targons padding down the ramp at her side.

"Chancellor, welcome to Valo." The greeting was given by Lonisa City's mayor, a pleasant Valon by the name of Nas Lariin. "We have been looking forward to this visit for many cycles."

"As have I," Soh said, bowing in the traditional Valon manner. "May I introduce my son, Kitrep."

She turned to usher in an awkward-looking boy, whom Elzar would put at about seventeen standard years. Tall and rake-thin, the lad was wearing a loose hooded jacket and dipped his head stiffly in greeting, long curtains of black hair falling in front of his face, obscuring, Elzar noticed, green eyes that kept flicking over to Mayor Lariin. No. That wasn't right. He wasn't glancing at Lariin but at the mayor's son, a handsome-looking boy called Jom.

Soh was introduced to everyone in turn, the chancellor taking particular care to acknowledge Samera and Elzar himself before introducing the rest of her party; her deputy, her aide, and of course her Jedi escort. Stellan immediately caught Elzar's eye, and Mann allowed himself a ghost of a smile before welcoming Nib Assek and her towering Padawan. The final figure, standing at the back of the group, was a human female whom Elzar recognized as the reporter that had been assigned to document the fair for posterity. Elzar looked away as her cam droid's lens focused on him, feeling solidarity with the hragscythe back at the zoo. Thankfully, the spherical droid soon swept along the line, leaving him be.

The formalities concluded, Samera led the chancellor to the row of gleaming aircars waiting at a discreet distance, the driver droids ready to whisk Soh to the Republic embassy for the first of many briefings that had been scheduled before the opening ceremony. Elzar held back as the committee followed the chancellor, falling in beside Stellan and the other Jedi. Stellan, of course, looked resplendent in full Temple attire, the stole over his shoulders identifying him as a recently elevated member of the High Council, a temporary addition to his robes that Stellan would be glad to leave behind once the appropriate period of time had passed. Stellan spotted Elzar glancing down at the fabric's embroidery, a smirk on his face.

"Don't."

"I didn't say a word."

"You didn't have to."

"It's very . . . impressive," Elzar said, pursing his lips. "You wear it well."

Stellan looked pointedly at Elzar's own vestments. "And your Temple robes—?"

"Are where they belong. In the Temple."

Stellan shook his head. "I'm surprised you brought them."

"I tried to forget," Elzar admitted, "but my attendant droid helpfully stowed them in my Vector."

"How much did you yell at the poor thing?"

"Enough to rupture its audioreceptors."

Stellan laughed, knowing all too well how much Elzar hated his gold-and-whites and would find every excuse not to wear them if he had a choice, in the same way that Elzar knew that Stellan couldn't stand seafood or dancing at state functions. The latter had always surprised Elzar. After all, Stellan never seemed to mind being in the limelight, for the good of the Order of course.

It was good to see him, though. Elzar could already feel his mood lifting, even though Stellan's blue eyes were now fixed attentively on him.

"What is it?"

"You look good."

"And you sound surprised."

"I've just been worried about you. The last time we spoke . . ."

The last time they'd spoken, Elzar had still been troubled by his vision of the future, a vision he was now convinced he had averted by his presence on Valo.

Elzar shrugged, trying to make light of things as usual. "What can I say? Valo agrees with me. Who would have known."

"The Force?"

Elzar fought the urge to roll his eyes. That was peak Stellan right there. "Well, yes . . . naturally."

"Well, I'm glad to see you so relaxed. How has it been?"

"The preparations? Remarkably straightforward, thanks in no small part to Samera."

"Coordinator Ra-oon?"

Elzar cursed himself for his slip. The last thing he wanted Stellan to think was that he was getting overfamiliar.

"She's quite extraordinary," he said quickly. "Nothing seems to faze her. She takes everything in her stride and sees solutions when others see problems."

"Sounds like you think we should recruit her."

Elzar chuckled. "I think she's a little too old to start training. Besides, I don't think she's particularly Force-sensitive, just talented."

"There's no *just* about it."

Elzar felt rather than heard the sadness in his friend's words. "Stell?"

Stellan smiled, a little embarrassed. "You reminded me of something Rana used to say."

"You miss her, don't you?"

"She is with me all the time."

"In the Force."

Stellan nodded.

"Not to mention on your belt."

Stellan's hand went instantly to the long silver lightsaber hilt he obviously thought Elzar hadn't noticed, tucked away beneath his robe.

"Shouldn't that be in the repository?" Elzar asked.

"It will be," Stellan told him, subconsciously pulling his cloak around him so the light couldn't glint off his late Master's lightsaber. "When I have learned everything she has to teach me."

Elzar's eyebrows rose in mock surprise. "You mean the great Stellan Gios doesn't already know everything?"

He felt a little shove from the Force, the equivalent of a nudge in the ribs, a lighthearted reminder to behave that Stellan had employed since they were younglings. He raised his hands in surrender.

"I'm just saying."

"You're always just saying something."

Stellan fell quiet, and they walked in silence for a moment before Elzar asked: "Did you feel it?"

"When she passed?"

Stellan took a moment before completing his answer. "I knew long before the call came from Coruscant."

"Followed by your call to the Council Chamber. I wanted to be there, you know, at your elevation . . ."

"You had your duties."

That was true enough, Elzar thought, thinking of the waves of Ashla.

"Besides," Stellan continued. "Avar was there."

"She passed on my congratulations?"

"She did. She was there when I found Rana's lightsaber waiting for me in my chambers in the Temple. One last lesson from my Master, that Jedi come and go, but the Order remains. We are all just part of its story, me, Rana . . ."

"Vern."

Stellan smiled again at the mention of his former Padawan. "Vernestra Rwoh, Jedi Knight. She's going to do great things, that one."

"A chip off the old block."

"Less of the old."

"Well, if you refuse to dye that beard of yours . . ."

They had reached the transports, the party coming to a stop. Elzar shifted uncomfortably when he realized that Stellan's eyes were on Samera. Maybe he hadn't shielded his feelings about her as well as he thought. No, not feelings. That was overstating things. Friendship. Fondness. Either way, he would have to be careful now that Stellan was here.

"So what was it Rana used to say?" he asked, trying to distract his old friend.

"Hmm?"

"About talents."

That did the trick. Stellan was back in teacher mode, his happy place. "Oh, only that the talents of others are a reminder of our place in the universe. Here we are with our gift and abilities, and then there are folk like your coordinator over there . . ."

"She's not my anything," Elzar cut in a little too quickly.

"You know what I mean."

Elzar had a horrible feeling he did.

"Samera Ra-oon with no particular connection to the Force and yet as able as any Jedi, all without a helping hand from the galaxy at large. It's humbling."

Not to mention a little patronizing, Elzar thought, but he let it slide. Besides, the retinue was now clambering into the aircars.

"Shall we?" Stellan asked, stepping aside so Nib and Burryaga could take their places in an aircar before climbing into a seat himself. "Elzar?"

Elzar's attention had been taken by a second shuttle descending from the sky, this time in gleaming red-and-white livery, the colors of a Jedi craft.

"That's from Starlight," he said, not bothering to disguise the excitement in his voice as he started back toward the landing pad.

"Elzar, wait!"

"I'll catch up," Elzar called over his shoulder as the aircars started sliding away. Stellan would give him merry hell about this later, but he couldn't let the moment pass. Starlight meant Avar, and Elzar needed to make sure she was greeted in style. It was a little odd that the chancellor's retinue was already speeding away without the Hero of Hetzal, but time and Samera's schedule waited for no one, even the marshal of the Beacon.

And yet, when the shuttle touched down, it wasn't Avar Kriss who gracefully stepped through the hatch but a short figure wearing a bulbous helmet above his mission robes. Elzar had only met Starlight's archivist at the dedication ceremony, but the Ugor had made a distinct impression: mainly the ability to bore the wings off a Drethi. Elzar had only made it through their conversation by imagining what OrbaLin looked like beneath his containment suit. Few people had seen Ugors in their natural form, which Elzar believed resembled a cytoplasmic blob, their suits manipulated by wriggling pseudopodia that also facilitated the creature's senses. OrbaLin was the only Ugor to be accepted into the Order, a fact that the archivist had mentioned at least seven times during their brief encounter.

"Master Mann?" the Ugor said as Elzar stopped in front of the ramp, the archivist's thick accent crackling past his helmet's speaker. "What a pleasant surprise. Have you come to help with the artifacts?"

"Artifacts?" Elzar looked expectantly up the ramp but there was still no sign of Avar, only packing droids pushing a long line of hovercarts loaded high with crates.

"For the Starlight Pavilion?"

"No, well, of course I will, but . . . where is the marshal?"

"Marshal Kriss? Why, she is on Starlight."

Elzar frowned. "She's cutting it a bit fine, isn't she? The opening ceremony is tomorrow."

OrbaLin shook his helmet. "She isn't coming."

"I'm sorry?"

"She cannot. The Drengir threat. I have come in her place."

Elzar's mood darkened, and for the first time in months he felt the shadows of his vision return. Avar wasn't coming. He had been so looking forward to spending time with her again, to hearing her voice, her laugh, without the hiss of a holoprojector. No wonder Stellan had told him not to wait. He'd known she wasn't on the shuttle, the sanctimonious puffbag.

"Well?" OrbaLin said. "We have plenty to transport to the pavilion if we're going to set up in time."

Elzar didn't try to hide his sigh. "Fine. Show me what needs doing?"

OrbaLin produced a datapad, excitedly scrolling through an itinerary while Elzar stewed. This was just typical. However keenly he felt his disappointment, Avar's absence also highlighted how far apart they had drifted. He glanced up at the sky, spotting a single star among the blue. She was out there right now, keeping the frontier safe while he was here on Valo, shifting ancient trinkets from the back of a transport. Tomorrow she could be leading Jedi into battle for all he knew, while he would be gawped at by diplomats and tourists.

Like a hragscythe in a cage.

Chapter Seventeen

Republic Avenue, Valo

Stellan was worried. His friend Elzar had always been a man of deep feelings, but like all Jedi he strove to keep them in check. Yes, he was at times unconventional, but he was never unstable. Now his frustration was palpable. Stellan had felt the surge of emotion the moment Elzar had stalked into the reception hall after helping OrbaLin. It wasn't difficult to guess the reason.

Avar wasn't coming.

Perhaps he should have warned him the moment Avar had decided to stay on Starlight, but he had no idea that Elzar would respond so fiercely. The look that he'd shot Stellan when their eyes had met across the room ... Thank the Force Elzar got himself under control when the Togruta ambassador had hurried up, eager to speak to him.

Now the pair were walking happily together as the chancellor's party was given its first tour of the park. The delegates were strolling up Republic Avenue, the long thoroughfare that ran from the park gates to the edge of Lake Lonisa, where visitors would gain access to the repulsor islands that floated above the water. Trees ran the length of the promenade, carefully imported from dozens of worlds across the

Republic, and Stellan could see glimpses of the attractions beyond, the various pavilions organized into four distinct zones: Technology and Science, Sport and Adventure, Arts and Culture, and finally Faith and Life, where the Starlight Pavilion was to be found. As they walked, Coordinator Samera Ra-oon was pointing out highlights, such as the impressive hoverball stadium or the lookout tower, but Stellan couldn't concentrate. Instead he was focused on Elzar, wondering what was going on beneath his friend's forced smile. Perhaps he should join Elzar and Ambassador Tiss. The last thing they needed was a diplomatic incident between the Jedi and the Togrutas. Some days it seemed that the respect that the Togrutas shared for the Order was the only thing that was stopping them from openly declaring hostilities against the Republic. The fact that the Togrutas were even here was a miracle, and testament to Chancellor Soh's diplomacy. If Elzar said the wrong thing . . .

"Master Gios, are you all right? You seem . . . distracted."

It was Nib, breaking off from a conversation with OrbaLin to check on him.

"I'm sorry, Jedi Assek," he began. "I just need to—"

He was about to make his excuses when Samera Ra-oon's confident voice interrupted him. The party had finally reached the edge of the harbor, the majesty of Lake Lonisa stretching out toward the horizon.

"My friends," she said, smiling proudly, "here we find ourselves beneath the crowning glory of the Republic Fair experience—the sky-islands." She looked up, directing everyone's gaze toward the magnificent repulsor platforms. Some were no larger than a shock-ball pitch, but most were gigantic, the buzz of their hoverpods noticeable, although that would change when the fair's sound system started blasting out atmospheric music.

"Incredible," Soh said happily, her teenage son standing sulkily beside her.

"I'm glad you think so, Chancellor," Samera acknowledged before returning to her prepared spiel. "Forty-two individual islands, each representing a key member of the Republic. Here visitors will be able to experience everything the Republic has to offer, from the golden beaches of Spira and island spires of Bestine, to the bustling markets of Jaresh and fashion emporiums of Alderaan."

"How will visitors travel from one to another?" Larep Reza asked.

"An excellent question. Guests will be transported in unique repulsorpods, decorated with designs appropriate to the native system of the planets themselves. Pods, incidentally, that will be available to buy in miniature from every gift stall and toy shop within the park."

Stellan smiled politely as a chuckle rippled through the party, using the opportunity to glance at Elzar. His friend was sharing a private joke with Tiss, the ambassador obviously enjoying the moment. Elzar seemed to have relaxed. Perhaps Stellan should do the same.

"You worry too much," a voice seemed to say in the back of his head. Avar's voice, an echo from years ago when he had first brought up Elzar's black moods. *"Elzar knows what he is doing. He's a good Jedi, Stellan. And besides, even if he wasn't, he's got you to watch out for him."*

Avar was right. Avar was *always* right. No one was free of frustration, not even legends like Grand Master Veter. Stellan had realized that soon enough in his first Council sessions, but like Veter, Elzar could control his grievances. All would be well.

"We were hoping we would be able to give you a sneak peek of just a couple of the pavilions, starting with lunch on the Hetzal platform. The grilled vando-fruit in particular is to die for, especially after a long journey."

"An excellent idea," said a heavily accented voice. "Am I too late to join you all for lunch?"

Everyone turned to see a jowl-faced Sullustan hurrying toward them, with a mountain of an Orzrelanso in a suit that did little to disguise his physique striding after him.

Norel Quo and Larep Reza reacted as one, stepping in front of Soh as if the newcomer was about to pull a blaster on the chancellor.

"Senator Toon," Reza said in a tone that could freeze lava, "how marvelous it is to see you again."

"And you, my friends," Toon replied, acknowledging the rest of the group, bowing his head particularly toward Stellan. "Council Member."

Stellan returned the gesture, turning on his most diplomatic smile as the Sullustan turned to the chancellor, bowing extravagantly.

"Madam Chancellor."

Quo and Reza were forced to step aside as Soh approached the newcomer, her targons padding with her. She extended a hand, which the senator took with good grace. "Senator, we weren't expecting you so soon."

"I arrived earlier today. I have a number of meetings to attend before the festivities begin. One of the benefits of the fair. So many visiting dignitaries. Perfect for business."

"Business of the Senate or the SoroSuub Corporation?" Reza asked with ill-disguised venom.

Toon didn't seem ruffled by the vice chancellor's tone. "Both," he admitted pleasantly. "I am here to represent my people *and* the Republic."

"And this is—?" Quo inquired, giving the Orzrelanso the most damning of side-eyed glances.

"My personal secretary, Ratko."

Quo didn't pretend to hide his incredulity. "Your *secretary*? Isn't he a little . . . big?"

The Sullustan looked shocked. "Big? Whatever are you suggesting, Norel?"

That was obvious to them all. Ratko had *security guard* written all over him.

Fortunately, Samera jumped in, trying her best to avoid fireworks while also steering the proceedings back to her schedule. "We would be happy for you to join us, Senator. You and your, um, associate. In fact, we have repulsorpods waiting for us all." The coordinator turned, indicating a number of hoverbuggies, similar in design to the pods used by representatives in the Senate chamber on Coruscant although each of these was staffed by a discreet pilot droid built into the chassis itself. "Those vando wraps won't eat themselves."

Reza tried his best to guide Lina Soh away from Tia Toon, but the Sullustan wouldn't take the hint, attaching himself to the chancellor like a mynock to a fuel line. Reza glanced up, finding Stellan's eye. The implication was clear—stay close. Surely Reza didn't consider Toon a threat, physical or otherwise. There was the Orzrelanso, of course, with his long prehensile lobes and ridged forehead, but Stellan could sense no malice from the giant, intimidating as he was. Nonetheless, Stellan maneuvered himself so he joined the chancellor in her pod. Behind him, Elzar was already leading the Togruta ambassador to the second pod along with Nib and the other Jedi, all of whom had read the situation perfectly. Rhil Dairo joined the remaining dignitaries and officials in the third and final pod, although her cam droid still hovered above them all, taking footage from all angles. Stellan reached out with the Force, noting that Elzar was doing the same, ascertaining if there was any real danger. Their eyes met and Elzar nodded subtly, obviously having come to the same conclusion. Toon was an irritant, nothing more, the heightened anxiety in the group due to the worry that he would turn what should be a pleasant lunch into another opportunity to push his DFP agenda.

The fears were only heightened when Lina Soh turned around and called for Ambassador Tiss to join them at the front. Elzar was forced to stay in the second pod as the Togruta accepted the invitation, Senator Toon grinning from jowl to jowl.

"Excellent," Samera said, doing her best to ignore the worried looks from her colleagues. "Is everyone ready?"

"Indeed we are, coordinator," the chancellor said, playing to Rhil's cam droid. "Let's sample the delights of the Republic."

The pod lifted from the ground with the gentle purr of a felinx, the delegates' chatter shifting from pleasantries to wonder as the full beauty of the park became apparent from the air.

As she had on the ground, Samera pointed out key buildings while they rose, from the awe-inspiring Starlight Pavilion housing treasures from the Archives on Coruscant, Devaron, and the Beacon itself to the fair's spectacular main gates. Like the sky-islands, what had been dubbed the Unity Arc was a marvel of repulsor technology, twenty-two floating spheres, one for each of the Republic's Core Founders, forming a majestic arc.

But Stellan's eye was drawn to the city beyond the gates. Lonisa was already teeming with the thousands of visitors who had arrived early for tomorrow's opening ceremony. He had never been here before but knew the work that had gone into the city, from the construction of the new spaceport to the east to Valo's own Jedi Temple, currently in the finishing stages of being rebuilt from its more modest predecessor, like many of the outposts across the frontier. All of life was here on the very edge of Republic space, testament to the rapid expansion of the last few centuries. While Rana Kant would have been the first to remind him that a Jedi thought only of the present, Stellan saw nothing wrong in acknowledging the promise of a bright future. It gave hope, and hope fueled the Force.

Ahead of him, Larep Reza shook his head in wonder. "You said we'd do it," he told the chancellor, "and you were right."

"The Republic can do anything," Soh said proudly, absently ruffling Matari's crimson head. "Together we are strong, as I hope the Togrutas will come to believe, Ambassador Tiss."

Tiss acknowledged the comment with a slight bow. "The fair is an amazing achievement, Madam Chancellor. I am sure the regasa will be most impressed."

Reza and Quo shared a meaningful glance, seizing on the ambassador's words. If Soh's gamble to invite Elarec Yovet paid off, her dream of the Togrutas joining the Republic would move one step closer. And yet their cautious smiles vanished as Tia Toon opened his wide mouth.

"Yes, a fortune in galactic credits *can* do anything. The site is truly impressive, Madam Chancellor, as I always knew it would be. After all, when you spend that much money, anything less would be, shall we say, disappointing."

"The fair will bring much investment to Valo and the surrounding systems," Samera cut in. "In fact, it already is. Transport, passage, tourism . . ."

"Increased security, numerous grants . . ." Toon said, picking up the litany.

"Do you not feel the credits are well spent?" Ambassador Tiss asked, regarding the Sullustan with eyes the color of a burnt sunset.

"Oh, they will bring much pleasure to those lucky few who make it here." Toon looked up at the approaching island.

"More than a few," Soh said calmly, although Stellan could feel the frustration roiling in her belly. "We expect thousands to pass through those gates every day."

"Thousands compared with the trillions who make up the Republic as a whole."

"While others, who cannot make the journey, will be able to watch from their home," Soh continued, indicating the cam droid hovering just above them, recording every moment of the conversation, although Stellan doubted any of this would make the official broadcast.

"Yes," Toon agreed. "They will sit, huddled together in habs too small for them, watching a flickering image on a holoscreen, safe in the knowledge that their taxes have paid for all this, when they could have paid for so much more."

Reza's face had darkened, a flush covering his cheeks. "Senator, I hardly think now is the time—"

"And when would have been the time, Vice Chancellor? On the numerous occasions when I requested meetings with yourself and the chancellor, or when my concerns were dismissed on the Senate floor?"

"Nothing was dismissed," Soh said firmly. "We listened to every argument regarding the Defense Force Program . . ."

"And continued without pause or consideration."

"Because we already have the Republic Defense Coalition."

"Which is haphazard at best and absent at worst." Toon raised his hands to signal a pause in the conversation and turned to the Togruta ambassador with well-practiced sympathy written all over his face. "I apologize for any embarrassment this conversation may bring, Your Excellency, but I admit to having my doubts about this venture, doubts I hope and pray will be proved wrong. The fair, I am sure, will be a marvelous success." Now he acknowledged Samera, who was obviously trying hard not to shatter the datapad clutched tightly in her hands. "And I am also sure that Valo will benefit from the fame and investment, but I cannot help but wonder if, considering the current climate on the frontier, the money could not have been better used to shore up our defenses against the growing Nihil threat."

The slightest irritation had crept into Soh's voice when she responded. "As the Senate has been informed . . . and has accepted on numerous occasions . . . our security budget has not been affected by the fair . . ."

"It has not been *increased*."

"Nor does it need to be. The Nihil situation is being contained."

"And the Drengir?"

"Again, the situation is under control. The Jedi are already working with Republic authorities to stop the spread of the Drengir across the sector."

"That's not *all* they are working with, of course," Toon said, not letting the chancellor reply before turning the conversation back to the ambassador. "Have the Togrutas suffered much at the Nihil's hands, Your Excellency?"

"Senator Toon—" Soh tried to interject, only to be cut short by Tiss's reply.

"There have been raids, of course, as there have been for many years. Unfortunately, the Nihil are a way of life in, what do you call it . . ." The Togruta searched for the words, glancing at Reza and Soh.

"The Outer Rim," Toon offered quickly, keen to keep in control of the conversation, "although of course for you, it has always been your own territory. The . . ."

"The *Caramendary,*" Tiss provided. "The Center."

"The Caramendary, yes," Toon repeated, savoring the word. "Yours is such a beautiful language. And one I hope to learn more of as our great cultures work together. I am looking forward to meeting Her Majesty . . . if I am permitted to join the reception?"

"Of course," the chancellor cut in. "As a valued member of the Senate you are always welcome, both at the reception and here now." She looked up as the pod docked at their destination, the doors sliding silently open to let them disembark. "Ah, we have arrived."

"Indeed we have, Madam Chancellor," Samera said, pitching her voice up so the other groups could hear. "Welcome to Hetzal. Senator, if you would like to follow me?"

Toon allowed himself to be ushered out of the pod, giving Stellan a self-satisfied smile. Stellan watched them go, Samera pointing out just a few of the exotic meat-fruits that hung from the brightly colored trees, Chancellor Soh following with Ambassador Tiss, trying to salvage the situation.

"That looked like fun," Elzar said, appearing behind Stellan.

"Like fighting your way out of a doashim pit."

"We must do that again sometime. And that crack about our allies?"

Stellan frowned. "How could you hear that?"

"Lip-reading. Not easy with a Sullustan, I can tell you."

Stellan crossed his arms. "I thought he was going to start complaining about the Hutts there and then."

Elzar mirrored the gesture, although Stellan doubted it was subconscious. Elzar never did anything subconsciously.

"It's no secret that Avar is working with the slugs."

Stellan raised a judgmental eyebrow.

"Sorry, sorry. All life is sacred, I know. But you can't blame Toon. Who knows what the Hutts are planning?"

"Avar trusts them, and therefore so do I."

"I'd feel better if I could ask her about it myself," Elzar said, nodding toward Toon who was now helping himself to the vast buffet that had been prepared for their arrival. "Do you think he's going to be a problem?"

Stellan shook his head. "I sense no malevolence in him. Mischief, maybe, but no malice."

"He enjoyed making the chancellor squirm, that's for sure."

"They're old rivals, but he *is* sincere. Whatever his agenda, Toon loves the Republic. He's a complication but not a crisis in waiting."

"Are you sure?"

"Yes. Whatever happens, I think we can leave Senator Toon to the chancellor. She knows what she is doing."

Elzar patted Stellan on the arm. "Spoken like a true diplomat. Shall we join them? Looks like Burryaga is eyeing the horned melons. I don't want to miss out."

Stellan allowed himself to be guided to the buffet, happy that the tension between him and Elzar seemed to have evaporated, for now at least.

Chapter Eighteen

Grizal

Ro strode back to the *Squall Spider,* his thoughts as black as the clouds above him. Pan Eyta was becoming a problem. It was expected, of course, but Ro hadn't thought it would happen so quickly, and stunts like the one he'd just pulled with the electrified mask would only work so many times. Dowutins valued strength above all things. Thrown out of their family nest at an early age, the brutes were forced to fend for themselves or die trying. Bigger always meant better for their kind, and Pan was one of the biggest Dowutins he had ever met, nearly two hundred kilograms of solid muscle, one for every year of Eyta's life. There was no way Ro could beat the Tempest Runner in a fight, so he was forced to show his superiority in other ways—hence the trick with the mask. If he survived, Pan would be shamed into obedience, at least for a little while longer, and if he didn't, well, perhaps it was time to disband the Tempests altogether, to combine the Nihil into one force, headed by Ro alone. Lourna and Zeetar would be given new positions of power, of course, relative to his own, but a new structure would solve any further insubordination. Ro's father should have restructured the Nihil years ago, but for all his so-called strengths,

Asgar had never been a man of vision, which was probably why he was dead. For all Ro knew Pan had been the one who had turned the knife in his father's back, not Kassav as he had originally thought. Ro's eyes flicked up to the *Gaze Electric,* hovering high above the forest, a constant reminder of his sovereignty, even when he was offworld. Asgar had loved that ship and all it represented; a relic of a bygone age. But now Ro had an even older relic, and one that would be more effective than any laser bank or torpedo launcher.

"Ro? Ro, wait up!"

Ro had half expected Pan's voice to echo over the rain-soaked courtyard, and yet it was a high-pitched squeak that stopped him in his tracks. He turned to see Kisma Uttersond hobbling toward him as fast as the rotund doctor's mechanical leg could carry him. Even though they had worked together for months the Chadra-Fan was still something of a mystery to Ro. He had seen Uttersond conduct the most brilliant experiments, constructing torture devices so exquisite they would make a Galderian salivate, and yet the diminutive surgeon lurched around on a rusty old prosthetic liberated from a 1-1A medical droid. You would have thought the bat-faced doctor would have built himself something a little more efficient, but Uttersond cared little for elegance, as his filthy lab coat and greasy fur ably demonstrated. Only the work mattered. Ro liked that, admired it even, whatever his first impressions of the Chadra-Fan had been. Plus, such undivided focus meant that there was little chance of Uttersond betraying him, unlike the others.

"Well?" the doctor demanded. "Did you get it? The Great Leveler?"

Not many people would dare talk to Ro like that, but he let it pass. Uttersond was excited, his mismatched eyes peering through smeared glasses, one pupil forever blown, the result of a failed experiment years before Ro had become aware of the scientist's particular talents.

Ro pushed wet hair from his own eyes. "Still encased in the ice, ready to be transported up to your laboratory on the *Gaze.*"

"The refrigeration unit worked?"

"It did."

That seemed to please the Chadra-Fan, who chirped happily.

"And the Talortai?"

"Was completely overwhelmed by the experience."

Uttersond licked already moist lips. "Excellent. Did he survive?"

"Unfortunately not."

The scientist nodded as if this were the most natural thing in the world. "A pity, but the subject is ready for testing."

Ro put a hand on the Chadra-Fan's shoulder. "Patience, my friend. We need to take our time. There is no telling what damage the defrosting process could cause."

Uttersond removed his glasses, wiping the lenses absently with a callused thumb. "Of course, of course. Once I have the dimensions of the ice block, I can fabricate a heating rig."

"A heating rig for what?"

Ro withdrew his hand at the sound of the voice. He turned to see Pan marching across the exercise yard, flanked on both sides by his fellow Tempest Runners, Zeetar's hydraulics steaming in the cold rain. The Talpini had picked up a studded battle hammer. Interesting. Perhaps Ro had misjudged the antagonism between the two Runners. A pity. At least none of Zeetar's Nihil seemed to be around. Not yet at least. Pan's own ship—the *Elegencia*—was standing nearby, members of Eyta's crew playing sabacc beneath its massive hull. They also looked up from the cards, hearing the edge in their Runner's voice.

The Dowutin looked past Ro and Uttersond at the *Squall Spider*. "Just where did you take that old heap, Ro?"

"All will be revealed," Ro said, glancing down at Pan's hands, his jaw clenching as he saw the twisted remains of his mask in the Dowutin's massive hands.

"Why wait?" Pan said, throwing his arms wide so everyone could see the crumpled helm in his grip. "We're all here. Tell us. Tell us why you ran off to Wild Space. Why you left the *Gaze Electric* hanging in the sky like the overblown museum piece it is." His arms finally dropped down to his sides, but the challenge in his voice remained. "Why you told no one where you were going."

"He told me." Ro tried not to wince as Uttersond piped up, seemingly unaware of the aggression in Pan's tone. For a brilliant doctor—not to mention a talented sadist—the Chadra-Fan could be remarkably dense when it came to reading the room.

"Well, that's all right then," Pan said with a sarcastic snort. "If the bat knows, you might as well tell everyone." Pan's crew were on their feet now, and other Nihil were gathering at the door to the nearest block, attracted by the tension in the air, like bloodflies to fresh meat. "We *all* want to know, don't we?"

Ro glanced at the other Tempest Runners, taking in each of their expressions in turn. Zeetar was chewing his lip, a tell that had lost him many a digotto hand over the years, but Lourna was as inscrutable as ever. Ro had no idea what was going on behind that impassive face, with or without her mask. Was the Twi'lek with Pan or with Ro, because that was the line that was being drawn out here in the rain. Everyone knew it. The Tempest Runners. The gathering crowd. Ro himself.

"You know how this works, Pan," Ro said before raising his chin slightly to address everyone in the yard. "We all know how it works. When the time is right, I will inform you, and you will inform the Storm."

"The time is now," Pan barked, throwing the two halves of the mask to the ground. They bounced and rolled, an oxygen tube coming loose and flopping down on Ro's boot. He resisted the urge to kick it away, waiting to see who would draw a blaster first, if that was how this was going to go down. One thing was certain: Pan wanted a crowd, a circus, and by the Paths he'd get it.

Ro's hand went to his stolen lightsaber.

Pan tensed, preparing to strike first.

"Don't," Lourna's voice rang out. The Twi'lek was standing, hand resting atop her disruptor, which, thankfully, was still in the holster.

Was she threatening him, or Pan? Ro couldn't be sure. But there was no way Lourna could miss, not at this range, not with her aim. If she sided with Pan, Ro would be dead long before he could draw the Jedi's weapon. *Don't react,* he told himself. *Don't yell. Just stare her down. Stare into the barrel of the gun. Let no one see your fear.*

"What are you doing?" Ro asked, focusing back on the Dowutin, keeping his voice steady.

"What we should have done a long time ago," Pan told him.

"Interesting." Ro turned to Zeetar. "And you are with them? The Tempests united."

"I stand with the Storm," the Talpini replied, the battle hammer held tight in the powersuit's hands.

"I *am* the Storm," Ro reminded him.

"You used to be," Pan sneered. "Things are going to change, Ro. Things *have* to change." He stomped forward, kicking Ro's broken mask aside. "You have done much for us, that I grant you. You have brought us together, given us the Paths."

"*My* Paths," Ro reminded him.

Pan stared him down. "Are you sure about that?"

Ro felt his blood turn to coolant in his veins. He didn't ask Pan what he meant. He didn't have to, because the Dowutin hadn't finished, not by a long shot.

"We know, Ro. We know about the old woman hidden on your ship. We know she gives you the Paths. And she'll give them to us just as easy."

"Not without my authority."

That was a mistake. Ro knew it from Pan's triumphant grin as soon as the words were out. He'd just confirmed Mari San Tekka's existence in front of everyone.

Pan waited, not saying a word. Ro should have finished him off when he had the chance.

"And what are you going to do? Kill me? Storm the *Gaze*?"

The Dowutin made a show of considering this. "It's a thought, or you could step aside. We know your secret now, and the secret of your father. I hear the woman isn't long for this world, and what then, Ro? What would you offer?" His eyes flicked to the crate. "Whatever's in your little box?"

"You have no idea what I can offer."

"Then tell us," Pan bellowed, throwing his hands wide. "Explain why the Storm needs an Eye. Why we shouldn't take everything from you?" This time Pan didn't give him time to respond, turning to the horde of Nihil who were looking more interested by the minute. "Because we could, couldn't we, my friends? We could take the *Gaze,* we could take your old woman with the Paths in her head, and then what would we have? Certainly not someone telling us that we have to cower in the back of beyond. We should be out there! Writing our names across the stars! Are you with me?" A few of the crowd shouted back, mostly from Pan's and Zeetar's Tempest, but enough of Lourna's warband to be a concern. "Are you with me?"

Ro needed to act.

"And what then?"

Pan tensed at Ro's voice, raised just enough to echo around the former exercise yard.

"Where exactly are you going to strike first?"

Pan turned back to him, a sneer stretched across that ugly, smug face. "Anywhere we want, *Eye.*"

The title was an insult, not a tribute.

What are you going to do now? wheezed a voice in the back of Ro's head, a voice that needed to be silenced along with the others.

Now I win, Ro thought back. *Maybe you've forgotten how it is done.*

Marchion Ro took a step forward, addressing not the Tempest Runner but the Nihil in all their number. "Pan is right. Of course he is. You could strike, like he ordered over Cyclor. Where Starbreaker and every member of his Cloud died at the Jedi's hands."

The Dowutin's sneer turned into a scowl, but Ro didn't give him a chance to respond.

"You could also kill me now." He threw his arms wide, pushing out his chest, providing them with a target. "It would be easy enough. And you *could* take the *Gaze Electric*, squeezing every last Path from the Oracle, the woman who has been loyal to my family for centuries."

There was no going back now. The Nihil knew of Mari San Tekka's existence, but he'd be damned if they knew her true name or what she could do.

Because then you would have nothing, said the voice, but Ro knew that was a lie. He had all he needed.

"The Oracle has served me well," he continued. "She has served the Nihil, through me and my vision."

"Vision?" Pan scoffed. "What vision is that?"

But no one was looking at the Dowutin. All the Nihil were looking at Ro. Pan didn't yet realize his error in trying to usurp Ro with an audience, or at the least waiting before firing a shot. The only way he could've won was to shoot Ro in the back before Ro even knew that Pan was there, but, as always, the Dowutin was more concerned with showboating than actually seizing control. It would be his undoing, maybe not now, in this moment, but soon enough. One thing was certain: Ro had the Nihil and wasn't about to let them go. Not to Pan. Not to anyone.

"You ask me where I've been? I've been out there," Ro continued, pointing up into the gathering clouds above their heads, "in the very stars Pan wants to burn, the stars we all want to burn. And do you know what I've seen? The Republic . . . The Jedi . . . *Her.*"

Pan snorted, ready to shout Ro down, but instead Lourna spoke up, asking the question he had planted in all their heads.

"Who, Ro? Who is out there?"

The Twi'lek hadn't drawn her blaster. Her hand still rested on its grip, but Ro knew where her loyalties lay. With whoever was stronger, and Ro was about to prove he was the strongest of all. His head high, the Eye of the Nihil uttered three powerful words.

"Chancellor Lina Soh. Everything that woman does is an affront to our way of life. She comes into our systems," he said, thumping his chest to punctuate the words, "our territories, our space, tells us how to live, how to think. And so we strike back. We strike time and time again. We smash her hyper-lanes. Ravage her worlds. Kill her Jedi. And what does Lina Soh do? She laughs at us. She *taunts* us. We strike at her, and yet her Republic grows day by day." Again, he pointed to the sky. "I've seen it for myself. Even now, Lina Soh is planning a spectacle to end all spectacles—the Republic Fair. Millions of her advocates, her followers . . . her *sheep*, arriving from every system to march beneath her colors. And not just the Republic. Their allies, even their *enemies* are invited. The Mon Calamari . . . the Togrutas . . . And why? So their numbers continue to swell. So their influence grows—but I say no! No more!"

Ro paused, letting his cry echo around the square, before making a solemn vow.

"They didn't invite the Nihil, but by the stars we will be there. And we will crush the real enemy, the symbol of their hope and their resilience.

"Death to the Chancellor," he cried out in conclusion, punching the air with a fist. "Death to Soh."

The chant went up, the warband seizing on his words in an instant, Zeetar leading the chorus like the good little soldier he was.

Death to the Chancellor.

Death to Soh.

Finally Lourna drew her blaster, swinging it up, not to shoot Pan or Ro, but to fire bolt after scarlet bolt into the sky as she too joined the throng.

Death to the Chancellor.

Death to Soh.

Death to the Chancellor.

Death to Soh.

All around, the assembled Nihil followed suit, weapons raised, blasters firing.

Only one being stood unaffected by the fervor, fists clenched and shoulders taut. Pan Eyta glared at Ro, murder in his eyes. Ro looked back calmly, challenging the Dowutin to make good on his threat. But Ro knew he wouldn't. He couldn't, not with the Nihil firmly behind their Eye.

Instead, all Eyta could do was join the rest of the retinue, bloodless lips barely moving as the camp reverberated to Ro's cause.

Death to the Chancellor.

Death to Soh.

Death to the Chancellor.

Death to Soh.

Death to the Chancellor.

Death to Soh.

Chapter Nineteen

Lonisa City Spaceport, Valo

The day had finally come after years of planning. The opening of the Republic Fair. Stellan stood, his eyes closed, considering using the Force to quite literally take the weight off his feet. He hadn't stopped since morning meditation, accompanying the chancellor here, there, and everywhere as the final preparations had been made.

"Feeling it, too, eh?"

Stellan opened his eyes at the sound of the voice. Elzar Mann stood in front of him.

"What I wouldn't do for a dip in that lake."

"Or a moment of peace and quiet," Stellan agreed.

They were back at the spaceport along with every other official on the planet, Stellan in his Temple robes, Elzar still—notably—in his day-to-day garb. But Mann's face was beaming, which was a distinct improvement from the day before.

"You've spent too much time in temples," Elzar said, breathing in the air as if he savored the reek of fuel. "I was worried when I was first posted here . . ."

"That's an understatement."

"Worried I'd be *bored*," Elzar continued, ignoring the interruption. "But now . . . can't you feel it, Stellan? The excitement in the air. The anticipation. So much life. So much energy. The Force is strong here."

He was right, of course. Even out here, far from the city, the atmosphere was electric, and Elzar, more so than any Jedi Stellan had ever met, was affected by his surroundings. Others saw it as a failing, but Stellan knew it as the way Mann connected to the Force, how he thought the way he did. They really weren't that different, although Elzar seemed to have less of an issue with the cam droids that swarmed around them like bloat-bottles. Stellan had coped with Rhil Dairo's cam on the *Coruscant Dawn*, gotten used to it even, but an army of the things was a different matter. Stellan glanced over to the media corps, who huddled behind barriers to the side of the chancellor's party. Rhil was among them. She had clearance to be with the official welcoming committee but had chosen to join her fellow reporters. A diplomatic move? Maybe, although Stellan suspected the young woman was keeping her ear to the proverbial ground, on the lookout for new leads. She was a shrewd customer and belonged in this world, while Stellan was feeling surprisingly out of his depth. Everyone thought he was taking this all in his stride. He knew what the others thought of him—most of his close friends teased him often enough. *Stellan Gios likes the sound of his own voice. Stellan Gios can't get enough of the limelight.* All of that couldn't have been further from the truth. Elzar was right. Stellan *had* spent most of his career in temples. Teaching. Advising. Coaxing. Elzar and Avar—they were the pioneers, they were the *explorers.* He was a mentor, not used to the public gaze, no matter how the Order positioned him as the bright young thing on the Council, an example to all. He didn't particularly like it, but if it was the will of the Force, who was he to argue or complain. Jedi were supposed to be an example, a guiding light. He should take this as the opportunity it was. The blessing.

As if to test his new resolve, a cam droid dropped down in front of his face, its lenses zooming in for a close-up. Rhil's droid, T-9. Stellan forced a smile, hoping it looked genuine, and breathed out in relief as the droid darted away, distracted by the sudden whine of a descending shuttle.

"Don't worry," Elzar whispered as the party shuffled itself into the lines that Samera had preordained. "You'll be out of the crosshairs soon enough." Mann shielded his eyes to gaze up at the landing ship. "All eyes will be on her."

The shuttle was certainly beautiful, its hull long and tapered, long wings swiveling up as the landing rig silently deployed. Its hull gleamed like polished bronzium, the engines all but silent as it gently touched down.

"Was all well at the hotel?" Stellan asked, adjusting his cloak.

"Everything checked out . . . again." Elzar didn't even try to disguise the irritation in his voice. "Do you know how many times Tiss has asked me to sweep the royal suite? And that's *after* the Valo Security Force gave the place the thumbs-up."

"He is just being thorough."

"That's one word for it. The others are beneath a Jedi."

Stellan tried to suppress the smile that tugged at his lips. "I'm glad you realize. The important thing is that the regasa feels safe."

"Yes Master. Thank you Master."

"Oh, shut up."

They both fell quiet as the ramp began to descend. Chancellor Soh stepped forward, her targons staying obediently where they were beside her son. Kitrep Soh looked as uncomfortable as Stellan felt in the glare of the cam droids, but, as Elzar predicted, every lens immediately shifted to the figures emerging from the shuttle.

First came guards carrying traditional Shilian weapons, the long, barbed pikes known as kiavene. The soldiers were dressed in long tunics, their faces hidden beneath near-featureless masks that were framed by their montrals, the distinctive horns capped with silver plating. Moving in unison, they marched forward, only to sharply double back, lining up on either side of the ramp. When they had snapped to attention, a vision in long, flowing robes began her descent. Elarec Yovet was simply stunning, her skin flawless orange and her montrals adorned with delicate golden metalwork that glinted in the sunlight, similar but far more ornate than the ear cuffs worn by the Valons. Her long head-tails hung down in front of her shoulders, past the high collar with its fur detailing and the heavy chain that marked her high office. Regasa of Shili, Supreme Huntress of the United Tribes, Ruler of Togrutas far and wide. Time seemed to stand still as she approached the chancellor, her guard falling in beside her. The two women appraised each other, as was the Togruta way, before Soh finally spoke.

"Most High Regasa, I welcome you to Valo, a proud member of the Galactic Republic. *Tara macane vara numara narak.*"

Stellan was impressed. Soh's mastery of Togruti was flawless, no doubt the result of many hours of practice with various protocol droids. And there was no mistaking the look of respect on Elarec's face as she returned the traditional greeting.

"Tara sootan koora manera narak."

May the Force guide your path.

May the Force bring you home.

Home—specifically the Togruta homeworld of Shili—had been the biggest stumbling point when the Republic had first ventured into Togruta space nearly 150 years earlier. Members of the species were fiercely protective of their world and its surrounding moons, considering the ground beneath their bare feet sacred. Stellan glanced down. Sure enough, the regasa wore no shoes. Most Togrutas wore boots when they were offworld, but the High Huntress always went barefoot wherever she was. He had never met her, of course. Few in the Republic had. Those early encounters hadn't gone well. The Togrutas had known about the Republic for centuries, just as the Republic had known about the Togrutas. There had been a mutual respect, many such as Jora Malli even leaving the Togrutas' home planet to become Jedi, but having the Republic on Shili's doorstep was a different matter. There had been clashes, some unscrupulous pioneers misreading the Togrutas' apparent pacifism. Lines had been drawn that still remained nearly two centuries later. But here was the regasa, standing on a Republic world, the official guest of the chancellor. Stellan knew how important this meeting was to Soh's plans. Having the Togrutas join the Republic was the culmination of what the media delighted in calling her Great Works, a lifelong ambition that she would do everything in her power to realize before her term of office came to a conclusion in four years' time.

"Here we go," Elzar muttered beneath his breath as the monarch was led along the line of dignitaries, bowing to each and every one as they were introduced. Stellan felt a stab of irritation. Couldn't Elzar take anything seriously? It was fine back when they were Padawans, even young Jedi Knights, but now the eyes of the galaxy were upon them. Quite literally as it happened. Stellan felt a bead of sweat roll down his back and for a moment considered that Elzar had been right not to wear his heavy Temple robes.

Before long, Elarec was in front of him, being introduced by the chancellor.

"Lord Jedi," the regasa said, using an honorific that the Jedi themselves hadn't used for millennia—but the Togrutas refused to let slip into antiquity. "I see from your raiment that you are a member of the Council on Coruscant."

"I am, Your Majesty."

"Then you knew my great friend Jora Malli. I miss her terribly."

"She was a wise and honorable Jedi, who now dwells in the Force."

Regasa Elarec nodded sagely. "Of course. I had hoped to visit her station."

"Starlight Beacon."

Another nod, the gems on Yovet's headdress catching the sunlight.

"Maybe you should," Elzar cut in without waiting to be introduced. "I'm sure Marshal Kriss would be happy to welcome you and your retinue."

"That would be most gratifying," the regasa said, turning to Soh. "With the chancellor's permission, of course."

"It would be our absolute pleasure," Lina Soh responded, apparently unperturbed by Elzar's disregard for protocol.

Stellan waited for the chancellor to lead Elarec farther down the line before he turned to raise his eyebrows at Elzar, who mouthed a characteristic *What?*

Some things never changed.

Chapter Twenty

The *Dynamo*

Mantessa Chekkat's ship was spotless. This, Ty Yorrick could appreciate. Her own ship, now safely docked on Port Haileap, was old, but it was never messy. Ty was a firm believer in a place for everything and everything in its place. It was one of the few things that she and her admin droid agreed on. The *Dynamo,* however, was something else. An army of tiny droids was constantly rolling from deck to deck polishing and sanitizing until every console gleamed and the filtered air smelled like a medcenter.

Considering her obvious predilection for cleanliness, it came as no surprise when Mantessa had taken one look at Ty's ship and insisted that they traveled on the *Dynamo,* much to the chagrin of both KL-03 and R0-VR, who had whined like the lovelorn puppy the astromech so often resembled. If she was honest, Ty appreciated the break from both droids, although she was beginning to worry that she'd be decontaminated if she stood in one place for too long.

The gig had been a simple one. Mantessa wanted a bodyguard. That was fine. Ty had performed enough babysitting gigs. They were largely without incident, and if things did take a turn for the worse, she could

handle herself, which she guessed was the point. So far, so good . . .
and then Ty had heard where they were going and flat-out refused.

Not Valo. Uh-uh. Not the Republic Fair. She didn't mind the crowds
and she certainly didn't mind the weather, but there was no way in this
reality or the next that Ty was going to a planet that would be crawling
with Jedi.

Of course, K-L had other ideas and had pointed out how the stabilizer still needed to be fixed. And the fuel intermixers. And the entire
sensor array. And just about everything else for that matter.

Ty had allowed herself to be swayed by the droid's logic (known in
other parts of the galaxy as "incessant nagging") and now found herself studying maps of Lonisa City, her eyes wandering repeatedly to
the partially completed Jedi outpost near the Republic Fair site. Yes,
their lack of credits was the only reason she was going near that thing,
definitely not the tiny voice in the back of her head that kept telling
her that this was the path she was supposed to tread. Why did she get
the feeling K-L wasn't the only force in the universe that wouldn't take
no for an answer?

"Would you like something to drink?"

Ty ground her teeth. She'd been asked the same question at least
four times since the ship had taken off. Trying not to sigh, she glanced
up at the girl standing on the other side of the holotable. Mantessa's
daughter, Klerin, looked to be about twenty years old and was as meek
as her mother was commanding. There were other differences, too. Unlike Mantessa, Klerin had a strip of closely cropped hair running from
her brow to an admittedly elegant neck. Ty wondered what her mother
thought of that, or how Klerin had avoided having one of the cleaning
droids shave it off while she slept. As acts of defiance went it wasn't the
most rebellious, but it displayed at least a glimmer of individuality in
what was otherwise quite a timid creature. Klerin spent most of her
time playing with the oversized bangle she wore on her wrist. Of course,
there were also the looks that she kept flashing in Ty's direction

between inquiries about hot beverages. Ty could recognize a crush when she saw one, and in all honesty wouldn't have been opposed to exploring the option in another time or place, but this wasn't the moment, especially with the daughter of a client who was still very much an unknown quantity.

Although . . .

Ty flicked off the map and sat on the table. A nearby cleaning droid let out a worried beep, but she ignored it. She'd changed pants before she'd come aboard. Mantessa had insisted.

"So," she said, turning on charm that she rarely required, "do you do this often?"

Klerin flushed, spinning that damn bangle around her wrist. "What?"

"Employ bodyguards."

Klerin breathed out, obviously a little relieved.

"Every now and then," she said, "especially when we're going somewhere . . . dangerous?"

That was a new one. "Somewhere dangerous? Like the Republic Fair?"

Klerin looked flustered. "I just go where my mother goes."

"And your mother is a . . . businesswoman?"

"An inventor."

"An inventor," Ty repeated as if Klerin were the most fascinating girl in the world. "And is that why we're going to Valo? To demonstrate her inventions at one of the pavilions?"

Klerin took a tentative step forward, warming to the conversation. "No, we have an important meeting. With a potential investor."

"An investor in what, exactly?" Ty raised a hand. "You don't have to tell, but your mother was, shall we say, a little vague on the details. I think I'm just supposed to stand around looking impressive."

"That shouldn't be too difficult," Klerin blurted out, her eyes going wide as she realized what she'd said. "Sorry, I . . ."

Ty let the girl blush. "Nothing to apologize for."

Klerin bit her lip and glanced in the direction of the flight deck before looking back to Ty. "Would you like to see it?"

Gotcha, Ty thought. K-L would be proud. Ty Yorrick, making a connection with another living being, even if it was for ulterior motives. But hey, a guard needed to know what she was guarding.

Not that she was much the wiser when Klerin led her to the *Dynamo*'s storage bay.

"This is it?" Ty asked, frankly a little disappointed.

"It's my mother's pride and joy," Klerin admitted, sounding a little sad.

Ty couldn't see why. The big blue crate was pretty nondescript, polished to a shine obviously, but standard all the same, like countless other crates in countless other storage bays. It was tall, coming up to her chest, but had no markings whatsoever to indicate what lay inside.

"Can I have a peek?" Ty asked, pushing her luck.

"We probably shouldn't," Klerin said. "In fact, we should probably go."

Ty cocked her head. "You're not going to offer me another drink, are you?"

The bangle went around the girl's wrist again. "It's just my mother doesn't like anyone getting close to it."

Something about the way she said it made Ty's phantom tendril prickle.

"Why?" The warmth dropped from her voice. "It's not dangerous, is it?"

"Most definitely not."

Klerin spun around at the sound of Mantessa's voice. The inventor was standing in the door of the storage bay, her ever-present sanitizer ball hovering beside her even on the ship.

"Mother, I was just—"

Mantessa didn't let her daughter finish, barely giving her another glance as she strode in, her focus target-locked on Ty.

"I have just forwarded an advance to your admin droid," she said, her tone clipped. "Half the fee as agreed, so she can start repairs to your . . . vehicle."

"I'm much obliged," Ty said, standing with her back to the crate.

"I can, of course, cancel the transfer."

"That won't be necessary."

"I hope not. I thought I'd made myself clear when I employed you. I need a bodyguard, not a confidante, someone who will do their job, no questions asked."

"I only asked if our cargo was hazardous."

"Which is a question."

"But one that is surely acceptable, considering the situation."

"And what situation is that?"

"That we're heading to a location where there are going to be an awful lot of people."

"And that worries you?"

"I would rather know what I am getting into."

Mantessa considered this, and for a second Ty wondered if she was about to find herself dropped off at the next spaceport.

Instead, Mantessa laughed humorlessly. "I like you, Ty."

Ty wasn't sure she could repay the compliment.

"You'll have to forgive me," Mantessa continued, pointing a perfectly trimmed fingernail at the crate. "I've put everything we have into that box. I have become a little guarded about it."

Ty raised her eyebrows. "Well, now you have *me* to guard it."

"Indeed I do, and while I hope you'll forgive me if I keep some secrets close to my chest, you should probably know what will be required of you when we meet our potential benefactor." She paused, her eyes falling to Ty's waist, specifically her holster.

Now Ty's missing tendril was *really* starting to itch.

"Would you like something to drink?" Mantessa asked, indicating the door. "I have a number of questions about that lightsaber of yours . . ."

Chapter Twenty-One

The Unity Arc, Valo

The crowd gasped as a drift of Vectors streaked overhead, flying in perfect formation. Stellan had to admit that it was the perfect end to a perfect afternoon. The regasa's arrival had gone like Muun clockwork, much to the obvious delight of Lina Soh, and now the chancellor's entire retinue was standing on a platform in front of literally thousands of people who had gathered in front of the fair gates for the official opening ceremony. Then there were the billions who would be watching on the holonet. It truly was a wonder to behold, although that didn't stop Stellan from wishing that he was up there with his fellow Jedi, joining the drift as they dropped into a perfect Sunburris cascade, one of Nib Assek's favorite maneuvers. Nib was leading the Vectors, Burryaga piloting a craft of his own, a recent development after years of flying with his Master. The Ithorian Jedi Mikkel Sutmani had joined them in the air, alongside Master Kunpar of the local temple. Regasa Elarec burst into applause as the Vectors made one last bank and sped off into the horizon, the crowd following the queen's lead. Stellan scanned the throng waiting to flow through the Unity Arc, picking out just a few of the familiar faces in their number. There was Cherff Maota, Avar's former Master who now scoured the galaxy as a Seeker, searching for Force-adept youngsters to be trained by the Order, and Nooranbakarakana, a Frozian Jedi whom Stellan knew by reputation alone. Then there was Torban Buck, the hulking Chagrian medic who was famed as much for his bizarre insistence that everyone call him Buckets of Blood as for his medical expertise. Buck saw Stellan looking his way and fired off a jaunty salute, leaving the Council member wondering if he should return the gesture.

Fortunately the decision was taken out of his hands when Soh took a step toward the dais where Matari and Voru had been sitting patiently throughout the display.

"We thank the Jedi," the chancellor said, resplendent in a long gown of nanosilk, her amplified voice echoing off the buildings of the harbor square. She swept a smile across the crowd, a gesture expertly designed to take in as many cams as possible. "It is good to see so many of you here today. Citizens from the Core, from the Inner and Mid Rim, and of course here from the frontier, the latest members of our galactic family." She raised her hands wide, as if she could see the entire Republic in front of her.

Maybe she could.

"For that is what we are. *Who* we are. A family, many but connected. Brothers, sisters, guardians, clan-kin, loved ones, and friends . . ." With that, Soh made a point of turning to Elarec, seated with Ambassador Tiss, her royal guard never far, lined up toward the rear of the platform. The regasa inclined her head in acknowledgment of the sentiment.

"Some have traveled far, some are close to home," Soh continued. "But we all are one. We are all the Republic, and this fair is for all of us. *This day* is for all of us. Together we will experience new things. Together we will witness marvels from across the sectors. Art. Music. Drama. Innovation. They belong to us and they bring us together. This is a chance to understand one another; to realize once again what we all bring to the Republic, each and every one. This is our time. And it is only the beginning."

A roar of engines sounded across the lake. The crowd craned their necks, looking past the chancellor, past the fair gates. The dignitaries on the platform turned, Stellan included, to see a squadron of Cyclor Skyhawks sweeping forward, their lights blinking against the sunset. And they weren't alone. Stellan could make out at least three Vectors traveling alongside it, not part of the display but ships that had traveled from the shipyards, one of them hopefully being flown by a recovered Bell Zettifar. This time, however, no one was looking at the Vectors. Instead, all were captivated by the breathtaking sight of the *Innovator* sweeping toward them. The holos Stellan had seen back on Coruscant had been impressive enough, but the ship itself was simply stunning. It was long and tapered, like a pristine arrowhead, its hull as white as a shark-boar tusk. Sensors lined a raised area near the rear of the vessel where Stellan knew from the schematics that the operations center was housed, a vast viewport flaring white in the sunlight. It was simply the largest ship Stellan had ever seen, dwarfing both the *Coruscant Dawn* and the Jedi's own flagship, the *Ataraxia*. Best of all, the *Elite*-class vessel wasn't a warship or a destroyer; it was a pioneer. After being displayed at the fair the ship would set out on a voyage to explore and map previously uncharted areas of space, the first of a new fleet of science vessels. While Starlight and Soh's planned network of Beacons were there to support and protect, the *Innovator* and its line would broaden all their horizons.

The Republic starfighters streaked overhead, followed by the Vectors. Stellan reached out in the Force as they passed, catching a hint of Indeera Stokes's presence along with the legend that was Porter Engle. There was someone else, someone he had never actually met, a younger Jedi who could only be Bell Zettifar. So the young Jedi Knight *was* out of the bacta tank and back at the controls of a ship, accompanied, Stellan presumed, by the charhound he had heard so much about. Stellan beamed. This was a good day. Not just for the Republic but for the Jedi as well. Surely now, for all the fear the Cyclor attack had caused, there could be no doubt that the Republic was safe. The Nihil had tried to take the *Innovator* and yet here it was swinging into position and lowering on perfectly tuned repulsors onto the floating dock that had been built to house the ship for the duration of the fair. The Jedi had proved, once again, that they were strong in the Force. Together they and the Republic could do anything, no matter who opposed them. The light was on their side, now and forever.

A cheer went out as the *Innovator* touched down, the crowd whooping and applauding, drowning out both Skyhawks and Vectors that had come about to rocket back toward them.

But Soh's voice was heard, booming over the speakers and transmitted to every planet in the Republic and beyond. "Nothing gives me greater pleasure," she exalted, throwing her arms wide, "than to declare the Valo Republic Fair open. This is our Republic, my friends, our family. The spirit of progress. The spirit of democracy. The spirit of unity."

With perfect timing, the combined starfighters streaked overhead as Soh completed her speech, and the pilots flicked a switch in their cockpits. Colored smoke trailed from hidden canisters, painting the sky gold and white as a specially composed anthem blared from speakers across the square. The music swelled, and the chancellor's platform started to rise steadily into the sky, finally allowing access to the gates that now were embellished with holographic letters, the chancellor's final words—and the motto for the fair as a whole—writ large for all to see: THE SPIRIT OF UNITY.

Stellan looked over to the rostrum and saw Lina Soh watching the people . . . her people . . . streaming into the park with tears in her eyes. Despite everything, despite the dark days following the Great Disaster, despite being told that the Republic Fair would never happen, she had proved everyone wrong. At that moment, Stellan believed that the chancellor could do anything. Centuries from now, the people of the galaxy would look back and see this day as a turning point, one that set the Republic's course for all time, and he for one was glad that the Jedi were at the heart of it, where they belonged.

Chapter Twenty-Two

The laboratory

Loden Greatstorm dreamed he was in the past. For a moment he was on Elphrona, riding a steelee across the rust plains, Bell behind him on his own mount. The young Padawan was laughing, his braids bouncing up and down, Ember running at the steelee's feet.

Loden breathed in the hot Elphrona air, imagining the smell of Porter Engle's famous Nine-Egg Stew already bubbling in the kitchen, and felt a jab in his neck.

He woke to find himself in torment.

This, of course, was nothing new. In fact, it had quickly become the norm, the life he had endured ever since he had been captured by Marchion Ro. His broken leg had healed, but pain remained, making it impossible for him to focus, to escape. To call on Bell.

I am here, my apprentice. I am still alive.

That in itself was debatable. Was he alive? Really? Some days he doubted it. Some days he thought himself insane. He had every right to be. The doctor—that sniveling, crawling, sadistic Chadra-Fan—had killed the other prisoners one by one, some still in their cells, some in front of Loden so he could see the light fade from their eyes, so he could smell their blood on the air. He'd watched them die, and there was *nothing* he could do.

Loden Greatstorm was a Jedi, and yet he was as helpless as a newborn.

The indignity burned at him night and day.

He had spent the endless days since his capture in a laboratory, strapped to a metal rack. A strict regimen of drugs had robbed him of both his strength and the ability to sleep. Whenever he began to slip away, as he had done minutes before, a hypo was pressed against his neck. The same click. The same hiss. The same rush through his veins, snapping him awake. Not that he could close his eyes. They had been clamped permanently open, his head held in an immovable vice. He couldn't turn his neck, couldn't even look away as lights strobed in front of him, a shifting kaleidoscope of colors, some he recognized, while others seemed new, almost as if he had forgotten their hue. And all the time a cacophony of screams and static was blasted from floating speakers, discordant sounds both organic and synthesized. Loden caught one of the speakers during the early days of his confinement, a glorious giddying moment when he managed to center himself, to reach out with the Force. He'd squeezed, shattering the unit, shards of sharp plastic cutting his cheek. That pain he didn't mind. It meant he had changed his environment, made a difference. It proved he still had a modicum of control.

The punishment had come later that night. He knew it would, although he had expected more than a simple surgical saw in his doctor's hands. Really? That was it? After everything else his captors had done to him? After the lights and the sounds and the madness. What did he have to fear from a saw?

The answer, it turned out, was nothing. The door had slid open, and the man he'd learned was called Ro walked into the lab. The Chadra-Fan had offered him the saw, but the Nihil leader had shaken his head, pulling instead a familiar weapon from his belt. Loden's saber. Loden's saber in the hand of his torturer. His blood had burned with outrage until Ro had ignited the lightsaber and reached for Loden's lekku.

Loden had no idea how much time had passed since then. Every day was the same.

Lights.

Screams.

Injections.

Blood.

Lights.

Screams.

Injections.

Blood.

And all the time, Ro stood on the other side of the observation window, watching, his dark eyes cold and unreadable. He never entered the laboratory again, never talked to his prisoner. The Chadra-Fan's squeaking rasp was the only voice he ever heard.

Until one day there was another.

Who are you?

I do not know you.

Loden thought he'd imagined it. Dreamed it maybe, wondering if the stimulants had stopped working or if he was one step closer to the end.

Are you even real?

Loden could ask the same of her.

"I don't know."

The Chadra-Fan had looked up from his datapad when Loden spoke, his notched ears crammed with plugs to protect them from the noise.

The voice laughed. Loden liked the sound. It was pleasant. Musical. A balm in the midst of horror.

I've had the same doubts. I know I used *to be real. Once upon a time. A long time ago.*

The dishevelled doctor had limped from the lab. He was standing on the other side of the glass now, talking with Ro. Loden tried to look past the glare of the lights to study their faces.

You can do it.

"I can't."

That doesn't sound like you.

"How do you know what I sound like? I'm not sure I even know anymore."

I know a lot more these days. See so much more. Look harder.

"Yes, Master."

The lights faded. Loden could see his jailers now, Uttersond showing Ro something. Results? Maybe.

They're hurting it.

"Hurting what? Hurting me?"

No. The ancient one. It's been hurt before, but not like this. The ice melting away.

"I don't know what you are talking about."

That makes two of us.

Another laugh.

Keep looking.

Loden couldn't focus. He didn't know how. He could see their lips moving, but couldn't make out the words. The final test. A last step along a Path. They were talking about something they'd found . . . that *Ro* had found. The Great . . . what? Betterer? Lessener? What was it?

You'll know soon enough.

"Can you help me? Can you set me free?"

Of course not, silly. You can only do that for yourself. But the time will come. Soon. When he is near.

Then the voice had gone silent, for a day, maybe two. When it returned . . . when *she* returned, she was talking nonsense, a jumble of numbers and words that meant nothing, but Loden listened all the same.

Maybe he was mad, maybe *she* was mad, but at least this way, they could be mad together.

Chapter Twenty-Three

The Starlight Pavilion, Valo

Stellan spotted Bell Zettifar the moment he entered the Starlight Pavilion. The space had seemed vast when he had first seen it on his tour of the fair yesterday, but now it was packed with dignitaries from every corner of the Republic and beyond. They were standing in small clusters, nibbling on snacks delivered by serving droids or gazing in admiration at the spectacular hologram of Starlight Beacon that was turning slowly in the center of the chamber, the most detailed three-dimensional light display most people had ever seen, Stellan included. It cast the faces of its admirers in a golden light that seemed appropriate for a beacon designed to illuminate the darkest corner of space.

Bell entered alongside Indeera and Engle and was immediately set upon by the other veterans of the Hetzal disaster—Nib, Burryaga, and Mikkel—who talked animatedly to the young man, Burry looking like he wanted to gather Bell into a well-meaning, but potentially bone-crunching, hug. All the time Bell's charhound sat obediently at his feet, looking up at the newcomers and glancing every now and then at her master, as if checking Bell was all right. But was he? The boy was smiling, but the expression seemed tired, forced even. Stellan knew that feeling. For the last half hour he had been engaged in a riveting conversation about the intricacies of carbon score removal with a member of the Ardennian Guild of Technicians. Of course, *engaged* was a relative term. Stellan had merely been smiling and making encouraging noises at the appropriate moments in the conversation. This was his moment both to escape and also to check that the Padawan had recovered from his ordeal above Cyclor.

"Have you toured the exhibition, Delegate Retar?"

The Ardennian shook his head, keen to steer the conversation back to matters of ship maintenance.

"Oh you should," Stellan said quickly, catching the eye—or at least the atmosphere helmet—of archivist OrbaLin. "It gathers treasures from every major Jedi collection. Absolutely fascinating." Thankfully, OrbaLin had taken the hint and stomped over, his movements as fluid as you'd expect from a blob of constantly shifting mucus operating a humanoid space suit. "Archivist," Stellan said, "I was wondering if you could accompany Delegate Retar around *Secrets of the Jedi*? I think he would be particularly interested in the Cassadrean Matrix."

"Of course, Master Gios," OrbaLin burbled, a vocoder translating the movements of the slime within the suit into spoken words. "It would be my pleasure."

Relieved of the conversation, Stellan waited patiently for OrbaLin to guide his charge toward the ornate double doors that led to the exhibition. When the coast was clear, Stellan made for Bell and the others, his progress hindered every few steps by delegates wanting to make the acquaintance of a member of the Jedi Council. Stellan made his excuses each time, trying his best not to cause offense but determined to make it to the group of Jedi before they disappeared into the crowd.

"Master Gios," Indeera exclaimed when he finally drew near, "it is good to see you."

"And you, too, Jedi Stokes. I am pleased that the Force led you safely through the raid."

"Some more than others," Porter Engle grunted. "I thought that young Zettifar was going to go the same way as Loden."

The directness of Engle's comment drew a startled mew from Burryaga, not to mention shocked looks from the other Jedi.

"This is why you should never become a counselor, Engle," Nib Assek scolded. "I hope your clawfish chowder is better than your bedside manner."

Engle frowned at the woman, his expression voicing a silent *What?*

Fortunately, Bell raised a hand, waving away any concern. "Master Engle is right. I barely made it out alive." Stellan allowed himself to breathe again. There was no animosity in Engle's clumsiness, and his lack of tact was as legendary as his lightsaberwork. Bell, however, seemed to take it all in his stride, although the pain that had stabbed the boy's heart had been palpable. "I wouldn't be here if it weren't for Indeera and the arrival of Master Engle's drift."

Graceful and diplomatic. Stellan knew at that moment that he was going to like young Zettifar.

"Would you like to see the exhibition?" Stellan asked, Bell's eyebrows raising slightly at the sudden invitation.

"Um . . . yes . . . yes of course." The Padawan turned to his fellow Jedi. "Would you like to come?"

Engle looked as if he was about to say yes before Indeera cut in. "No, we need to discuss tomorrow's display. You go ahead."

Stellan offered his thanks to Bell's Master and guided Zettifar through the throng. "It will be a little less crowded there."

"That would be a welcome change." Bell glanced down at his feet to check that his charhound was still at heel. "I've never seen so many people, at least not in such close quarters."

"It can be overwhelming, especially after a period in a bacta tank. I'm intrigued to hear about the experience. When I was a Padawan, Master Kant would have us meditate in a sensory deprivation field so we could be truly one with the Force. I assume that it's a similar sensation."

A shadow passed over Bell's face. "I think I would prefer the field."

There it was again. The sadness Stellan had sensed on Bell's arrival. He was in no way as empathetic as Burryaga, but he couldn't help recognizing the emotion.

He stepped back to allow Bell to climb the steps to the exhibition doors. They parted obediently, the steward managing entry to the exhibition not likely to turn away a member of the Council. Inside, Stellan felt Bell relax, the Padawan's shoulders falling slightly. Bell took a deep breath, spotting a spiral of pink flowers swirling gracefully in a repulsor field.

"Are those—?"

"Uneti blossom," Stellan confirmed. "From the Great Tree on Coruscant. Master Wishan has manufactured incense from its petals. I can arrange to have a box sent to you, if you'd like?"

"That would be incredibly kind."

"Not at all. I brought some with me on the *Coruscant Dawn*. I found it invaluable during meditation."

He walked the young Padawan toward a cabinet containing a collection of small medallions arranged on velvet pillows.

"What are these?" Bell asked, fascinated by the tiny disks, each marked with a Coremaic rune.

"Tythonian Mastery Tokens," Stellan replied, happy to be teaching again. "A common practice back in the early days of the Order. They were awarded when a Jedi Knight was elevated to the rank of Jedi Master, both to the Jedi Knight themselves and to the Master who had trained them."

"Fascinating." Bell was looking down at the display case, but Stellan wasn't convinced he was actually looking at the coins.

"How is your meditation?" The directness of the question broke Bell's trance. He looked up, a flicker of panic on his face, the sharp emotion mirrored by a sudden growl from the charhound. Bell covered his embarrassment by scolding the dog.

"Ember. Sit."

The hound hesitated before complying, the red patches in her coat smoldering in the low lighting.

"I'm sorry, she . . ."

Stellan raised a palm. "Please don't apologize. Animals don't like me."

Bell flushed. "I'm sure it's not that."

"Maybe not, but it's true nonetheless. Back when I was a youngling, I had trouble bonding with animals. I think Master Gidameen was about to give up on me before my final Padawan trials."

"What happened?"

"I scraped through . . . just." The truth of the situation was more complex, of course. Stellan had been asked to influence the flight of a bora-finch but had been failing terribly until Elzar had prodded the finch with the Force, putting the little yellow-and-blue bird back on track. It wasn't exactly cheating, as Jedi were expected to help one another, but neither did it quite meet Gidameen's strict requirements. Fortunately, the old Master hadn't noticed.

Bell started to wander through the exhibit, not really paying attention to the treasures from a thousand generations of Jedi. Instead, he seemed preoccupied with Stellan's question, as Stellan had assumed he would be.

"You asked about my meditation . . . It has been difficult."

"Since the battle?"

"Since before then. Ever since Master Loden disappeared."

"You are struggling to clear your mind, to touch the Force."

Bell looked as though he wasn't sure how or even if he should respond. Stellan could understand that. He was talking to a Council member after all. The hesitation was the only answer he needed.

"When Master Kant passed, I also struggled . . ."

Bell looked shocked. "You?"

"Yes, even me. Every Jedi, no matter their age or experience, associates meditation with their Master. We are taught the basic principles from our arrival in the temples, but it is only when we become Padawans that our understanding of the process deepens. We spend hours, days, weeks in meditation with our Masters, sitting side by side, exploring the Force together. There's a connection that is never fully broken. Then suddenly our Master is gone, and we can never experience it again in the same way. It had been many years since I meditated with Rana Kant, and yet I felt her passing deeply. To lose your Master as a Padawan . . . that is bound to have an impact, especially with a Master like Loden. He was the best of us."

Bell pursed his lips as if trying not to let them quake. "Yes," he said, his voice cracking. "Yes, he was."

Stellan reached out, placing a hand on the boy's shoulder. "It will come back, I promise. That serenity. That peace. Loden is part of the Force now, so in a way the two of you are closer than ever. But in the meantime, you can always come to me."

Bell shook his head abruptly, wiping a tear from his eye. "No, you . . . you have duties. I wouldn't presume . . ."

"My duty," Stellan reminded him, "is to the Order, and the last time I looked, Padawan Zettifar, you were part of that Order."

Bell laughed and cleared his throat. "Yes. Yes, I am."

"Then I will hear no more arguments. What is the motto of this fair?"

"The Spirit of Unity."

"You'll see it on enough posters over the next few days, but it's true, not just for the Republic but for the Jedi. For *us*. No Jedi is ever alone. We are united in the Force."

The memory of Elzar guiding the finch flashed across his mind again, but this time it was followed by a shadow, a sense of trepidation.

"Master Gios?"

Bell was searching Stellan's face for answers, concerned at the Council member's sudden hesitation. Even Ember leapt up, uneasy once more. "Is everything all right?"

Stellan shook his head. "No. Something is very wrong."

Chapter Twenty-Four

The Starlight Pavilion

Council Member Gios excused himself and hurried from the exhibition. Not knowing what to do, Bell stood in front of the display cabinets, trying to work out what had just happened. The last day had been so surreal, slipping from the bacta tank, running his fingers across the synthflesh over the freshly closed wound in his belly. It felt so strange to the touch, so unreal, as disconnected as Bell felt from the world. Since then everyone had been buzzing around him like soka flies. The med droids checking to see if his new intestinal implants were operating correctly, Indeera never leaving his side. And then there had been Porter Engle. Bell didn't even know when the gruff Ikkrukki had arrived and wasn't overjoyed when he announced his intention to stay. It was ungrateful, he knew, but, like Indeera, Porter reminded him of Elphrona, and Elphrona reminded him of Loden, who was the last person he wanted to think about right now. *Especially* now. Bell hadn't gotten a moment's peace since the attack, which was why he'd jumped at the chance to accompany the *Innovator* into Valo airspace in his Vector. Anything to be alone, except for Ember, of course. The charhound had been his only comfort as the science vessel rocketed to the Valo system, not demanding anything of him save the odd scratch behind the ear.

But now the dog was scampering out of the exhibit, heading after Stellan Gios!

"Ember, wait!" Bell called after the dog. "Where are you going?"

The charhound was out of the exhibition doors before Bell could stop her. He chased after her, only to find the dog in the crowded hologram chamber. At least he didn't have to reach out with the Force to find her. He could see Gios making his way through the crowd and knew that the dog would be just behind him. And the man had said he wasn't good with animals. Why the stars was she following him?

He pushed his way through the delegates, apologizing as he stepped on both feet and tentacles. So much for the grace and elegance of the Jedi!

Meeting Stellan had been as odd as everything else. Bell hadn't known what to do when he saw the Council member making a beeline for him. As if meeting Nib, Mikkel, and Burry after all this time wasn't overwhelming enough. He was sure that one of them would notice what he was trying to hide. Maybe Stellan's interruption had been a blessing. At least Gios didn't know him as well. And then there was all that stuff about lost Masters. It was all Bell could do not to run all the way back to his Vector. Why in the Republic's name was Ember leading him back to the man?

Bell saw a flash of gray and red just behind Stellan and caught up with the dog moments before she jumped up onto the Master's robes. Stellan was back with Indeera and the others, asking about another Jedi.

"Have any of you seen Elzar Mann? He was here just a few minutes ago."

Stokes shook her head. "I haven't seen him."

"Neither have I," Nib admitted, the others saying the same.

Stellan looked vexed.

"You said something was wrong," Bell spoke up, Gios whirling around to face him, a look of annoyance in a face that had been so kind minutes ago.

"Not so loud!"

Bell blinked at the reprimand. "I'm sorry."

Stellan's expression softened. "No, I'm sorry. I felt . . . not exactly a disturbance in the Force but a sense of unease, emanating from Elzar. I must find him."

"We'll help," Nib said, beckoning Engle over from where he was perusing a tray of spiced rycrit strips.

"No," Stellan told the older woman. "You must stay here. People will be concerned if we all leave at once. I'll go."

He made for the door, nearly tripping over Ember who insisted on trotting at his feet.

"Bell? Could you?"

Bell apologized—again—and told Ember to sit. The dog ignored him, scurrying after Stellan. What was she doing?

"Looks like someone has a new friend," Nib chuckled, watching the dog follow Gios out of the pavilion.

"Yes, because Stellan is such an animal lover," Indeera replied. "I hope he doesn't break the little lady's heart."

"I better get after them," Bell said, wishing he'd never come to the reception in the first place. This was the last thing he needed.

He found Stellan standing in the fair's main thoroughfare, looking forward and then back as if trying to spot Elzar in the crowd. Bell couldn't help. He'd heard of Mann but had never laid eyes on the guy. Ember was hopping around like an excitable puppy at Stellan's feet, her tail wagging furiously. She barked as Bell hurried up, ready to pull her away if necessary.

"I'm sorry. I don't know what's gotten into her. We'll get out of your way."

"No need. Hold this, will you?" Stellan said, pulling his lightsaber from its holster and handing it to Bell. The Padawan looked at it in confusion as Stellan proceeded to unbuckle the holster and pull it from his waist.

"I told you Elzar and I go back a long way," he said, smiling at Bell's obvious bewilderment. "We had different Masters, but we were taught in many of the same ways, especially when it comes to looking after our equipment." Stellan sniffed the leather and grinned all the wider. "Muttamok oil. We've both been using it since we were Padawans."

Stellan crouched down and offered Ember the leather. She sniffed it once and then once again and then scooted off into the crush of people. Stellan jumped up, the holster grasped in his hand, and took back his lightsaber before taking off after her.

"Maybe I'm getting better with animals," he shouted back as Bell chased after them both. "Proof you're never too old to learn."

They would have run straight past Mann if it weren't for Ember. They had followed the charhound out of the fair park into the heart of Lonisa City itself, only for her to lose the scent at the last minute.

Bell had felt Stellan reach out with the Force in an attempt to locate his old friend, but Ember had barked sharply and scurried around the corner of a droid dealership that was making the most of so many tourists being in town. They pelted along a crowded side street and would have come bursting out of the other end if Ember hadn't suddenly skidded to a halt and barked sharply, looking up to the roof of one of the buildings.

The street was illuminated by lanterns strung from building to building, and yet the glow-bulbs around this particular roof were all out. Stellan put a finger to his lips, then dipped into a narrow alley between the building in question and a noisy saloon—the Lake's Rest. Before Bell had gone after him, Ember at his heels, Stellan had leapt from the ground to the roof, leapfrogging from one wall to the next.

"You stay there," Bell told Ember before following the Council member, using a second-story windowsill to bounce up to the roof. At first neither Jedi saw Mann, but then their senses came into focus and they spotted him crouched near the edge of the flat roof. A look of annoyance crossed his face, and he beckoned them over.

"What are you doing here?" he hissed through gritted teeth. "Get down, for void's sake."

"We're looking for you," Stellan said as they scrambled down to where Mann had been hiding, using the Force to mask his presence.

"Master Gios sensed something was wrong," Bell explained, choking slightly at the dust they had kicked up.

"Did he now?" Mann glared at Bell. "And who are you?"

"This is Padawan Zettifar," Stellan explained.

Mann grunted.

"Ah. Greatstorm's apprentice. Just keep yourself covered. I don't want anyone to see that we're here."

"Why?" Stellan asked. "What are you waiting for?"

"It's what *he's* waiting for that I'm interested in." Mann pointed out an open window on the third floor of the cantina. A Sullustan was deep in conversation with a heavy-set Orzrelanso with long drooping earlobes and shoulders that wouldn't have looked out of place on a Gamorrean.

"Tia Toon," Stellan breathed.

"As large as life."

"Which one?" Bell asked, watching the Sullustan pace around the thug in the suit.

"The small one," Elzar told him. "The senator for Sullust and a royal pain in the backside."

Stellan crossed his arms. "Spoken like a true Jedi."

Mann shrugged. "Look, I was sent to Valo to sweep for trouble, yes?" He jabbed a gloved finger at the Sullustan. "That guy has been on my scope ever since he crashed Samera's reception. The Force is telling me he's up to something, and the Force is never wrong."

"But our interpretation of it can be."

Mann blew out. "Don't give me that. You said you sensed it."

"I sensed that *you* were troubled, not that Toon was up to no good."

Ouch! thought Bell. *That didn't sound like a loaded statement, at all! What was going on between these two?*

"You've been troubled for weeks."

"Something is coming," Mann said gravely. "I can feel it, you can feel it, and Zettifar could feel it if he weren't trying to close himself off from the Force." Mann looked straight at him, and Bell felt his mouth go dry. "What's that about anyway?"

"I . . . I was injured recently," Bell stammered, knowing the explanation wouldn't hold water. "I've found connection to the Force . . . painful." At least that part was the truth.

Weak or not, Mann seemed to accept the excuse, or at least was too busy to worry about it right now. He turned back to Stellan. "Toon is up to something. He's supposed to be at the outpost in an hour for the chancellor's tour."

"We *all* are," Stellan reminded him.

"And yet he's here," Mann continued, ignoring his superior. "Above this dive. With his bodyguard. What kind of senator needs a bodyguard anyway."

Stellan peered over the edge of the building. "I've seen worse."

"The bodyguard?"

"The bar!"

Elzar snorted a short laugh. "Because you're *always* hanging out in tapcafes. But whatever you think about it, this is the last place you'd expect to find a senator."

"He said he had meetings."

"But with who? That's the question. If Toon has something to do with what I've been feeling . . ."

Mann's voice trailed off, and he and Stellan shot a look at the window. Even Bell felt it, shielding himself from the Force as he was. There were more people in the room now, at least three, maybe more. They couldn't see who, only shadows thrown against the wall and Toon standing with his side to the window, talking to the newcomers, the Orzrelanso at his side.

Beside Bell, Mann rummaged in a pouch connected to his belt and pulled out a small dish that he connected to the end of a comlink, screwing it tightly into place.

"Is that a listening device?" Stellan asked as Mann pointed the dish at the open window.

"We can't rely on the Force for everything," Mann told him, adjusting a dial on the back of the unit.

"Neither are we secret police."

Mann shot a glance at Stellan's still-pristine robes. "Not wearing that you're not."

Stellan looked like he was about to retort and then thought better of it. Elzar Mann gave the dial another sharp twist, and the senator's voice crackled from the comlink, Bell's heart skipping when he heard what it said:

"Is that a lightsaber?"

Chapter Twenty-Five

Above the Lake's Rest, Lonisa City

"**I**s that a lightsaber?"

Ty Yorrick tried not to shift under Tia Toon's scrutiny. First rule of negotiation: Never let them know you're uncomfortable, even if you are—and nothing about this made her comfortable. Repairs or not, Ty should have told Mantessa where to stick her bodyguard job, especially when she found out exactly what she was expected to do. *This* was why she'd used the Verazeen stones for so long. The Verazeen stones had never tried to change her mind.

"Are you a member of the Order?" the senator asked when she didn't answer right away.

Ty shook her head briskly. "I am not, sir."

The Sullustan cocked his head, his large black eyes narrowing. "Interesting. And then where did you acquire the hilt?"

To Ty's annoyance, Mantessa jumped in with an obvious lie. "They're surprisingly easy to purchase, if you know who to talk to."

"Is that so?"

The inventor nodded, only getting herself in deeper. "My own father had a large collection himself. Relics of the Sith Wars, no less. Absolutely priceless."

"Fascinating. Do you still have them?"

Mantessa clasped her pristine hands in front of her. At least her sanitizer was safely stowed in her pocket. The unit's constant hiss was really getting on Ty's already fractured nerves. "Sadly not," the Kuranu continued, using the opportunity to direct the conversation back to the reason they were here. "I sold them all to finance my work."

The blue crate was standing behind her on the repulsorsled that Ty had pushed all the way from the *Dynamo,* its contents surprisingly heavy.

"Of course," Toon said. "The reason we are here. And you developed this yourself."

"Working with my daughter."

"And she is . . . ?"

"On our ship. She's a clever girl, but nervous in crowds."

Ty couldn't help but feel a little jealous. She would give anything to be back on the *Dynamo* about now.

"Valo is particularly crowded at the moment," Toon said, looking eagerly at the crate. "So, may we see?"

"Naturally." Mantessa said, punching a code into the combination lock on the side of the crate. Ty couldn't help but be intrigued as the seals clicked open. Mantessa had explained what needed to happen, but not what to expect when the case swung open. The answer, it turned out, was not much. The device inside resembled a portable comm array or maybe even a moisture vaporator, albeit one smothered in exposed wiring and flashing diodes. *That* was what she was guarding?

Toon obviously shared Ty's disappointment. "I thought it would be a little more . . . polished," he admitted, stroking his jowls.

"It is a prototype," Mantessa said quickly. "A *working* prototype."

Toon took a step forward, his Orzrelanso muscle shifting beside him. Ty had already discounted the overgrown oaf, whom the senator had hilariously introduced as his "secretary," Ratko. He looked impressive, but Ty had already formulated at least three different ways to incapacitate the brute. It always paid to be prepared.

"And how exactly *does* it work?"

Mantessa smiled, pulling a small remote from her sleeve. She pressed a button and the unit started whirring, lighting up like the *Dynamo*'s control console.

"The finished unit will be far less conspicuous," she explained. "Not to mention much smaller, meaning it can be mounted on walls or roofs without drawing attention."

"I'm glad to hear it," Toon said, peering at the device, which, rather disconcertingly, was starting to steam.

"At its heart is a recainium core," Mantessa continued, unperturbed, "which is currently spinning within a vortex chamber."

Toon took a sharp step back. "In which case you can turn it off! Recainium is illegal!"

"Only in its raw form."

"In *every* form," Toon insisted. "And for good reason."

Mantessa wasn't giving up. "But as you will see, the four-seven nullifier will be an excellent reason for the Senate to revisit that decision."

Ty's stomach tensed. She knew what she was about to be asked to do and didn't like it, or the way the Orzrelanso's hand had moved none-too-subtly to the bulge beneath his jacket.

"Turn it off," Toon insisted.

Mantessa's eyes flashed with frustration. "But you said you wanted a demonstration." She turned to Ty. "Yorrick, if you would be so kind?"

Ty breathed out, snatching her lightsaber from her belt. The purple blade snapped on, and the Orzrelanso finally pulled his blaster, the idiot going so far as to squeeze off a bolt. This was not how this had been meant to be. Ty swung, sending the energy slamming harmlessly into the wall. The Orzrelanso's finger tightened again and Ty threw up a hand, pushing him back a little too forcibly. He crashed into the wall, cracking his domed head on the stonework, his blaster skidding across the floor toward Toon's feet. The senator dived for it, coming up to fire at Ty, who again batted the bolt away.

This was definitely not what Ty had signed up for, and that was *before* a figure in white and gold flew through the window.

Stellan had been ready to jump the moment a lightsaber had been mentioned, but Elzar had held him back.

"Wait. We need to know what they are doing."

But there had been no stopping the Council member when the first shot had been fired. Stellan ran for the edge of the roof, using the Force to leap farther than was humanly possible, rolling through the window to spring up, his own lightsaber already blazing.

The senator was on the floor, blaster in hand, a Tholothian with an ignited lightsaber looming over him. Stellan took in the others in the room: Toon's hulking "secretary" slumped against a wall and a Kuranu woman shielding what he assumed was the recainium device.

"Drop the weapon," he instructed the Tholothian.

She stood her ground, her blade buzzing menacingly.

"Only if you do the same."

He almost laughed. Was she really calling him out?

"This is your last warning."

For a second she looked as though she was going to comply before Elzar and Bell leapt in behind him, their hands going for their own sabers.

The Tholothian's response was immediate. She swept up her free hand, the fallen Orzrelanso crying out as he was plucked from the floor and crashed into Elzar and Bell, Elzar's lightsaber spinning from his grip. Then she went for Stellan, her purple blade sweeping in from the side. He parried the blow, going on the counterattack, but she was ready for him. Their blades clashed over and over, Stellan all too aware of their relatively cramped surroundings.

"Protect the senator," he ordered Bell. Elzar dived between the flashing sabers, risking his head to scoop up his hilt and roll back up to his feet in front of the Kuranu woman who suddenly found herself facing a plasma blade of her own.

"What does that do?" Elzar demanded, pointing at the machine, but the woman actually chuckled.

"You'll see."

"What's that supposed to mean?"

All the time, the Tholothian stayed on the offensive. Everything about her screamed Jedi, from the way she held her lightsaber to the raw talent of her form, although the snarl on her lips and frustration he felt at her core spoke of a life without discipline, far from the light. Was she dark side? No, they would have sensed that the moment they'd seen her, but if she had been trained, she had certainly veered from the path.

Nothing proved this more than the moment when they found themselves in deadlock, Stellan's blade crossed against hers.

"Submit," he demanded, glaring at her across the hissing plasma. In response she pulled back her head and clapped her metal skullcap hard across the bridge of his nose. He went down hard, dazed, only dimly aware of Bell coming to his aid.

Without even pausing, the woman turned on Elzar, bringing her lightsaber around. Sensing the attack, Elzar brought his own blade up, using the Tholothian's momentum against her. The locked blades completed a perfect arc, Elzar slamming the tip of her saber into the ground. Elzar slid his blade up the length of hers, the plasma screeching as he aimed for her hands, but she realized what he was doing and landed a boot in his chest. Elzar was knocked flat against the wall as the strange-looking machine reached its crescendo, the whine almost unbearable. Stellan shouted out a warning, but the Tholothian struck, burying her saber up to its hilt in Elzar's chest.

"No," Stellan yelled, calling on the Force to pull the woman away from him. She flew across the room, slamming into the wall, her lightsaber spinning from her fingers. Bell raced to Elzar who had his hand to his chest, but when the Padawan pulled it away there was no hole through Elzar's heart, only bloodstains where the woman's spiked hilt had punctured his skin.

"What?" Stellan breathed, keeping the Tholothian pressed against the wall.

"Look to your own lightsaber," the Kuranu said, ridiculously animated considering the situation. "Light it."

Stellan drew his lightsaber up to his hand and thumbed the activator. The emitter spat, but no blade extended from the hilt, the quillons remaining locked. None of this made any sense.

"Padawan?" Stellan asked, and Bell tried to light his own saber only to have the same result, or lack of it. Elzar's was the same, all three weapons incapacitated.

"It's the machine," the Tholothian hissed. "It extinguished our blades before I struck the killing blow."

"And you knew that would happen?" Elzar asked, pushing himself up.

"No," the woman scoffed, and Elzar took a step forward before stopping himself.

"Someone needs to explain what she means," Stellan demanded, his head thudding from the throb of his nose and the pulsing of the Kuranu's device.

"I agree," Toon said, stepping up to join Stellan, his eyes fixed on the woman.

"Only once you release my associate."

"You are in no position to make demands, Ms. Chekkat," the senator snapped, surprising all of them with the fury of his words.

The woman raised her hands as if they could somehow protect her. "Very well. The nullifier generates a frequency that can disrupt any energy weapon, from the humble blaster to, yes, the weapon of a Jedi."

"And why *exactly* would I be interested in such a device?" Toon demanded.

The woman looked at him confused, as if the answer was obvious. "Your opposition to the Jedi is well known, and the nullifier . . ."

"The nullifier swamps everyone in a ten-meter radius with danger-ous radiation," Toon snapped. "Turn it off. Turn it off this instant!"

Chekkat swallowed, shaken by the senator's tone. "But—"

"You heard what he said," Stellan warned.

Chekkat sighed and hit a button on her remote. The hum dropped away and Stellan's weapon crackled back to life, as did Elzar's and Bell's blades. Still pinned to the wall, the Tholothian raised a hand to call her own lightsaber to her, but it flew in the opposite direction, landing in Elzar's hand instead.

"Hey, that's mine!" she snapped.

"And definitely of Jedi design," he responded, examining the hilt closely, "although it's been modified over time."

"Who are you?" Stellan asked.

"Ty Yorrick is my bodyguard," Chekkat said, and Stellan felt a stab of annoyance from the young Tholothian. Perhaps she had wanted to keep her identity a secret. Stellan had certainly never heard of the name, but he would check with the registry back on Coruscant. The woman had obviously been trained by a Jedi at some point in her life, maybe even been a Padawan, but had never been Knighted, otherwise she would have been immortalized in the Corridor of the Lost in the Great Temple. Granted, she could have been expelled, but then he would have heard of her. Such removals were rare in the extreme, espe-cially these days.

"And your name is Chekkat?" Bell asked, his lightsaber still burn-ing.

"Mantessa Chekkat," Toon supplied for her. "An inventor who ap-proached my people with a device she said could be used by the De-fense Force Program."

"Which I have ably demonstrated," Chekkat reminded him. "I thought you of all people would see its potential."

Toon stepped up to the woman, his fists clenched. "I see something that is foolhardy and dangerous; a potential weapon that could be used *against* both Republic and Jedi forces."

The confusion on Chekkat's face deepened. "But what you said in the Senate . . . your speech about the Republic's reliance on the Jedi—"

"Does not mean that I oppose the Jedi themselves," Toon said, keeping his voice under control with a supreme effort. "The Jedi have long been our allies, and I pray that will continue for many generations to come."

"Then why are you campaigning for the Defense Force?"

Stellan couldn't help but wonder himself.

"Because I believe the Republic should be able to defend itself without relying on the Jedi alone. Because—stars forbid—if anything happened to the Jedi, where would we be?" He jabbed a finger at the nullifier. "But this is recainium. You have brought an illegal substance onto a Republic world, I'm assuming without the correct permits or permissions."

Mantessa visibly swallowed. "I thought . . ."

"You thought that because you were meeting me, you were above the law. I'm afraid, Ms. Chekkat, that you are woefully mistaken."

There was a clatter of footsteps from outside, followed immediately by the sudden arrival of armed Valo Security officers.

The lead officer took in the scene and turned instinctively toward Stellan. "We received a report of an incident."

Toon stepped forward, drawing the lawman's attention back to him. "And arrived in the nick of time. I shall send my compliments to Captain Snat." He turned to face Chekkat and her mysterious bodyguard. "Arrest these two and impound their device."

Stellan tried not to let his annoyance at being circumvented show. "Senator Toon, all things considered, I think that the Jedi should handle this."

"I have no doubt you do, Council Member, but this is a *Republic* matter. These criminals came to me, breaking Republic rules in the process. They are my responsibility." He lifted his head, challenging Stellan to contradict him. "Do you agree?"

"Of course," Stellan said, glancing at Bell, who returned his saber to its holster.

"Although we would like to study this lightsaber," Elzar added as Stellan released Yorrick into the security officer's supervision, the Tholothian having the sense not to struggle as binders were snapped around her wrists.

"Be my guest," Toon said dismissively. "Maybe you will share any information it proves about these criminals with the appropriate authorities."

Stellan bowed magnanimously. "Naturally. Thank you, Senator."

Toon took a step forward, his voice dropping. "No, thank you, Council Member. You jumped in to protect me, despite my reputation in the Senate, and it is appreciated, no matter what you think of me."

Stellan went to protest, but Toon waved the sentiment away.

"I meant what I said, Master Gios. We *are* allies. I just wish for the Republic to stand on its own feet from time to time, especially following the events of Hetzal. You do understand that, don't you?"

There was no duplicity in Toon's words. Stellan nodded, saying, "We are all the Republic."

Toon smiled. "Indeed we are, Council Member. Indeed we are."

The senator swept from the room, his Orzrelanso aide limping after him. Mantessa was bundled out next, followed by Yorrick who called back over her shoulder:

"I'll need that back."

Elzar didn't reply as the remaining security officers puzzled over what to do with the nullifier.

"Help them, Bell," Stellan said, "We should get that thing offworld as soon as possible."

"At once, Master," Bell responded, although Stellan could tell he had a thousand and one questions. He wasn't alone.

"Shall I go with them?" Elzar asked. "See what I can get out of Yorrick?"

Stellan shook his head. "We need to play by the rules. Toon's right. This is Republic business."

"But we're *all* the Republic," Elzar reminded him.

It drew a sigh from Stellan.

"Elzar, I mean it."

"She's obviously Jedi. Or at least used to be. Aren't you curious about that?"

"Of course I am. But she isn't going anywhere."

"You honestly think a Valon cell will hold her?"

"The local detention center is more than capable of containing Force users."

"But—"

"But nothing. I mean it, Elzar." He pointed at the stains on Elzar's tabard. "Go and get those checked out."

"Says the man with the swollen nose."

Stellan risked probing his own injury, wincing at the pain.

"Broken."

"I don't think so."

"Shame."

"El!"

"You need to change your robes," Elzar snapped, storming from the room, Yorrick's lightsaber still in his hand. "I'll put this someplace safe."

Stellan let him go. When Elzar was in this kind of mood there was no talking to him, but he was right about something. His nose might not be broken, but it had bled all over his Temple robes. He really hoped this wasn't the sign of things to come.

Chapter Twenty-Six

The Faith and Life zone

The party was in full swing, and Kitrep Soh hated every minute. Everywhere he looked there were laughter and excitement, delighted faces, and happy voices. Dancers from a dozen worlds whirled on stages across the park—riots of silk, ribbons, and bangles—while children pulled at their parents' hands, wanting to run in seven different directions at once.

The only place Kip wanted to run to was his mother's suite in the Hotel Republica. Mom had, of course, already given him the usual pep talk, just after she'd unveiled his outfit for the evening. The septsilk jacket had come complete with a golden bloom pinned to his lapel. Since when had he worn flowers, not to mention pants with seams so sharp that they looked like they could blunt a lightsaber?

"Just look interested," she had said. "That's all I ask."

"You sure about that?" he asked, yanking at the collar of his shirt.

She'd adjusted the fastening, smoothing it against his neck before resting a hand against his cheek.

"Okay, you can have that one. I know it's a lot, and I know you didn't want to come to Valo in the first place."

He'd started to contradict that one, but thought better of it. Lina Soh knew all too well what her son thought. She wasn't a bad mom. He also knew that she had a galaxy to run. She'd always been ambitious, even before she'd been elected chancellor. More so, probably. And yes, he understood why. His family had come from Daghee, and Kip had seen firsthand how difficult it was to gain respect when you were from a backwater world, especially when you had a son in tow. But she'd always made time for him, even when running from one meeting to another, from one *planet* to another.

That didn't mean he had to like it. It didn't mean he wanted his life plastered all over the holonet. His mom thrived beneath the spotlight, but not him. He'd rather everyone focused on Matari and Voru, forgetting Lina Soh even had a son. At least they were interesting.

But like it or not, he was stuck on a seemingly never-ending circuit of receptions and tours, watching his mom walk side by side with the Togruta regasa while he trudged behind, forced into making small talk with delegates he barely knew and avoiding Norel Quo at all costs. The last thing he needed was the creepy Koorivar nagging him to "stand up straight" or to "smile like you mean it" for the umpteenth time.

It wasn't all bad. He liked Rhil Dairo, even though he suspected she was just warming him up for an interview.

"What do you think?" the reporter asked as they were treated to a preview of the *United in Song* exhibit in the Faith and Life zone.

"The coordinator was right," he stammered. "It's very . . . catchy."

The reporter had leaned in, smiling conspiratorially. "So's Dantari flu."

That made him laugh, although he could have done without the blasted tune crawling into his head. The performance itself had been created over a twelve-month period, children from dozens of Republic worlds recorded individually and then mapped together as part of a gigantic holochoir that numbered in the thousands, standing side by side on a revolving stage. Kip pitied anyone working nearby. He couldn't

imagine anything worse than hearing the saccharine lyrics looped over
and over again.

> We are one, we are many,
> We are me, we are you,
> So much joy, so much love,
> So much peace, it is true,
> From distant worlds, distant planets,
> We stand together and sing,
> The future's bright and united,
> Let the galaxy ring.

"You'll be humming that all night," a voice said beside them. Kip
turned to see the mayor's son beaming at him with his perfect teeth
and mop of ginger hair.

"Yeah," Kip stammered, suddenly finding it impossible to speak.

"Although he doesn't look very happy about it," the boy said, indicating an Ikkrukki Jedi who was frowning so hard, it looked like his
face would crack.

Kip laughed, drawing a smile from Rhil.

"I'll leave you to it," she said, turning to go.

"You don't have to," Kip told her, a little too quickly.

"Needs must," she said, her cam droid swooping after her as she
walked off. "Places to go, soundbites to gather, but don't think I've
forgotten that we have an interview booked in the morning, Jom."

"I'll be there," the mayor's son said, before adding a quick "no, I
won't" under his breath as soon as the reporter was out of earshot. "I
don't know about you, but I'm determined to avoid the cam droids as
much as possible."

"Me, too."

Jom grinned. "Maybe we could avoid them together . . . unless you'd
rather spend time with Ms. Dairo."

"No," Kip said, flustered. "I mean, she's great and everything . . ."

"Pretty, too."

"Yeah, I guess, but . . ."

"Not your type."

"No. Not at all." There was a moment of awkward silence. "I'm Kip, by the way."

"I know."

"And you're Jom."

"I am."

"Great . . . great."

More silence. Too much silence. Kip desperately tried to think of something to say. How difficult could it be? He was the chancellor's son, for stars' sake.

"Moving on," Norel Quo said, ushering the group toward the next stop on their itinerary. "Moving on."

"Maybe I'll see you later then," Jom said. "I think they're putting on some kind of spread at the Melahnese Pavilion. Hope so. I'm starving."

"Me, too," Kip said hopelessly as Jom started to walk away. The young Valon was heading toward a dark-skinned Jedi in Padawan robes. An extremely good-looking Jedi.

"Er, have you heard about Rhil," Kip said, catching up with Jom and the Padawan.

Both Valon and Padawan shook their heads. "Should we have?" Jom asked.

"She's quite a big deal, according to my mom." Yes, because that's *exactly* what Kip needed to do in this situation, talk about his mother. "She got sacked from her first job."

"Your mom?"

"No, Rhil. There was a fight."

"Okay, now I *have* to know what happened."

"I saw it," Kip babbled. "I mean, I wasn't there. It's on the holonet, if you know where to look. She was covering wildfires on some planet or another, and discovered that the local fire chief was charging people to save their homes."

The Padawan—Bell—looked suitably appalled. "That's . . . that's awful."

"Yeah. Rhil lost it, right on cam. Told him that *he* deserved to burn."

"Harsh," Jom said, "but probably fair."

"That's not the best bit." Kip was in full flow now, talking animatedly. "The fire chief is telling her that it's none of her business and she just grabs a hose from the nearest firefighting droid and lets rip."

"Putting out the fire?" Bell asked.

"No. Putting *down* the fire chief. Liters of foam, right in his face."

Jom laughed. "I've gotta see that."

"It's so funny. Of course, she lost her job, but the clip went galactic. Soon everyone wanted to hire her, and she ended up on GoNet. Mom watches her all the time."

"And that's how she got this gig?"

"I guess. I think the network wanted to send Sine Spenning. Do you know him?"

"I can't say I do," Bell admitted. "We don't have much call to watch the holonet."

"You wouldn't forget him if you saw him," Jom told the Padawan. "Typical news anchor—all flashy suits and crazy teeth. I mean, really, *really* crazy."

"Whiter than the moons of Dutar," Kip agreed. "Anyway, Mom wouldn't hear of Spenning covering the fair. Said Rhil was a hero. That she'd stood up for what was right."

"Sounds like she's quite a fan of Ms. Dairo," Bell said.

"She is, yeah . . ."

Jom gave Kip a lopsided smirk. "Still don't want to be interviewed, though."

He grinned back. "Me neither."

And so the evening rolled on; the music, the dancing, the Ikkrukki Jedi unaware he was humming "United in Song." Elsewhere in the park, preparations for the following day continued. Nib Assek and Mikkel Sutmani helped the local Bonbraks service the Vectors, while

Tia Toon entertained investors from the Arkanis sector in the Technology and Science zone.

Farther afield, noted soprano Madam Trangess Conserra arrived at the spacedock, her harassed Toydarian manager, Pall Sleko, secretly pleased that the journey was over, especially as the Mon Calamari diva had insisted on spending all seven hours warming up the most heavily insured vocal cords this side of Brentaal Minor.

Meanwhile, the only music on the bridge of the *Innovator* was the Ualaqian jazz that played over the flight deck speakers as Vam Targes worked alone, taking the opportunity to analyze the data he'd collected during the Cyclor attack. Tomorrow he would be too busy answering a thousand and one questions, but for now he was at his happiest, crunching numbers and finding patterns.

The night drew in, and the crowds began to thin, although the celebrations continued in the Melahnese Pavilion in the Arts and Culture zone. Regasa Elarec was the star of the show, everyone wanting to talk to her. Ambassador Tiss was never far, permanently fretting even though Stellan Gios—resplendent in fresh robes and with his nose back to its correct size thanks to the ministrations of Torban Buck—stayed close, keeping a watchful eye on the proceedings.

On the other side of the pavilion, Kip and Jom never stopped talking. Any embarrassment had long since evaporated, as had any misplaced jealousy about Bell Zettifar, his charhound enjoying the treats that Jom slipped her when he thought the Padawan wasn't looking.

Kip had never been happier, but that couldn't be said for Elzar Mann, who had found a balcony that was perfect for brooding. That's where Samera Ra-oon found him, approaching with two long wine flutes in hand and a smile on her lips.

"Ingot for your thoughts?" she asked, offering a glass.

He took it, surprised by how friendly she sounded, considering the temperature of their relationship of late. "Oh, you know. Scanning the crowd for trouble."

"Protector-of-the-peace stuff?" She took a sip of her drink.

"A Jedi never rests."

"That's a pity."

For once Elzar was lost for words and so took a sip himself. It was Serennian wine, light and fruity. He hadn't tasted it for years.

"So . . ." he ventured, not sure where the words would take him. "Are you . . . happy?"

"With the fair?"

"Yes."

She took another sip, turning to look at the view that stretched out in front of them. "Yes. Everything is perfect."

"Just as you planned it."

She graced him with a sideward glance, one perfectly maintained eyebrow raised. "Would you expect anything less?"

He shook his head. "Of course not."

They stood in silence for a moment, enjoying each other's company, their free hands resting on the railing in front of them, millimeters from each other. Elzar felt the tip of one of Samera's fingers brush his own and turned to find her looking intently at him.

Their heads came together, lips parted, arguments forgotten.

Elzar couldn't be sure that Samera hadn't timed the moment to coincide with the beginning of the fireworks display, the skies above them erupting in color and sound. All across the park—across the city—delegates, citizens, politicians, and Jedi looked up, all except for Elzar and Samera Ra-oon. They were otherwise occupied.

Chapter Twenty-Seven

The Republic Gardens, Valo

The sun shone brightly the next morning as Stellan joined the chancellor's party on a tour of the botanical gardens at the edge of the Technology and Science zone. All around, everything was as he'd expected. A steady stream of visitors flowed through the gates, and spirits were high, but for some reason he couldn't fathom Stellan was on edge. Before the tour, he had dropped into the administration building, checking on Captain Snat and Coordinator Ra-oon. The Valon had seemed a little flustered when he walked through her door, but he soon put that down to a Jedi Master sticking his nose in when everything was running as it should. She certainly didn't need him interfering, and so he had made his excuses and left.

Now, as he followed the group, archivist OrbaLin delivering an in-depth monologue on a spectacular display of Selabbian roses that had been cultivated on Starlight, Stellan meditated on the cloud that marred the otherwise perfect morning. Something in the Force felt heavy. At first, Stellan put it down to his duel with Ty Yorrick the previous evening. She had fought like a Jedi, but there was no record of anyone with her name in the Jedi roster. He hoped that Elzar's examination of her lightsaber would uncover something, but surely a rogue Force-user wasn't the cause of such unease. He glanced at Indeera Stokes, noting that she was frowning. Did she feel it, too? He reached out with the Force, sensing the people that wandered the gardens and the walkways beyond. Yes, there were concerns out there: Parents worried about losing sight of their children in the crowd, exhibitors fretting over headaches with their displays, and the park's chief gardener who wanted to point out to OrbaLin that *he* was the one who was supposed to be giving the tour. Then there was the Togruta guard captain, Maramis, who was becoming increasingly agitated that spectators were gathering on the periphery of the gardens to catch a glimpse of Regasa Elarec. None of these things, important though they were to those in question, justified such a sudden sense of foreboding. What *was* it?

He was still pondering the question when Indeera drew near.

"You felt it?" she asked, keeping her voice low.

"As did you. Have you any sense what it is?"

The Jedi cocked a single brow. "Maybe. The chancellor's son. When did you last see him?"

Stellan scanned the small group. Indeera was right. Kip Soh had been with them as they approached the gardens but was now nowhere to be seen, and neither was the mayor's boy. Stellan didn't know his name. Star's breath. They were supposed to be watching the chancellor's party. How had they missed it?

Stellan reached out to Bell, who was talking to Rhil Dairo as her cam droid captured footage of Soh and Yovet, nudging the Padawan to subtly attract his attention. Bell glanced over and, noticing Stellan's expression, made his excuses to the reporter and walked over to join them, Ember at his feet. Stellan was already on the comm to Coordinator Ra-oon, who was scrolling back through security footage at his request in the administration building.

"Aha," Ra-oon said as she found something. "The sneaky so-and-sos."

"What is it?"

"The boys followed you into the garden but ducked out when they thought no one was looking."

"Heading where?"

"I'm not sure. They disappeared into the crowd. They're not showing up on any of the feeds."

"How is that possible?"

"Do you know how many people we have in the park, Council Member? I can have Idrax Snat put a call out for them?"

"Is there a problem?" Stellan looked up to see that Norel Quo had spotted the group of Jedi huddled together and had come to investigate.

"The chancellor's son seems to have absconded," Stokes said before Stellan could interject, alarm immediately flashing across the aide's face as he looked around in near panic.

"Kitrep? Gone?"

"I am sure there is an innocuous explanation," Stellan said quickly. "He appears to be with the mayor's son."

"Jom," Bell offered helpfully. "Jom Lariin."

"You were talking to them last night, weren't you?" Stellan asked.

"Yes. Kitrep wasn't enjoying being in the public eye, at least at first."

"I know the feeling," Stellan said, glancing up at Rhil's cam droid, which had spun around in their direction.

"Did they mention their plans for this morning?"

Bell laughed. "They didn't mention sneaking away, if that's what you mean, and they certainly wouldn't have told me. Jom did mention he was looking forward to touring the *Innovator*, though."

"The official tour isn't until this afternoon," Quo pointed out.

"Perhaps they decided to go early," Indeera suggested.

"They'll be lucky," Samera chimed in over the comm. "The queues are already around the block. That ship is the star of the show."

"But the chancellor's son isn't exactly another visitor standing in line." Stellan looked down at the VIP pass clipped to Quo's belt. "I assume Kitrep has one of those?"

The aide blew out an aggravated breath. "That boy will be the death of me. Yes, he has a pass. Access to all areas."

It was a long shot, but it was the only lead they had. Stellan turned to Indeera. "May I borrow your apprentice?"

"Of course."

"You want me to head over to the *Innovator*?" Bell asked.

"Hopefully between you and Ember, you'll be able to track them down before anyone notices."

"I'll have Snat dispatch a security team," Ra-oon suggested over the comm, only to be shot down by Quo.

"We need to keep this quiet," the Koorivar said. "If anyone found out that the chancellor's son is missing . . ."

"I think the chancellor may have worked it out for herself," Stokes said, turning toward Soh, who was pointedly looking at the four of them from across the garden.

Soh's aide sighed. "I'll go tell her."

"And I'll find them," Bell said, confidently. "I promise."

Stellan had no doubt that Bell would be as good as his word, but still couldn't shake the nagging doubt at the back of his mind.

"Coordinator," he said before closing the comm. "How is traffic into the sector this morning?"

"Space traffic?" she answered from the administration building. "As busy as you'd expect. But everything is under control. The portmaster certainly hasn't reported any problems. Would you like me to double-check?"

Stellan looked up into the cloudless skies. "If you wouldn't mind . . . It's probably nothing, Kitrep's disappearance is making me jumpy."

"Now you've got *me* worried," Ra-oon said. "I thought Jedi didn't get jumpy, only us mere mortals. I'll report straight back."

Stellan thanked her, and the connection closed. He looked over to see Quo talking to the chancellor, both trying their hardest to pretend that nothing was wrong with so many reporters in the vicinity. Near them, the Togruta head of state glanced his way, and he returned the look, turning on a smile he wouldn't quite feel until he received the all-clear from Samera.

"All will be well," Indeera said quietly. "Bell will find them soon enough."

Stellan knew Stokes was right. That had to be what was wrong, the exploits of two young teenagers throwing an intricately planned day out of kilter. If Elzar was here, he would tell him he was worrying over nothing. He just wanted everything to be perfect; for the chancellor, for the visitors, for the Republic as a whole. And it would be, Force willing, Stellan was sure of that.

Chapter Twenty-Eight

Fair park, Valo

The temperature continued to rise, the day even hotter than the meteorologists had predicted.

The chancellor's party progressed around the gardens, Lina Soh reassured that her son would be found and already composing the scolding she would deliver when they were alone.

Bell Zettifar pressed through the crowds, thanking those who stepped aside and waving at the children who excitedly pulled at their parents' arms to say that they'd just seen a Jedi.

In her office, Samera watched his progress on her screens, having just commed ahead to check if Kitrep and Jom had been spotted at the *Innovator*. They hadn't, and neither had any problems been reported by the portmaster. The line of cruisers and shuttles continued their ordered progress through the Valo system, ready to be assigned a landing spot. She drained the last of her caf, raising the mug to attract a serving droid who immediately beeped and trundled over, refill in pincer. Samera tried not to let Master Gios's rudeness rankle her. He had just been doing his job, and if something was wrong, she would rather know about it, even if it meant being ordered about by a Jedi who bordered on the pompous. She smiled as she sipped her caf. At least not all Jedi were like Stellan Gios.

Elsewhere other Jedi went about their business. Nib Assek and the other members of the display drift were fielding questions about their Vectors, now parked near the Starlight Pavilion for a later demonstration, while inside medic Torban Buck was delighting a bunch of youngsters with stories about his past exploits that their parents thought were just on the wrong side of gory but the kids thought were all kinds of awesome.

A family of Krantians from the Mid Rim were standing in the exhibit, the youngest of three children already wondering how long it was until lunchtime and imagining the delights of the rycrit wrap his mother had promised him. Not far away, other parents were "enjoying" the *United in Song* exhibit while secretly hoping they could drag their children to the next exhibit sooner rather than later.

High above them, repulsorpods slipped effortlessly from one sky-island to another, and down in the theater Mon Calamari soprano Madam Conserra started the first of six planned performances, the opening stanzas of the *Wildwater Cycle* filling the auditorium from the orchestra droid pit.

Conserra's voice soared from the stage, mixing with the hubbub of life on the promenades, just one of myriad musical styles that were playing across the park. Mantessa Chekkat had been particularly looking forward to hearing Fi Yona and the Hyper-Gazers play on the stage, but was currently reclining in a Valo security cell, her disgraced bodyguard across the corridor trying her best to trip locks that were complex enough to frustrate even the most adept Force-user.

Across the park, the youngest Krantian child finally slid his hungry mouth around the rycrit wrap and was already thinking of the bantha milkshake he wanted for dessert. The chancellor's party left the garden as Bell reached the *Innovator* and the portmaster confirmed that no spatial anomalies had been picked up from the second scan Samera had insisted upon. Everything was running to plan, missing dignitary offspring notwithstanding. The Mon Calamari diva finished her aria, the audience applauded, food was cooked, visitors queued, demonstrations were made and children laughed, the animals in the zoo roared and squawked and chirped and chittered, and everything was how it should be.

All except for Elzar Mann, who woke with a start. For a moment nothing made sense. He wasn't in the Temple or any of the quarters in the administration building. The sheets beneath him were soft, the mattress firm, but not as unforgiving as the slab he used back in his own chambers in the Temple Outpost. The air was sweet, the faint hint of floral incense permeating the room, masking the musk of his own sweat. He ran a hand through sleep-tousled hair and groaned as comprehension dawned, memories slipping back into his mind like the light spilling through the painted shutters.

He leapt from the bed, screwing up his face as he realized he was naked. Ashla's Light, how could he have been so stupid?

"Samera?"

There was no reply as he scanned the room for his robes, finding most of them scattered across the carpeted floor, his tabard thrown across a tall-backed wicker chair.

He pulled the jerkin over his head, recalling the touch of her lips on the reception balcony, the sudden yearning that had enveloped him as she had pulled him closer, their bodies crushing together. He had no real memory of getting back to her apartment, crashing through the door, their hands exploring, caressing, pulling at the many layers the Order insisted its Jedi wear . . . for very good reason, it seemed. But peeling off belts and vests had done nothing to cool the pair's ardor. If anything it had increased the anticipation, the thrill, and Samera's dress hadn't taken half as long to slip to the floor.

Damn. Damn. Damn. Damn.

He tried her name again, snatching his pants from beneath the chair and sending it crashing over onto its back.

She didn't come running, either to her name or to the sound of the chair knocking a sideboard, which in turn sent a delicate vase toppling over the edge. Elzar threw up an arm and the ornament hovered in the air, suspended in the Force. A sweep of his hand and it was back where it belonged. If only he could so easily fix the rest of the mess he was in, and he didn't mean the chair.

He pulled his pants over one leg and hopped to the bedside table where his chrono lay. A glance at the digital readout brought another stream of expletives, most just as unworthy of a Jedi as the act he had enjoyed last night . . . acts, plural . . . Samera's velvet skin so soft, her breath so warm against his neck.

"Not helping," he told himself, rushing to retrieve his tabard and looking around in a sudden burst of panic for his lightsaber. It was there, in its holster, at the foot of the dresser, Yorrick's confiscated lightsaber next to it. That was a blessing, at least. Explaining why he was late to Stellan was going to be bad enough, especially when the man could read him like a chrono, but losing the weapon . . . that would have been unforgivable. Now the only thing that seemed to be missing was his cloak . . . and the self-restraint he had so enthusiastically abandoned a few short hours ago . . .

Across the city, the fair continued as Elzar searched Samera's empty apartment. The coordinator's own thoughts were focused on the ebb and flow of the morning's events. Everything was working as if it had been planned in exhaustive detail, which of course it had. Her eyes flicked from screen to screen, watching repulsorpods ferrying visitors between the floating islands, while across the various zones music played, artists performed, experts lectured, and storytellers enthralled. She saw Bell Zettifar reaching the *Innovator* to make inquiries about two teenage boys, while at the opera house Chancellor Soh and Regasa Elarec met with Madam Conserra and her manager, Pall Sleko. Samera allowed herself a moment to enjoy what she was seeing, focusing in on a Krantian family who were waiting in line to tour Rothana Heavy Engineering's latest walker. She turned up the audio feed and chuckled as their youngest son, whose name was Sarry, tried to persuade his mother that he was still hungry even after a rycrit wrap *and* a bantha milkshake. That was what this fair was about, not nagging kids and fast-food stalls, but families from across the galaxy, creating memories together.

But no one would forget what happened high above the planet moments later. Space traffic controller Milon Thakkery had just given permission for a shuttle of excited schoolchildren from Wukkar to make its approach when a cruiser third in the line exploded into silent flame. Alarms blared and Thakkery's dashboard lit up as emergency protocols went into overdrive.

"Who was on that ship?" Milon asked.

His assistant, a timid Peasle named Skuun, checked the registry. "A troop of Jinda dancers from Eriadu."

"Had the ship been scanned?"

"No," the orange-shelled insectoid replied, "it was next in line. The portmaster wants to know what's happening."

"Tell him it's under control." Milon flicked a switch, switching channels. "This is space traffic control. Dispatch medical teams to help the wounded." He turned back to Skuun. "Is there any damage to any neighboring craft in the queue?"

"Nothing major," the Peasle said, obviously fighting the natural urge of her species to roll into a ball at the first sign of danger. "Although scans are detecting a strange radiation signature. It looks like a conflagrine leak."

"Conflagrine? What the hell were Jinda dancers doing carrying conflagrine?"

Skuun never had the chance to answer. She had been so preoccupied by the manageable and yet worrying accident that she'd failed to notice the signal of a ship hyperjumping into Valo's atmosphere at a point where no jumps were supposed to be possible. The signal was joined by another and another and another until there was no missing the myriad signals that appeared on the scope seconds before Thakkery and everyone on the space traffic control satellite were vaporized in the explosion that tore the station apart.

Chapter Twenty-Nine

The *Innovator*, Valo

Bell spotted the boys on the far viewing platform at the rear of the *Innovator*. Two platforms had been set up overnight to allow visitors to stand on top of the ship's hull, the perfect image scan opportunity, with the floating islands to the side and the shimmering lake out front. Kip and Jom were laughing, Kip looking far more relaxed than he had been last evening, even from this distance. Bell was on the other platform, near the bow just next to the dock. Ember wagged her tail happily, feeling her master's relief as Bell raised his comlink to his mouth.

"I've found them," Bell reported, wondering how long it would take him to head down into the bowels of the vessel and make it to the back of the ship. At least he wouldn't have to follow the route laid out for the visitors. His time exploring the ship at Cyclor meant he knew at least a dozen routes through it, shortcuts that the Cyclorrian workers would surely let him take, especially after everything they had all been through during the Nihil raid.

"Master Gios?" That was odd. Stellan hadn't responded. Bell waited before switching channels, thinking for a moment that he must have knocked the settings when he pulled the comm from his robes. No, he'd been on the correct channel, there was just no response, nor on the Republic channel he flicked over to when he couldn't raise Coordinator Ra-oon, either.

Ember growled, drawing a startled look from a nearby Lannik male.

"Settle down, girl," Bell said, resisting the urge to shake the comlink to see if it was still working. "It's probably just a bad transmitter."

"I don't think so," a voice said to his right. Bell turned to see Vam Targes pushing his way through the crowd, a few of the visitors also checking their comms. "I heard you were back on board, Padawan. Do you know what the problem is?"

"Problem?"

"With communications. Every channel seems to be blocked. Internal comms within the ship seem to be fine, but we've lost contact with the administration building in the city."

That wasn't good. Clipping his comlink to his belt, Bell lowered the defenses he'd placed around his connection to the Force and almost staggered as a wave of dread swept over him.

"Padawan Zettifar?"

Bell swallowed, trying to steady his stomach that had suddenly lurched as if he were standing on a storm-tossed sailing ship rather than a moored star cruiser. "You said that internal comms are online?"

"Yes."

"Then contact the other viewing platform. The chancellor's son is there with the son of the local mayor. We need to make sure they're safe."

Targes's mandibles quivered. "The chancellor's son? Why wouldn't he be safe?"

Bell didn't answer. Instead he looked up to the sky, Ember not caring what the Lannik thought and barking as dots appeared on the horizon, dozens and dozens of dots that were approaching rapidly. Bell used the Force to blank out the noise around him so he could better focus on the new arrivals. They were ships, some large, some no bigger than a Vector, but all of them were filled with an unmistakable hatred, the same hatred he'd felt over Cyclor.

They were Nihil.

Bell spun around, sensing that they weren't alone. Sure enough, more ships were rushing in from the east, dropping down into the air above the mountains on the far side of the lake.

"Get everyone off the platform," Bell said, as calmly as he could muster.

"Are they . . ."

"Vam, please. You need to save the people. Too many people have already died."

"Died?"

Other voices joined the rising babble.

"Did they say 'died'?"

"Are those ships?"

"Is this another display?"

It was no display. Bell felt waves of emotion. The panic setting in for those who had noticed. The concern of his fellow Jedi, who had also realized the danger. The cries of too many souls high above the planet, cries suddenly cut short.

"Get everyone away, Vam," Bell shouted, vaulting the rail and landing nimbly on the hull of the *Innovator*. "Get them to shore or down below. I don't care which, just get them off the platform."

Bell ran, flooding his body with the Force, driving him faster, his feet pounding along the *Innovator*'s hull plates. Ember kept pace beside him, head down, ears flat against her head. Even before he'd started, Bell knew he wouldn't make it. He was moving fast, but the raiders' ships were faster. They swept in like the horde they were, their thrusters kicking up plumes of water from the lake. He could feel their pilots' excitement, along with the countless thugs that filled their holds, all of them clutching weapons designed to cause as much damage as possible. It was almost euphoric, the agony of waiting for the carnage to start, the Nihil captains working their crews into a frenzy. Bell glanced at the front viewing platform, searching for Kip and Jom in the crowd that was being herded belowdecks. He couldn't see Kip's dark-blue jacket or the flash of orange from Jom's sweater. But he could see a solitary Rodian ignoring the steward's calls to move, remaining on the observation deck, captivated by the approaching craft. Bell willed the green-skinned male to move, to snap out of his trance, instead of staring death in the face like a rocan caught in a speeder's glare.

"Get down," Bell screamed as he raced forward. "Listen to the steward. They're going to kill you!"

The Rodian stayed rooted to the spot, even as Bell felt the order being given in the approaching craft, a thumb pressing down hard on a trigger. Fire spat from the nearest fighter, raking across the *Innovator*'s stern. Bell never saw the Rodian die, but he felt it as keenly as he had felt the spacers screaming in terror high above them when the Nihil armada first struck, or those dying beneath his feet in the crush of fair visitors trampling over one another in panic.

The Nihil craft screamed over Bell's head, streaking toward the city, laserfire slamming into the hull on either side of him. Ember yelped as she tumbled into the gaping hole that opened up beneath Bell's feet, her master following seconds later, arms pinwheeling as he tumbled into the abyss.

Chapter Thirty

The *Elegencia,* above Valo

A grin stretched across Pan Eyta's broad face as the chaos played out on the planet beneath him. His ship, the *Elegencia,* hung over Valo like a scavenger waiting to feast on a fresh kill, a swarm of Zeetar's scav droids already picking over the corpses of the wrecked cruisers and transports that just half an hour ago had been waiting patiently to make planetfall. Pan guessed that the bounties would be few and far between, although there would be plenty of credits that had been saved for years to spend at the fair. They would boost his coffers, and there would be parts for his fleet of course, but any monetary or technological gains paled in significance compared with the carnage that was unfolding on the planet below. That was the main event. That was what they had come for. They were here to destroy, not loot, to write their name across the Republic's precious frontier once and for all. Most of all, they would write *his* name. Yes, the other Tempests were involved, Lourna herself leading the land assault and that idiot Zeetar chasing after the ships that had cut and run when the attack started, abandoning their place in line to flee for their lives. Zeetar's Storms would cut them down long before they could raise the alarm, and even if they did, neither the Republic nor the Jedi would be able to get there in time, not with Kriss and her merry band occupied on Miluta.

The comlink beeped on Pan's opulent command chair. He didn't answer it, waiting for his navigator to accept the call. Why keep a bassa hound and bark yourself?

"Well?" he growled at the olive-skinned Rybet who swiveled in his chair, a webbed finger pressed against the comm bud in his ear.

"It's the Eye."

Pan hefted his weight in his chair.

"Of course it is." He waved a thick finger languidly. "Put him on main speakers."

There was an audible click, and Pan made sure he spoke first.

"We were *supposed* to be maintaining comm silence."

His grin returned when he heard just a hint of annoyance in Ro's reply.

"And you were supposed to report in."

That was new. Usually Ro didn't demand field reports. In fact, he actively discouraged them. The Eye of the Storm was rattled. He knew he was losing control. Good. Pan scratched at the burns on his palms where he had gripped the Eye's electrified helmet. Let Ro squirm for once.

"The *Innovator* is sinking," he grunted, watching footage from one of the fighters.

"And?"

"And we need to be left to do our jobs, unless you're thinking of joining us for once."

The Rybet writhed in his seat at the navigation console, sweat glistening on the amphibian's skin, or maybe it was mucus. It was hard to tell with those damn frogs.

"Just get it done and scatter to the prearranged coordinates," Ro said. *"We don't want a repeat of Cyclor."*

"We know what we're doing," Pan said, cutting the transmission.

At the navigation console the Rybet made a deep croaking noise.

Pan's eyes bore into the brown markings on the back of his head. "Do you have a problem, Breet?"

The Rybet swiveled to face him.

"No, Tempest . . . I just . . ."

"Yes?"

Breet swallowed. "I just wonder if it's wise to antagonize the Eye. He—"

Pan's blaster bolt threw the Rybet back against the navigation console where he slid down, landing in a charred heap on the deck.

"Someone clean that up," Pan said, slipping the blaster back into its holster and breathing in the agreeable reek of burnt ozone, charred flesh, and unmistakable fear that pervaded the bridge. He caught the Morseerian at the helm glancing nervously at him through his breath mask.

"You got something to say, Chell?"

Morseerians famously had difficulty recognizing facial expressions, but even the methane breather couldn't mistake the corpse cooling beside him.

"No, Tempest," he said, turning quickly back to his controls.

Pan let his eyes drop back down to the screens and sniffed loudly. Everything was proceeding exactly to plan.

"Communications are down," Stokes reported as the Nihil fighters swept around for another pass. Stellan could barely hear the Jedi above the screaming, fair-goers running in every direction at once to find shelter. He turned to OrbaLin who, minutes before the attack, had been regaling Sleko with what the archivist considered a fascinating lecture on the ancient texts of Brus-bu.

"Lin, can you get to the comm tower?"

The archivist's helmet bobbed. "Of course, if I knew where it was."

"I can get you there," Rhil Dairo cut in, already running as explosions sounded outside. "This way."

The archivist waddled after her, T-9 bobbing after them both.

"I'm going to help in the air," Indeera said, looking up at the Vectors that had already scrambled. "Unless you need me here."

"No, go," he told her. "And may the Force be with you."

Stokes was already running as Stellan turned toward the chancellor and Yovet, the Togruta's guard forming a circle around them, their kiavene ready for battle.

"We need to get the regasa to safety," the guard captain said.

"And we will," Stellan promised, looking up as cries sounded from the other side of the stage curtain. Stellan pushed it aside with a wave of the Force to see the tallest of the three repulsor tiers still in the air. The other two were down, the audience members running for cover, but the last stall was still suspended high above the ground.

A steward ran up. "We can't get it down. Something has gone wrong with the controls."

"I can help them," Sleko shouted, the manager's wings thrumming as he shot up to the stricken audience members.

"Sleko, wait!" Stellan called out, but it was already too late. The Toydarian had barely reached the right-hand side of the stall before the crowd rushed toward him, desperate to be the first to be flown to safety. The sudden shift in weight was enough to overload the struggling repulsors. The right-hand side of the stall suddenly dropped, flinging the audience in the air. The tier dropped like a stone, Stellan throwing his hands up to try to catch as many fair-goers as he could. It wasn't enough. At least a dozen hit the ground as the stall itself came crashing down, landing first on its end before toppling over to crush those who had survived the fall.

"No . . ." Stellan moaned, knowing even before he reopened his eyes that he'd only managed to catch five of the fifty audience members waiting for the next performance. Another, a small Bivall child, was cradled in Sleko's arms as he flew back to the ground, the Toydarian's blue skin blanched with grief. There was no way of telling if the youngling's parents were still alive.

Stellan went to run forward but a firm hand clasped his arm. He tried to yank it away, but Larep Reza's fingers held fast.

"You need to get the chancellor to safety," the Kalleran said, his dark eyes resolute. "I will help the injured."

"As will my guard," Elarec Yovet added.

"Regasa, no," the guard captain said, the knuckles around his pole-arm white.

The queen took a step forward, displaying serenity worthy of a Jedi Master, whatever was happening around her. "Their need is greater than mine, Maramis. You will come with me, while the rest of the guard will help the vice chancellor. Do you understand?"

"As you command, Supreme Huntress," Maramis said, bowing to his sovereign before ordering his charges to assist the wounded.

"Thank you, Regasa," Larep said, chasing after them to join the stewards who, along with Mayor Lariin, were already at work assessing the injuries of those who had survived.

Stellan turned to the remainder of their party. In addition to Soh, Elarec, and Maramis, there was Norel Quo to worry about, not to mention the two targons and Madam Conserra, who had stayed with the chancellor when the rest of the company had turned and fled, gambling that a full company of Togruta guards would keep her safe, a bet that now looked less sensible than it had.

"We need to move," Stellan said, trying to block out the panic and sorrow all around. The roar of the marauders' engines was already increasing as they came around for another strike.

"We should go to the Republic building," Soh said as they hurried from the stage.

"No. We'll head for the Jedi outpost."

"The outpost?" Maramis repeated incredulously. "It is not completed."

"But the vaults beneath the surface are," Stellan insisted. "Both the chancellor and the regasa will be safe down there."

Soh gripped his hand as he helped her down the stairs. "And what of my son, Council Member? Is Kip safe?"

"Padawan Zettifar will protect him," he assured her, offering a silent entreaty to the Force that Bell had survived the first strike.

Chapter Thirty-One

The opera stage, fair park, Valo

Panic had taken hold. People were running away from the approaching marauders, the ships flying low, their laser cannons already spitting crimson fire.

"They're heading for the lake," Chancellor Soh realized. "There's nowhere to go but the water!"

She stepped forward, waving her arms, trying to direct people back to the harborside, but Stellan knew they wouldn't listen. Herd mentality had set in, feet, tentacles, and in some cases wheels determined to get away from the danger whatever the cost. A fleeing Echani barreled into Soh, knocking her from her feet. That was all it took for her already stressed targons to pounce, Matari leaping for the Echani who had barely noticed what he had done. He would notice a targon's jaws closing around his head, that was certain. There was no time to try to create a bond with the animals. Instead Stellan raised his arms, using the Force to hold both beasts back. They writhed and twisted in his grasp as the Echani ran away as fast as he could. Good. The last thing they needed was innocent passersby getting mauled by the chancellor's overprotective pets.

Soh jumped back up to her feet, facing the animals, her palms raised, telling them that everything was all right, that *she* was all right. The beasts relaxed, no longer fighting Stellan's grip over them, and he released them, relieved when instead of attacking they surrounded their mistress, although their long teeth continued to flash menacingly at anyone who got near the chancellor.

Stellan looked up at the Nihil craft, which were gaining by the second. Bays opened in their bellies and bombs dropped, whistling down to the ground. Stellan leapt forward, putting himself in front of the chancellor and her animals, Captain Maramis doing the same for his queen. Stellan's hands were raised again, ready to push back at the inevitable fireball, but the flames never came. Instead, each bomb detonated with a sharp crack, thick yellow smoke billowing out.

"What is that?" Madam Conserra cried out.

"A war-cloud," Stellan replied, looking around for shelter. The Nihil's gas meant only one thing—the pirates would be attacking on foot as well as in the air, protected from the noxious fumes by respirators. Why hadn't he insisted that all Jedi carry breathers as standard? The answer, of course, gnawed at his belly. He'd believed their hubris, really believed an attack would never happen here.

The fighters zoomed overhead, firing at the ground indiscriminately. Stellan jumped back, using the Force to pluck his lightsaber from its holster, igniting the blade before the crossguard hilt was even in his hand. He swept his blade around, batting away one of the bolts, feeling satisfaction as it slammed into one of the fighters at the back of the formation. Thick smoke belched from the impact, but the marauder flew on, unhampered by the damage.

The wall of gas rolled toward them.

"Get close," Stellan yelled, deactivating his lightsaber. "I'll try to clear the air."

"Won't you need that?" Quo asked, his eyes flicking toward the lightsaber's hilt.

"Not unless I want to burn you."

It wasn't a threat, but a statement of fact. They'd all have to cram close if he was to shield them from the smog. Stellan raised a hand, pushing back against the noxious fumes. It wasn't easy, not in the midst of such clamor, the focus he required made all the more difficult by the understandable panic of the group. Not that there was any hysteria in Lina Soh's voice when she asked where they should go. Stellan thanked the Force and focused on the chancellor, drawing strength from her resilience, feeling the gas push back just a little bit farther.

Unfortunately, Norel Quo was anything but calm. "Well? Is anyone going to answer?"

"There," Captain Maramis said, pointing through a gap between two pavilions. The Rothana experimental walker stood abandoned, its platform open to the elements but hopefully higher than the approaching gas.

"Can you protect us, Lord Jedi?" Elarec asked.

Stellan felt a twinge of doubt, which he did his best to subdue. "Yes, if we move slowly."

"Slowly?" Quo squawked.

"This will be difficult for him," the regasa said, looking deep into Stellan's eyes. "But we are grateful. What was the expression Jorra Malli taught me? For light and life."

"For light and life," Stellan repeated, grateful for her support. He repeated the mantra over and over as the group moved forward, Regasa Elarec and Lina Soh picking up the refrain along with him, as much to draw strength for themselves as to help him, although the result was the same.

For light and life.

For light and life.

The progress was painfully slow, and with every shuffled step the air surrounding them became staler as Stellan kept the toxins at bay.

"Can't we go quicker?" Quo asked, only to suffer a rebuke from his chancellor.

"Not if you want to breathe, Norel. I think that's an acceptable trade-off, don't you?"

The aide fell silent, and they continued toward the walker, their eyes stinging despite Stellan's protection, disorientation immediately setting in. A scream cut through the smoke to their right, the cry of a small child, distorted by the fog. A shadow appeared, materializing into the shape of a pale-skinned Krantian female, carrying a youngling, who ran straight into the group, barging into Stellan. He took a step back, his concentration broken, and the fog rolled in.

"What do you think you're doing?" Quo snapped at the woman, who sobbed openly with tears prompted by grief as much as the caustic smoke.

"My family. I can't find them. I . . . I think they're dead. There was an explosion . . ." She was covered in blood, her child, a boy of no more than five years, clinging to her, terrified out of his wits.

Stellan leaned into the Krantian's sorrow, using it as fuel to push back against the smog, to protect the woman and her child.

"What is the name of this little one?" Elarec said, supporting the woman who looked like she was about to collapse.

"Sarry."

"And you are?"

"Lerahel." The Krantian was answering automatically, the regasa's tone commanding but compassionate.

"We haven't time for this," Quo told them.

"Then we make time," Soh said, putting a supportive hand on Lerahel's arm. "Come with us, and we will do everything we can to keep you safe. Do you understand?"

Stellan didn't see the woman nod. He was too busy trying to work out which way they should be traveling. The drama with the mother and child had disoriented him. He barely knew which direction they were facing anymore.

"The walker is that way," Maramis said, pointing ahead, as if reading Stellan's mind.

"Are you sure?" Norel Quo said, rubbing his inflamed eyes.

"He is," Stellan said, nodding in thanks. He had heard stories about Togruta montrals, that the conelike horns gave the species a form of echolocation, but had never seen it in action until now. The Force told him he could trust it. They moved on as one, Stellan wishing he could help poor Sarry who wailed pitifully in his mother's arms, but it was all he could do to keep them breathing clearly, let alone calm their minds.

"Surely we should have reached it by now?" Madam Conserra burbled, fear getting the best of her.

"Reached what?" Quo snapped back.

"The walker, of course."

"We're nearly there," Soh said firmly. "Isn't that right, Council Member?"

"We are," Stellan replied, although for a moment he wasn't so sure. Had they walked straight past the REW? Surely not. It had to be just ahead.

"There!" Maramis cried out. "There it is."

The warning came just before Stellan could blunder into the gigantic metal leg that swam out of the smoke like a tree in front of them.

Norel looked up, the structure disappearing into the smog above them. "How are we supposed to get up there? Climb?"

"I won't be able to do that," Conserra spluttered in alarm.

"There was a stairway," Stellan reminded them, remembering the walker from their earlier tour.

"Stellan's right," Soh agreed. "Leading up to the deck."

"This way," Maramis said, guiding them beneath the metal belly of the beast, heading toward its head, which had been facing the harbor. It was exactly as they remembered, steps rising up into the fog.

"How do we know it's safe?" Norel asked, peering up into the murk. "Up there."

Stellan felt a pressure through the Force, an urge to get everyone up as soon as possible. He turned, sharing a look with Maramis. The guard captain had sensed something too, in the smog. Something was coming toward them, moving fast. Stellan felt the danger even before they heard the clank of armor and the unmistakable hiss of rebreathers.

Stellan's lightsaber ignited and Maramis lowered his kiavene.

"What is it?" Quo asked as Matari and Voru padded forward to flank the combined forces of Jedi and Togruta guard.

"Not what . . ." Stellan replied gravely, "Who."

Chapter Thirty-Two

The *Elegencia,* above Valo

Pan Eyta watched the war-cloud blossom like flowers across the fair. He could almost smell the panic, Republic scum scurrying like ants ready to be crushed beneath his boot. This was how it had been meant to be. People running in fear, knowing that death was upon them, death brought by him. If Ro thought he was taking credit for this, he was sorely mistaken. Pan had been alone since he was eight years old, thrown out of the nest to fend for himself. He'd nearly died that first night on the tundra, mauled by a manatrix. He still bore the scars across his chest where the beast's talons had cut deep. By all rights he should have bled out on the ice, but he endured, dragging himself to the nearest cavern, enduring the fever that almost took him, surviving on the meat of the eight-legs that hid between the rocks, their juices running down his chin horns as his strength slowly returned. Oh, how he'd savored tracking down the damn manatrix when he was hardy enough, breaking its neck as the north wind blew, roasting its carcass over a spluttering fire in the cave. He'd vowed never to go hungry again, even if that meant getting off Dowut.

He'd walked kilometers to the nearest spaceport, finding a ship ready for takeoff and sneaking aboard before the hold was sealed. The star traders hadn't even known they had a stowaway, not until they felt his knife on their throat. The spacers hadn't tasted half as good as the manatrix, but their ship had served him well for many a year, even after he'd fought his way into the Nihil. Nothing had come easy to him, and he hadn't wanted it to. Not like Ro. Pan hadn't been handed the Nihil on a platter. Pan hadn't expected everyone to bow at his feet because of his name, but after today that's exactly what they would do.

Pan thumbed a control, opening a channel to the ground using the secure line Zeetar's Tempest had developed, a way to remain in touch even after all other comms had been blocked. Maybe the scrawny Talpini was good for something after all.

"Are the salvage parties ready?"

Lourna's voice crackled back, as cold as ever, even through the distortion.

"Raiders are already on foot, speeders and track runners moving in."

"Remember, the objective is to cause as much damage as possible . . ."

"I haven't forgotten."

"But that doesn't mean we can't help ourselves to a few goodies along the way. Shared equally among the Tempests, of course."

"And with Ro."

There was the hint of a question at the end of her statement. Pan didn't provide the answer.

"Just get out and burn what's left. Understood?"

"Understood. Releasing the blaredroids now."

Pan growled to himself. Another of Zeetar's innovations, the droids were designed to fly into the war-cloud, their speakers pumping out a mix of white noise and wreckpunk, anything to further disorient their prey. Pan thought they were an unnecessary addition, but he was willing to see what difference they made. And if they didn't work? Well, then he'd stuff one down Zeetar's throat.

"Here come more survivors," Chell Trambin reported as a wave of ships shot up from the planet, fair-goers and dignitaries trying to escape the carnage.

They wouldn't get far.

Technically, Pan should leave them for Zeet's crews, but why should he let the Talpini have all the fun?

"Looks like we've got ourselves a little target practice," he told his crew with a satisfied sneer. "Light 'em up."

Chapter Thirty-Three

Lonisa City Detention Center

The universe was punishing her. That was the only possible explanation. Life had been fine when Ty Yorrick used the Verazeen stones. Every big decision was a fifty-fifty chance. Take the job. Don't take the job. Nice and simple. Sure, she often ended up in jails such as this, but it was never her fault, only the stones'.

Outside, the explosions continued, and with them the chorus of screams and shouts. Something bad had happened, and Ty knew exactly what it was. She had known as soon as she'd heard the screech of the Path engines, even before the kid who had been thrown into the next cell not long after their own incarceration had tried to warn the prison droid what was coming.

"Raiders sabotaged the comm tower. I think they were Nihil."

The droid had laughed, cackling even more when the boy—Ram—claimed he was a Jedi Padawan and that he'd been arrested by mistake. Now the same droid was running about like a headless tip-yip, calling for backup that would never come.

Ty didn't like it, but she needed the kid to step up.

"Look, kid," Ty said to the boy who was pacing up and down in his cell, "things are going to get messy. Can I count on you?"

"Can you count on *him*?" Mantessa repeated behind her, the Kuranu's voice shriller than ever. "I was supposed to be able to count on *you*!"

Ty ignored her. The woman hadn't stopped complaining since they'd been taken into custody. *Can't you do something, Ty? What about your Jedi friends, Ty?* Jedi friends? Ty had just tried to stab one in the heart in a fit of pique. No. This wasn't the time to think about that. The Jedi had pushed her too far, and he wasn't dead yet, although that might all change when she caught up with him. For now, Ty had to focus on the kid.

"Well?"

Ram scratched his chin, still thinking about it. She could see why the droid hadn't believed him. The kid was a mess, dirty goggles pushed up on his forehead and robes that were smothered in grease and oil, but Ty knew a Jedi when she saw one, even a Jedi as timid as this. He just needed to make up his mind.

Finally, after what seemed like an eternity, the boy spoke up, although his eyes were still swimming with doubt. "Tell me what you need."

What Ty needed was time to speak, but she didn't get it. Instead, the detention center door slid open, and a hail of blasterfire reduced the guard droid to pieces. Ty jumped back, putting herself in front of Mantessa, professional to the end no matter where they'd ended up.

A Nihil stomped in, tall and broad with an imposing hand-cannon. Like all his kind he wore a heavy respirator mask, its three lenses marking him out as a Gran.

"Lookee here," he said, swinging his blaster around to face the kid, "target practice. It's my lucky day."

Not for long, Ty thought and raised a hand. "You will release us from these cells," she said, trying to impose her will on the thug. Usually Ty found mind tricks impossible. She always had, but she needed to do something. At the very least, it would gave the Gran a blinding headache.

To her amazement, the Nihil paused, letting out a confused, "Errrr."

"Try again," Mantessa hissed, and Ty fought the urge to smash her own head against the bars.

"I said . . ." Ty began, but the Gran nodded stupidly before she could complete the command, his gas mask bobbing up and down.

"I release you from the cells," he mumbled, shuffling toward the cell controls.

"That's it," Ty coaxed, thinking that perhaps the universe wasn't such a bad place after all. "That's it. Reach for the buttons."

The Gran's hand came up and . . .

"Zarabarb!" shouted another voice from the door. "What are you doing, man?"

The Gran whirled around, confused as his trance was broken, and unleashed a hail of blaster bolts. The newcomer—a Mon Calamari in a cracked visor—jumped back, narrowly avoiding the storm of blasterfire, but Ty knew what was coming. So much for the universe. For all she cared, it could take its help and shove it where the stars didn't shine.

The cell block erupted into a war zone as the Mon Calamari at the door retaliated, joined by more raiders who didn't care who they were shooting at as long as they caused as much damage as possible. Zarabarb's body danced in the blasterfire as the Nihil piled in, a stray bolt nearly taking off Ty's head.

Well, two could play at that game.

"Ram!" she shouted above the onslaught, hoping that the kid was still breathing. "Push them back, together."

She didn't wait for a response, pushing out with the Force. The blasters stopped as the marauders flew back, smashing painfully against the wall.

Ty glanced over, seeing Ram in his cell, a shaking hand held high. He looked pale but unhurt, although this was no time to rest on their laurels.

"Blasters," she shouted. "Now!"

They both pulled with the Force, snatching weapons from dazed Nihil hands, at least a couple of fingers snapping as they were disarmed. Ty found it hard to sympathize as a carbine clanged against the bars of her cell. It fell to the floor, just out of reach. Ty called out with the Force, but the blaster didn't budge.

"Get it, will you?" Mantessa barked.

"I'm trying," Ty snapped. Using the Force wasn't just a case of waving your hands and waiting for the magic to happen. It took effort, especially for the likes of her.

She'd just have to do it the old-fashioned way.

Ty dropped to the floor and reached through the bars up to her shoulder.

Near the door, the Mon Cal came to and spotted what she was doing.

Ty groped for the weapon, willing it to move.

The Mon Calamari raised his bowcaster, the quarrel locking into place.

She wasn't going to make it.

The Nihil yelped as his 'caster sparked, smoke billowing out its inner workings. It clattered to the floor, and Ty glanced at Ram. The kid was grinning. Had *he* done that? Maybe he wasn't so timid after all.

He had also put himself in the firing line. A Nihil with blotched purple skin shoved past the Mon Calamari, her blaster aimed directly at Ram's head. The Padawan's smile dropped away as he stared into the muzzle, and Ty decided he wasn't going to die today. The carbine jumped to her hand and she fired, delivering a head shot that sent the Nihil woman spinning into the bars of Ram's cell.

The Mon Cal turned on her in fury and went the same way. Suddenly Ty wasn't feeling so tired. Freedom had a way of doing that to her.

She brought the blaster up a third time and shot out the control panel, the bars sliding back. Mantessa barged past before Ty could even move, while Ram stood shell-shocked in his cell. He was a good kid but would have to look after himself. Like it or not, she still had a job to do.

Chapter Thirty-Four

The *Innovator*

Bell grunted as his body jerked to a halt half a meter from a deck plate that could have broken most of the bones in his body. He had reacted out of instinct, cushioning both his and Ember's fall using the Force, although the sudden stop had sent a worrying stab of pain through his newly healed core. He couldn't concern himself with that now. He had vowed to get Kip and Jom to safety, and the *Innovator* was listing wildly, obviously taking in water. He could feel the anguish of those trapped inside, the panic, but also the resolve of those among them who were trying their best to escape, taking as many survivors with them as they could. He focused on that, drawing strength from their courage.

He scrambled up, splashing in the cold lake water that was already pooling around his ankles. He called upon the Force to orient himself, working out which way was forward and which was aft. All around, the ship groaned like a wounded garral, the superstructure creaking as the deck continued to tilt.

"This way," he told Ember, heading toward a metal door as the sounds of battle filtered through the gaping hole above his head. Trails of vapor were drifting across Valo's sky. If he could jump back up, out of the ship's belly, he might be able to reach the stern from outside before the vessel sank beneath the water. He prepared to make the jump, gathering Ember into his arms, the Force charging his already tired muscles with the energy needed to make such a superhuman leap, when the charhound barked, wriggling from his grip. She landed in the water, yapping at the closed door in front of them.

"What is it, girl?" he asked, casting his mind beyond the metal to be rewarded by a sudden surge of fear. There were people on the other side.

"Good dog," Bell told the faithful charhound, striking the button that should have sent the door sliding back into the bulkhead. It didn't budge. He flipped open an access panel, uncovering a gleaming control port. An astromech would override the lock in seconds, but Bell didn't have an astromech. He had something better. He had a lightsaber.

Ember jumped back from the molten metal that splashed from the door as Bell cut a near-perfect circle, leaping through the freshly carved gap as soon as he was done. Bell followed the hound, finding himself in a sloped corridor illuminated by strobing bulbs.

"Help us," came a frightened female voice. "Can you help us please?"

Halfway down the corridor, a female Pantoran was hunched over a human attendant trapped beneath a pile of jagged metal. A section of the ceiling had collapsed, bringing most of the next deck down with it on the man who was screaming in agony.

Bell and Ember rushed over, the charhound instinctively nuzzling her nose against the trapped man's cheek as Bell slipped his lightsaber back into its holster.

"I can't get him out," the Pantoran said, her light-blue skin splattered with the attendant's blood. "It's too heavy."

Bell tested the weight of the metal. It shifted with the effort, and the human cried out again, more out of fear than any increased pain as far as Bell could tell.

"It's going to crush me."

It was already doing that. From what Bell could see, the heap of metal was delicately balanced. One false move could cause everything to shift with devastating consequences, not to mention the very real possibility that more wreckage could tumble from above at any moment. Bell reached out with the Force, trying to see if he could support the debris, but there was little he could do with telekinesis alone. He just wasn't skilled enough to keep everything in place while trying to get the attendant out. For all he knew, there were metal shards in there ready to puncture the man's chest or stomach if he made a mistake. Bell's recent experience told him how dangerous that would be, not to mention excruciating. Still, he had to do something. There was no telling how extensive the man's injuries were under all that junk.

Bell knelt in the shallow water beside him. "What's your name?"

"Denis," the man replied, trying his best to remain calm as Ember gently licked his cheek. "Can you get me out?"

"I'm going to try."

"I can't feel my legs."

He was starting to panic again.

"Do you trust me?" The attendant didn't reply. "Do you trust me, Denis?"

The man bit his lip. "Yes."

And there it was, the blind trust that the Jedi would save the day, whatever the situation. Bell hoped he could live up to the reputation of those who had gone before him.

"I'm going to try to lift the metal. Just a little bit. Is that okay?" The attendant gave another nod. Bell blew out slowly, centering his mind. Raising his palms, he closed his eyes and willed the metal to rise.

The Force will provide. The Force will guide.

The metal shifted, almost imperceptibly, but the result was the same as before. The entire heap creaked, metal fragments tumbling into the water. Denis gasped, the sudden intake of breath more terrible than a ragged scream. Ember barked, as if sensing sudden calamity.

Above them, the constant drip-drip-drip of water became a trickle. Bell carefully withdrew his influence.

"I'm sorry, Denis, but we're going to have to think of another way of getting you free."

"Couldn't you cut him out?" the Pantoran asked. "Like you did with the door?"

"I'm afraid not . . ." He paused, allowing the female to fill in her name.

"Senza. Senza Mulak."

"I'm afraid not, Senza. A sudden shift in the debris could cause it to collapse, plus of course there's a risk that I could cut Denis along with the metal."

Bell's heart was beating almost as fast as his thoughts were racing.

"Then what are we going to do?" Senza asked. "We can't just leave him here. He was trying to get me out when the ceiling came down."

Ember barked again, this time looking up at the hole in the ceiling. Something was moving on the deck above them.

"Hello?" Senza called out, scrambling to her feet. "Is anyone up there? We need your help."

Bell put a hand on her shoulder. "Don't."

She looked at him as if he were mad. "Why not?"

"Because we don't know who it is."

"What does that matter? They might be able to help."

They might, but there also was no way to tell if the newcomers making their way over the shrapnel of the upper deck were friend or foe. Those had been Nihil ships in the skies above the *Innovator*. Maybe the pirates were picking over the ship's corpse before it sank to the bottom of the lake, back to claim what had been denied them above Cyclor.

The deck lurched, sending Senza crashing into Bell. Denis screamed, a sharp, shrill sound, the wreckage shifting dramatically. Bell reacted out of instinct, shooting out a hand to steady the debris through the Force. Now *he* was trapped. If he let his concentration slip, even for a moment, Denis would be crushed by the wreckage, and yet at the same time a pack of bloodthirsty Nihil could appear above their heads at any moment, and he was the only one who could hold them back.

Ember barked, reminding him once again that whatever happened, she had his back.

But first, he had to get the Pantoran out of the firing line.

"Senza?" he asked softly, reaching for his lightsaber with his free hand. "I need you to step toward the wall."

The Pantoran's eyes went wide as she realized Bell was going for his weapon. "Why? Are we in danger?"

Denis snorted a little bitter laugh. "I would say on a scale of one to ten, that's a big, fat eleven."

"It could be nothing," Bell told him.

"But on the other hand it could be the people that sank the ship?"

"We're not sunk yet."

Bell wished he sounded more confident.

"Can't you tell who it is?" Senza asked, waving her fingers beside her head to mime Jedi powers. "You know, with your . . . *hooby-dooby.*"

"My hooby-dooby?"

"Your *magic.*"

Bell sighed. "It's not magic, and it doesn't always work that way." He didn't tell the terrified woman that it probably would, if his senses weren't being swamped by her understandable panic and the effort of keeping the debris from grinding Denis into the deck. Instead he turned his attention to his charhound, his eyes locked on the hole above their heads.

"Ember, you need to be ready, okay?"

The dog growled, ready to defend them all without hesitation, smoke curling up between her bared teeth.

"What is *that*?" Senza squeaked.

"Ever heard of fire-breathing dragons?"

"Only in fairy tales."

"Well, Ember is very real, as is her flame. I'd advise you to keep your distance."

"Maybe I'll stay where I am," Denis offered weakly, producing a grim smile from Bell. Even in the face of such peril, everyday folk like the attendant still amazed him, using humor—no matter how dark—to draw strength. If Denis could joke in the face of such uncertainty, he could fight a bunch of cowards like the Nihil.

No, Bell, he thought to himself, *you can do better than that. You will fight them off and you will win.*

Lightsaber in hand, Bell Zettifar waited for the inevitable.

Chapter Thirty-Five

The fair gates

This was his fault. All of it. Not the fact that he had been caught with his pants down—quite literally as it happened. No, it was worse than that. Elzar Mann had been so full of himself, so supremely *arrogant,* that he had believed, *really* believed, that the disaster the Force had deigned to show him had been averted by his arrival on Valo, as if his mere presence had been enough to stop death running amok.

His feet pounded on the ground as he raced into the fair, his senses assaulted by the wall of sound that hit the park, smashing glass and filling the air with a shrieking, discordant scream. Elzar staggered, teeth gritted, his hands clamped over his ears, convinced for a second that his eardrums had burst. If only. That would have been a blessed relief. The noise was absolute, bouncing off the wrecked buildings, just as the Nihil wanted. They had robbed their victims of sight and smell with the war-cloud and now were completing the disorientation, flooding the smog with white noise.

Elzar let go of his ears, trying to center himself amid the cacophony, calling upon the methods he'd been taught as a youngling.

Focus on the planet beneath your feet. Focus on the gravity holding you in place,

*grounding you, connecting you to one moment in time and space. One moment.
One moment. One . . .*

He felt himself falling, not to the ground, but back into the terrible
future he'd glimpsed on the Starlight Beacon, the vision echoing from
the depths of his mind. The mutilations. The terror. The world gone
mad.

And not just any world. This world. Valo. He had been given a vision of this very moment, the noise and the chaos, and what had he
done? Kidded himself that he could solve it all on his own, the brilliant Elzar Mann: iconoclast, trailblazer . . . idiot!

He would never forgive himself. Never allow himself a moment of
peace. He didn't deserve it. All this blood, all this terror, was on his
hands, and it would *never* wash away.

With a primal roar, Elzar lit his lightsaber and plunged deeper into
the nightmare the Nihil had created. His eyes streamed from the
smoke, and his skin burned, but he didn't care; in fact he welcomed it.
He deserved it. Every scar the smog inflicted was a reminder that he
needed to make amends. He needed to put things right.

A scream sounded ahead, followed by the growl of a chainsword.
Elzar felt the pain of a victim and the perverse joy of their attacker and
pushed himself to run faster, his lightsaber gripped tight.

He would bring justice.

High above the war-cloud, Indeera Stokes didn't hear Mann's lightsaber slice through a Nihil chainsword before driving deep into its
wielder's thick body. She was too busy trying not to get blown out of
the sky.

The fight above Cyclor had been bad enough, but this was so much
worse. The Nihil marauders were everywhere at once, strafing the
ground, strafing the sky-islands, strafing the Republic Skyhawks. There
was no rhyme or reason to their attack. They followed no pattern of
formation that she could recognize. Their only tactic seemed to be killing as many people as possible in the shortest amount of time.

Indeera homed in on a stubby fighter that was hanging off the tail of a Republic flier. The Skyhawk was weaving back and forth, trying to present a moving target, but had already taken a hit, black smoke billowing from its starboard wing. The marauder was moving in for the kill. The last thing Indeera wanted was to end a life, but if she showed mercy then the Nihil pilot would go on to kill over and over. Even if she could get them to bail out, they would only continue their reign of terror on the ground.

Indeera jabbed her trigger, and the marauder erupted into flame. She took no pleasure in the moment. Every death was a failure, not a victory, even as the rescued Skyhawk waggled its damaged wings in thanks.

She brought her Vector around and looked for another regret to add to her tally.

Elzar Mann didn't think of the souls he was sending to the Force. He cut through the Nihil like a clinical instrument. He'd started by remaining true to his teaching, disarming instead of killing as a good Jedi should, but the Nihil didn't know when to give up. He ripped the masks from their faces, taking their weapons first and then their arms, but still the brutes kept coming, fueled by bloodlust or drugs or most probably both. Elzar didn't know, and for one terrible moment he didn't care. The Nihil were acting like animals, and like animals they'd be put down.

The fight wasn't going well. More marauders were joining the fray every second—those who survived their sudden, shocking arrivals on Valo, that is. Indeera wouldn't have believed it if she hadn't seen it with her own eyes. The Cloudships were hyperjumping directly into Valo's atmosphere. It was utter madness, not to mention nigh-on impossible. Most defied the odds by staying in one piece, maybe something to do with the bizarre engines bolted onto the back of each battle-scarred hulk. Others either exploded the moment they hit Valo's gravitational field or plummeted to the ground, blazing balls of death that would only add to the inferno already raging across the park.

Right now a large cruiser had arrived, three lightning bolts painted jaggedly across its nose, and was unleashing its laser batteries on what remained of the sky-islands. Almost half the repulsor platforms had gone down in the first wave, larger islands smashing into their smaller counterparts as they dropped like stones. Indeera could only pray that the attractions were relatively empty this early in the day, although each island would have had countless attendants already in place to welcome visitors that would now never come. Indeera felt a wave of despair wash over her every time a platform went down, adding to the all-pervading sense of terror that rose up from the ground below. She knew her fellow Jedi would feel the same behind the controls of their own Vectors: Porter, Mikkel, Nib, and poor empathetic Burry, who, out of all of them, would be finding the level of anguish unbearable.

Bolts lanced past her canopy. She'd picked up a tracker. She didn't hesitate, pulling into a roll so extreme that any other pilot would've instantly lost consciousness. Her pursuer didn't stand a chance as she dropped behind them and mashed her triggers.

Above her another of the platforms dipped worryingly. Indeera's heart leapt to her mouth as she saw dots tumbling from the island. What planet did the platform represent? Boz Pity? Bestine? It didn't matter. Each of those dots was a life, and there was nothing she could do. Even if she somehow managed to get beneath one of the falling souls, catching them on the back of her Vector would smash every bone in their already doomed bodies.

That dreadful truth didn't lessen the horror as she watched a Nihil swerve to hit one of the falling victims, smearing them across its windscreen. Indeera gripped her yoke tighter as she felt the pirate's glee. Sadistic bastard! It wasn't the most Jedi thought, but it was an honest one. Despite years of training, for a moment all she wanted was revenge.

Porter Engle saved her from acting on the impulse. Her Vector rocked as he roared past her, oily smoke billowing from his engine. There was no way he could pull up, but he had somehow wrestled the craft into a collision course with the Nihil. Time seemed to slow down, Engle's canopy detaching as the Ikkrukki bailed out, shooting straight up as the Vector plowed into its target, both Jedi and Nihil craft destroyed in one neat explosion. Indeera swept through the fireball, only sensing the Blade of Bardotta a fraction of a second before he landed on top of her Vector, grabbing one of her wings to ride her craft like a skyboard. Indeera had heard the stories of what Engle had been in his youth—she even believed some of them—but this was something else. She had no idea how he was hanging on, or how he'd managed to land on top of a ship flying this fast, but she knew instinctively what he planned to do—and it was in every way as impossible as the stunt he had just pulled. They had no comms, and yet somehow the rest of the drift appeared at her wings. Was this Porter calling the others to them? It had to be. What else would explain the broken images that flooded her mind? Eggs cooking on a stove. Engle's Vector screeching out of hyperspace over Cyclor. A distant terror, from years ago, a lightsaber slipping from broken fingers.

He was trying to communicate, but the message was as scrambled as the eggs she could almost smell. She reached back, calming his thoughts, easing the memories that threatened to overwhelm her. Was this how Engle viewed the galaxy, the past and the present constantly in flux? What had happened back then? What horror had the Blade of Bardotta witnessed?

Not now, she imagined him saying. *Now we save lives.*

Suddenly everything was clear. There was no more confusion, only certainty. Engle, Indeera, Mikkel, Nib, and Burryaga of one mind and one resolve.

The drift came about, dropping effortlessly into a formation, Porter still miraculously standing on her Vector's back, anchored in place. Whether it was by force of will or will of the Force, she didn't know, nor did it matter. All that mattered were the people falling to their deaths.

Porter Engle was about to perform the impossible.

No, not just him. They all were.

Together.

For light and life.

Chapter Thirty-Six

The Faith and Life zone

Get to the comm tower. That had seemed easy enough before the war-cloud had rolled in and all sense of direction had gone out of the window. Worst of all, Rhil's connection to T-9 had been severed along with every other line of communication on Valo. After so many years linked permanently to the cam droid, it felt as if she had lost a limb, or more accurately part of her own brain, the droid's data no longer scrolling through her implant. At least the loyal little unit was still recording, the red light by its lens flickering intermittently. If they made it out of all this alive, these moments needed to be seen by the wider galaxy. This was a turning point in history, she knew it in her gut, and she was here, right in the thick of it.

Granted, she couldn't breathe, let alone see. She only knew where she was going because she was holding tight to OrbaLin's gloved hand. She had to admit she couldn't believe how fast the archivist could run in that atmosphere suit, but she had to trust that he was still going in the right direction. So much for her leading the way.

"Up here," he said, leading her up steps. That wasn't right. The communications tower didn't have steps, did it? They burst through a set of doors that closed silently behind them. Rhil choked as the air cleared, although she still couldn't see. She wiped her eyes, but that only made the pain worse.

"Don't rub them," OrbaLin burbled, and Rhil felt his hands press against either side of her head. There was the slightest pressure, and her vision cleared.

"What did you do?" she asked, although the question was soon followed by another, far more accusatory query. "Where have you brought us?"

"Starlight Pavilion," he responded as if the answer was obvious.

She shook her head, not quite believing this. "Please tell me we haven't come to rescue a bunch of Jedi treasures."

The Ugor actually sounded a little hurt. "No, of course not."

"But Stellan said—"

"Stellan said for us to get to the communications tower, but it soon became obvious that we'd never make it, especially with you in that condition. However, we have everything we need right here in the exhibition."

"We do?"

"Hopefully."

"*Hopefully?*"

The Ugor started across the empty space, which was now missing its showcase hologram of Starlight Beacon, the projectors dim. "We still have a number of artifacts in storage, scheduled for appearance later in the fair."

"Do you really think there's going to be a later?"

"We must not talk like that," OrbaLin said without looking back. "One particular curio was set to be loaned out to Crozo Industrial Products for their upcoming communications showcase."

Now he had her interest. "Communications?"

"An ancient deep-space transmitter from the temple of Vrogas Vas."

"And you think it still works?"

"That, Ms. Dairo, is what we need to find out. Of course, even if it does we'll still need to bypass the Nihil's jamming signal, but that's where you come in."

"Me?"

"You are our resident communications expert."

He paused, realizing she was no longer following. "Ms. Dairo?"

"Rhil," she said, looking down at the holoprojectors that had wowed the chancellor's reception with the top-of-the-line, three-dimensional image of Starlight Beacon. "Call me Rhil."

"What is it, Rhil?" he asked, moving back to join her. She nodded down at the projector cradle. The lenses weren't just dim, they were missing, yanked out roughly, leaving only a tangled nest of cables.

"The Nihil," she said quietly. "They've been here."

A crash sounded from the exhibition room. OrbaLin spun around to face the smashed doors. "And maybe they never left."

The archivist flicked out his wrist and a short lightsaber appeared in his waiting hand, delivered from a secret compartment in his suit. For all his quirks, the archivist had class, but would it be enough to keep them both alive?

"Where is the storeroom?" she asked, keeping her voice low.

The archivist pointed at the smashed doors with his lightsaber hilt.

"On the other side of the exhibition, eh? How did I know you were going to say that?"

"Maybe it was the Force."

"Or maybe I worked out that the galaxy never makes things easy."

"That does seem more likely, yes."

More clatters and crashes rang out, followed by the sound of a shattering display case.

The archivist turned to face her. "Are you ready?"

"As I'll ever be. I just wish I could send Tee-Nine to see how many Nihil are in there."

"No need," OrbaLin replied, igniting his blade. "Whether there are five or fifty, I'm getting you to that transmitter."

Chapter Thirty-Seven

The Unity Arc

"This way," Ty shouted, racing into the Nihil's war-cloud.

"We need to get to the *Dynamo*," Mantessa yelled after her. "Klerin could be in danger."

Try as she might, Ty had trouble seeing Mantessa as a caring mother. Still, dodging laserfire and explosions could force you to reconsider your priorities.

"Ty—we're going the wrong way!"

Ty wanted to scream at the woman that they weren't, but she needed to concentrate. The smoke was thick, and Ty hadn't had time to recover the rest of her belongings, which had been taken as evidence, including her respirator. All she had was the Nihil's carbine and the Force, and she couldn't listen to the latter's leadings with Mantessa's constant whining.

A scream rang out ahead.

Behind her, Mantessa gasped. "That's her. That's Klerin. You found her."

Ty threw back a hand, parting the smog like a curtain. Sure enough, the Kuranu girl was ahead of them, shrieking as a Nihil raider tried to pull that damn bangle from her wrist. Breaking into a run, Ty brought up the carbine and fired.

Nothing happened.

Ty squeezed the trigger again, but no bolt brought the Nihil down. The damn thing was out of gas. Never mind. There was more than one way of skinning a tooka.

"Hey!" Ty shouted, her voice coarse from the smoke. The Nihil turned, and Ty flipped the carbine in the air, grabbing its still-warm barrel. She swung hard, and the Nihil's head snapped around, taking at least two of his vertebrae with it. The impact shattered the blaster, the rusty barrel snapping off in Ty's hand, but the Nihil was down. Ty gave him a sharp kick just to make sure.

"You're safe, you're safe," Mantessa wheezed, pulling her daughter into an awkward hug. It was clear the pair never usually touched, and Klerin froze, not quite knowing what to do.

"I was looking for you . . ." the girl said, her eyes streaming, more from the cloud than emotion. "I went to the meeting place and then when I couldn't find you there, I came to the park. And then, when those ships came in, I didn't know what to do."

Ty had been checking the Nihil's respirator, but now that she had realized it was too big for her, it was time to nip this touching reunion in the bud.

"We need to move," she told the Kuranu.

"Back to the spaceport?" Mantessa asked.

Ty shook her head sharply. "No."

The Kuranu looked at her as if she was mad. "But we've already found Klerin."

Ty didn't have the time or the inclination to admit that she hadn't been looking for the girl.

"Follow me," she barked and ran toward the harbor.

Chapter Thirty-Eight

The Arts and Culture zone

"Hurry up! They're coming!"

Stellan couldn't protect anyone from the smog now, not if he was going to protect them from the far more pressing threat of rampaging Nihil. Luckily none of the chancellor's group needed persuading to clamber up the steps to the walker, especially when they were being urged by Conserra's unparalleled vocal talents.

"Mooove!"

Soh and Yovet had immediately shepherded the Krantian mother and child ahead of them, a selfless act that only seemed to infuriate the Mon Calamari opera singer. Living up to her title, the diva all but barged the Togruta monarch out of the way, but neither queen nor chancellor complained. The slate of rank and privilege had been wiped clean by the choking smoke.

Stellan blinked, calling on the Force to grant him the strength he no longer felt. Sheltering the others had already exhausted him; it was all he could do to keep his lightsaber from shaking. If Maramis noticed, he didn't say anything, the captain of the royal guard standing like a statue, kiavene lowered, ready for action. Stellan could feel his anticipation, as well as the power coiled in the muscles of the chancellor's targons waiting for the enemy to rush them, Matari to Stellan's left and Voru to the guard captain's right.

"Are you ready?" Stellan asked as five figures appeared in the smog; lumbering shades carrying outrageously large weapons.

Maramis didn't waste time with an answer but instead pressed a hidden trigger on his kiavene, a bolt of brilliant disintegrator energy shooting from the tip of the blade. There was a flash of light deep within the fog and five figures became four, the odds evened.

So there was more to a kiavene than met the eye. Stellan hoped that could be said of all of them as he raised his lightsaber into a defensive position. In days gone by, the merest hum of his blade had been enough to have potential enemies lay down their weapons, but the Nihil were different. They didn't respect the Order. They didn't respect anything.

Maramis didn't wait for their opponents to emerge from the smoke, disappearing into the fog like a wraith. The targons followed, leaping in after him with a growl, but Stellan kept his ground. A Jedi never attacked, only defended. Instead, he tried his best to send out a warning through the Force, anything to avoid further bloodshed.

You don't want to do this. This is wrong. Surrender and you will live.

He heard the roar of targons, the slash of Maramis's blade.

It doesn't have to be this way.

The smoke parted in front of him, a vibro-ax slashing down, ready to cleave his skull in two.

The way was set.

Stellan stepped aside, letting the momentum of the weapon drag the Nihil with it. A body was pulled out of the fog, the ax-head slamming into the ground, sparks erupting where it struck. It was a Trandoshan and a bulky one at that, its reptilian face hidden behind a thick mask. The lizard dropped into a roll before springing up to its feet, ax in one hand, a heavy slab of a shield in the other. It charged forward, its shield raised. Stellan threw up a hand and pushed back with the Force. There was a thick crunch as Trandoshan steel met air that now had the density of a blast door. The Nihil grunted, and Stellan stumbled back, gasping at the intensity of the impact, but was still prepared for the ax that came swinging in. He brought his lightsaber around, slashing through armor and flesh. The Trandoshan bellowed in pain, Stellan planting a boot firmly in the brute's chest. The Nihil fell back with a thud, the shield clattering away.

"Stay down," Stellan barked, his voice hoarse from the smoke. "I do not wish to kill you."

"That is why you are weak!"

The Trandoshan had lost both its arm and its shield, but that didn't stop it using its thick head as a battering ram. Bony ridges thudded into Stellan's gut, knocking what little wind was left from his lungs. He fell, the back of his head cracking on the floor, stars exploding behind his eyes as his lightsaber flew from his fingers. The Trandoshan was on him, its one remaining hand tight around his throat, the grip like durasteel. Stellan gagged, unable to breathe, his only defense his smog-stung hands that tried to pry the monster's fingers from his neck. No. There was something else. There was always something else. He was Jedi.

Stellan pushed out with the Force. There was no focus, no aim. His senses were too dulled for that, his strength fading. Instead, the Trandoshan shot into the haze as if caught in a tractor beam, its claws raking Stellan's throat as it was forced to let go. Stellan's cry was drowned out by a crump of muscle against metal, followed by a second terrible crash that shook the ground beneath him. He jumped up, clutching his throat, knowing what he had done even before a keening wail cut through the smoke. Stellan stumbled forward, trying to part the mist in front of him, all too aware of what he would find.

The Trandoshan had flown back, striking the walker's ladder with such force that the metal steps had toppled over, clattering into the ground. Norel Quo was lying where he'd fallen, his eyes screwed up, not from the sting of the gas, but from the agony of the leg he had broken. Stellan pressed a hand over Quo's forehead to send waves of serenity into his mind, telling the Koorivar there was no pain when there obviously was. A simple enough trick, and one that wouldn't last, but Stellan had other concerns. He looked up, throwing up an arm to part the smoke, and saw Lina Soh dangling from the side of the walker.

"I can reach her," Elarec Yovet cried, making a lunge for the chancellor as Krantian infant and Mon Calamari diva engaged in a competition to see who could scream the loudest.

The regasa found Soh's hand a second too late. Unable to hold on, the chancellor tumbled away from the ledge, her arms spinning.

"All will be well," Stellan croaked, raising both his hands. At any other time, catching a falling woman would've been simple, if it wasn't for two things; first was that Stellan was tired to the bone, while the second was the sudden appearance of the enraged Trandoshan charging out of the smoke to slam Stellan's face into the walker's leg.

Chapter Thirty-Nine

The *Innovator*

Ember bared her teeth, sparks dancing across her dark tongue. The water was gushing down from the ceiling now, Denis spluttering as it splashed over his face, unable to move, the heap of metal only kept in place by Bell's connection to the Force.

The scrabbling feet from above finally reached the edge of the yawning gap.

Bell ignited his lightsaber.

A head appeared, followed by another, two sets of compound eyes reflecting the glow of Bell's blade. Bell relaxed, snapping the lightsaber off as the Cyclorrian engineers clambered down into the corridor, their bare hands and feet sticking to the walls. Both knew not to touch the precarious pile of debris, wary of causing more damage.

Senza let out a yelp of alarm as the nearest insectoid jumped down into the water to scamper to Denis, its antennae twitching in readiness.

"It's okay," Bell assured her. "They're friends."

Extremely able friends for that matter. The pair had already gone to work, buzzing busily to each other as they pulled laser-welders and gravity jacks from their belts. Bell watched without question as they slipped the jacks into gaps in the wreckage, activating repulsors designed to lift delicate machinery so repairs could be made. Now they were stabilizing the detritus so they could cut Denis free.

Bell carefully withdrew his own support, thankful for the Cyclorrians' timely arrival. The Force had provided, as always. He stepped back, allowing the larger of the two engineers to add much-needed gravitational support to a beam that threatened to garrote the trapped attendant. Beside him, Ember barked, keen to get moving.

"I know, girl," Bell said, raising his voice to be heard above the cutting tool. "We should just wait for a minute longer, in case they need our help."

"Were you looking for a way out?" Senza asked, hugging herself as the engineers carried on their work.

Bell shook his head. "No. I'm looking for the chancellor's son."

"He's on this ship?"

"I think so."

"I hope you find him," she said sincerely, her teeth chattering from the cold. Bell shrugged off his long outer robes.

"Here, wear this."

She glanced at the cloak in surprise. "No . . . I couldn't."

"Please, you look cold."

"I am. Thank you." She took the robe and pulled it over her shoulders, smiling as the dark material all but swamped her. "I thought they'd be rougher. I mean, you're monks, aren't you?"

He returned the grin. "More or less."

Ember barked again, scampering back a few steps before looking at him, her eyes full of meaning. He raised a hand.

"I know, I know. Just another minute."

Bell reached out with the Force, trying to ascertain the extent of the attendant's injuries, and was gratified to find that Denis's legs were moving now the weight had been lifted.

"You'll be all right," he told him. "The Cyclorrians will get you out."

"You're leaving?"

"There are others I must help. Be well, Denis."

"And you." Color had even started to return to the attendant's face. "Thank you. For everything."

Bell turned to leave, convinced that Denis would be safe. How wrong he was. Ember was already bounding back up the corridor when an explosion sounded deep below them. The deck pitched and Bell crashed down into the water that was now gushing from the ceiling.

"What was that?" Senza cried out as the debris tumbled away, taking not only Denis but the smaller of the two Cyclorrians. Bell shot out a hand, grabbing the twisted edge of a hull plate to stop himself from falling into the dark pool that swelled beneath them.

"The debris must have formed a dam," Bell realized as Ember hopped on a ledge and barked at the rising water as if she could frighten it away.

"Where's Denis?" Senza asked, before losing her grip and sliding toward the water herself. Bell reached out to her, but the remaining Cyclorrian got there first, grabbing hold of the hood of her borrowed robes. She jolted to a halt, the Cyclorrian's hand squeaking along the wet metal as it desperately tried to hold both their weight. All the time, Senza was repeating her question: "Where is he? Where's Denis?"

Bell wished he knew. He'd hoped the attendant would swim back up, but there was no sign that either Denis or the Cyclorrian was even still alive.

With a bark, Ember dived into the water, disappearing headfirst. Bell yelled after her, but the dog was already gone, bubbles breaking in her wake.

Bell looked up at the cascading water, raising a hand to shield his face. There was no way any of them could climb to safety, but he wasn't about to let these people drown in the dark. He thought of Indeera sealing the hole in his Vector during the shipyard attack, using debris from the ship itself. Could he do the same? Surely not. Indeera had years of experience on her side, and what was he: a Padawan who tried to cut himself off from the Force so others wouldn't see how much he was hurting?

No, that wasn't it, was it? He hadn't shut himself off to hide away. He had done it because he was afraid of what he'd find if he stretched out into the Force. Or rather what he'd miss—*who* he'd miss—but now he didn't have a choice, not if these people were going to live.

Bell closed his eyes, imagining himself reaching down into the water, feeling its chill against his arm, his fingers brushing against the metal that had formed a barrier. He could sense Denis and the Cyclorrian, trapped in the tangle of bent metal, Ember scrabbling to get them free. All three were running out of air. He needed to act now. He needed to believe.

The Force is strong.

Bell pulled the wreckage toward him. Senza gasped in surprise as hull plates and metal beams erupted up from the water, whistling past the young Jedi to slam into place above his head. Now Bell pushed up, crushing the detritus together, wedging it into place. Less water ran down into the corridor. Bell started again, repeating the process, more wreckage bursting from below to plug the gap above. The downpour became a trickle, but the layers of metal, thick though they were, creaked ominously. The seal was holding, but the pressure was building by the second.

The Force is sure, he told himself, not letting go. *It will never let us down. We are . . .*

One thought crystallized in his mind, the truth that had evaded him for so long. The truth everyone had been trying to tell him.

We are not alone.

Bell's eyes were still closed as Senza shouted out: "The water level! It's dropping."

We are not alone.

Could it be true? Was the water really draining away?

We are not alone.

But what of Ember and the others? Were they safe?

We are not alone.

Bell grinned as he was rewarded by the sound of the charhound breaking the surface along with the splutter of the Cyclorrian she'd rescued. Still he couldn't look, even as the dog dived back down to search for the missing man. Bell longed to take her place, but he knew that would spell doom for them all. The dam wouldn't hold by itself.

We are not alone!

"Denis! Oh, thank the stars!"

This time Bell whooped with joy, listening to Ember bark and the two Cyclorrians helping Senza haul the retching attendant to safety.

Good girl, Ember. Good girl.

"You all right up there?" Denis asked, gasping for breath.

"I am now," Bell replied, finally allowing himself to open his eyes. Ember barked up at him, looking as though she wanted to leap up and take the strain of the dam herself. If only, but she had another job to do.

"Get them off the ship," he told her, the charhound whimpering slightly, confused by the command. "You know the way out," Bell continued, nodding at the hole he'd cut through the bulkhead. "You can find a path, I know you can."

"What about you?" Denis asked, shivering beneath the robe that Senza had transferred to his shoulders.

"I need to hold the water until you're clear."

Ember barked, more forcibly this time.

"It's okay, girl," he said, despite the weight of the water bearing down on the metal high above his head. "I'll see you again, I promise."

The look in her eyes broke his heart. He had no idea if she believed him or not, but he needed her to listen to him before it was too late. With one final whine, Ember did as her master commanded and leapt from one foothold to another, the orange spots beneath her fur shining like miniature beacons in the dark. The others followed, scrambling toward the hole Bell's lightsaber had carved, following the hound as she disappeared out of sight. Bell could still hear her, in the next corridor, barking encouragement as the Cyclorrians helped Denis and

Senza through the gap. The Pantoran was the last to leave, Ember already leading the others to safety.

"Are you coming?" she asked, looking down at Bell.

He shook his head, hand still raised toward the mass of metal that was keeping the water in check. "You go. I have work to do."

"On your own?"

"I'm not alone. Not really."

"Are you sure?"

"Yes," he said, meaning it for the first time in months. Stellan, Indeera . . . even Loden . . . had all been right. Bell *was* ready to take the next step, ready to stand on his own two feet, not as a Padawan, but as a Jedi Knight. And Loden would be there when it happened, closer than ever.

"May the Force be with you, Senza," he told the woman.

"And also with you," she replied, her face creasing into a frown. "Sorry. Is that the right thing to say?"

He smiled at her warmly. "It's perfect."

The Pantoran hesitated for a second before an urgent bark called her away. Bell imagined Ember finding a safe path up to the deck, leading the others out into the light.

Above him, the metal creaked, water starting to pour through the gaps. Bell knew what he had to do, but wasn't scared. Why should he be? Like Ember, he had a job to do.

Bell let go.

Chapter Forty

The skies above Valo

Slow down.

There were no words, but every Jedi in Indeera's drift followed the instruction to the letter, easing back on their throttles at the exact same time, decelerating at precisely the same rate. They were working as one. No one Jedi had issued the command, not even Porter, who was still perched on the back of her Vector. They had just known what to do and when to do it.

Indeera had heard there were a pair of Kotabi on Starlight, twins from Sagamore who shared such a strong bond that they almost operated as if they had one mind split across two bodies. Indeera had never met them, but imagined that this must be what it was like. One mind. Multiple bodies. A perfect union.

A perfect union that was about to perform the impossible, but, hey, wasn't that what being a Jedi was all about?

Ahead of them, people were still falling. Indeera counted three bodies . . . no . . . four. She felt Engle reach out for them as calmly as if he were practicing levitation in a training gallery, his mind at peace for the first time in years.

No, it was more than that. They were *all* reaching out, keeping one another centered. They felt the fear of those who were falling, saw them as if suspended in time. There was a human male, a blunt-faced Thodian, and a fur-covered Sneevel. And then there was the fourth: a Nihil raider who had crashed into the island, surviving only to fall to his death when his comrades in arms had opened fire on the final platform. Poetic justice? Maybe, but his was still a life. Who were they to say who lived or died.

The drift flowed through Engle, using him as a conduit, catching those in peril and pulling them toward their ships. The fear was still there, maybe now stronger than ever, mixed with confusion and just a glimmer of hope. Indeera felt rather than heard a barrage of thoughts: *There are Jedi here. We're gonna be safe. What if they drop us? What if their magic fails? Kill the Jedi. Feed the Storm. The Storm triumphant. The Eye forever.*

That was the Nihil. The Jedi blocked out the negative thoughts, pulling every survivor toward them, regardless of their faction, one for each Vector. The entire maneuver probably took less time than the single beat of her heart and yet the work was done, Indeera only vaguely aware of the Sneevel dropping onto the nose of her fighter, long skinny arms holding on tight.

"You're safe," she told him, even though there was no way he could hear, even with ears like that. She glanced right and left, checking the rest of the drift. The human male was with Nib, the Thodian clutching onto Burry's craft, her large eyes screwed shut. The Nihil had clamped hold of Mikkel's Vector, glaring at the kindly Ithorian through the canopy, teeth bared and barking obscenities. It didn't matter. Let the wretch hate. They were safe. All safe.

All safe.

The words reached Elzar Mann on the ground below, even as he fought a hulking brute in Nihil armor. There was no way of knowing which species lurked beneath the visored helmet with its spikes and tubes. All Elzar cared about was the energy-mace that was swinging around to slam into the side of his head.

Nice try.

Elzar flipped back, lightsaber still in hand, and the studded mace passed harmlessly beneath the heels of his boots as he brought them up and over his head. The Nihil snorted in frustration, only spotting something in his peripheral vision a moment too late. He turned to see a lamppost flying toward him. Long and distinctly solid, it had been toppled in the first few minutes of the attack, maybe even by the Nihil's own gunship. Now it smashed into his head, cracking his helmet and most probably his skull.

Elzar Mann landed back on his feet seconds before the unconscious Nihil crashed to the ground. He brought the post around, not letting it clatter back to the ground but sending it up above his head like a baton twirler in a Founder's Day parade. It swirled around and around, pushing back the war-cloud so he could see up into the sky.

Yes. That had been what he felt. Four Vectors were turning to fly out of the park; each fragile fighter had a person hanging on to the outside. What's more, another figure was riding the back of the central Vector like a Drumian wing-walker, his long beard flowing behind him.

"Engle," Elzar breathed, his voice husky from the smoke, unable to believe what he was seeing. At any other time Elzar would have laughed at the audacity of what his friends were attempting, but he could see what they couldn't, a Nihil cruiser dropping behind them, three jagged lines of paint slashed across its nose and its weapons preparing to fire. It was coming about the last remaining sky-island, dropping toward the Vectors like a shark diving on its prey. As he watched, the ship's central fin scraped the bottom of the sky-island, finally knocking out the repulsors that had been trying so valiantly to keep the platform in the air. It fell, snow tumbling from artificial mountains that would crush everyone below.

The Nihil ship accelerated, ready to blast the drift from the sky.

"No," Elzar spat. "Not today. Not now."

He dug deep, unleashed every emotion he had tried so hard to re-press in the months since his vision, the anger and the fear. All at once he was back on Starlight, his legs buckling, blood gushing from his nose, overwhelmed by what he had seen. Lights strobing, screams ring-ing out. Stellan dead. Chancellor Soh dead. The Council ravaged. En-tire planets on fire. He pushed further, mining the disappointment he'd felt when Avar pushed him away on Starlight, the embarrassment of her hand on his chest, mixed with the equal if not greater blow of seeing OrbaLin waddle out of the shuttle in her place. He'd felt so hurt that Stellan hadn't mentioned it to him, so out of the loop. His oldest friends and yet neither had trusted him. Could he blame them? He'd neglected his duties, seeking out Samera's bed rather than remaining vigilant. It wasn't the sex, that meant nothing; it was the realization that he had let everyone down for a moment of pleasure. Emotions roiled around him, through him, in him, like a storm out at sea, pow-erful and dangerous, but he could control them, he saw that now. He could control the frustration and the anger and the guilt and remorse. He could shape them, mold them, bend them to his will. He could use it all for good. He could put everything right.

Elzar lashed out, his hand outstretched, his fingers spread wide. The Force rushed through him like a wave, up into the air toward the falling island.

Unstoppable.

Defiant.

Indeera felt her concentration waver, just for a second. They all did. It was clear to see why. The final sky-island was falling, but even that, terrible though it was, wasn't their biggest danger. A Nihil ship was almost upon them, laser cannons glowing and ready to fire. There was nothing they could do. If they broke formation and scattered, the bond they'd achieved would falter and the people would fall; Porter, too, for that matter. If they fought back, the same result would follow. The people they had worked so hard to save—human, Thodian, Sneevel, and Nihil—would die the most horrible death.

Words flashed across Indeera Stokes's mind, words she hadn't used since she was a Padawan, words that had brought a stinging rebuke from her Master.

It's not fair.

But the universe was rarely fair; she knew that, as did every member of their drift. All they could do now was strive to calm those who had been caught up in the conflict, whose hope was about to be snatched away.

And then the world changed once again.

She felt the wave of emotion hit before it happened. One second the Nihil ship was preparing to fire, and the next it was obliterated. The sky-island had changed direction, slicing up where moments before it was tumbling down, soaring through the air like a discus thrown by a giant.

It continued out into the bay, carving a looping arc through the Nihil armada to splash spectacularly into the lake, but Indeera wasn't looking, she was shouting an order in the confines of her cockpit, the Sneevel hugging the nose of her craft.

"Down! As quickly as possible."

Nib and the others couldn't hear her, but they obeyed the command all the same, the drift dipping down. They had been given a second chance, but Indeera couldn't ignore the chill that wouldn't leave her. The wave of emotion she'd felt, that had saved all their lives, had originated from a Jedi, but was fueled by the darkest of passions.

Whoever had wielded such power would pay a terrible price.

Chapter Forty-One

Fair park, Valo

Elzar Mann knew what he had done, what he had unleashed. The drift was safe, the sky-island sinking to the bottom of the lake far from those it would have crushed. He had saved lives, but he had also taken them. So many lives. The Nihil on those ships, on his rampage through the park, even the brute who lay nearby, his skull caved in. He couldn't even remember killing him.

But he remembered what it felt like to send the island spinning through the sky. Such a feat should have left him exhausted, but he wasn't, and that scared him most of all. He felt energized, more alive than he had for months, years even. He ran a shaking hand over his face, glad that the war-cloud had rushed back in, hiding him from sight.

These waters were deep. These waters would drown him, unless . . .

Unless.

Elzar drew the word to him, hugging it close as if it was a life buoy in the sea. There was always another way. Always *hope.*

He would go to Stellan and Avar, tell them what he had done, how he had touched the darkness, *used* the darkness and, for a moment, reveled in it. His friends would understand. They would see what had brought Elzar to this point, and they would help. There would be no more secrets. No more going it alone. No more distractions. Even if he had to become a Padawan again, he would not walk this path.

He was Jedi.

Still shaking, Elzar drew his lightsaber and turned to rejoin the fight. He didn't see the weapon that came swinging out of the smoke, but felt it connect to his head, a supernova bursting across his vision as he smashed back to the ground.

The blow would have killed another man, but Elzar had come too far to be killed today. He looked up, blinking through his own blood to see the Tholothian woman with the missing tendril and the indigo eyes. The Tholothian woman who was holding the discarded Nihil mace in her hands.

"Where is my lightsaber, Jedi?" Ty Yorrick spat with undisguised venom. "Answer me now."

Chapter Forty-Two

The Starlight Pavilion

If Rhil had been impressed with OrbaLin *before* he charged into battle, she would never forget the sight of him running headfirst into the exhibition hall, helmet down and lightsaber glowing.

A quartet of Nihil were on the other side of the doors, cramming priceless treasures into sacks. With their bulky and frankly *terrifying* helmets it was difficult to see what species they belonged to, although there was no mistaking the towering Lamproid with its curved neck and bony legs, each ending in a clawed pincer. Two of the six grippers had been replaced by crude mechanical claws, but all were busy looting a stand filled with ancient lightsaber hilts.

"Dee!" the Lamproid cried out as OrbaLin charged out of the smoke. "We have company!"

"I see him," a masked Twi'lek with long green lekku replied, drawing twin blasters and firing on the archivist at point-blank range. "Get the others out of here, Amarant. Take everything you can."

"I'm afraid I can't allow that to happen," OrbaLin informed her, batting the bolts into the nearest Nihil, a human wearing a complex respirator. The pirate dropped, smoke curling from the burns on his chest.

The Lamproid and—was that a Kitonak?—joined the assault, unloading their blasters into OrbaLin, the bolts ricocheting away from the Jedi but somehow avoiding any of the priceless treasures scattered around.

"Surrender and you will live," the Jedi promised, drawing a bark of disbelief from the Twi'lek who had answered to Dee.

"There's three of us and one of you, Jedi. What *exactly* do you think you're going to do?"

"What I do best," OrbaLin replied, his lightsaber a blur. "Give a lecture."

"*What?*"

The archivist didn't miss a beat. "There are many fascinating artifacts here in the exhibition, many I see you have been trying to plunder." More bolts struck his lightsaber, not one reaching him through the whirling blade. "Although one of my favorites was noted just last night by a member of the High Council."

"Typical Jedi," Dee sneered, holstering her blasters to grab the glaive that was slung low on her back, the edge of its jagged blade crackling with energy. "Just doesn't know when to shut up."

From her hiding place by the doors, Rhil was inclined to agree as the Twi'lek lunged forward, her glaive clashing against OrbaLin's lightsaber. Was this *really* the time for a history lesson? And yet still the archivist continued unabated, somehow managing to deflect every bolt and blade that came his way, all without sounding out of breath.

"Tythonian Mastery Tokens are among some of the smallest items on display," he said, blocking the woman's pike and shoving her back with a none-so-gentle Force push. "Although I notice that their display case has been rather savagely smashed. By your associates, I would assume. Such a waste."

"We'll be sure to pick up the pieces," Dee said, slamming her blade into the floor to stop herself from sliding back. "We'd hate to cause a mess."

She sprang forward, twirling the polearm into another attack.

"You are mocking me," OrbaLin burbled, parrying every strike with consummate ease. "This in itself is nothing unusual, but I worry that you're not seeing what's in front of your face." The archivist flicked his wrist and Rhil suddenly found herself swiveled around to face a nondescript door on the other side of the hall. That had to be the storeroom, but her path was blocked by the Lamproid and its venomous tail.

And all the time, the galaxy's most obstinate Ugor babbled on and on, *and on.*

"I can understand why you have discarded the tokens," he said, sweeping his lightsaber down to slice the glaive in two. "They have little monetary value." Dee threw her bisected weapon aside, drawing a pair of vicious-looking sickles that had been strapped to her legs. "Neither are they particularly beautiful, although they meant much to their original owners."

Sparks flew as the curved blades tried to find a way past OrbaLin's defenses.

Rhil felt a nudge in the small of her back. T-9 was still hovering above her head. It had to be OrbaLin. Surely the maniac didn't expect her to get past the Lamproid? She'd be dead as soon as she broke cover.

The archivist sliced through the first of the sickles with ease, the metal, dense though it was, little use against a lightsaber. Dee hissed, slashing at the atmospheric seal of OrbaLin's helmet with the other blade. The Jedi stepped back, only narrowly avoiding the blade.

"They were, however," he said, still blathering about the bloody tokens, "minted from crude barabbian, which as I'm sure you know is remarkably dense, especially when propelled at high velocity, as I will now demonstrate."

Something small and round whipped up from the floor and streaked past Rhil's head. Was that—? It was! OrbaLin had used the Force to snatch up one of the tokens that he had been obsessing about. Two others joined the first now, whirling around the room as if caught in a hurricane. She wasn't the only one who had noticed them. The Lamproid called a warning but was a dash too late, as each swirling projectile suddenly found its target.

Spluk.

Spluk.

Spluk.

OrbaLin had been correct. The tokens were surprisingly dense as they punched through helmets and respirators, dropping the Lamproid and Kitonak to the ground. Only the Twi'lek was still on her feet, her helmet obviously constructed of stronger stuff. In desperation she threw the sickle at OrbaLin's head, flipping back head over heels to liberate an antique staff from a smashed cabinet. The archivist's fight was far from over, but at last Rhil's path was clear.

She pelted forward, leaping over the stunned Lamproid, and crashed through the storeroom door, T-9 nipping after her.

Behind her the duel continued, OrbaLin now facing one of his own antiques, but the archivist had more than proved he could look after himself. As for Rhil, she had a job to do.

Chapter Forty-Three

The Rothana experimental walker

Stellan never heard the chancellor hit the ground. He couldn't hear anything. His ears were ringing and one of his eyes had swollen shut. All he knew was that the Trandoshan was on top of him, punching down with his remaining fist, each strike loosening more of Stellan's teeth. Stellan had no idea where his lightsaber had fallen or even how to summon it. He couldn't think. Couldn't breathe. Couldn't function.

That's when he saw his Master's face. Not physically, of course, Stellan could be blind for all he knew, but Rana Kant was there all the same, her features creased with age but kind, gentle, and so, so strong.

Stellan wanted to go to the old woman, to throw his arms around her in a way he had never done when his Master was alive. He wanted to be at peace in the way the old Jedi was at peace, one with the Force in a place beyond pain, beyond duty.

No, her voice seemed to say. *A Jedi is never beyond duty. A Jedi should always feel pain; the pain of those who are oppressed, the pain of the powerless. It is not your time, Stellan, but I am with you. Always.*

Stellan's hand slipped beneath his robes, not to his empty holster, but to the hilt clipped to his belt. Grazed fingers wrapped around the cylinder, finding grooves molded into the leather grip by another hand, a metal stud beneath his thumb. Stellan pulled Kant's lightsaber from its clip, angled the emitter, and pressed hard. He barely heard the green blade ignite, barely smelled the flesh burning as the plasma punched through the Trandoshan's torso and out of his back.

The hits stopped coming, and the reptilian slumped to the side, breathing his last beneath his respirator.

Stellan let the blade die. He wanted to rest, to let his starved lungs catch their breath, if such a thing was even possible in the Nihil fog. At least the heavy gas had risen slightly, the pungent air just a little clearer. Everything suddenly felt calm, although a thought nagged at the back of his mind, something he had forgotten. Something important.

The chancellor!

Stellan jumped up, his vision still blurred. He had to find Lina Soh and assess her injuries. He was no Torban Buck, but there would be something he could do, unless he was already too late.

He stumbled forward, his free hand stretched out in front of him, the pain in his head stopping him from using the Force. There was every chance he had a concussion, but he would have to deal with that later. He stumbled, realizing to his horror that he'd kicked Quo who was still lying on the ground, passed out from the pain from his leg, but where was the chancellor? Where was Lina Soh?

"Chancellor?" Stellan croaked, and he was rewarded by a shout from above.

"Up here. Please. We can't hold on!"

Stellan forced himself to concentrate, trying to get a clearer picture of what was happening. Lina Soh was still hanging from the walker. He must have slowed her descent after all, long enough for Elarec Yovet to have lunged toward the chancellor, almost sending herself over the edge as she'd grabbed Soh's wrist. Now the others were there. The Krantian mother—Lerahel—even Madam Conserra, her hysterics forgotten, all reaching down to help haul Soh to safety, working together to save a life.

The Spirit of Unity.

Stellan gripped Kant's lightsaber, drawing on its strength, feeling her presence. He raised his other hand and called on the Force once again, cushioning Soh's body, pushing up just enough so the others could grab her arms, her dress, anything to get her on board.

"She's safe," the regasa called down. "We have her."

Relief flooded through him, so potent that his legs nearly buckled, and yet the fight wasn't over. He was hurt, he was bleeding, but he could not give up.

Something moved in the smog.

Stellan whirled around, dizziness overtaking him for a moment.

He steadied himself, muttering beneath his breath. "The Force is with me. The Force is strong."

Whatever was coming, he had to be prepared. The mantra would help; already he could feel strength creeping back into his limbs, clearing the fog in his head if not in the atmosphere all around.

"The Force is with me. The Force is strong."

This was his duty. His calling. He would not stop until everyone on the walker was safe.

"The Force is with me! The Force is strong!"

Stellan's lightsaber shot out of the smoke to his left, finding his open hand. He held Kant's hilt tight, igniting both blades at once, and stood, ready to defend them all.

The shadows in the fog solidified into three shapes running toward him. Stellan tensed as Matari and Voru bounded out of the cloud, followed by a familiar flash of red armor.

Stellan relaxed, letting his sabers drop as Captain Maramis came to a stop in front of him. The Togruta was breathing hard, a vivid slash down his cheek oozing blood.

"The Nihil?"

"Dealt with," the captain told him, shouting to be heard over the raider's aural assault. "At least, the few foolish enough to take on a couple of angry targons."

The targons were nuzzling Quo, who was lying worryingly still.

Stellan holstered his lightsabers and jogged over to the aide, Maramis running behind him, the guard glancing up at the walker, which was once again shrouded in fog. "What happened? The regasa . . ."

"Is safe, and brave beyond measure."

"I could have told you that."

The targons parted to let Stellan kneel beside Quo. He checked the Koorivar's pulse, finding it weak but steady. "He's gone into shock."

"That break looks bad."

"It is. We need to get him up to the others."

"Where are the stairs?"

"Wrecked." Stellan didn't have time to get into all that right now. He pointed in the direction of the Trandoshan he'd killed. "There's a Nihil over there. He had a shield."

"Had?"

"He won't be needing it anymore. Can you get it . . . and his ax, too."

"You want his weapons?"

"Please," Stellan said, trying not to get frustrated. "Just do as I say."

Maramis complied, returning with the armaments, which he threw to the ground, along with a bandolier filled with vials.

"They're all wearing them," the guard captain explained, pointing out a needle connected to the contraption. "This was connected to a shunt in the Trandoshan's remaining arm. I think they're stims to keep the brutes fighting even when injured."

"That explains a lot," Stellan said, remembering his assailant's tenacity, which was impressive even for a Trandoshan. The stims could come in useful, but for now he had Quo's injuries to worry about. As Maramis watched, Stellan drew his lightsaber and sliced the blades from the Nihil ax. Next he used his now blood-splattered stole to bind the shaft to Norel's leg. The splint was crude, but it would have to do.

"Now for this," Stellan said, turning the shield pommel-side down beside the aide. It looked roughly the right size.

"The right size for what?" Maramis commented, and Stellan realized that he must have been talking out loud. Maybe his head injury was worse than he'd imagined. "Lord Jedi?"

Stellan didn't respond. Instead he reached out with the Force, lifting Quo as gently as he could onto the shield. Like the splint, the makeshift stretcher wasn't ideal, but it would allow them to move Quo without inflicting more damage . . . hopefully.

Placing the bandolier of drugs on Quo's chest, Stellan quieted his mind as much as was possible. He raised both his hands, and the shield rose haltingly with them. The effort made Stellan want to throw up, but he knew he had to remain strong. If his concentration wavered, even for a moment, Quo would come crashing down for a second time, and no amount of Nihil stims would help him.

Stellan pushed up, feeling the shield rise into the haze.

"That's it," a voice called down from above. The chancellor, safe from her ordeal. "You're doing it, Stellan. We nearly have him. Keep going."

Stellan focused on her words and the encouragement of the other survivors who leaned out to grab the shield as it came into reach, lifting Quo over the edge and onto the platform.

Stellan waited, not releasing his influence until he was sure that the aide wouldn't roll from the shield, not until he'd heard that Quo was safe on board. Then and only then did he relax, his knees buckling. He pitched forward, Maramis rushing to catch him before he fell.

"Stellan."

"I'm fine," Stellan told him, grabbing the captain's arm gratefully. "The Force is with me."

The sound of fighting reached them through the smog.

"I'm glad to hear it, because we're about to have company."

Stellan pushed himself up, gratified that he didn't immediately slump back to the ground. To their right, Voru growled. Stellan pushed the fog aside to see the targon pawing the toppled stairway.

"Can we get it upright?" Maramis asked, running over to the targon.

"Maybe," Stellan said. "Although there's no guarantee it'll take our weight."

"It's either that or climb the legs."

Stellan looked over to see Matari already doing exactly that, scaling the walker's leg as if it were a pinnoc tree on the targons' native world. Force or not, there was no way he could do that. He doubted he could even manage a jump right now.

"Stairs it is," he agreed, helping Maramis haul them back up. They were heavier than expected, but Stellan had enough strength left to call on the Force to help. The steps clanged into place, and they shoved them as close as they could get to the side of the walker.

With a bloodcurdling scream, more Nihil burst from the cloud, clubs and axes raised. Maramis drew his own weapon, taking down two of the raiders with a succession of blasts from his kiavene.

"What are you waiting for?" the captain yelled, taking out a third. "Move!"

Stellan wasn't stubborn enough to argue. Jedi or not, Maramis was in better condition than he was, as became painfully apparent when he was forced to grab hold of the stairs' railing to haul himself up to the walker. The structure shook worryingly, but he made it to the top, Regasa Elarec helping him over the edge, the second of the targons following him. Then it was Maramis's turn, racing up the stairs, ignoring how much they swayed.

"Look out!" Madam Conserra shouted as Nihil charged up after him, but they wouldn't get far. Stellan waited until Maramis vaulted the edge before giving one last push with the Force. The stairs toppled this time. Stellan spun around, grabbing a nearby seat to steady himself. Chancellor Soh had clambered into the walker's cockpit and was activating the control, the metal giant taking its first thunderous step.

"We're moving," Lerahel cheered, hugging her child to her as blaster bolts shot up from below to ricochet harmlessly off the walker's belly.

Stellan staggered to the front, ignoring the scream of the Nihil who found himself under one of the walker's feet as they lumbered forward.

"I didn't know you knew how to pilot one of these things," he said to Lina Soh as he reached the cockpit.

"Neither did I," she admitted, peering into the smog, which thankfully was a little thinner this high up. "So where do we go?"

"Forward," Stellan said, pointing in the direction he hoped was Valo's temple outpost. "Always forward."

Chapter Forty-Four

The *Innovator*

*L*et's go and *see the* Innovator *on our own,* he'd said. *I can get us in,* he'd said. *No one will miss us.*

What an idiot.

"Kip, take my hand."

Jom reached down to Kitrep, ready to pull him up a stairwell that was now leaning the wrong way. It had gotten so that they couldn't tell what was floor, wall, or ceiling, not that it mattered as long as they got out before the ship sank.

Kip's fingers found Jom's wrist and the boy heaved, Kip grabbing the banister with the other hand to steady himself.

Behind him, the Quarren they had found wandering the corridors alone wheezed wretchedly. Kip looked back, worried about the old guy. He was going downhill fast, the nasty gash across his left eye still bleeding. Kip had spotted him with a woman back on the viewing platform, but now he was alone, and there was no mistaking the tears in the Quarren's eyes. The only thing they knew about him was his name and the fact he was finding it hard to breathe.

"You okay, Nwo?" Jom called down. "Do you need a hand?"

"He doesn't speak Basic," Kip reminded the mayor's son, climbing back the way he'd come to help. Luckily for all of them, Quarrenese was just one of the many languages his mom had insisted that he learned.

"Not far now," he said to the old-timer, only for the Quarren to shake his head bleakly.

"Leave me."

"No way. We stick together."

It wouldn't be difficult. There were only four of them, after all; just Kip, Jom, Nwo, and Leesa, the human fair attendant who had gotten them off the platform when the Nihil attacked.

"Let me get behind you," Kip said, maneuvering himself around the Quarren. "Give you a leg up."

Still grumbling, Nwo allowed himself to be pushed up the stairwell, Jom grabbing the Quarren's waterlogged robes.

"But where are we going?" Nwo burbled when they reached the top.

It was a good question. He turned to Leesa, who was consulting a cracked datapad.

"Where now?"

The woman dragged a finger across the map on the display, rotating the device to make sense of their location.

"This way," she said in an accent that Kip didn't recognize. She was pointing to a half-closed door that had stalled on its runners.

Jom pushed on ahead and tried to open it, muscles bunching under his wet shirt.

"It's moving," he reported through gritted teeth.

Leesa slipped the datapad in her waistband and went to help, pulling where Jom was pushing. Kip joined them while Nwo leaned heavily on the wall, catching his breath.

The door creaked on its runners. "That's it," Jom said. "It's beginning to give."

And give it did, in spectacular fashion, sliding suddenly back as if freshly oiled. Leesa let go, but Kip and Jom were carried forward by the sudden movement, landing in a heap on the floor, a mess of tangled arms and legs.

"Look out," Jom said, grabbing Kip tight before he could tumble back down the stairs. Kip clung to the Valon, the boy's body firm against his own. He'd spent the previous night fantasizing about what it would be like to hold Jom so close, but now wasn't the moment to make good on his dreams. The pair disengaged, scrambling up to their feet just as Leesa disappeared through the now open door.

"This way!"

They followed her as she tracked their location on the map, turning first one way and then another. Kip had no idea where they were heading but had little choice but to trust the woman as she led them down groaning passages, beneath pipes that had crashed through broken ceilings and over toppled equipment. Nwo slipped when navigating what looked like a vending machine, sucking in breath through his fronds as his foot caught in the twisted chassis. Kip and Jom helped him after that, his arms thrown around their necks as he half hobbled, half hopped after the attendant.

"Are you sure you know where you're going?" Jom asked.

"No," came the honest reply. "But if I'm reading this correctly we're on deck six. There's a shuttle bay three decks down, which I think we should be able to get to via a turbolift up ahead."

"What good will a shuttle bay do us?" Kip asked.

Jom had worked it out. "If there's a shuttle, we might be able to open the bay doors and escape."

"If the doors aren't underwater."

"You're a little ray of starlight, aren't you?" Jom teased. Kip tried not to let the rebuke sting. "Even if they are, the shuttle should still be able to get us back up to the surface. We've got to try."

He was right. They couldn't go back and had no other way off this thing. Still, it seemed like a long shot.

"Here we are," Leesa said as they reached the lift doors, the lights flickering on and off above them.

"I don't think you're supposed to use lifts in emergencies," Kip said, slipping from beneath Nwo's arm.

"I doubt it's working," Leesa admitted, flipping open an access panel to reveal a lever. She yanked down, the doors unlocking to reveal an empty shaft complete with a ladder and a bottomless drop.

"This thing has a light on it," Leesa said, finding a control on the datapad. A tiny bulb flicked on, dazzling Kip for a moment as she tucked the unit, bulb-side out, into her belt.

"I'll go first," Jom said, swinging over to the ladder.

"What about Nwo?"

"I will manage," the Quarren said in his own language, having picked up the meaning of Kip's question. "You go first."

"Are you sure?" Kip asked in Quarrenese, and even though Nwo nodded, he could tell by the quiver of his tentacles that the Quarren was anything but.

That makes two of us, Kip thought, reaching across for the ladder.

The rungs were wet, water running down the shaft from above, and Kip's arms and legs soon began to ache as he started his descent, Nwo struggling step by step above him, followed by Leesa. They made their way in silence, Kip's breath sounding far too loud as he groped for the next rung with his feet, too scared to look down. He was sure he was going to slip, but managed to hang on as they passed deck four's closed doors.

"Just one more to go," Leesa encouraged, although it turned out not to be that easy.

"We've got a problem," Jom called up.

"Just the one?" Kip retorted, finally looking down to see what he was talking about. It was a problem all right. The shaft had filled with water, forcing Jom to a halt.

"How much farther to the next doors?" the Valon asked.

Leesa's voice came down from above. "It can't be far."

"But it's so dark," Kip said. It was true. Even with Leesa's flashlight it was like trying to peer into oil, the water as black as pitch.

"Is there a way to open the doors from in here?" Jom asked.

"Yes," Leesa told him. "There should be a lever like the one I used before. Throw the lock and you should be able to yank the doors open."

"Even underwater?" Kip asked.

"I guess."

That didn't sound reassuring.

"What are you talking about?" Nwo rumbled.

Kip translated for the Quarren, who sighed deeply. "I shall swim down to open the doors."

"You can't. You're not strong enough."

"I'm as strong as a keelkana," Nwo claimed, puffing out his chest before collapsing into a coughing fit.

"Is this a private argument or can anyone join in?" Jom asked.

"He said he can swim down there."

"Not in that condition he can't."

"Hence the quarrel with the Quarren."

"Lucky for you guys I've been swimming in this lake since I was knee-high to a beeta-grub. Time I took another dip."

Before Kip could stop him, the Valon took a deep breath and plunged down into the water.

"Jom!"

"He'll be fine," Leesa said, but Kip wasn't sure. Neither did he know whether he should drop into the water to help. He'd never been a strong swimmer, and the thought made his stomach flip, but if Jom got into trouble . . .

Bubbles broke on the surface, at first small and then larger. Kip realized he was holding his own breath, especially when the sudden flurry of pops was replaced by no bubbles at all.

"Jom?" The water was ominously still. "Jom!"

That was it. He *had* to jump. Willing his fingers to let go of the rung, Kip drew in a ragged breath and prepared to plunge headfirst into the darkness.

The water dropped away, Leesa cheering as it drained through a set of open doors, weak emergency lighting illuminating the shaft.

A head appeared through the doors, ginger hair dripping wet.

"Well?" Jom said, grinning up at Kip. "You waiting for an official invitation?"

They clambered down, Jom helping them swing into the corridor, which like the rest of the ship was listing to the side. Nwo's wheezing had gotten worse than ever, but even he leapt forward to make a grab for Leesa as the vessel suddenly lurched and she lost her footing.

"We've got you," Kip said as they pulled her from the shaft, but nothing could stop the datapad from tumbling from her waistband to plop into the water that had settled beneath the open doors.

"Please tell me you don't need me to go after that?" Jom asked, peering into the murky liquid.

"No need," Leesa said, steadying herself on the wall to stop herself from slipping. "The shuttle bay's down here."

Luckily they didn't have to go far, but that didn't stop Nwo from taking a tumble or two, each fall prompting Kip to wonder if the old-timer would make it back to his feet again.

"Not far now," Leesa promised as they rounded a corner, finding that the shuttle bay itself was in a worse state than Nwo. Barrels and containers had tumbled from one side of the hangar to the other, collecting on the far wall, cables hanging from a ceiling that looked dangerously close to collapse. But there was one glimmer of hope in the shape of a sublight shuttle that had slipped with the barrels but looked like it was still in one piece.

"The hatch is open," Leesa called as she clambered aboard.

"Is it dry?" Jom asked.

"As a Chaaktil night." Lights flashed on within the cabin. "And we have power!"

They helped Nwo through the hatch, finding two rows of seats, three at the back and two behind the flight controls. Leesa slipped into the pilot's seat, flicking switches on the console and frowning.

"What is it?" asked Jom, noticing her expression.

"We may have power, but the hangar bay doesn't." She peered through the shuttle's transparisteel viewport at the huge double doors that would usually lead out into the vacuum of space. "Those things are jammed shut."

Jom and Kip joined her, Jom dropping into the copilot's seat. "And there's nothing we can do from here?"

The buttons beneath Leesa's fingers beeped helplessly. "The system is blown."

Kip turned to climb back outside.

"Where are you going?"

He turned back to Jom. "There must be a manual control, like in the lift shaft."

"I don't like the idea of pulling those back by hand," Jom admitted. "Not with a lake on the other side."

"Do we have any other choice?"

"Does this thing have weapons?" Jom asked.

Leesa checked a readout. "I think so. The bare minimum, at least. Simple lasers, nothing more."

"Enough to punch through the doors?"

She continued to check controls. "There's only one way to find out, but the real problem comes when we make it out . . ."

Kip's heart sank. "You don't know how to fly."

"Not in the slightest. I'm great at turning on power and not at all bad when it comes to identifying systems, but getting us back to the surface? Well, that's a very different matter."

Jom swore.

"You can say that again."

"Well, I don't know how to do it." He swiveled around to look expectantly at Kip.

"Me? Why would I know how to fly a shuttle?"

"You must have been on a lot."

"As a *passenger*."

"Oh, for the love of Dac, move aside." They all turned at the sudden outburst of Quarrenese to see Nwo heaving himself toward Leesa, his wrinkled hand flapping her away. "Go on. Scoot. Scoot."

Even without fully understanding him, the attendant moved aside, letting the Quarren flop into the flight seat.

"You're a pilot?" Kip asked.

"*Used* to be a pilot, but they can't have changed things too much."

Nwo started flipping switches with his webbed fingers, and the engines hummed, as did the comm, a voice crackling over the line.

"*—this is Vam Targes, the designer of this vessel. I am attempting to jettison the main processor which contains vital research about the hyperspace anomalies the Nihil seem to be using. The flight deck is rapidly filling with water and—*"

The sound of an explosion boomed over the speakers, which would have been worrying enough if the hangar bay didn't suddenly lurch backward. They all screamed, grabbing hold of anything they could as the shuttle shifted, sliding toward the back wall. There was an almighty crack as the bay's ceiling finally gave way, water cascading from above. Something very large and very loud struck the top of them, the shuttle's ceiling bowing. They jolted to a halt, Jom craning his neck to peer up.

"We're caught beneath a beam."

"What kind of beam?" Kip asked.

"The kind that would need a dozen Wookiees to shift."

The hangar bay was filling fast, the water level already halfway up the viewport.

"Do you think the ship's gone under the lake?" Kip asked.

"There's no way to know," Leesa said. "But it's likely."

"Then what are we going to do," Jom whined.

"Hold on to something," Nwo burbled, firing the engines. The shuttle shook more violently than ever, and for a split second there was a terrible scraping noise as it tried to break free of the beam.

"It's no good. We're stuck," Kip said, leaping up and opening the hatch.

"What are you doing?" Jom shouted over the engines.

"Seeing how I compare to a dozen Wookiees."

Jom and Leesa scrambled after him, but it was useless. Try as they might there was no way they could lift the beam. They were wedged tight.

"Maybe there's cutting equipment in the shuttle?" Jom suggested.

"Even if we worked out how to use it, would we have time to cut through the metal?" Kip asked, before deciding not to waste more time by waiting for an answer. "Never mind. I'll go look."

He started toward the hatch but slipped on the wet roof, sliding over the edge. Taking a deep breath, he closed his eyes and waited for the cold water to hit him. Instead, he found himself floating in midair, arms whirling.

"Try to remain calm," came a voice from above. Kip twisted around as he was lifted back to the top and saw a figure looking down from the deck above, one hand holding himself steady while the other traced Kip's journey back to safety.

"Bell!"

The Padawan leapt down to join them, landing with impossible grace.

"Having fun?"

"Not really," Kip replied. "But thanks for, you know, the floating."

"It's the least I could do." Bell turned to look at the beam. "You'll never move that. You need a cutting device."

"That's what I was going for."

"No need." Bell drew his lightsaber, the green blade igniting. "Get back aboard."

Kip wiped water from his eyes. "What about you?"

"Let the Force worry about me. Go."

They did as they were told, slip-sliding down to the open hatch, which Leesa shut behind them.

"We can't leave Bell up there," Kip said, but she was already pulling a restraining belt over her lap.

"You heard what he said. He's a Jedi. That's what they do."

"Commit suicide?"

"No," Bell's voice shouted from outside. "Is everyone ready?"

Kip told Nwo what he thought Bell was planning, and the Quarren nodded.

"Yeah. We're good to go."

"Then hold on tight."

There was a hiss, and sparks rained down onto the viewport. Kip winced but the transparisteel didn't crack, at least for now.

The sound of screeching metal stopped, and Bell's footsteps clanged over their heads as he crossed to the other side of the shuttle. He gave a muffled sound, but they couldn't make it out over the noise of the water.

"What did you say?" Kip yelled.

"I've cut through the beam on the right-hand side," came the reply. The water had reached the top of the viewport now. They thought Bell said that he was going to start at the other end, but it was too difficult to make out.

"Ready the cannons," Nwo burbled at Jom, who looked at him none the wiser.

"The lasers," Kip translated.

"In front of you," Leesa added.

"Where?" Jom asked, his voice going up at least two octaves.

The sound of cutting started again.

"Here and here," Nwo said, leaning over and jabbing buttons. The bay doors appeared on a tactical display in front of Jom, a red target overlying the image.

"Just press this when I say, yes?" Nwo said, and this time Jom got the meaning.

"That's how we fire the weapons, yeah? Pew pew?"

"Yes, weapons," Nwo confirmed, adding a "pew" in Basic to underline the point.

On the roof, Bell's feet shifted.

"He's got to be nearly finished," Leesa said.

Nwo primed the engines, placing a hand on the thruster control.

"Not yet," Kip urged, but Nwo wasn't willing to wait. The water had completely covered the window now, and there was a sudden crack. Was that the transparisteel finally giving way?

"Yes, now," Nwo said, pulling back the lever before Bell had finished cutting. Kip cried out to wait, but his shout was lost in the sound of tearing metal as the shuttle shot forward.

"Fire!" Nwo barked in Basic, grappling with the flight yoke as the shuttle barreled toward the doors. "Pew, pew!"

Jom pressed the trigger, and there was a blinding flash of light followed by a tsunami of water as the doors disintegrated.

Nwo shouted something else, but Kip didn't hear what it was. He was too busy trying to grab hold of a chair. There was another crack, and water started to spray through a now very obvious crack in the viewport. Kip couldn't see where they were heading, or even if they were out of the *Innovator,* but seconds later the water stopped pouring in and the gloom was replaced by smoke-filled skies.

Jom punched the air while Kip fought not to be sick as Nwo brought the shuttle around sharply, heading back toward the harbor. There was no sign of the *Innovator,* and the park itself was shrouded in a thick yellow fog that clung to the ground. There were fires and there were explosions, starfighters dancing around one another above them. The sky-islands were gone as were most of the pavilions, downed aircars burning on the dock, bodies strewn in all directions.

"My mom's somewhere in there," Kip said quietly as Nwo brought the nose of the shuttle down.

"We're going in too fast," Leesa cried, but Nwo just yelled at them to brace, pulling back on the yoke with all his might.

Kip had sat through enough flight safety holos in his life and called for them all to curl forward, their hands over their heads.

The shuttle hit the ground and screeched to a juddering stop, throwing them against their restraints. Kip looked up, surprised to still be alive. Jom was already out of his seat, opening the hatch.

"Is it safe?" Kip asked.

"Better than in here. We don't know if this thing is going to blow."

They stumbled out, Kip helping Nwo even though he wanted to scream at the selfish old fool for leaving Bell behind.

Outside, the air was rank, screams and explosions drowned out by what sounded like a madman's definition of music. Kip choked on the foul stench; his legs buckled, taking Nwo down with him.

Jom was beside them in a second, checking that they were all right.

"Of course we're not," Kip spluttered, pushing Jom aside. "We just left a Jedi to drown on a sinking ship."

Jom looked wounded at the anger in Kip's voice. "I know."

"He was one of the good guys, Jom. Tell me—what does that make us?"

As if in answer, a dog barked somewhere in front of them. Kip looked up to see a gray-and-orange hound running toward them full pelt. *Bell's* hound. Did she know what they had done? Was she about to take revenge for abandoning her master? Matari and Voru certainly would to anyone who had done the same to his mother.

He held up an arm to protect himself, but the dog shot past, bounding up the side of the wrecked shuttle. Kip's mouth dropped open as he saw Ember leap into the arms of a figure sprawled on the shuttle's sloping roof, a figure in drenched Jedi robes.

"Bell," Kip shouted, scrambling back to his feet and running to the shuttle. "You made it!"

"I told you the Force would take care of me," the Jedi said, trying to stop the charhound from licking him to death. "Although hanging on wasn't fun as you took out the doors."

"Yeah, about that . . ." Jom began, shamefaced.

Bell leapt down from the shuttle, Ember bounding after him. "We got out, that's the important thing, although I'm afraid my lightsaber went down with the ship."

"That's a shame," Leesa said. "I think we're going to need it."

"I've gotta find my mom," Kip blurted out, and Bell laid a supportive hand on his shoulder.

"We will, if we stick together." Something caught Bell's eye behind them, and he smiled. "All of us."

Kip turned to see a Pantoran woman and a pair of bedraggled Cyclorrians helping a wounded human in a tattered attendant uniform.

"Denis?" Leesa said, recognizing the man. "Are you—"

"I'll live," the man replied, smiling wearily at the Jedi. "Thanks to Bell. It's good to see you again, kid."

"You too," Bell replied, "although this really isn't the place for a reunion. I hope you're ready."

"For what?" Jom asked.

Bell turned to face the Nihil's cloud. "Getting off the ship was easy. Now comes the real challenge . . ."

Chapter Forty-Five

Fair park, Valo

The mace could have killed the Jedi. *She* could've killed the Jedi, for the second time in so many days. Ty knew it and regretted what she had done, just as she had regretted going for his heart the previous evening, but no one took her lightsaber. No one.

She could cope with being locked up—that had happened often enough—but that weapon was one of the only links she had to her old life, before all the monsters and the gangsters. Back when she was good.

"Ty? Ty, what the hell are you doing?"

It was Mantessa, stumbling out of the smoke behind her, Klerin a few steps behind. "We need to leave now."

"Not until I get what is mine," Ty said, keeping her eyes locked on the Jedi, who was struggling to get up, stunned by the blow. His cheek was already swollen, maybe even fractured, but Jedi could cope with pain, she knew that. She had learned the lessons herself.

"You don't want to do this," the Jedi said, his words slurred. "You're only making it worse."

Worse than being a fugitive? Even in the middle of the Nihil attack, running from the authorities was another black mark in her ledger, helpful Padawans or not.

"Just give me my lightsaber and I'll go," she told him, holding out her hand. "You'll never see me again."

"And what if I don't want to?"

Ty dropped back into a fighting stance as the Jedi lurched up to his feet, swaying slightly. "I don't see how you have much choice."

"Is that so?"

The mace was yanked from her grip, flying into his hand. Ty swore, bunching her fists instead. If only she'd managed to recover the rest of her arsenal from the jail. This was a bout she couldn't win, even with the Jedi in this state, and the smug bastard knew it.

Still, she had never run from a fight.

"Yorrick!" Mantessa hissed from behind.

"You go," she called over her shoulder, not taking her eyes from the Jedi, who had the mace down by his side, his eyes surprisingly clear for a man who had just been half brained to death. "I'll find you later."

"Don't bother," came the reply, and Mantessa pulled Klerin into the smoke. Good. That was two fewer people to worry about. It wasn't as if she expected to be paid anyway, not after how badly the gig had gone. A decision made then. No more bodyguard jobs. From this day on she'd do what she did best—bringing down monsters—and for that she'd need her lightsaber.

"Well?" she said, eyeing the mace.

"Well what?"

"Are we going to do this?"

She sounded confident. That was good, because without a weapon in her hand she was feeling anything but. Any other Jedi might disable her, shoving her back with the Force or trying a mind trick, but she'd seen what this guy had done with the sky-island. It had been a long time since Ty had stepped foot inside a Jedi temple, but she remembered enough of the teachings to know the difference between light and dark. What he'd just pulled was definitely dark.

Ty pushed forward, kicking out, aiming for the chest she'd attempted to run through the night before. He feinted back, avoiding the kick and the punch that followed it.

"Don't," he warned.

"I have to."

"Very well."

The Jedi raised the mace across his chest and . . . threw it away.

She peered at him, unsure how to respond, especially when he reached inside his robe to produce her lightsaber.

"Here."

Ty blinked.

"What?"

The Jedi took a step forward, the hilt held out toward her. "You want your saber? You can have your saber."

"Just like that."

"Just like that, although I need something in return."

Ha! Now, wasn't that just typical? The world was going to hell around them and this joker was trying to make a deal.

"What the hell would you need from me?"

He opened his hand, and the lightsaber floated toward her.

"Your help. Whoever you are, you were trained as a Jedi. That much is obvious. I don't know what happened to turn you away from the Order, but I know this is how you can make amends."

She snorted, the lightsaber still hovering between them. This had to be a trick. "You don't know what happened to turn *me* away? Says the guy who did *that*." She jabbed a finger toward the space where the sky-island had been. "What's next, eh?"

"Next, I'm going to make amends." The Jedi pushed the lightsaber closer to her, challenging her to take it. "Look, the sky-island is why I can't be alone. I need someone . . . to keep me on the right path."

She laughed. "Me?"

The Jedi shrugged, his hand still outstretched, the lightsaber shaking slightly in the air. "You're the only one here, and people are dying.

They need me, which means I need you. The Force knows it, I know it, and I think, deep in your heart, you know it, too. Will you help me? Please."

Ty stared at him, studying his face, trying to work out if this was all a trick. He looked sincere enough, but wasn't that always the way. As a last resort, she reached out with her feelings the way she had been taught so long ago and felt a mass of doubts and regrets, and an over-whelming resolve to put things right.

The guy was on the level. He could have killed her where she stood, but needed her . . . really needed her in a way that bordered on over-whelming.

Ty snatched her lightsaber from the air, checking to see if he had disabled it. Everything looked in order. Now the tables were turned. She was the one who was armed, and he was vulnerable, in more ways than one.

She looked up and met his pained, haunted eyes.

"Well?" he asked, his empty hands turned toward her.

"Thank you for this," she said, tapping the hilt against her hand, and made another decision. "But it's not my fight. I'm sorry. About everything."

Ty Yorrick turned and ran into the fog before she could change her mind.

Chapter Forty-Six

The Starlight Pavilion

Rhil had been using communications equipment for years and yet had never seen something as sophisticated and just plain beautiful as the Jedi comm relay with its gilded panels and antique dials. Of course, it didn't look half as elegant now that Rhil had jury-rigged it with cables she'd yanked from a nearby computer terminal. She hoped OrbaLin would forgive her, although judging by the various crashes and yells, the archivist still had his hands full in the ruins of his beloved collection. T-9 hovered at the door, watching the fight, ready to bleep a warning if anyone came their way. Their link may have been severed, but the cam droid could still be helpful.

Which was more than could be said for the relay booster. Turned out the antique unit was as useless as it was exquisite. It was hardly surprising considering its age and the fact that communications lines were down everywhere; on the ground, in the air, even, as far as she could tell, out in space.

Then something caught her eye. She had cast her net wide, and the gilded terminal, ancient though it was, had picked up something, the merest hint of a signal. Was that an echo or someone else desperately trying to get a message out to the stars? Rhil turned a dial, trying to lock onto the frequency. There was another blip. Yes. Something was definitely there, although the relay couldn't lock on. That didn't matter. She knew something that probably could.

"Tee-Nine? Over here."

The cam droid obeyed instantly, whizzing over to her.

"Can you get this panel open?" she asked, tapping a silver-edged access point.

The cam droid went to work, extending a hidden manipulator arm to pry open the panel that had so far confounded Rhil.

It was the work of a moment for the cam droid's arm to flip the panel open, revealing a nest of wires below.

"Yes," she said, examining the inner workings of the unit. "This is exactly what I need."

T-9 whistled worriedly as Rhil pulled out a handful of cables and spliced together a connector that would allow her to hook up the relay unit to the implant on her face.

"Don't worry, Tee," she told the droid as she plugged herself into the transmitter and attempted to establish an interface. "I know what I'm doing."

She didn't, of course, which became abundantly clear as raw data washed over her, accompanied by a wave of searing pain. Her implant's receptors tried their best to shut down the rogue signals, but she switched off the safety protocols and gritted her teeth.

None of what she was doing should have been possible, not according to the manufacturer's original specs, but Rhil had spent the last few years customizing and just plain meddling to the point that, if she prodded the right inputs, she could see sound waves as clearly as if they were physical objects. And there it was, the echo, on the very edge of her perception. She shut everything else down, effectively cutting herself off from the physical world—another modification that probably invalidated her warranty—and boosted the frequency. The echo swam into focus, solidifying until she was rewarded by the faint hiss of words that she felt rather than heard.

"Main Strike, prepare for third run. Ride the storm."

Ride the storm. She had found a Nihil frequency, one that bypassed their jammers. It made sense. Why would raiders handicap themselves if there was a way around it? She heard commands bounce between ships and marauders, as well as out into deep space. And if they could get a message out to the stars, so could she.

She would have to be careful. She couldn't just broadcast on the Nihil frequency—the pirates would hear that—but if she could piggyback a signal, she might be able to get a distress call to Starlight or the nearest outpost. There would be no way to direct the call, but at least she would be heard.

Something bashed into her head. Rhil flicked her head, switching back to her organic senses, and was shocked to see T-9 lying on the relay terminal in front of her, smoke rising from his broken chassis. What in star's name had done that?

The answer came as the Lamproid loomed over her, her own terrified expression reflected in its visor.

OrbaLin heard Rhil scream over the whir of his blade, not that he had much time to react. By Surik's Blade, the Twi'lek woman was impressive. Try as he might, he couldn't force her back, her quarterstaff still in one piece despite numerous strikes from his lightsaber. That in itself wasn't surprising. The staff dated back to the Blood Moon Uprising and was forged of phrik, one of the few substances that wasn't susceptible to a lightsaber's blade. Had she known what she was grabbing? Maybe, maybe not, but it was hardly important right now. OrbaLin had been trying to buy Ms. Dairo time, but her cry—and the fact that the recovered Lamproid was missing—meant extreme action had to be taken quickly.

The need for urgency only intensified as Dee got lucky, the end of the phrik staff catching his lightsaber hilt and sending it spinning from his hand. He'd barely had time to react before she delivered a blow that cracked his visor. OrbaLin tumbled onto his back, and Dee struck, slamming the staff down into what she assumed was his brain with a cry of victory.

If she had been fighting any other Jedi the fight would have been over, but Ugors were quite literally a different breed. The mass of jelly that usually resembled a face tightened around the end of the staff and held tight. She could wreck his helmet, but there was no way she was having one of his artifacts.

Calling on the Force, OrbaLin pushed with all his might.

The Twi'lek shot into the air like a rocket and didn't stop when she met the ceiling, smashing through the pavilion's roof to be thrown high into the poisoned air. OrbaLin never heard her land, but felt the crunch of her bones on the avenue outside. He would meditate on that later, but for now he had a life to save.

Yanking the staff from his helmet, the archivist jumped to his feet and raced toward the storeroom.

The Lamproid lifted Rhil from the floor, hissing through its cracked mask. She struggled but couldn't free herself, not from its grip or from the now taut cables that were threatening to rip her implant from her face.

Her vision blurred with pain, but she saw a whirl of fabric and heard a dull thud as a containment boot met the side of the Nihil's helmet, smashing its already weakened structure. The Lamproid grunted, dropping Rhil into a heap, and whirled around to face Orba-Lin, who had landed from his flying kick and dropped into a defensive stance, the staff the Twi'lek had been using ready for battle.

The Lamproid lunged forward, knocking OrbaLin onto his back. Even if she couldn't help him, Rhil knew she had to get the signal through. She hauled herself up the relay unit, checked the connections, and locked onto the Nihil signal.

"To anyone who can hear my voice," she said, trying to ignore the fight that raged behind her, "this is Rhil Dairo of the GoNet news team. Valo is under attack by Nihil forces. Please send assistance. Repeat, Valo is under attack. We need your help."

She slammed a control on the terminal, sending the message out on a loop.

Beside her, OrbaLin was in trouble, pinned under the Lamproid, using the Force to deflect its venomous stinger that was trying to stab down at him. The alien had managed to yank the staff from the Ugor's hand, flinging it to the side. Pulling the cables from her face, Rhil lunged for the weapon, funneling all her anger and rage into a swing worthy of a speedball batter. The Lamproid's head snapped around, but it didn't let up, continuing to press down on the archivist. Rhil tried again, but this time the Nihil was ready. It grabbed the staff with one of its pincers, twisting hard to break her grip. The world went white as the end of the staff found her head, sending her spinning back into the wall.

Hissing, the Lamproid threw the weapon clear, slashing across OrbaLin's chest with a serrated claw. If the Nihil expected blood, it was disappointed: Green jelly gushed up into the Lamproid's face, OrbaLin's true gelatinous form finally flowing free of the containment suit. The Lamproid thrashed and twisted, but there was no escape, the archivist encasing his opponent within seconds.

Who needed a lightsaber?

As Rhil watched in ever-so-slightly grossed-out fascination, a snakelike pseudopod stretched up from the top of the cocoon, forming a rough approximation of a mouth, complete, it seemed, with vocal cords.

"The signal?" OrbaLin asked, his voice wet and garbled.

Rhil scrambled back to the relay unit and saw to her horror that the message had stopped transmitting. Had the Nihil discovered it? She pressed buttons and turned dials, trying not to look at the smashed remains of her cam droid to the side of the unit's main screen.

Her cry for help had transmitted, of that she was 99 percent certain, but there was no way of knowing if it had been heard.

Chapter Forty-Seven

Fair park, Valo

Elzar didn't even have time to curse beneath his breath as Ty disappeared into the war-cloud. The roar sounded almost as soon as she vanished, followed immediately by a scream. Without thinking he raised a hand, doubts banished as his lightsaber flew back into his palm. Elzar hadn't even known when it had fallen, but the Force knew. The Force hadn't deserted him, no matter what he had done. That had to be worth something.

Now all he had to do was to get back to the business of saving lives.

He found them not far ahead, Klerin Chekkat rooted on the spot, screaming in terror as a monster crouched in front of her. Elzar had no idea if the Nihil had released the animals from the zoo on purpose or by accident, but the result was the same. The hragscythe was out of its cage and feeding on what could only be the girl's mother.

This time, Elzar really did curse. Why hadn't the pair stayed where they were, waiting as Ty demanded her saber? Why had they blundered into the smog, half blinded by the gas? Perhaps he should have just handed over the weapon, instead of trying to recruit Ty to his cause. Would Mantessa still be alive? Would he not have another death on his conscience?

No, that was the darkness talking, trying to reel him back in, but he wouldn't listen.

"Get away," he yelled, waving for Klerin to run, disturbing the hragscythe from its grisly meal. All three of its heads snapped up, and it leapt forward, one of its great paws pinning Klerin to the ground. There was no way it was going to give up its next feast, Jedi or no Jedi. What Elzar had to remember was that the beast bore none of them any malice. It was only doing what came naturally and was obviously spooked. That Elzar could understand.

He killed his blade, hoping that something in the animal's brains would recognize the trust implied in the act. Slipping the weapon away, he raised both hands, showing his palms.

"All is well. Do you understand? All is well."

He edged toward the creature. The hragscythe's growl intensified, and he stopped again.

"Listen to me," he said, keeping his voice as steady as possible. "*Feel my words. We are one. Joined through the Force. One mind, two bodies.*"

He should have known this was going to be difficult. The events of the morning had taken their toll, images sweeping over him like a tidal wave. A Nihil ship jumping in above the zoo, its engines overloaded, its pilot out of control. The explosion had killed most of the creatures in their cages, but the hragscythe survived, the walls of its enclosure twisted out of all recognition. He saw the animal leap from its burning cover, heard the screams of the wounded as it thundered into the chaos, snapping at anyone who passed, finding the Chekkats, pouncing on Mantessa even as she screamed for the bodyguard she'd abandoned minutes before.

The only trouble with a connection like this was that it could go both ways. The hragscythe saw what Elzar had done, saw the platform smashing through the Nihil ship, saw the raiders burn, felt Elzar's rage, and in an instant decided that he was a threat.

The great animal pounced, slamming Elzar onto his back, the full weight crushing down on him, the tip of a razor-sharp claw piercing his shoulder. Elzar screamed in pain, trying his best to hold back all three of the beast's heads with the Force, anything to give Klerin Chek-kat the time she needed.

"Run!" he bellowed, not knowing if she could hear him over the 'scythe's roar. She ran all the same, not looking back as she disappeared into the fog. Now he just had to save himself, which proved easier said than done. The claw pushed deeper into his shoulder, and Elzar's concentration faltered, taking with it his grip on the hragscythe's jaws. He felt the beast's breath wash over him, stale and rank, hot drool pouring into his eyes. The hragscythe howled in victory . . .

. . . and a flash of purple streaked past his eyes, accompanied by the tang of seared meat.

Elzar opened his eyes in surprise as two of the beast's severed heads slapped down on either side of him, the third knocked away along with its body in a sudden tsunami of the Force.

"What the crik is wrong with you?" Ty yelled, her lightsaber humming in her hands. "Who faces a hragscythe with their saber still in its holster?"

"What's wrong with *me*?" Elzar jumped up, the world suddenly very much in focus, thanks, in part, to the pain radiating from his shoulder. "I was trying to calm the bloody thing."

"Then you didn't do a very good job," the mercenary snarled, glancing to where Mantessa lay, regret registering across her cold features. "Damn."

"I'm sorry. Did you know her well?"

"No. And what little I knew I didn't like. Where's Klerin?"

"She ran . . . that way," Elzar said, trying to point in the direction Klerin had escaped and wincing.

"Is that your saber arm?"

"No."

"That's something at least."

"Says the woman who's nearly killed me twice."

He glanced down at her blade, which was still very much activated. "Did you come back to finish the job?"

She clicked her hilt, and the purple blade slid up into the spiked grip.

"Look, what you said . . ." Her eyes narrowed as if this was difficult for her to admit. "You're right. People *are* dying. It's bad enough that the Nihil are swarming all over the place, but if the zoo animals are free . . ." She nodded at the hragscythe's severed necks. "I didn't want to do that, but I can't catch them all by myself."

A shriek echoed above them. Elzar waved a hand, pushing at least some of the smog aside. What he saw made him wish he hadn't looked.

"Are those . . ."

"Sanvals," Ty confirmed, watching the animals that whirled in the sky.

"And do they usually travel in pairs?"

The saber-for-hire shook her head. "They're rarely seen away from their natural habitat, and trust me, that's a good thing. Just wait until I meet the genius who decided to exhibit apex predators from a dozen systems. It won't be long before those two start swooping down and picking off survivors."

Elzar drew his lightsaber, wondering what good it would do against a creature that size, let alone two. Both sanvals must have been twenty meters from nose to tail, with wingspans as broad as their dragonlike bodies were long.

"We need to stop them."

"Finally something we can agree on," she said, "although it's not their fault they're here."

"Animal control?"

"That's where you come in. It's never been my forte . . ."

"I used to think it was one of mine, before the hragscythe."

"Which is why we need each other. I could barely manage it when I was being trained, and struggle even more with it now. I need someone to help me focus, someone with more training than I ever had."

She raised her right hand, its palm toward him.

Elzar swallowed. This was definitely more than he'd bargained for when he'd asked for her help. "Are you sure you want to do this?"

"No, but teaming up was your idea."

"I *had* just suffered a blow to the head."

"Don't make me give you another."

He took a breath and stepped forward, pressing his own palm against hers, the tips of their fingers touching. She was shaking, nervous about what they were about to do. He felt much the same way, as she was about to find out.

"Are you ready?" she asked.

"No," he answered honestly.

"You and me both."

Elzar reached out with his mind and Ty did likewise. He had done this before, but only with Jedi he knew. Jedi he trusted. Master Quarry. Stellan.

Avar.

The Force joined them as one.

Why, why, why had his last thought been of Avar before their minds touched? To be honest, the memory her name threw up probably explained it, the memory he always had, back when they were Padawans, back when they were happy to bend the rules. All at once he saw Avar's quarters, felt the sheets beneath their bodies . . .

"Wow," Ty said out loud. "You dirty dog. I'm impressed."

He banished the memory, although it was already too late. He could feel Ty's amusement, not to mention her *attraction.*

"Keep your shirt on, Mann," Ty teased him. "You're not my type."

He tried not to sound disappointed. "Seems to me that I'm the only one sharing anything. This won't work unless we're completely honest with each other."

Ty didn't respond, although he felt her defenses lower just enough to confirm his suspicions about her past. He saw Ty as a youngling. As a Padawan. She shifted slightly, uncomfortable, wanting to break the connection but knowing she couldn't. Faces formed in his mind, an Azumel in Master's robes, a teenage boy with scruffy hair and a mischievous grin. Names floated on the edge of her memories. Cibaba. Teradine. He saw them train, heard them laugh, and then felt shadows fall. A decision made. A life lost.

Elzar felt Ty wanting to break away and slipped his fingers through her own, squeezing her hand tight, not to stop her but to show her that for the first time in years she wasn't alone. That he understood. Force knew what she had seen from his own past, what regrets she'd shared, but they were here together now and probably always would be.

All at once they were back on Valo, staring into each other's eyes. They heard the cry of the sanvals, felt their fear and confusion.

We are one, Elzar thought, as much to the winged beasts in the sky as the woman standing in front of him.

We are connected, Ty responded.

For a second, Elzar felt as though he was looking through the eyes of the larger sanval, looking down at a man and a woman standing face-to-face in the swirling fog, their hands pressed together.

Your will is our will. Our wants and needs aligned.

The sanval shrieked, its companion . . . no, its *sibling,* echoing the call. They were hungry.

Your will. Our will.

The sanvals dropped into a dive, jaws gaping, talons bared.

Our will. Your will.

Elzar felt the wind against his face, smelled the blood of the sanvals' prey . . . felt the anticipation of the kill, of the meat, the fat, the gristle.

Our will. Our will. Our will.

The sanvals landed softly on the ground and curled around Ty and Elzar. They weren't hungry anymore. They didn't want to eat. They wanted to help their friends.

Elzar broke the connection, although he still held on to Ty's hand.

"Well," she said, sounding breathless. "That was . . ."

"The Force working through us," Elzar said, feeling strangely bashful and not just because of the things Ty had seen. It had been years since he'd allowed himself to get so close to someone, Samera included. The experience he'd just shared was deeper than any physical contact, more intimate.

He felt her fingers try to pull away and released his grip. She smiled awkwardly, turning instead to the sanval that waited patiently beside her, its large triangular head flat on the ground. Elzar did the same to the smaller of the two sanvals, patting its flank.

"It's been a while since I felt anything like that," Ty admitted. "Not since Loreth."

"What happened on Loreth?"

She laughed. "You mean we still have some secrets?"

An image sprang to Elzar's mind, a horned creature that he didn't recognize. There was so much he wanted to ask her, but this was neither the time nor the place.

"So what now?" he asked, the sanval nuzzling his palm. "We round up the other animals?"

"If they are still alive," Ty replied, leaping onto her lizard, straddling the beast like a dewback. "And along the way I'm sure our new friends wouldn't be opposed to a little monster hunting of their own." She looked up at the Nihil marauders who could still be spotted through the smog. "I know I'm not."

Stars, he liked this woman. Elzar mounted his own beast in a single bound, the sanval baying with anticipation as he settled between her wings.

"After you?"

Ty shook her head, a wry smile upon her face. "I don't think so. Secrets or not, I still want you where I can see you. Jedi first."

Elzar snorted and patted his mount's thick neck. "Okay, girl. Time to see what you can do."

Chapter Forty-Eight

The skies above Valo

Jedi were taught to see the best in people from an early age. Friend or enemy, all were to be respected. The belief ran deep. There was good in the darkest of hearts. Such conviction marked the Jedi out from other Force-users: They were always ready to give someone a second chance. They were always ready to try again. To do otherwise would have been a betrayal of everything the Order stood for.

Unfortunately, the Jedi occupied a universe that didn't share this sentiment, a universe that constantly tried to prove otherwise. The Jedi's greatest strength was also their weakness, the gap in their armor.

Indeera's drift swept out of the park, their charges still hanging on for dear life, Porter Engle keeping them all in place. That's when the Nihil on Mikkel's nose struck, punching down with the power gauntlet on its curled fist. The electrified glove smashed through the Vector's thin skin, plunging deep into the workings. The result was instantaneous, the suicidal act of hatred robbing Mikkel of his controls. His Vector dropped out of the drift, breaking not only the formation, but also the Force-enabled connection among the pilots. The other survivors slipped ever so slightly, the Jedi reaching out to grab them, Porter

Engle nearly tumbling from his perch as Mikkel corkscrewed out of the sky.

Below the drift, Chancellor Soh had managed to get the walker out of the fair park, trudging over what was left of the Unity Arc. The gates had been smashed, the spheres of the founders lying like broken Life Day decorations on the ground. The Alderaanian sphere smashed beneath the walker's tread as the REW lumbered on. On its back, Stellan and Maramis stood with their faces to the sky, Stellan batting away strafing runs from passing marauders while the guard captain took shots at their engines with a kiavene almost drained of energy. All the time, Regasa Elarec kept the others huddled nearby, away from most if not all shrapnel. Stellan's body ached and his mind reeled from the horror that had befallen the fair, but he kept going, for light and life and the frightened souls in his charge. This was why he had become a Jedi. This was his duty.

At the controls, Soh pulled up sharply as a Vector streaked from the sky and plowed into a nearby stone tower, sending debris rocketing out in all directions. The blazing craft hit the ground and skidded into a café where survivors were sheltering. The building came down, sending a plume of dust out into the already fogged air. Stellan shuddered as he felt a Jedi life enter the Force. Was that Mikkel Sutmani?

"We must help them," the regasa shouted, peering over the edge of the walker.

Stellan would have agreed, but the decision was taken out of his hands.

"I'm taking us down," Lina Soh shouted back from the cockpit.

"Do you think that's wise?" Maramis asked, only to be silenced by his queen.

"Captain . . ."

"As you command, Supreme Huntress."

At a flick of a switch, the REW's legs folded down so its riders could disembark. Soh and Yovet led the charge, racing toward the survivors,

Matari and Voru following close behind, with Stellan and Maramis bringing up the rear in case of ambush.

The building was a mess, the survivors even more so. Stellan did what he could to support the structure using the Force while the others pulled the injured clear. Even Madam Conserra forgot her airs and graces to finally get her hands dirty.

"Can anyone hear me?"

Stellan almost missed the tinny voice over the cries of the wounded and the Nihil's aural assault. It was only when it sounded again that he realized what it was.

"Is anyone there?"

Stellan activated the comlink on his wrist. "Vernestra?"

Relief filled his former Padawan's voice. "Master Gios? Is that you?"

"The same. What are you doing on Valo?"

"It's a long story. It's good to hear you."

"And you, Vernestra. OrbaLin and Rhil must have gotten the comms up and running."

"Not us," the archivist said, joining the conversation. "Although we might have gotten a message offworld."

"*Might* being the operative word in that sentence," Rhil Dairo added, speaking over OrbaLin's connection.

"Then who?"

"I brought some friends," Vern told him. "The Padawans from the *Star Hopper.*"

"Master Yoda's charges? Is he here, too?" That would be too much to hope for.

"Not that I know of. Sorry."

"Don't apologize. You've done the Force's work today." Stellan extended the frequency to encompass all Jedi and Republic officials.

"Valo security forces. Assembled Jedi. This is Stellan Gios, please respond. Repeat, this is Stellan—"

They didn't wait. The voices came thick and fast. Jedi he knew were on the planet, others who must have arrived after the pomp of the opening ceremony.

"This is Cherff Maota. I hear you, Stellan."

"Idrax Snat here, with Vice Chancellor Reza."

"As is Jedi Bakari from the Bromlarch outpost."

"Nooranbakarakana checking in."

"Um. Padawan Ram Jomaram, here. Sir."

"Buckets of Blood is ready for action!"

"As are Lula Talisola and Zeen Mrala. Master Buck, we didn't know you were here!"

The names came thick and fast, from Jedi on the ground or in the sky, now all able to talk, it appeared, thanks to the work of Padawan Jomaram, who seemed to be from the local outpost. There were some worrying omissions. Elzar Mann was still nowhere to be heard, although Coordinator Ra-oon reported that she had gotten a number of senators to safety, including the troublesome Tia Toon and his Orz-relanso associate who had suffered a broken arm. Stellan was waiting for one name above all, the young man he had connected with before all this began. He couldn't help but call him out.

"Padawan Zettifar? Do you read me?"

The sound of a charhound barking came over the comm seconds before Zettifar's voice. "I'm here, Master Gios, and I have Kip and Jom, not to mention an ever-growing group of survivors we picked up on the way."

Stellan thanked the Force, not just for Bell's successful mission but that so many Jedi voices had survived the Nihil's best efforts. But their job wasn't done yet. Now they had to get everyone else to safety.

"Okay, listen up. Gather as many citizens as you can and take them to the Temple."

"I thought it wasn't completed?" Indeera Stokes asked from her Vector.

"Not completely, but it will be more defensible than any Republic building."

The Jedi signaled their understanding, although Nib Assek had one last question.

"Master Gios, our drift was practicing united meditation, but Mikkel went down. Do you know . . ."

She would know the answer, of course. Having worked with the Ithorian for years, she would have felt him slip into the Force, but even the most experienced Jedi sometimes needed to hear the truth from someone else.

"He is at peace, Nib."

There was a moment's pause before she responded. "The Force is with him."

"The Force is with us all. Stellan—"

He meant to sign off, to let the Jedi go about their mission, but something in the millennia-old phrase made him pause. Us *all.*

Like everyone caught in the attack, the Jedi had been cut off from one another to fight alone, but not anymore.

"All Jedi," he said quickly, before the others could call off. "Are you still there? I have an idea."

Chapter Forty-Nine

The Unity Arc

Not for the first time, Stellan wished that Avar were here. Her unique talents would have helped so much. There would have been no need for comms at all. He dreaded to think how much bloodshed could've been avoided.

But what he did have was some of the finest Jedi he had ever served with, and others whom he knew were about to prove their mettle. He had faith in them. He had faith in the Force.

"We need to lift the cloud . . ." So far so blindingly obvious. "Each of us can push back the fog to a limited degree . . ."

"But together we can clear the smoke completely."

Stellan smiled, even though his bruised face hurt like the blazes. Bell was already ahead of him. That Padawan was good.

"More unified meditation?" asked Stokes over the comm.

"Maybe not even that coordinated. My old Master used to tell me to keep things simple . . ."

"She was a wise woman," Porter Engle grunted, the sound of his humming lightsaber buzzing over the connection. Was the Ikkrukki in the middle of a fight?

"If we call on the Force together, at exactly the same time . . ."

Buckets of Blood's gruff voice came over the comm. "Yeah, yeah, we get it. What are we waiting for?"

"I need to know everyone is on board," he told Buck, understanding the Chagrian's impatience.

All at once the various Jedi signaled that they were.

"Good. On three, push toward the lake. One . . . Two . . ."

"Three," they all said in unison.

Elzar pushed out with the Force, feeling his fellow Jedi doing the same, some near, some far. The sensation was dizzying, just as it had been when he'd joined Avar's chorus above Hetzal Prime all those months ago. Together they could achieve anything. He had known it before, but it was confirmed again. The war-cloud rolled away as if blown by a great wind, and it didn't stop, the other Jedi pushing out from where they stood, the fog lifting all across the park and out into the city. All at once they could see, as could the thousands of scared survivors.

As could the enemy.

"Lourna, what's happening?"

Pan sat forward in his command lounger, peering at the screens. What was the damn woman doing down there? It was bad enough that communications on the planet had been restored, but now the war-cloud was dissipating in front of his eyes.

"Lourna," he yelled into his comm. "Can you hear me? Are you there?"

There was nothing. No reply at all. On screen, he saw Nihil standing dumbstruck, surprised by their sudden unveiling. There was plenty of devastation, that was for sure, and a hell of a lot of bodies, but now the Nihil had lost their advantage. Now the Jedi could see.

"Prepare the death charges," Pan snapped at his crew. "If Lourna's Tempest can't do their job on the ground, we'll raze the damn planet from the skies."

Thank the Force for that, Indeera thought as she reduced another of the Nihil's infernal speakers with a careful shot from her Vector's laser cannons. Throwing the ship into a spin, she targeted the next spiked probe and sent it the same way before turning her attention to a Nihil marauder that was zeroing in on a civilian ship that had taken off when the war-cloud had lifted.

She took no pleasure in denying the pirate its life, but was happy to see the cruiser continue on its way, safe from attack. The people they had saved now safely deposited on the ground, Indeera's drift had returned to the air and were fighting alongside the last of the Republic pilots, trying to put Mikkel's passing from their mind. There had been so much loss today, but Mikkel was a part of them all now. He was still in the fight, and always would be.

A pair of thermal missiles shrieked toward her. She jerked to the left, the Vector responding perfectly. The missiles streaked past her wing, straight into the Nihil raider that had picked up her tail. Destroyed by their own ordnance. The universe brought its own justice with or without the Jedi. She flew straight at the fighter that had unloaded its missile launchers at her. The pilot was firing wildly, laser bolts zipping past her. She didn't flinch, and she didn't respond, not until she knew her own weapons were in range. When her shot came, it was clear and clinical, the fighter blossoming into flames.

Indeera had to admit, she was impressed in a funny sort of way. Once Stellan's plan had dissipated the smoke, the uncovered Nihil had frozen for a split second, but their stunned silence hadn't lasted long, replaced by more bloodcurdling war cries over the thud of their damn "music," if such a word was appropriate. They had rejoined the battle with renewed vigor, more feral than before, no matter how many of the speakers the Jedi brought down to cut short the aural bombardment or how many marauder craft were sent plummeting from the skies. They were like the battle hydra of legend. Cut off a head, and four more would grow back in its place, but whatever the odds, the Jedi would never stand down. Not now. Not ever.

Indeera grunted as her Vector took a hit from behind. She glanced over her shoulder, seeing smoke billowing from her tail. Another Nihil fighter was right behind her. The last strike had been a glancing blow, causing little damage, but the next might rupture her fuel reserves, unless she took a leaf out of the Nihil's book.

"You guys like smoke, right?"

She flicked a switch, activating the second canister of dye that she had been carrying since the opening ceremony. Red vapor flowed out of her exhaust, billowing over the Nihil, blinding its pilot. And yet her grin fell away as she realized that the marauder hadn't fallen away. Whoever was behind the stick was good, staying on her no matter how she weaved and rolled. The smokescreen hadn't stopped them and neither did the g-inducing climb she pulled in the hope that the Nihil's aircraft would stall. Instead the Nihil climbed with her, higher and higher, sending salvo after salvo across her tail, each volley nearer than the last. She made one last turn, but still the Nihil stuck to her like hull sealant. She felt the marauder's crosshairs lock onto her and prepared herself for the blast that would tear the Vector apart.

The blast never came.

Indeera swiveled in her seat, looking back to see a gigantic winged creature soar behind her, the mangled remains of the Nihil's cockpit in its jaws. She laughed out loud as she saw who was hunched on the sanval's back, robes blowing in the wind.

Elzar Mann was riding a dragon into the middle of a dogfight.

Because who else would it be.

Chapter Fifty

The skies above Valo

They were winning. Stellan's plan to clear the war-cloud
had worked, just as Elzar knew it would the moment he'd heard his
friend's voice come over the comlink. He hadn't been able to respond
personally. He was too busy trying not to get thrown off the back of a
bucking sanval as he and Ty took to the air. His mount was feisty but
flew straight into combat without complaint. The Nihil didn't know
what hit them. Those who weren't knocked out of the sky with a flick
of the sanval's tail soon found themselves staring down its gullet, the
dragon's teeth making short work of their canopies.

The Jedi Vector they'd rescued waggled its wings in thanks before
zooming off. Elzar had no idea who was behind the controls, but was
glad they had survived to fight another day.

He patted the sanval's hide, feeling freer than he had in months, his
head finally clear. All the disappointment and frustration were gone.
He couldn't forget what he'd done earlier that day, but he could start to
make amends.

And hey, if he could do it in style, so much the better.

"Someone is looking happier," a voice crackled over a comlink. Ty swooped in on the back of her own sanval, tendrils pushed back by the rush of air.

"Right back at you," he yelled into the comm.

"How many have you taken down so far?" she called over as their mounts came alongside each other.

"It's not a competition."

"You do remember I've seen inside your head, right?"

He was about to respond when laser bolts tore between them. He craned around to see a single-seater Nihil fighter attempting to bring down a Skyhawk. Ty didn't wait. With a cry she brought her sanval around and dropped on the marauder like a hawk, the reptile biting clean through the Nihil's wing. The fighter spun to the ground, smashing into an already wrecked pavilion, its pilot dying instantly.

Ty whooped in triumph, reminding Elzar how different they were. She may have been trained as a Jedi, but she'd wandered far from the path. Perhaps this was the reason they'd been brought together, part of his atonement. If he could show her the way it should be . . .

He scanned the ground below him, finding the perfect opportunity. A Nihil speeder bike was bearing down on a blood-soaked Crolute who was running for his life. The saggy-skinned amphibian wouldn't get far, not at the rate the speeder was traveling, its outriggers tipped with pointed bayonets that would impale the runner in seconds.

Luckily for the Crolute, Elzar's sanval was faster.

He urged the dragon into a dive, and the beast opened its maw wide, ready to swallow the Nihil whole.

No. Not like that, girl, Elzar thought. *There's been enough death.*

The creature's jaws snapped shut and instead the sanval skimmed low, pushing what was left of the war-cloud aside with the beat of her wings. The Nihil twisted in their saddle, their eyes widening behind grease-smeared goggles as the sanval closed the gap. With a swing of her scaled head, the sanval thwacked the Nihil from their perch, the now pilotless vehicle rolling straight for the Crolute. The amphibian tripped, landing in a heap of blubber, the speeder passing harmlessly over them, guided by a helpful nudge from Elzar. Nearby, the grounded Nihil watched their bike explode against a wall and, snatching a blaster from their belt, prepared to take their revenge against the helpless Crolute.

Typical bully, Elzar thought as he brought the sanval back up, *too scared to pick on someone your own size.* He probably shouldn't have enjoyed the dragon flicking the Nihil shooter into the air with the tip of her tail, but was sure the Force would forgive him in the long run, especially as it would be a lesson to Ty that she didn't always have to kill.

But there was no sign of the Tholothian as they climbed back into the sky. In fact, the air was remarkably clear, not only of the noxious gas but of the Nihil forces as a whole. Was the attack over? Had the tide finally turned?

Elzar glanced up and realized that the answer to both questions was a definite no . . .

Chapter Fifty-One

Fair park, Valo

What was Pan *thinking*? They were still on the ground!

The force of the first explosion knocked Lourna Dee from her feet, aggravating the injuries she had endured when that damn Jedi had thrown her through the roof. Her shoulder had been dislocated and, although she had rammed it back into place, was still raging with pain, as were the ribs that were obviously broken. The fact she could still run was a minor miracle, as was the fact that her skull was still in one piece. The last thing she needed was to be vaporized by one of her own bloody bombs.

Lourna pushed herself up, crying out as bones grated together.

The plan had been clear since the beginning. The raid would end with a carpet bombing, the charges dropped from the edge of Valo's atmosphere, one final indignity—but only when her Tempest was clear!

"Pan? Pan!" she screamed into her comlink as she forced herself on. "Can you hear me?"

The comm came apart in her hands, damaged beyond repair in her fall. Lourna threw it aside in disgust, spotting three of her own Tempest running for cover as the bombs continued to fall.

"You three! Wait!"

The Nihil brought their weapons up, surprised by her shout, the largest of the trio—a maskless Alzarian with scales the color of pus—unleashing his flamethrower in her direction. Lourna leapt over the stream of ignited conflagrine, the pain in her shoulder almost worth it for the satisfaction of loosening the reptilian's jaw with the heel of her boot. If the other two Nihil didn't recognize her without her mask, they sure as hell recognized the brutality of the kick. The Alzarian thudded to the ground, blood gushing from his ruined mouth. Lourna reached down and snatched two of the syringes that were strung through the idiot's bandolier. The first she punched into her own arm, the second she slammed into the Alzarian's broad back. He may have provoked her wrath, but she still needed the horned brute on his feet, even with a jaw that was hanging loose.

"You have a ship nearby?" she barked at the two Nihil who could still talk—a bear of a human wielding a large plasmaul and a female Weequay who glared at Lourna with venom. "Well?"

The Weequay pointed at a junker on the other side of the debris-strewn park. It was ugly, but it would do until Lourna got back to her own cruiser. For now, though, Lourna wasn't looking at the ship. She was looking at what was in front of it. *Who* was in front of it, in all her finery. Suddenly the indignity Lourna had suffered at the hands of the idiot Jedi in the containment suit seemed worth it. Even the bombs seemed easier to forgive. Here was her prize.

Lourna held out her hand for the plasmaul, not expecting to have to ask. To his credit, the human handed over his weapon without question, flexing his knuckles in anticipation of the fight ahead. Lourna tested the maul's weight, activating the energy field that covered the hammer's blunt heel.

Yes, that would do nicely.

Her course set, Lourna Dee broke into a run, four simple words reverberating around her head:

Death to the chancellor.

Chapter Fifty-Two

The Unity Arc

The bombs had been a surprise that even the Force hadn't warned them about.

"Regasa, we must get you away from here," Maramis told his queen, who was helping Madam Conserra carry a wounded Forshul from the wrecked building, its long gray hair matted with blood. The Supreme Huntress didn't look much better, once-glittering robes soiled with gore from the victims, her regal face streaked with dirt.

"We must help," she said as the ground shook from another explosion.

"No, the captain's right." Chancellor Soh joined them, similarly disarrayed, the hem of her long dress ripped and torn where she had used the material for bandages. "What you have done is beyond our expectations, Regasa, but my duty now must be to get you to safety. Don't you agree, Council Member?"

Maramis looked at Stellan expectantly as the chancellor addressed him. Of course he concurred. The bombing was proof that the danger was far from over. Would these devils never stop?

As if to answer his question, long-range lasers lanced down from above, carving deep fissures into the ground. They swept toward the wrecked building, vaporizing anyone in their path.

"Back into the walker!" Stellan shouted.

Elarec Yovet looked around in despair. "But the wounded ..."

"Take who you can," Stellan told her, drawing his lightsaber. "I'll protect those who are too injured to move."

"As will I," Maramis said, his kiavene already in his hand.

Stellan shook his head. "No, Captain. I need you to protect the regasa and Chancellor Soh. Will you do that for me?"

Maramis held out an open hand. "You have my word, Lord Jedi."

The two men grasped each other's wrists. "Then I know they will be safe."

The sound of running boots broke the moment. Stellan turned to see a small band of Nihil charging at them, led by a Twi'lek with death in her eyes and a plasmaul burning in her hands.

Maramis let loose a volley of blasts from his kiavene, hitting one of the Nihil in the shoulder. The brute, an unmasked Alzarian with a slack jaw, spun with the force of the blow but somehow stayed on his feet.

"It's their wretched drugs," Maramis snapped as the chancellor ushered everyone who could walk onto the walker. "The *talagret* don't know when to lie down and die."

Stellan didn't recognize the Togruti word, but could guess its meaning.

"We're all on board," Soh shouted down from the walker.

Stellan reached for Kant's saber, igniting both weapons.

"Go, Captain. Get as many as you can to safety."

The Togruta hesitated for a minute before running to join his queen.

But they weren't leaving Stellan alone to face the Nihil. The chancellor's voice rang out from where she had taken up the controls herself.

"Matari. Voru. Stay with the Jedi. Protect him as he protects us."

The targons obeyed their mistress without question, bounding from the walker to stand by Stellan, Matari to his left, Voru to his right. Stellan didn't look to the chancellor to thank her or to see the experimental walker start to rise, but he was pleased to have the animals with him. With the targons by his side, he just might survive the day.

Elzar's sanval keened as a laser bolt almost punched its way through her wing.

"Steady, girl," Elzar urged his mount, not taking his eyes off a Vector that was trying to shake off not one but two marauders. He could tell from the flight pattern that the pilot was inexperienced. The Wookiee, Burryaga? It could be, and there was no sign of Nib. Force willing she was still airborne, but even if she was, the Padawan needed help now. Burry was slewing left and right, doing his best to avoid being shot down, but could neither shake his assailants nor double back to go on the offensive.

"Time to even the score. Get me nearer."

Elzar reached for his lightsaber as the sanval's wings beat faster, pushing them toward the skirmish.

"That's it. That's it."

He lit the blade.

"Just a little closer."

A bomb whistled past them from above, the shock causing the sanval to buck in the air, nearly throwing Elzar from her back. He pressed an open palm against the beast's neck.

"Steady, girl. Steady."

The sanval calmed, sweeping nearer to the firefight. Nearer. Nearer. Just near enough.

Elzar drew back his arm and threw the lightsaber with all his might. The blade pinwheeled through the air like a plasma disk, Elzar guiding its flight so it dipped down into the path of the first fighter. The Nihil had no time to pull up. His mount howled in triumph as the spinning blade sliced through the fighter like a circular saw, the marauder bursting into flames as plasma met fuel. The sanval pulled up to sweep over the explosion, Elzar calling out in the Force to draw the now extinguished hilt back to him. He glanced down at the weapon, gratified that it showed no signs of damage, although the same couldn't be said for the second Nihil fighter, who suddenly found itself peppered by bolts from Burryaga's cannons.

The Wookiee peeled away to find his Master, although Elzar could feel the Padawan's gratitude and prepared himself for a bone-popping hug when all this was over.

"Nice trick," a voice came over the comm. "You'll have to teach me how to do that sometime."

Elzar looked back to see Ty coming up fast on their tail, her own sanval panting heavily.

"So you're my apprentice now?" he asked.

Ty barked a sharp laugh. "You wish."

She brought her sanval alongside him, and Elzar couldn't help but notice the blaster burns on the creature's side.

"What happened to you?" he shouted across. Ty had peeled off not long after they had engaged the Nihil. Elzar losing her in the theater of war.

"You asked whether sanvals fly in twos? Turns out it's threes."

"There's another?"

Ty's sanval bucked beneath her. "Apparently these two are the babies. Mom was still out there, trapped by a bunch of Nihil in the middle of the crazy exhibit with creepy singing holograms."

Now it was Elzar's turn to laugh. "United in Song" was still playing, even through all of this. He hoped it had given the Nihil an earworm they would never forget.

"But you got her out?"

Ty patted her sanval's neck. "This little fella came to Momma's help and took a bruising in the process, but he'll live."

Elzar scanned the skyline. "So where is she now?"

"Safe and sound with a group of Padawans. You'll be pleased to know the place is now crawling with Jedi. Never thought I'd be so glad to see it."

"The Force provides . . ." he began, before looking down to the ground.

"What is it?" Ty asked, as Elzar clambered to his feet on his sanval's back. "And what in stars' name are you doing?"

"You've handled the momma . . . Reckon you can handle both kids at once?" he asked, igniting his lightsaber.

"Do I have a choice?"

"No," Elzar replied and leapt into the air.

Chapter Fifty-Three

The Unity Arc

Stellan met the Nihil at a run, the Alzarian unleashing a torrent of fire from a bulky flamer. Stellan somersaulted over the gushing flame and came down in front of the raider, severing the weapon's barrel before bringing the pommel of his hilt up into the Alzarian's already damaged jaw.

The reptilian stumbled back, his place in the skirmish taken by the Twi'lek wielding the plasmaul, the weapon's energized hammer bouncing off Rana Kant's blade. The targons were already on two of her cohorts—Matari knocking the thug of a human to the ground while Voru tackled the Weequay. Neither pirate would last long, their armor little use against a targon's claws. That didn't stop the human from punching Matari in the face, a decision he soon regretted as the chancellor's protector closed his jaws around the Nihil's throat.

The Twi'lek, however, was a different proposition. While the others were little more than brutes, she fought with skill and precision, the heel of her plasmaul slamming repeatedly against Stellan's twin blades.

He had no time to check on the animals, but the scream that issued from beneath Voru told him that their enemy's number had been reduced by one more. He spun and blocked, kicked and jumped back, fighting two Nihil at once, as the Alzarian rejoined the fray, snatching up a blaster from his fallen comrade. Neither would give ground, fighting with supernatural strength. Was it the Nihil's cocktail of drugs running through their veins?

The Alzarian got too near and Stellan punched him with the fist that wielded Kant's blade. A dirty move, but Stellan was exhausted. The reptilian staggered back, his finger locked around his trigger. Blaster shots raked the ground, Stellan avoiding losing his feet solely by jumping back. Recovering, the Alzarian brought up his weapon, only to holler in pain as Voru sank her claws into his wide back.

The Alzarian landed on his face, Voru's full weight bearing down on him. Stellan turned to look for the woman, who had targon trouble of her own. The red fur darkened around his mouth, Matari jumped, but the Twi'lek was quicker, swinging her maul at the animal's head. The hammer connected and Stellan felt rather than heard the targon go down. Voru abandoned the Alzarian to run to her brother's aid, but the Twi'lek leapt, using the targon's back to propel herself at Stellan. He crossed his sabers to protect himself, but his arms were like lead. The Twi'lek's hammer struck the blades with the sound of a thunder-crack, the force of the blow knocking both lightsabers down. Stellan toppled forward, overbalanced, and the Twi'lek brought the pole of her weapon up, catching him under the chin. Stellan tasted blood as he was flipped over by the impact, his lightsaber hilts clattering beside him as he hit the ground. If he had been capable of rational thought he would have expected to feel the maul cracking his skull like an egg, but instead he could only lie stunned. The world spun as he tried to push himself up, flashes of yellow and red streaking past him.

He looked up, trying to focus. Matari and Voru were racing after the woman, who was running full pelt toward the lumbering walker. She was going after the others, going for the regasa and the chancellor. All things being equal, Maramis would be able to take the woman, but what had been equal about today? Stellan pushed himself to his feet, not really sure what he expected to do before his legs gave out. He threw out an arm to break his fall, but it folded beneath him, unable to stop him thudding to his side.

It was down to Matari and Voru now, although the red targon was wavering, still suffering the effect of the plasmaul's blow. It didn't matter. Stellan smiled through bloodied teeth. The Twi'lek may have bested him, but she couldn't outrun one, let alone two targons. And yet, as she neared the oh-so-slow walker, Stellan saw the woman pull a device from her belt. A weapon? No, a grappling hook that shot up toward the back of the REW. It found its target, locking into place, and the Nihil flew up into the air, the cable retracting. The targons leapt, but she was already out of range of their claws, speeding toward her victims, her plasmaul gripped tight.

"No!" Stellan cried out, as if his shout alone would be enough to bring her down. He crawled forward, desperate to save the people he'd pledged to protect, desperate to do *anything*.

Boots smacked down beside him, a fingerbreadth from his head. Was it the Alzarian, still jacked up on the stims, ready to finish him off?

"Stellan!"

Hands grabbed him, turning him over. A face swam into view. Elzar? Where had he come from? It didn't make sense.

It also didn't matter.

"Stop her," he wheezed. "The Twi'lek. She's going for the chancellor . . . for Regasa Elarec."

Elzar took off at a sprint, pulling back his arm to launch his lightsaber into the air. The blade shone as it arced toward the REW, slicing through the Nihil's cable before she could reach the top of the walker.

The Twi'lek dropped, releasing the maul as she fell. Stellan didn't know if Elzar would get to her before the targons took their revenge, but he knew it was finally over. The chancellor and everyone on the walker was safe. Stellan could relax as long as someone stopped that dreadful whistling that was coming from above.

The bomb hit the ground between Elzar and the walker and everything turned red.

Chapter Fifty-Four

The skies above Valo

The onslaught needed to be stopped, and Indeera Stokes was the Jedi to do it. She had almost died at the hands of the Nihil, and the Force had given her another chance, working through Elzar Mann. Now she had to make it count.

She was pushing her Vector to the limit, and she wasn't alone. Nib Assek was with her to starboard, Burryaga to port, engines gunning, eyes fixed on their target. Behind the Vectors, the last remaining Skyhawks struggled to keep up, their starfighters unable to match the Jedi's speed.

The Nihil ships hung in the sky above them, circling an imposing battle cruiser that was almost beautiful in its brutality. The Vectors were hideously outgunned, of course, even with Jedi at the controls, but among them they would find a way to bring the Nihil down.

They just had to.

"We have incoming," Chell informed Pan Eyta aboard the *Elegencia*.

"How many?" the Dowutin grunted.

"Three Vectors and a handful of Skyhawks."

Pan snorted. "The remnants of the glorious Republic."

He thumbed a control, broadcasting to the fleet. "Continue the bombardment. These gnats are mine."

Indeera's life was saved for the second time by a sudden stab of intuition. She pulled her yoke to the right, Nib swerving to avoid her. A barrage of turbolasers streaked from the belly of the main Nihil ship, missing her port wings by millimeters. The Skyhawk that had been climbing behind her wasn't so lucky. The fighter burst into flames that were instantly extinguished in the weak oxygen, the wreckage tumbling back to Valo. Indeera aimed at the cannon to return fire but was still out of range.

She needed to go faster.

Pan grunted as the Jedi evaded his shot, although the destruction of the Skyhawk had been a worthy consolation. As the rest of the Tempest continued to shell the planet below, Pan switched from one cannon to another, scattering the attackers as they targeted the *Elegencia*'s bombing bays.

Ha. Some chance.

He took out another Skyhawk with a blast from the ventral laser, only for the cannon to be obliterated by the lead Vector. Pan thudded a meaty fist down on the console. Damn their eyes, whoever that Jedi was, they deserved a fiery death—which he would be more than happy to provide.

Another charge dropped into the clouds. Indeera reached out with the Force, trying to nudge the shell as it whistled down, shifting its course so it would splash into the lake. At least that was the plan. She would have no way of knowing if she'd succeeded until it plunged beneath the water. In the meantime, she would have to be content with making a difference up here.

Indeera turned her Vector on its head, streaking across the battle cruiser's undercarriage. One of the ship's three bomb bays lay straight ahead. Indeera could only imagine the Nihil at work, preparing another barrage. They would be disappointed. Indeera raked the dreadnaught's belly, the last few bolts finding their way through the open doors.

Flames gouted from the bay as the bombs detonated in their cradles, the shock wave buffeting Indeera's Vector as she dropped into a sharp turn to stop herself from being immolated in the blast.

The *Elegencia* shook violently as a chain reaction ripped through the lower decks. Pan swore, yelling for a damage report. It came back better than the quake had suggested, although there were numerous fires raging down below.

"They'll pay for that," he bellowed, spittle spraying from his thick lips. "Release the scav droids. Gut them like fish!"

The first wave came out of nowhere, swarming out of hatches that sprang open along the cruiser's long keel. Hundreds of scav droids, manipulator arms grasping, dropping into the atmosphere like locusts. A Skyhawk was the first to fall prey to the robotic scavengers, laser cutters slicing through the starfighter's thin canopy. The small craft went into a spin, taking out another Skyhawk in the process. Only one of the Republic starfighters remained, and there was little the Vectors could do, the Jedi just as vulnerable to the droids' advance.

Burryaga mewed over the comm as Nib's Vector all but disappeared under a mob of the metallic scavengers, although his Master responded to the crisis with customary grit.

"Steady yourself, Padawan. It'll take more than a few scavvers to send me packing."

Indeera felt a flutter in the Force as Nib used the energy field to strip the droids from her hull, although the Vector's thin skin showed numerous scars where the droids had already started to mine it for parts.

Burry barked happily, but the celebrations were premature. A laser blast shot down from the main Nihil cruiser, slicing through Nib's already damaged wing. Her Vector went into a tailspin, falling away.

"Looks like I'm out," Nib said, her canopy popping as she bailed out. "See you on the ground."

Indeera felt concern radiate from Burryaga. "The Force will protect her, Padawan," she told him. "Stay with me."

The Wookiee responded as any apprentice should, banishing his fears and dropping into position as they raced toward the next bay.

"Oh no you don't," Pan growled as he saw the two Vectors move in for the kill. Switching controls, he unleashed a barrage of laser bolts, laughing as the Jedi fighters were forced to peel off, scav droids locking onto their heat signatures.

Chell was still worried, but Pan didn't care. He was having fun.

One of the Jedi seemed more experienced than the other. He sent a command to the droids to focus on the lesser of the two pilots.

"Always look for the weakest link," he muttered as they latched on to the Vector's hull.

Burry was in trouble and Indeera knew it. The Wookiee just wasn't centered enough to scrape the scav droids from his Vector's skin as Nib had so ably demonstrated moments before. She reached out to calm him, but instead felt a warning from the Force. Lights were flashing on the back of each and every droid.

"Burryaga," Indeera shouted, realizing in an instant what the commander of the dreadnaught had planned. "Push them away! Do it now!"

The urgency in her voice was the focus Burry needed. He pushed out with the Force, sending the droids spinning, but it was already too late. The scavengers exploded as one, the blast buffeting Burryaga's Vector. Anyone else could be forgiven for thinking that the sudden destruction had been caused by Burry's actions, but Indeera knew

STAR WARS: THE RISING STORM

better. The Nihil commander had activated the scavengers' self-destruct, sacrificing the droids to take Burryaga with them.

Indeera's warning had saved the Wookiee, but he was out of the game, smoke belching from his engine.

"Get out of here, Padawan," she ordered him, gambling that his Vector would make it to the ground. "You've done enough."

The Wookiee moaned over the comm as he dropped away.

"You too, Burry," she responded. "We'll see each other soon."

Whether that was true or not remained to be seen. Indeera brought her Vector about, flinching as the last Skyhawk dissolved into a blaze of superheated metal. She was on her own now, one Jedi against a Nihil fleet.

So be it.

There was no way she could get to the bomb bay, not with a swarm of scav droids on her tail. She swung around, leading them a merry dance along the length of the ship, shooting past its nose, out into the upper atmosphere. She pulled into a roll, coming about to face the mammoth warship, the scav droids perfectly matching the turn. Now it was only a matter of time, seeing who could run faster.

Indeera opened her throttle, shooting headfirst toward the dreadnaught, her laser cannons blazing hot. Force willing she would land a direct hit to the Nihil flight deck. The other options were that she would be dismantled by the scav droids or reduced to atoms by the cruiser's battery. Either way, she'd always believed that one Jedi was all it took to make a difference. Now it was time to put her theory to the test.

Chapter Fifty-Five

The *Elegencia*

"Jedi Vector, coming right at us," Chell Trambin yelled as the *Elegencia*'s viewport lit up with laserfire.

"Then that's how they'll die," Pan said, locking onto the fighter.

The *Elegencia* shook, not from the Vector's attack or the exploding ordnance in its belly, but from above.

"What the hell was that?" Pan growled, grabbing hold of the console to stop himself being thrown to his own deck.

"Ships arriving out of hyperspace, Tempest Runner," Chell reported shrilly, checking his scope. "Multiple signals. At least twenty so far."

"No!" Pan cursed, forgetting about the Vector and switching to a tactical view of the space above them. A damn transmission must have got through, reinforcements finally arriving. But from where? The Republic? The Jedi? Who?

Indeera had never seen ships so graceful. They weren't from the Order or any Republic world, their lines as refined as the shuttle that had made the journey from Shili the day before.

A transmission came from the lead cruiser, which was already

STAR WARS: THE RISING STORM

barraging the Nihil dreadnaught. "Attention all fighters. This is Trido Tamaree of the Royal Togruta Fleet. Enemy craft must disengage or be destroyed. This is your first and final warning. We shall show no mercy."

Indeera didn't doubt it. Suddenly it was the Nihil who were outnumbered, more Togruta ships arriving with every passing second. An entire fleet.

Opening a channel, she issued a response, never taking her eyes off the Nihil's flight deck as she raced forward. "Togruta fleet. This is Indeera Stokes of the Jedi Order. The Force welcomes you to Valo. Now blow those junkheaps from the sky."

Pan scrabbled for his command lounger, damage reports streaming in from every ship that still functioned.

"Should we respond?" Chell asked as the deck continued to buck.

"Only enough to get us out of here," Pan barked back, opening a channel to what was left of his Tempest. "All Nihil, the storm has passed. Take to the escape Paths, now."

"Shall we cover the evacuation, sir?"

"What?"

"Protect the others while they leave?"

"What do you think we are? The Republic? Get us out of here!"

The Morseerian swiveled back to his console, punching in coordinates, as Pan sank back into his lounger. Reinforcements may have arrived to pull the Jedi from the fire, but they were too late. The strike—*his* strike—had been decisive. There would be no ignoring the Nihil now. There would be no ignoring him.

The *Elegencia* punched its way into the nearest Path, leaving the rest of the Tempest to its fate.

Chapter Fifty-Six

The Starlight Pavilion

"**I**s it working?"

Rhil Dairo tapped the side of her implant. Static was filling a vid-window only she could see. The Starlight Pavilion was still standing, more or less, OrbaLin back in his containment suit, lengths of his robes tied around the gash where he had so spectacularly revealed his true viscous form. The Lamproid was still on the floor, now bound in a legendary artifact apparently known as the Lariat of Armistice, an unbreakable cord that dated from the days of the Mystic Nine, when-ever that was. Rhil had been amused when OrbaLin couldn't resist giving yet another history lesson as she had helped him secure the Nihil and then the pavilion as a whole. First Stellan and now OrbaLin. These Jedi were true to type, a font of all knowledge whatever the situation. Lin and Stellan must have been a real hit at Jedi parties. But there was no malice in her thoughts. OrbaLin had saved her life, and as for Stellan . . . well, there was no telling if he was even still alive.

"Can I help?"

She shook her head. OrbaLin had already repaired T-9, stripping parts from a wrecked service droid as well as helping her establish a wireless connection to the replay unit. Communications with the Republic had been reestablished, even if they were still patchy, maybe something to do with the Togruta fleet, and Rhil wanted to get footage back to GoNet as soon as possible. The galaxy needed to see what the Nihil had done.

"Come on, Tee," she muttered under her breath. "Come on."

She turned a dial, and the static gave way to a grainy image, T-9's excited chatter scrolling over her heads-up display. No. Excited wasn't right. The droid was overwhelmed, and she couldn't blame him.

"What are you seeing?"

OrbaLin's question was almost lost beneath a distorted message from her producer back in the Core.

"We're getting it, Rhil. Star's End, what's happened there?"

Another voice crackled over the line. She realized she was listening to GoNet anchor Sine Spenning commentating over the footage, which was now being broadcast live to the galaxy.

"Rhil—can we come to you?"

"Live?"

"Yeah. We'll patch you in, audio only."

She nodded, realizing a second later that the producer couldn't see.

"Sure," she said, trying to hide the waver in her voice. She punched a control on the comm terminal, switching over to GoNet's frequency. A holoprojector whirred, beaming a flickering image against the storeroom's wall so OrbaLin could see for himself. T-9's pixelated footage was writ large in front of them, complete with GoNet's logo in the bottom corner, a ribbon of headlines scrolling beneath the imagery.

BREAKING: REPUBLIC FAIR HIT BY UNPRECEDENTED NIHIL ATTACK.

DEATH TOLL ROCKETING.

CHANCELLOR SOH'S WHEREABOUTS UNKNOWN.

Sine Spenning's smooth voice, grave and achingly professional, came over the speakers. Rhil killed it so they didn't get feedback when she replied.

"We are joined now by GoNet's very own Rhil Dairo, who is on the scene. Rhil, first things first—are you safe?"

Rhil tried to speak, but a lump formed in her throat as she stood transfixed by the footage of the wrecked park.

"Rhil? Can you hear me?"

"I . . . I can hear you. Sorry, Sine, it's . . . well, it's been quite a day."

"I'm sure it has. These pictures are devastating. Can you talk us through what we're seeing?"

Talk them through? What was there to say? What was that old phrase? A holo tells a thousand words?

In this case, the holo was nothing short of heartbreaking. A fleet of Longbeams had arrived, bringing more reinforcements, but on the ground buildings were smashed, rubble strewn across broken walkways. Wrecked fighters lay in smoking craters, while the bodies . . . the bodies were everywhere.

Rhil was talking, but had no idea if her words made any sense. She didn't want to be in here, little more than a spectator. She wanted to be out there where it mattered, helping those who were trapped or worse, the wounded and the lost, lying in the dirt. As she talked, T-9's cam focused on the image of a small child wandering the once-glorious Republic Avenue, a stuffed toy clutched to its chest, tears rolling down grimy cheeks. A sob escaped Rhil's throat. OrbaLin's gloved hand appeared at her shoulder, a sense of calm radiating from the Jedi. She brushed it away. She didn't want to be calm. She wanted to experience the moment in all its rawness. She *needed* to experience it.

"Rhil," Sine asked over the comm. "Do you need to take a minute?"

She brushed a tear away. "No. I'm good."

"We would totally understand. I cannot imagine the trauma you must have endured."

"Really. I want people to see this. I want them to know what it's like."

"Of course. And what of the Jedi?"

"What about them?"

"We've yet to see any evidence of them at work on the footage. Are they—"

"One's here with me right now. Archivist OrbaLin of Starlight Beacon. He saved my life. The Jedi . . . the Jedi fought bravely to keep everyone as safe as they could."

"Ah, yes—" Sine interrupted, safe from his studio half a galaxy away. "We can see some now—an Ikkrukki and a Mirialan. Do you know their names?"

She said that she didn't, apologizing as if it were important when what really mattered was what was unfurling on screen, the Jedi attempting to pull an unmoving Gungan from a collapsed ride. Who cared what the Jedi were called? The important thing was that they were here, trying to hold back the horror.

"And what do you say to those who are already saying that the fair should never have gone ahead?" Sine asked. "That the Senate was warned of the danger before the festivities began? As we speak, Senator Tia Toon of Sullust has issued a statement that reads—"

But Rhil wasn't listening. T-9 had picked up chatter on the droid channels, a worrying rumor.

"If I could stop you there, Sine. I'm receiving reports that Chancellor Lina Soh has been found. Our cam is on the way."

Spenning immediately picked up the commentary for their viewers, informing them once again that the chancellor hadn't been seen since an attack on the opera house. All the time, T-9 whizzed across the park, his cam picking up the twisted remains of a downed walker. Bodies were scattered around, some moving, some ominously still.

Sine continued to babble in Rhil's ear. "These are remarkable scenes. Can you confirm that we are seeing Regasa Elarec Yovet, queen of the Togruta?"

That was obvious, wasn't it? The woman's montrals were instantly recognizable, but still Sine kept asking banal questions as if the pictures didn't speak for themselves. The Supreme Huntress was standing in a cluster of people, one of her royal guards by her side. Nearby, another Jedi wearing dark robes, the Master they called Elzar Mann, was helping the wounded, but T-9 had zeroed in on a figure kneeling on the floor, cradling a body, the chancellor's targons standing guard.

"Oh Stars," Sine said, actually sounding as if he had been caught off guard for once in his glittering career. "Is that . . . Surely it can't be . . ."

But it was, and Rhil felt as if her heart had been ripped out.

Chapter Fifty-Seven

The Unity Arc

Somewhere in the back of his mind, Stellan knew the galaxy was watching. He could hear the whine of the cam droids, almost feel their lenses closing in, picking up every scrap of dirt on his robes, the injuries on his face, the tears in his eyes.

Jedi weren't supposed to cry. They were supposed to keep their emotions in check. But weren't they also supposed to feel compassion for those in pain?

For light and life.

For light and . . .

Stellan heard a whimper, but didn't realize it was his own.

There was no avoiding the suffering of those whose lives had been torn apart, no avoiding their pain. If he could, if the anguish and the misery didn't cut him to the quick, then what kind of Jedi would he be?

People were racing toward him. Togruta military, direct from Shili, running toward their queen. There were others, too; medics both Republic and Jedi led by a Jedi Knight he knew but couldn't place right now, a Chagrian, clutching a medpac.

And then there was Bell and his charhound chasing after a young teenage boy who was racing full pelt toward Stellan, yelling one heartbreaking word:

"Mom!"

Kitrep Soh crashed down on his knees in front of Stellan, in front of his mother who was lying limp in Stellan's arms. No one would blame Kip for his tears, no one would blame him for his grief. He wasn't a Jedi, he was just a son fearing for a mother who might already be dead.

Matari and Voru padded around to the teenager, nuzzling into him. Kip buried himself into the targons' fur, sobbing openly.

And Stellan wept with him.

Chapter Fifty-Eight

Grizal

The camp on Grizal reverberated to the sound of blasters fired repeatedly into the sky. Pan strode through the throng that had gathered outside the main complex. He would have rather been at the Great Hall in the depths of No-Space, but actually, there was something satisfying coming back to this varp-heap of a planet after the success of the raid.

He had led the largest Nihil attack in their long and torturous history. Pan Eyta, not Marchion Ro for all his brave words about Lina Soh. While Pan had rained terror down upon the Republic, how exactly had the so-called Eye whiled away his time? By skulking in his relic of a ship on a rain-drenched world as far from the action as you could get.

Who would the Nihil listen to now? Who would lead the Storm? Ro thought he had secured his position by ordering the assault on Valo, but all he had done was play into Pan's hands. Even Zeetar looked impressed as Pan swaggered toward the main doors, the Talpini having emerged from the building without his ridiculous powersuit. A sign of respect? Of submission? Maybe. Perhaps Zeet wasn't as big a fool as Pan had thought.

Pan smiled, slowly turning on his heels before disappearing into the building to meet with Ro. He wanted to savor this moment, to soak up the admiration of the assembled Tempests, to see the reverence in their faces, for them to see the strength in his. He stood, arms stretched wide, chest heaving with pride. As the blasters fired, Pan threw back his head and bellowed three simple but victorious words, once Ro's but now forever his.

"The Storm *triumphant*!"

The Nihil responded with a collective roar, the jubilant shouts intensifying. Some of the crowd had been with him in the attack. Others had heard about it from afar, but all were united behind the Tempest Runner who had secured the victory.

"The Storm triumphant indeed."

Pan turned at the voice. Ro stood in the doorway of the building, in full regalia: his father's ragged cloak flowing in the wind, Arratan wolf skin around his shoulders, that damned cyclopean helm replacing the one that Pan had reduced to scrap metal.

"Ro," Pan said in welcome, eyes narrowed, waiting to see how the Eye would respond.

"Tempest Runner," Ro exclaimed, clapping Pan's arm, his voice amplified by his helmet. At least that explained why the fool was wearing it, so everyone could hear, but as for the hand on his arm, it was all Pan could do not to snap the man's arm.

Who did Ro think he was? The two of them weren't compatriots, they weren't even comrades in arms. Pan had no need for Ro anymore.

And yet the Eye continued, turning to address the assembled horde like a damn politician.

"We congratulate you all on your victory. Today marks the beginning of a new reality. Never again will the Republic underestimate us. Never again will they consider themselves beyond our touch. Their power is a lie. The Jedi are a lie." He thudded his chest with a gloved fist. "This is our time. Yes, we lost many in the attack, and we honor their sacrifice, but we have gained so much. Tonight we drink. Tonight we celebrate. Tonight we are Nihil!"

Another cheer of approval erupted all around, but Pan rankled where he stood. They had lost many? They had lost some, that was true, as was to be expected, but Ro was playing a dangerous game. After everything Pan had done, after everything he had achieved, Ro dared to undermine his success. If there had been losses, they were from Lourna Dee's ground forces, not from the Tempest in the air.

That was a point. Where *was* Lourna? Pan could see some of her legion among the throng, but the Tempest Runner herself was not among them, nor had her ship been in orbit when the *Elegencia* had arrived.

He turned, as if alerted by a sixth sense, to see her in the shadows of the doorway. Realizing she had been spotted, she hobbled out. Like Pan, she wore no helmet, although unlike the Dowutin she had obviously suffered on Valo's surface. There was a pronounced limp in her gait, and her face was heavily bruised. Most of the cuts had already scabbed over, although the vivid burn down her right cheek would take longer to heal. It didn't look like a blaster burn, or even that of a lightsaber. Fire from the carpet bombs? It was a definite possibility if the fury in her eyes was anything to go by, fury that was at this moment directed at him. Pan tried not to let the others see him tense, ready for an attack he was sure was about to come. And yet the Tempest Runner merely fell in beside Ro and addressed Pan with the cold emptiness of a starless sky.

"Congratulations, Pan."

He nodded, still cautious. "And to you, Lourna."

She turned to the crowd, not needing an amplifier to make herself heard. "The Eye is right. We will feast and we will honor those who fell on the path to our victory. And then . . . then we shall avenge them."

Again the Nihil cheered, Ro raising his arms once more and declaring that the revels should begin.

Pan would enjoy them soon enough, albeit back on his ship where he could celebrate in luxury, but for now they had matters to discuss.

"We should talk," he told the Eye, who inclined his head.

"Of course. Shall we go inside?"

They gathered in a temporary hall Ro had established, a tactical slab stolen from a Mon Calamari cruiser set up at the far end. Ro walked around the table and glanced down at the star map on its surface.

"Aren't you going to take that off?" Pan rumbled as he stalked over to join him.

Ro looked up. "What?"

Pan pointed at the helmet. "Take it off."

"Why?"

"Because I say so."

"And I have to do what you say?"

Pan slammed a fist down on the table, cracking the display.

"Damn right you do. That victory you described. That was us. Not you. Lourna and me."

Ro cocked his head. "What about Zeetar?"

Pan growled beneath his breath. "He played his part."

"But I didn't?"

The other Tempest Runners were infuriatingly quiet. So be it. This was Pan's moment after all.

"Very well, you can hide behind that mask as much as you want, but I want to know what happens now."

Ro spread his hands. "You heard it yourself. Now we party."

"Not good enough. We've done what we said we'd do. We've established our reputation now and for all time."

"At great sacrifice," Lourna added.

Pan stabbed at the star map with a finger, pointing at Coruscant. "Yeah, but they don't know that, do they? They're scared."

Ro stared straight at him, that damn red light shining in Pan's eyes, forcing him to squint. "And what would you have us do?"

Pan snorted. Wasn't that obvious? "We strike now and we strike fast. We show them that there's no respite, no time to lick their wounds. We hit them again, where it hurts, letting them know we mean business."

Lourna was studying him intently. "Where do you suggest?"

Pan searched the map, indicating the first target on his list. "Here."

Ro barely even looked down. "The Cyclor yards? We've talked about this before."

"Yes. Before Valo. When they thought they had driven us back."

"But we proved them wrong," Lourna said coolly. "*You* proved them wrong."

Pan wanted to slam her irritating face into the table. "That was one Cloud. Now we return as legion, not just to smash, but to do what we do best: to take what is ours by right of conquest. We thought too small with the *Innovator*. Do you know how many ships are in that yard? How many ships that could be ours?"

Lourna crossed her arms, looking down at the display.

"It's an interesting target, but is it ambitious enough?"

"How so?" Zeetar asked.

"Cyclor is important to the Mid Rim, yes . . ."

"To the entire Republic," Pan reminded her.

"Again, I don't disagree, but hitting the Republic Fair was a hugely symbolic act. I suggest we need something equally momentous, equally devastating."

"Such as?"

She jabbed a finger at the edge of the board, Pan's eyes going wide when he saw where she was pointing. "Hetzal Prime?"

The Twi'lek looked him straight in the eye. "We've already shown that the Jedi can bleed. Why not break them altogether? Erase the scene of their greatest triumph. Prove to the galaxy that their Jedi cannot protect them."

Pan grinned. His pulse was racing, his adrenaline at a peak. He'd suspected a challenge from Lourna, not that she would throw herself behind his plans with such vigor.

"I like it. It would certainly send a message."

"And where next?" Ro asked, his voice low. "Alderaan? Chandrila? *Coruscant?*"

"Why not?"

"Because it is suicide!"

Pan couldn't believe what he was hearing. "How can you say that?"

"Because unlike you I see the bigger picture." Ro was circling the table now, coming around to face Pan. "You did great work, all of you, but forcing the Republic's hand is a mistake."

"Force their hand? We've laid them wide open."

"And they are hurting. My source within the Senate tells me that an emergency session has been called, blame is being applied. The chancellor is on her deathbed."

"Yes," Lourna spat. "And the bomb that hit her walker nearly killed me. I saw her, Ro, before I got away. I doubt anyone could survive that."

"You did," Ro pointed out.

"I'm hard to kill."

"And that's what makes us better," Pan snarled, turning on Ro who was now standing beside him. "You see that, don't you, Ro? We wanted Lina Soh dead."

"We *wanted* the Republic to realize the threat we pose," Ro snapped. "We wanted them to realize that their so-called Spirit of Unity is a lie. And we've done it. Now no one on the frontier will sleep soundly. No one will think the Jedi can help."

"Then we should strike."

"No, you should *listen.*"

Pan didn't know that Ro could move so quickly. The Eye's arm shot up and a yellow lightsaber appeared at Pan's throat, the blade so close he felt his skin burn. Big mistake. Huge mistake. Pan struck, grabbing Ro's arm and slamming it into the table, the glass cracking with the impact. That would have been the end of it, should have been the end of it, if Ro hadn't swung up with his other hand and jabbed . . . what . . . a needle into Pan's neck? Pan staggered back, his hand pressed tight over the puncture wound. He looked down, seeing some kind of device sliding back beneath Ro's sleeve, an injector on a tiny mechanical arm.

Pan tried to speak, to demand to know what the crik Ro had just stuck him with, but no words came. His throat was too tight, his vision blurred. He sagged, his weight suddenly too much for his legs to bear. His head bounced off the side of the table as he collapsed, but he hardly felt the pain against the fire that burned through his veins. All the time Ro was speaking, his words echoing as Pan's muscles started to shake.

"You see, this is your problem, Pan," Ro said, pointing at him with the lightsaber. "You're so quick to respond that you never see the real attack coming. We started a war today, and you can be sure that there'll be a response. But the Republic doesn't know where we are. The Tempests need to scatter, to rebuild, while fear and paranoia spread like a plague from one end of the galaxy to the other." Ro extinguished the weapon and returned it to his belt. "The Republic will tear itself apart and then—when *I* say—we will reap the harvest, but you, Pan with your ambition and your thirst for glory . . ."

Ro's fist came down across Pan's face, a hit for every word.

"You . . . will . . . not . . . see . . . it."

Pan tried to gasp as the onslaught ended but couldn't draw breath. The voices he heard seemed a million kilometers away, but he clung to them, even though he could barely tell them apart.

"Go start the revels. I will be on the *Gaze*."

Pan didn't hear Ro leave. He was already blind. He knew what this would look like, when his body was eventually found. They'd say he overindulged, took one too many stims. It's what he would do. Ro had taken it all from him . . . Pan's victory . . . his victory . . . and there was no way to make the bastard pay.

Was there?

Pan heard a hiss, felt a scratch cool against his skin. The pain subsided like a lowering tide, only to return as his starved lungs gasped for breath. The world came back into focus, colors bursting in front of eyes that could see again, the thump-thump-thump of distant wreckpunk threatening to split his skull in two.

Someone was in front of him. Pan snatched out a hand, grabbing a thin but powerful arm. An empty hypo clattered to the floor. Pan looked up and saw long lekku and cold eyes. Lourna. He released her arm, but she didn't wince, even though bruises were already forming where he'd gripped her.

"You saved me," he croaked.

"Should I regret it?"

Pan pushed himself up, willing the hall to stop spinning. "I should've known he had something up his sleeve." Pan coughed, his lungs aching. "And you for that matter. Did you know what he was planning?"

"No. Not at all."

"But you had an antidote."

Lourna drew a vial from her pocket and shook it. "Cypanid. Extracted from the bibfort males back on Ryloth. It's a general anti-toxin. You got lucky."

Pan leaned heavily on the display table. "I don't feel it. Where's the Talpini?"

"Enjoying himself."

"And Ro?" The name was like bile in his mouth.

"On his ship, no doubt doing the same. He thinks you're dead."

Pan clutched the edge of the table, dragging himself up. "Then I will rip that antique apart to prove him wrong."

"No." Lourna put a hand on his arm, her palm cool against skin that still burned from the poison. "You know what he's like. He never joins the revels. He'll be up there until the party burns out, and when he finally shows his face it will be too late."

"Too late for what?"

"For him." Lourna grabbed his face, holding it between her hands to stare into his eyes. "He wasn't there, Pan, on the ground. Neither was Zeetar, for that matter. They didn't feel what it was like. The *power*. We have the Republic on the run. You were right, Ro isn't thinking big enough. Not anymore. I say we keep going."

"Strike now."

"And strike fast. We give it a day, maybe two, see where the Republic shores up its defenses. The shipyard or Hetzal's bacta fields. And then, whichever is weakest—"

"—is ours."

Lourna pressed her lips hard against his. It was like kissing a viper.

"You rest," she said when she finally broke away from him. "Let the cypanid do its work. I'll start spreading the news. The Nihil belong to us now."

"And if Zeetar doesn't agree?"

She smiled, showing teeth filed into points.

"He's not wearing that armor anymore, is he? I've always thought that three Tempest Runners was one too many."

Chapter Fifty-Nine

The Communion Chamber, Valo

The Jedi Council was in session, as was right and proper considering what had happened, but it was also the last place Stellan wanted to be. Outside the nearly completed Jedi outpost, the relief work was well under way. Medical and support ships had arrived from the Core, and the large majority of Jedi were on the streets of Lonisa securing buildings and tending to survivors.

The outpost itself had become the center of the relief effort. The Republic administration building had been hit in the final attack and, while it was still standing, had been decreed structurally unsafe. What remained of Samera Ra-oon's staff had been transferred to the Temple and were doing their best to help folk get home when most of the transports in the spaceport had been destroyed. The job hadn't been expected of them. Samera and her team had simply taken the initiative, volunteering to oversee the cleanup.

"Is there word from Starlight?" The question snapped Stellan back to the here and now. It had been spoken by Keaton Murag, another relatively new member of the Council who had been elevated just prior to the Great Disaster.

"Yes," Grand Master Veter responded. "Although Marshal Kriss is still engaged at Miluta."

"Along with half the Jedi in the sector, it seems." Teri Rosason— always a combative member of the Council—had already been critical of Avar's handling of the Drengir affair, especially her alliance with the Hutts. Now she was positively scathing as news reached them that Avar had summoned more Jedi than expected to support her assault on the Drengir's supposed rootworld. "Marshal Kriss seems to think she can do what she wishes, with or without the will of the Council."

"Nonsense," Yareal Poof, the long-necked Quermian, interjected. "Master Kriss is operating well within the parameters we afforded her."

"And in direct response to Chancellor Soh's request to deal with the Drengir threat as quickly and effectively as possible," Master Adampo pointed out, the Yarkora joining the conversation for the first time since the holoconference began. Master Rosason made a response, but her words were lost in static, the Council's images scrambling for a moment. Communications lines had largely been restored, but the wider network was struggling to cope with the sheer amount of data beaming back and forth from Valo. At this rate Stellan was surprised no one had suggested breaking out the antique courier droids the Republic had used in their first push for the frontier a century or so before.

The Masters' holos swam back onto the walls, Yareal caught mid-sentence.

"—besides, Master Kriss had no way of knowing what was happening on Valo. None of us did until the reporter's message got through."

Rosason tutted. "Can you imagine what would have happened if the Togrutas hadn't responded?"

"But they did, Republic Longbeams close behind." Stellan's tone was more forceful than he'd intended, but had the gratifying effect of shutting up Rosason, at least for a moment.

Pra-Tre Veter regarded him with concern over the holochannel.

"Master Gios, are you sure you shouldn't rest? Your injuries—"

"Are not as bad as they look, thank you." While that wasn't a lie, it wasn't exactly the whole truth, either. Torban Buck had wanted to plunge him into a bacta bath, but instead Stellan had pulled rank, opting for simple rejuv washes instead. A medical droid had closed the larger cuts with microsutures, Buck warning him that the stitches might leave scars. Stellan waved the concerns away, insisting that the already depleted bacta supplies be redirected to those who really needed them. As a Jedi, Stellan could look after himself, relying on the Force rather than stims that could dull his senses.

"What of the Nihil?" Grand Master Veter asked.

This was better. Stellan wanted to deal with facts, not recriminations.

"Most escaped," he told the ancient Tarnab. "The Valon Security Force does have a small number of Nihil prisoners, but most are in critical condition. However, archivist OrbaLin did manage to subdue one raider, a Lamproid by the name of Quin Amarant. We have him in custody here in the outpost."

Veter's bushy eyebrows shot up. "You do?"

"At the request of Larep Reza who has assumed the position of acting chancellor while Lina Soh . . . recovers."

The mention of her name took Stellan back to those dreadful moments after the bomb had detonated. He had been convinced that Soh was going to pass away in his arms. The explosion had reduced the REW to scrap, throwing Soh and the others to the ground. Most had survived with some odd broken bones, Madam Conserra suffering a deflated lung, but Soh had been caught in the wreckage, her injuries severe. True to form, though, the chancellor had proved stronger than she looked. Torban Buck had worked wonders maintaining her condition before Republic medics could arrive. Now she was in the outpost's infirmary, in a clinical coma, ready to be transported back to Coruscant as soon as the doctors confirmed that she could be moved. Those same doctors weren't happy with two targons lying permanently at her side, but there was little they could do about it.

"And the Lamproid is being questioned?" Veter asked.

"Yes," Stellan confirmed, "although as yet he hasn't revealed any-thing of note. However, we do have this . . ."

Stellan pressed a button on his cuff, activating footage of the fight between OrbaLin and the same Twi'lek who had attempted to storm the walker. He let it play for a moment before pausing it, the woman freezing mid-attack.

"This is a recording captured by Rhil Dairo's cam droid, Tee-Nine. The Twi'lek appears to go by the name of Dee. As I said, Amarant hasn't revealed much, but the Jedi who last interviewed him reported a sense that Dee holds a position of power within the Nihil."

"You fought her yourself, did you not, Master Gios?"

Stellan felt his face burn at Rosason's question.

"Indeed I did."

"And she was largely responsible for your injuries."

"She is a . . . skilled fighter."

"So it would seem."

"I see. And what of the Drengir?"

Stellan frowned at the sudden switch in conversation. "We have al-ready discussed Marshal Kriss's mission . . ."

"I am not talking about Avar Kriss's crusade, Master Gios. I am talking about the fact that Drengir matter was discovered on Valo dur-ing the attack."

"I hear it was slightly more than that," Keaton Murag commented.

Stellan fought the urge to pinch the bridge of his nose to relieve the headache that was building by the moment.

"Yes, Master Murag. According to a report by Vernestra Rwoh—"

"Your former apprentice," Rosason cut in.

"My former apprentice, yes," Stellan acknowledged. "As you know, a number of Jedi were operating at the fair during the attack, although due to the comm blackout we were unable to communicate. During this time, the Padawan known as Ram Jomaram discovered Nihil troops planting what appear to be Drengir spores around the commu-nications tower."

"Suggesting the Nihil have found a way to seed the Drengir," Rosason pointed out. "Another weapon in their arsenal."

Pre-Tre Veter looked concerned. "This has already been raised in the Senate," the Tarnab told them. "Some even suggest that the Nihil are behind the Drengir crisis as a whole."

"What better way to spread fear along the frontier?" Murag asked.

"Keeping Starlight Beacon conveniently busy while they raise merry hell on Valo," Rosason added.

"I hardly think that's fair," Stellan injected.

Rosason actually went so far as to scoff. "Really, Master Gios. And why wasn't the Hero of Hetzal on Valo at the time of the attack? Why had she commandeered so many Jedi for her task force? Jedi who could have come to Valo's aid if they hadn't been occupied by an infestation of murderous plants. We have been played by these Nihil. Led to believe that they are little more than a rabble. But if this is all true, if this attack was all part of an elaborate scheme . . ."

"Then they are an army," Stellan said gravely, "with tactics and unexpected resources at their command."

"Finally we agree on something, Master Gios," Rosason conceded. "The real question is, if they are an army, who is their general?"

Stellan looked over at the hologram of the Twi'lek who had bested him.

"Do we know what happened to her?" Yareal Poof asked, as if reading his thoughts.

"She was gone when the smoke cleared," Stellan told the Quermian. "Master Mann believes she escaped in a nearby Nihil junker."

"Is there a possibility she was arrested by the Togruta military?" Rosason asked.

"Unfortunately, we have no idea," Veter said. "Now that Regasa Elarec has been recovered, the Togrutas have broken contact with the Republic. I attempted to contact the regasa myself but have been unable to talk to anyone in her court. I fear this incident has put back Shili-Republic relationships by several decades."

This Stellan could believe. The Togruta fleet had left as soon as Elarec Yovet had been evacuated, taking Ambassador Tiss along with them. Images of the monarch steeped in the blood of those she had been trying to save had replayed repeatedly on the newsnets, as had the footage of Stellan cradling the injured chancellor, his anguish laid bare. Like it or not—and Stellan did not—the picture of him openly weeping over Lina Soh's body had become a defining image of the atrocity. Tia Toon had obviously gone into overdrive, praising Stellan and the Order to the skies, while also using the image to tell the galaxy that the Jedi had been pushed to the limit. How many more lives would have been lost if it hadn't been for the timely arrival of the Togrutas, especially, the senator was keen to add, with the Longbeams arriving too late. Obviously all this fed into his narrative about establishing a central Republic defense force, but the worst thing of all was that he was right. The death toll on Valo was astronomical, but just how much had the Jedi held back the tide? How much difference had they actually made?

Stellan's thoughts were broken by a courteous cough at the chamber door. Stellan didn't need to look to see who it was. He could feel his friend's presence, troubled though it was, him and every other Jedi on the planet.

"Master Mann," he said formally, gesturing Elzar into the room.

Elzar stepped forward, bowing respectfully in front of the Council members.

"Apologies for the interruption, Masters, but the chancellor has requested Stellan's presence."

"Acting Chancellor Reza?" Rosason asked.

Elzar shook his head. "No. Lina Soh. I'm pleased to say she's awake . . ." He turned to face Stellan. "And she wants to see you."

Chapter Sixty

The infirmary, Valo Temple Outpost

Stellan wasn't surprised to find Rhil Dairo beside Lina Soh's bed, T-9 hovering at a discreet distance.

"She insisted on giving an interview almost as soon as she was awake," Larep Reza told him, with the weary look of a man who had recently engaged in an argument he would never win. "Thankfully Quo wasn't here to burst a blood vessel."

"How is Norel?" Stellan enquired.

"Doing well," Lina Soh said, her voice weaker than he had ever heard it, which was understandable considering what she had been through. The private chamber was devoid of medical droids, but only because Torban Buck had personally volunteered to care for the chancellor until she could be transferred onto the *Coruscant Dawn*—which had survived the assault, its crew fighting off a Nihil boarding party firsthand. Stellan looked over at Buckets of Blood, who was checking the chancellor's vitals. Buck was an acquired taste, but his medical abilities were second to none. Soh looked better than Stellan had expected, another reason why Reza had no doubt allowed the interview, which would go through a rigorous vetting procedure before being broadcast. Sensors had been placed on Soh's neck and temples, but she was free of breathing tubes, the scratches and cuts on her pale face either already treated or covered with bacta strips. Stellan fought the urge to look down at the bed, already having been briefed that Buck hadn't been able to save Soh's right leg. He wondered if that detail had made it into the interview.

He approached the medbed, Elzar waiting by the door. Rhil went to move aside, but Stellan made a point of smiling at her warmly. It was the first time he'd seen the young reporter since the opera house.

"We owe you a debt of thanks, Ms. Dairo."

Rhil blushed, shaking her head. "I don't think so."

"I do," Soh said from her bed. "From what archivist OrbaLin informed me, it was *you* who got the message offplanet."

Rhil's discomfort only increased. "I was just doing my duty, ma'am."

Stellan was impressed by the woman's humility. He knew reporters didn't like to become the story, but this needed to be said. "Be that as it may, without your actions the Togrutas would never have known that we were in danger."

"That their regasa was in danger, you mean," Reza muttered, only to be reprimanded by Soh.

"They saved us, Larep." Yes, the Longbeams came, but the Togrutas turned the tide. Weak or not, the chancellor was still a formidable presence. "I have placed Ms. Dairo's bravery and resourcefulness on the record in our interview; an exclusive she more than deserves."

"An interview I should edit," Rhil said, waving for T-9 to follow her. "My producer will be waiting."

She turned to leave, but Soh raised an arm, light glinting from the tube delivering painkillers to the back of her hand. "No. Please stay. Perhaps some shots of us talking would add a little color to your report, if the Council member doesn't object."

How could he? Not only was Lina Soh formidable, she was also a politician first and foremost, always looking for the perfect holo-opportunity, even now.

"I have no objections," Stellan said, hoping the Force would forgive him a little white lie. "Although maybe the footage should be picture, no sound?"

"Agreed," Reza said firmly. "Some of the conversation may be . . . sensitive."

Rhil took a step back, although her cam droid remained where it was near the ceiling. "Understood. You got that, Tee-Nine?"

The droid bleeped once and began recording again.

Stellan drew closer, trying not to feel self-conscious under the droid's gaze.

"I won't ask you how you are feeling."

A smile tugged at the chancellor's lips. "I think you just did."

"Giving an interview already. Most people would have at least waited until they were out of bed."

She cocked an amused eyebrow. "Are you saying I'm like most people?"

He shook his head. "Never."

Her face grew more somber. "The people deserve to see me. This is my fault."

"I don't think anyone—"

That hand came up again, stopping him before he could protest.

"Please, Stellan. We both know what the media is saying. And if they aren't saying it, they *should*. I was warned."

"We were *all* warned."

"And yet I carried on as if we were untouchable. How many people died because of my arrogance, Council Member?" Stellan assumed the question was rhetorical, letting her continue. "How many people will never return home from a 'fun day at the fair.' I take personal responsibility for each and every death."

"The Nihil are to blame," Reza reminded her darkly.

"And we allowed them to come, with our complacency. With our arrogance." Soh turned back to Stellan, her face grave. "Master Gios, from this point on, you have the full resources of the Republic at your disposal. Intelligence. Security. Whatever you need. Please . . . will you bring these villains to justice?"

Stellan didn't know what to say. He had expected for the Jedi to be asked to investigate, but this was something else. "I . . ." he began, searching for the right words. "I will consult with the Council."

"I mean it, Master Jedi. I still believe in my heart that we were right to vote against Toon's permanent defense force. The last thing the Republic needs is an army, but if you ask, I am convinced that every planet that flies the Republic flag will stand with you. Local security forces. Planetary guards—"

Now it was Stellan's turn to stop her. "The Jedi are not warriors, nor should we ever be."

"But you are symbols," she insisted, trying to sit up. "Especially now, especially *you*."

"Madam Chancellor—"

Soh reached up, grabbing his hand in hers. "Stellan, please. I've seen you on the holonet, after the attack. Everyone has. Holding me when . . ." Her voice caught for a second. "When it looked as though it was too late. The entire galaxy has seen the compassion in your eyes. Seen the resolve. That wasn't the face of a general or a politician. It was the face of a man who is better than those who would do us harm. A man who will protect us. A man who will be just. We need the Jedi, now more than ever. We need the light."

Stellan felt the eyes of everyone in the room upon him. Of Reza. Of Rhil. Of Buck and Elzar. Lina Soh didn't know what she was asking. There were so many who were better suited to the task. Avar. Most of the Council. *Yoda,* if anyone knew where he was. Stellan had been caught out like everyone else. Had he paid the price? He'd been wounded, yes, humiliated even at the hands of a lone Twi'lek. Stellan who had been so proud to show off his lightsaber prowess on the *Coruscant Dawn.* But what of the countless millions who would never recover from the Nihil attack, those who had lost their lives on Valo and those who now grieved, living in fear, constantly checking the skies for the sudden appearance of a war-cloud. Could he be a symbol to them? Should he even try?

"Council Member?" Soh asked, looking for an answer he struggled to provide.

Thankfully he didn't have to, not yet. Larep Reza's datapad bleeped, and the vice chancellor looked up at his superior with alarm.

"Larep?"

"It's Shili, Madam Chancellor. A secure channel."

"The Togruta military?"

The Kalleran ran his fingers across the 'pad, checking the data stream. "Not as far as I can tell. It seems to be coming from the royal court."

Soh sat up in her bed, adjusting her medical gown. "Ms. Dairo, if you could stop recording, please?"

The reporter nodded. "Of course. Would you like us to leave?"

"I think you of all people deserve to see this. Thank you, Larep."

Reza pressed a control and a large hologram appeared on the wall, Elarec Yovet's face close to the cam.

"Regasa," Soh acknowledged, with a slight bow.

"It is good to see you awake, Chancellor," the Togruta replied. "I must admit, I feared the worst."

"Elarec, I am so sorry . . ."

The Supreme Huntress shook her head. "It was not your fault, Lina. None of it."

"You were my guest."

"And I came freely, despite the concerns of my security council. I for one am glad I was there."

"I don't think Captain Maramis would agree with you, Regasa," Stellan said.

"On the contrary, Lord Jedi. Captain Maramis has been singing your praises ever since leaving Valo. As have I." Her eyes flicked back to Soh. "As for Chancellor Lina Soh of the Galactic Republic . . . Other leaders would have hidden themselves away at the first sign of danger, but not you. You stood by your people, pulling them out of the rubble with your own hands if need be, assuring them time and time again that all would be well."

"As did you, Regasa."

"Which is why we are kindred spirits, as are Captain Maramis and Master Gios. You protect those in need and weep for those you cannot save. You are the spirit of the Republic, a spirit you share with my people."

Soh leaned forward in her bed. "What are you saying, Regasa?"

"I am saying that the Nihil's cowardly attack showed us that isolation is not the way. Only together can we be strong."

"You are talking about an alliance?"

"At first yes, maybe more in time. It will not be easy. There are plenty in my government who disagree with me, but they will listen. I am their queen and I will be silent no longer."

Of this, Stellan had no doubt. Maybe another of the chancellor's Great Works was already in motion. Maybe there was still hope.

"In the meantime," the regasa continued, "as a sign of goodwill, I am sending you a data package containing information that my intelligence services intercepted, encoded messages from the Nihil communications network."

"From their comm network?" Reza repeated in disbelief.

"There were those who did not wish you to have it, preferring to use it for our own advantage, but I see no advantage in keeping secrets from our allies, for that is what we are, Chancellor. On that you have my word."

Reza's datapad bleeped. "I have the package."

On the holo, Elarec Yovet smiled. "Excellent. We will talk again, Lina Soh, whether our governments like it or not."

"The Senate will welcome your friendship," the chancellor responded. "Talks can commence whenever you are ready."

"We are ready now. My ministers just don't know it yet. To the Spirit of Unity, Chancellor."

"The Spirit of Unity," Soh repeated, and the hologram cut off.

The chancellor didn't waste any time, turning to Reza. "Have that intel analyzed and report back immediately."

The Kalleran was already striding from the room. "At once, Madam Chancellor."

The door slid open as he left, and Soh saw her son waiting in the reception room beyond, Jom Lariin at his side. There was no mistaking the tears that brimmed in her eyes.

"Now if you could all excuse me," she said, beckoning Kip in, "I would like a moment alone with my son."

Stellan indicated for everyone to leave them in peace, all except for Matari and Voru who jumped to their feet, purring loudly.

Stellan stood aside to let the young man in. Kip Soh ran to his mother and threw his arms around her, Lina Soh hugging him back.

Stellan watched them as the doors slid back, looking away sharply as he realized that Elzar was studying him.

"Well, that was . . . intense," his friend finally said.

"That's one word for it."

"You didn't give her an answer."

"No . . . I didn't."

Elzar crossed his arms. "So . . . what's it to be? I mean, if the Supreme Huntress of the Togrutas can stand up against her own government for the safety of the galaxy . . ."

Stellan raised a single eyebrow. "Have you finished?"

"Probably. Possibly. Maybe not."

Stellan turned and marched from the medical wing. "Well, maybe you should, because we have work to do."

Chapter Sixty-One

Lonisa City Spaceport

It was fair to say that the job had not gone as expected. Ty Yorrick had spent the best part of a decade trying to avoid Jedi entanglement. The nearest she'd come to the Order in recent years had been that business on Blarrum three months ago, and yet in the space of a couple of days she'd survived a lightsaber duel with a member of the High Council, shared prison time with an errant Padawan, and ridden into battle with a Jedi Master on the back of a sanval, all three lizards now safely back in a temporary enclosure at the zoo. One thing was certain, KL-03 would *never* believe any of this, if Ty ever saw the fussy droid again. The problem was getting back to her and the ship. The original plan was for Mantessa to drop Ty back when the gig was over, but now Mantessa was dead and the inventor's ship was in pieces, along with just about every other ship in Valo's spaceport.

The Nihil had done a number on every cruiser and transport, raiding the majority and scuppering the rest. The *Dynamo* was no different.

"No, no, no, no," Klerin moaned as they stood in the once-pristine ship. Ty had found Mantessa's daughter picking through its wrecked hold, the terminals smashed, cables strewn everywhere. In all honesty, Ty was surprised that the reactor hadn't blown. There was no way the ship would ever fly again.

"I guess we should get ourselves on a list."

Klerin looked at her in puzzlement.

"List?"

"For those needing transport. The Republic is putting on a number of Longbeams, although I can't see us jumping to the front of the queue anytime soon."

"Can't your friends help?"

"My friends?"

"The Jedi!"

Ty couldn't help but laugh. What she'd shared with Elzar Mann had been . . . intriguing, but she had no intention of pursuing that particular connection. She still wasn't convinced that Elzar was completely stable, and besides, their brief union had stirred up memories she'd tried hard to forget. Klias. The Yellow Shrine. No, she had gotten close enough. Worst of all, it seemed that the Jedi, conflicted as he was, had rubbed off on her. The old Ty would have let Klerin find her own way offplanet, but the new, improved Ty found it impossible to simply abandon the girl. Klerin had just lost her mother, albeit a mother who had carted around unrefined recainium. Ty thought back to the girl who had stumbled into a war-cloud looking for them after their arrest. There was no way Klerin could manage by herself. At the very least, Ty would get her to a waystation before returning to KL-03 and Rover.

However, if they were going to arrange transport, they needed to get a move on before all the spaces were filled, which meant Klerin had to stop flitting from computer to computer and go register.

"None of them are going to work," Ty told her as Klerin tried the fifth console in a row.

"You don't know that," the Kuranu replied and was proved right when the screen flicked on.

"What are you looking for?" Ty asked, peering over the girl's shoulder.

Klerin ignored her, working through an obviously fragmented file system.

"No," she muttered, quietly at first and then with more urgency as she flicked from section to section. "No, no, no, no!"

The last exclamation was punctuated with a fist to the keyboard, the computer beeping in indignation.

"They're gone," Klerin said, slumping in her seat.

"What are?" Ty's patience was wearing thin. "Talk to me, Klerin."

"Mother's plans . . . for the nullifier."

"And that's a bad thing, why?"

Klerin looked at her as if she was talking to a child. "Because the Nihil raided this ship . . ."

Ty's heart dropped to her boots as realization dawned. If the Nihil had access to a device that could knock out energy weapons . . .

She sighed, surrendering to the inevitable. "What was that you were saying about my Jedi friends?"

Chapter Sixty-Two

Valo Jedi archive

Valo Outpost's Jedi archive was not how its architect had intended it to look. The large chamber, with its sweeping staircases and elegant data stacks, had been transformed into an emergency operations center. Everywhere you looked, Republic and Jedi staff worked alongside each other, sitting at hastily installed comm terminals as they coordinated the evacuation of those who were stranded on the planet.

Elzar strode through the mass of technicians and officials, nodding a greeting at OrbaLin who was leading the Jedi's part in the proceedings. The archivist, his containment suit now fully repaired, was too busy to engage in idle chitchat, a fact that pleased Elzar, not out of any enmity, more because there was another conversation he needed to have.

"Hello, Samera."

The Valon looked up from her screens, the light of the displays reflected in her emerald eyes.

"Hello yourself."

Elzar was pleased that, save for a few cuts and grazes, Samera looked unhurt, although the dark shadows under her eyes betrayed an exhaustion that he guessed would only deepen in the days ahead.

As he stood waiting, she fielded three calls and authorized a request for supplies to the field medcenter that had been set up in the park's Technology and Science zone.

"Can I help you, Elzar?"

His mouth was dry.

"No, I just wanted . . . just wanted to see if you were okay."

She laughed with little humor. "Never better. You?"

"I've lived through worse."

He immediately regretted his choice of words.

"Then I'm glad I'm not you," she said, returning to her screens. "I never want to experience anything like that again as long as I live. When this is over I'm retiring to Sasoraan."

He walked around the terminals to stand beside her. "I've never heard of that. Where is it?"

Samera sighed, putting down the 'pad she was attempting to study, and looked up at him, a pained expression on her face. "Really? You want to do this now?"

Elzar did not want to do this now. He would rather face an entire pack of hragscythes.

"I . . . Well, we haven't seen each other since . . ."

"Since the night of the opening. Yes, I know. Things have been a little busy."

He laughed, acknowledging the understatement. "I just thought . . ."

"Thought what, Elzar?"

Saber's Grace, she wasn't making this easy.

"I just wanted to say . . ."

Samera ran her hands through her hair. "Okay, look. I know what you want to say and there's no need. It was fun. We had a good time, and then the world ended. Even if it hadn't ended, then that would've been the end of it."

Elzar couldn't help but feel a little crestfallen. "It would?"

She looked at him as if he had lost his mind. "Of course. You're a Jedi, Elzar, and I'm . . . well, I'm busy. Very, very busy."

For the first time in a long time, Elzar Mann didn't know what to say, so Samera said it for him: "We're good, okay? Job done. Line drawn."

"Line drawn," he confirmed as her console beeped to inform her of another incoming request. "I'll let you get on."

Samera had already answered the call. "This is Coordinator Ra-oon. How can I help?"

Elzar left her to it and walked as purposefully as was possible toward a tactical display that had been erected on the other side of the room. Stellan stood in front of the screen, scrolling through reports, but looked up as Elzar approached to glance over at Samera. "Should I ask what that was about?"

"Probably not," Elzar answered honestly, making a show of studying the board. "How are things going with the Togruta intel?"

"We're expecting it back any minute," Stellan said, scratching his beard. "The encryption is remarkably advanced. Which brings us to our next problem."

He tapped the screen, bringing up a new display. Elzar peered at the report and sighed.

"They have a pipeline into the Republic."

"So it would seem. Official communications lines. Data packages. Ship-to-ship communication. We've no idea how long they've been listening. Just something else to add to the list of things we don't know about them, including how they do this."

Another tap of the display brought up an image of a Nihil ship jumping into Valo's atmosphere.

"Arriving that close to a gravitation field should be impossible. At the very least, they should crash and burn."

"Some did," Elzar pointed out.

"So we know the process isn't foolproof, but if even one ship can make it past planetary defenses . . ."

"So how do we find out?"

"That is the all-important question." Stellan killed the footage of the Nihil junker, pulling down a picture of an Aqualish. "This is Vam Targes."

"The designer of the *Innovator*."

Stellan gave another nod. "Padawan Zettifar tells me that Targes was working on a way to predict the Nihil's incursions."

"Fantastic. Where is it?"

"With him at the bottom of the lake. A team of diver droids are being sent down to see what they can find, along with any bodies they can recover."

"Have you thought about bringing in Keven Tarr?" Elzar asked, thinking of the shy technician he'd met in the aftermath of the Great Disaster.

"Tarr?"

"He was behind the calculations on Hetzal. The guy's a genius."

"I'll mention it to Vice Chancellor Reza."

Elzar studied his friend's face. Even ignoring the bruising, Stellan looked beat.

"You can do this, you know that, don't you? We're all behind you. The chancellor, the Republic. Me. Anything you want, you just have to ask."

"A cup of uneti tea."

"I'm sure it can be arranged."

Stellan smiled, before peering a little harder at Elzar. "What about you, El? What do *you* need?"

So the moment had finally come. He knew it would. Stellan was preoccupied, yes, but could read Elzar like a datapad, no matter how he tried to bury it.

Elzar forced himself to meet Stellan's gaze.

"I think I need help."

Stellan didn't say anything, just waited for Elzar to continue.

"There was a moment, during the attack, when I gave in to the dark side. It was only for a moment, but the results were . . . devastating, in every sense of the word."

"Do you know why it happened?"

Elzar rubbed suddenly dry lips. "Yes. And I think it's been coming for a while."

Again there was a pause, but this time it was Stellan who broke the silence.

"We're all tested, each and every one of us. And yes, there are moments when we're found wanting. The important thing is that you've recognized it, and you've asked for help." He reached out and squeezed Elzar's arm. "You said you were here for me, and that goes both ways. We will get through this, all of it. We're not alone, not when we have the Force and we have each other."

"And what about Avar? Do you think I should tell her?"

"If you think it will help. Just like the old days, eh?" Stellan tapped Elzar's arm, his voice changing, becoming more formal. Someone was waddling up to the screen: archivist OrbaLin. Stellan turned and addressed the Ugor.

"Master OrbaLin, how can I help?" His eyes dropped down to the datareader in the archivist's gloved hands. "Is that—?"

"The analysis, yes, Master Gios. It appears the Nihil are mobilizing for another attack."

"So soon?" Elzar asked.

"According to the data, two of the leaders, a Pan Eyta and Lourna Dee—no doubt the Twi'lek we both encountered, Master Gios—have spread word that they are to choose between one of two locations."

Stellan took the reader and flicked through the text. "Which are—?"

"Hetzal Prime or the Cyclor Shipyards."

"Picking up where they left off," Stellan mused.

"Or where they began," Elzar pointed out. "If they wipe out the new crops, bacta supply would be put back years."

"Whereas the destruction of the Skyhawk yards would be a clear threat to Republic security." Stellan stopped scrolling, highlighting one particular paragraph in the report. "According to this, the Nihil have intercepted a request for an increased Jedi presence from Cyclor . . ."

"In case of another attack," OrbaLin confirmed. "A request we've been unable to fulfill, due to the current crisis."

Stellan turned back to the display, bringing up a star map. He tapped again, highlighting first Cyclor's position and then the Hetzal system's.

"Reading between the lines, they're waiting to see what we do next. If we send a contingent of Jedi to Cyclor . . ."

"They'll return to Hetzal," OrbaLin said.

"Whereas the shipyard will be the target if it looks like we're reinforcing the Rooted Moon," Elzar said, following the logic, even though he didn't like it.

Stellan fell quiet, his eyes flickering over the map.

"I know that face," Elzar said. "You have a plan."

"Possibly."

"So you should probably share it."

A mischievous smile played on Stellan's lips as he turned back to OrbaLin.

"Archivist, do you know where I could find Senator Tia Toon?"

Chapter Sixty-Three

The *Elegencia*

"**I hear your** concerns, Shipmaster Hazziz, and share them myself."

Pan Eyta was on board the *Elegencia,* listening to the feed the Republic thought was encrypted. There was a moment while an intermediary—a protocol droid or other such lackey—transcribed Senator Toon's words into Cyclorrian chirps and buzzes, and another when the shipmaster responded.

Pan smirked as the senator relayed the information that he'd been waiting to hear. "From what I can gather, our Jedi friends are going to ground. All Jedi have been instructed to return to that monstrosity of a space station in the Outer Rim, with only the smallest contingent sent to fortify Hetzal."

"Hetzal?" the shipmaster repeated in disbelief.

"What do you expect? Of course the Jedi would protect their vanity over all. I'm afraid that no Knights are being deployed to any of the places that really need them most, including Cyclor. It seems my deepest fears are being realized. The Jedi are abandoning us in our hour of need. We are all but defenseless."

There was another pause. Another translation. "Perhaps I can count on Cyclor's support at the next reading of the defense force bill? If the Jedi won't—or, Force forbid, *can't*—protect us, then we must defend ourselves."

Hazziz buzzed a reply, which seemed to flummox Senator Toon. "You want *Sullust* to defend the shipyards? If only we could oblige, my friend. Chancellor Soh likes to say that we are all the Republic. Unfortunately, since Valo, I think the reality of the situation is that we are all very much alone. That's why the DFP is so importan—"

Pan flicked off the communication, swiveling around to face Lourna Dee's holo. "Did you hear?"

The Twi'lek nodded from the safety of her own ship, still in geostationary orbit on the dark side of Grizal's moon. "It appears we have our target."

"And the Eye doesn't suspect?"

"The Eye is still on the *Gaze Electric*. All he cares about is his relics . . ."

Pan huffed, the sound becoming a rattling cough.

On the holo, Lourna looked concerned. "Pan?"

"It's nothing," Pan lied, wiping his lips with the back of his hand. He glanced down, seeing the spots of blood. His body still ached, but it was nothing compared with what he would do to Ro when they returned from the raid.

"So, we're set," he said, changing the subject. "We'll take the Tempests to Cyclor and then, when we get back—"

"We'll storm the *Gaze*," Lourna confirmed.

"And Zeetar?"

Lourna pulled a finger across her neck.

Pan sniggered. "Will you let me watch?"

The Twi'lek smiled playfully. "I'll even let you lick the knife."

"You little tease. Do we have the Path?"

Lourna leaned off-screen and pressed a button. "Coming over to you now."

The *Elegencia*'s navigation console bleeped, and Chell Trambin confirmed that everything was in order.

Pan gripped the arms of his command lounger, relishing the feel of the soft leather beneath his hands. Soon they'd be rid of Ro and his blasted legacy. They'd have his ship and his savant, plus whatever treasures the scud-fisher had been hoarding over the years.

The future had never looked brighter.

Chapter Sixty-Four

Valo Jedi archive

Senator Tia Toon sat back as the screen went blank. "How was that?"

"Spoken like someone who believed every word."

The Sullustan looked up at Stellan, his dark eyes searching the Jedi's face. "Do you think that little of me?"

Stellan shook his head. "You have strong convictions."

"But I am not so entrenched in my views that I am blind to the needs of the Republic. A Republic I love."

Stellan couldn't let the moment pass without at least asking, "And the DFP?"

"Is still a necessity as far as I am concerned, but until such a time as the Republic catches up with me, I will do everything I can to assist you and the chancellor. As I always have."

While Stellan didn't quite believe the latter half of the statement, he had no doubt that Toon wanted to help. The senator had certainly made the most of the situation on Valo, but had also pledged Sullust's unquestioning support to the rebuilding of the planet and securing the system.

Beside them, Rhil checked the transmitter controls.

"Did it get through?" Toon asked.

"To the Nihil? There's no way of knowing, but I'd bet my best ratings they were listening."

"And the order to mass on Hetzal Prime?" Elzar Mann asked from where he was standing with Bell and Indeera Stokes, Bell's ever-faithful charhound at their feet.

Rhil returned to the readout and nodded. "Also sent."

"Although no Jedi will ever receive it," Stellan told them, having provided Rhil with an antiquated frequency that OrbaLin had doctored to make it vulnerable to the Nihil tap.

"Then my job here is done." The Sullustan senator rose from his seat. "If you will excuse me, I have a consignment of prefabricated buildings arriving from SoroSuub, a donation to house those whose dwellings were destroyed by the Nihil."

"A gesture I'm sure the Valons appreciate," Stellan acknowledged. "As do I."

"I'm glad to hear it," Toon said, pausing in front of him. "I mean what I say, Council Member. I have only the greatest respect for the Order . . ."

"But believe that the Republic should be able to defend itself, yes, I know."

"We *are* all the Republic," Toon told him. "That is one principle where Lina Soh and I are in *complete* agreement."

"A Spirit of Unity?"

Toon chuckled. "That is all any of us can hope for, Master Jedi. Excuse me."

Stellan stood aside so that Toon could leave, the Sullustan crossing paths with the last person Stellan expected to see enter the operations room. It was all he could do to stop his hand from dropping to his lightsaber.

Elzar stepped forward to intercept the newcomer. "Ty?"

The Tholothian mercenary didn't waste time with pleasantries. "Elzar, I need to talk to you about the Nihil."

Chapter Sixty-Five

Valo Temple Outpost

Amarant's mouthparts clacked together in agitation as he was led down the corridor by an idiot of a security officer.

The Neimoidian—Snat or some such—had informed Amarant that he was being taken to a Republic ship for transport to a secret facility where he would be interrogated. *Good luck with that,* Amarant thought. He'd plunge his stinger into his own thorax before betraying Lourna Dee.

That said, at the moment he had no idea how to escape. His arms were shackled, the Neimoidian armed with a surprisingly heavy blaster rifle, and he was being marched through an outpost swarming with Jedi.

At least the transport itself didn't seem to have any more guards. The shuttle sat in the temple's open courtyard, the building having survived Pan Eyta's bombing runs. There were signs of hastily extinguished fires, the walls blackened with soot, but the main structure seemed untouched. Pity. Amarant would like to see the place burn. Maybe he'd return once he was free and raze it to the ground himself, after he'd sunk his fangs into Snat's stinking neck, of course. Amarant's mind wandered, imagining the indignities he could heap on the Jedi, especially that wretched Ugor who had encased him in his disgusting gloop.

"Captain Snat, wait up."

Now what? Amarant swiveled one of his eyestalks back the way they'd come to see a group of Jedi rushing up. At least he *thought* they were Jedi. Two were definitely in Jedi robes—both human, one with a beard, the other clean-shaven—while their companions were female, a Tholothian with a lightsaber at her hip and a Kuranu with no weapon that Amarant could see.

"Captain!" the clean-shaven male repeated, stopping the Neimoidian, who in turn told Amarant to wait. He considered slithering for it, but knew he wouldn't make it to the ship before Snat laid him out with that damn blaster rifle.

"Master Mann?" the security chief said, sounding irritated. "I need to get the prisoner on the transport as soon as possible."

"That will have to wait, Captain," the bearded human said, staring up at Amarant. "We have questions that need to be answered."

"I have nothing to say to you, Jedi," Amarant hissed defiantly, drawing himself up to his full height, not that it seemed to faze the young Kuranu who shoved past Snat to address him directly.

"You don't understand. Your people, they stole something from my ship, something that could be fashioned into a terrible weapon."

"Klerin, please," the bearded one said, grabbing her arm to stop her.

The Kuranu shrugged him off. "No, Master Gios. The stakes are too high. If the Nihil realize what they have—"

"What we have is victory," Amarant cackled. "Look at you, *Master* Gios. Your face bashed in, your precious robes covered in blood."

That got a reaction. Not from Gios, but the one they'd called Mann. The Jedi looked like he was seething where he stood. Good, Amarant wanted him to squirm. Amarant wanted him to get angry. Angry people made mistakes. Angry people got dead.

"Silence," Mann said, and Amarant knew he had him.

"Why should I? You lost, Jedi, you just don't realize it yet. But you will, when you remember what we did. When you remember how many people died at the hands of the Storm."

"Silence!"

Amarant cried out as he was thrown back into a column with such force that the stone cracked and the binders around his wrists snapped open. Not that he could escape. He couldn't even breathe. It felt like a fist closing around his windpipe, throttling the life from him.

Mann stepped forward, a hand raised in front of him, the fingers curled into a claw.

"Take that back," he spat. "Take it all back."

All Amarant could do was choke.

"Elzar, please!" Gios shouted, running forward to grab the maniac's arm. Mann's other hand shot up and Gios was sent flying as if he'd been backhanded by a Gamorrean. Captain Snat raised his blaster, but it was yanked from his hands and tossed aside, the Tholothian's lightsaber going the same way. The woman dived forward only for her head to snap violently to the right. She went down and never got up.

Only the Kuranu remained on her feet, a shaking hand raised to the furious Jedi.

"Please. Don't kill him," she begged. "We need to know where to find the Nihil."

Behind them, Snat sneered. "She's right, Mann. Do this and I'll report you to the Jedi Council. You'll never wear those robes agai—"

An invisible hand punched the Neimoidian in the chest, knocking him back.

"Not bad," Amarant wheezed. "You'd make a good Nihil."

The pressure on his throat increased.

"Tell me the location of the Nihil base," Mann hissed, drool dropping from his bottom lip. "Tell me now or I'll snap your neck."

Finally the Kuranu moved, slamming her fists against the Jedi. "Stop it! If you kill him we'll never be able to retrieve the weapon." Mann raised a hand, not to push her back, but to protect his face.

Amarant felt the grip ease. He could move. He brought up his tail, slashing at the Jedi with his stinger. Mann jumped back, stumbling over the prone Tholothian. By the time he'd righted himself, Amarant had the Kuranu in his pincers, his jaws dangerously close to her throat. "One false move, Jedi, and I paint this courtyard with her blood. Do you understand?"

To her credit the woman didn't struggle, whimpering quietly for him not to hurt her.

"You're safe with me," Amarant hissed as he started to slide toward the waiting ship. "Who else is on board?" he asked the Jedi who was standing, palms raised, unable to get to him without going through the woman.

"No one," Mann snarled. "The security detail has yet to check in."

"Then make sure they don't."

They had reached the ramp now.

"Leave the woman and we'll let you go."

Amarant clicked his fangs together, the nearest his species ever got to laughter. "I don't think so. If I so much as see a Vector, she dies, do you understand?"

Mann's shoulders slumped. *Now* he knew he was beaten. "Yeah."

They were at the top of the ramp, the Kuranu a living shield in case Mann changed his mind. He didn't, and Amarant hit the hatch control as soon as they were on board.

"Bye-bye," he jeered, as the hatch clanged shut.

The girl screamed as Amarant threw her to the side, the cry cut short as she stumbled, her head cracking against the bulkhead. She slid to the floor, but Amarant didn't care if she was dead or merely unconscious. She had served her purpose. Now all he had to do was get away.

"Do you think he bought it?" Elzar asked as the shuttle blasted out of the temple.

"You mean before or after he took Klerin?" Ty said, punching him in the arm.

"Ow!"

"Sorry, did that hurt? Why did you let him take her?"

"I didn't exactly have a choice."

Stellan stepped in, "recovered" from his battering, to break up the fight.

"It wasn't Elzar's fault. We had to let him get away."

"With a hostage?" Snat demanded, jabbing a finger at Elzar. "And was there any need to hit me so hard in the chest?"

"We had to make it believable," Elzar protested.

"Yes," Ty said, her arms crossed to stop her from whacking him again. "Klerin looked particularly scared. You're still all the same. Playing games with people's lives."

Stellan made sure his lightsaber was still in its holster. "No one's playing. Certainly not us."

"And besides," Elzar said, countering Stellan's gravity with what he hoped was a winning smile. "You're going to be on hand to make sure Klerin's safe."

Ty's eyes went wide as she put a hand to her chest. "Me? How do you work that out?"

Elzar answered her question with one of his own. "How long is it since you flew a Vector?"

Chapter Sixty-Six

The *Elegencia*

"Time to arrival?"

Chell Trambin checked his systems. "Exiting the Path in five."

"And the other ships? Has the Tempest signaled?"

"Not yet, Runner."

Pan grunted. This in itself wasn't unusual. Ship-to-ship communication while on a Path was tricky, but they would all be there, he was sure of that.

"Coming up on target," the pilot reported. "Entering realspace in three . . . two . . ."

The *Elegencia* thudded to a halt in front of Cyclor, a handful of Cloud and Strikeships exiting the Path at the same time.

Pan's mouth dropped open. He leaned forward, his command lounger creaking beneath his weight.

"What is this?"

The shipyards stretched in front of them, the hangars glittering in starlight, but they weren't alone.

"Sir, those are—"

Pan completed Chell's sentence with a snarl. "Skyhawks."

And that wasn't all. There were fighters from a dozen different worlds. Hosnian Prime. Corellia. Sullust. Iskalon. Even Shili.

"Where is the rest of the Tempest?" Pan barked, checking his displays.

Chell looked to his scopes. "Multiple signals coming in. It must be them now."

"Show me."

Holosquares appeared in front of him, feeding images from the aft. One by one, ships jumped into the system, but none of them were Nihil. They were Republic Longbeams and Jedi Vectors. Lots of Jedi Vectors, each cradled in a triangular hyperframe.

"It's a trap," Pan spluttered, the splutter turning into yet another hacking cough. This time there was no hiding the blood that splattered on the deck.

"They knew we were coming," the Strike at the comm station groaned.

"But how?" Chell asked.

It was a good question, but not the one they should be asking, mainly because Pan already knew the answer.

Where the hell was Lourna Dee?

"All wings, report in."

A litany of names came over the comm. Nib. Burryaga. Bakari. Porter. Vernestra and Imri. Other call signs followed, the Republic commanders adding their names to the roster, as did the members of the fleet that the Cyclorrian shipmaster had assembled following the bogus communication with Tia Toon. The Nihil had taken the bait, just as Stellan knew they would.

Only one thing worried him, a concern that Porter Engle immediately put into words: "Is that it?"

"Must admit, I thought there'd be more of 'em," Nib chimed in from her own Vector.

"Maybe there aren't as many as we thought?" Vernestra offered.

"Or they lost more over Valo than first estimated," Engle added.

"Then how about we add to that number?" said a new voice. It was the commander of the lead Togruta warship, keen to get the fight under way, but Stellan couldn't give the word, not until the Nihil took the first shot.

They didn't have long to wait. Completely surrounded, the Nihil had no alternative but to scrap their way out. Stellan felt the gunners scramble for their posts long before the turbocannons fired. *Now* they could act.

"All units, move in," Stellan said as calmly as he could into the comm. "The Force is with us."

Chapter Sixty-Seven

The *Gaze Electric,* above Grizal

"**A**re we ready for the final test, Ro?"

Were they? Ro wasn't sure. He had planned this for so long, studying the texts he had found in his father's collection, texts the old tyrant had forgotten, gathering dust in the *Gaze* library. The great Asgar Ro, the man who had remade himself, remade the Nihil. The man whom Marchion had found bleeding out in the Great Hall.

Help me, Marchion... please.

Such a fall from grace. In life Asgar had never treated his son with kindness, never treated him with respect. It was somewhat fitting that, bleeding out in his quarters, he was forced to beg that same son for help.

Ro hadn't even crouched down, standing over his father. "Who did this to you?"

Blood had spilled from Asgar's mouth as he replied. "I . . . I don't know."

"A shame," Ro had said. "That at least would have been useful."

The first kick had dislocated the dying man's jaw; the second fractured his cheek. The third had probably killed him, but there was no way to be sure. As for the fourth and the fifth and the sixth and the seventh, well, they'd just been for fun.

He'd stood there for an hour, not out of respect, but to commit the scene to memory. This was how he would remember Asgar Ro, not the larger-than-life despot who had made his life a misery, but a battered slab of meat.

"Marchion?"

Kisma Uttersond was eager. Ro could understand that. He should have felt the same, but something was holding him back, his father's voice in the back of his mind. Even after all these years, it was as if the old man was standing at his shoulder, his face little more than pulp.

Why are you doing this, Marchion? Do you really know? Don't you realize how much will change? Are you ready?

He looked up, meeting the imprisoned Jedi's bloodshot eyes through the laboratory window.

Look at him, Marchion. He knows. He knows how weak you are.

"Shut up!"

"What?"

Ro snapped around. Uttersond was staring at him. Confused. Concerned. "I only asked."

"We are ready when I say we are ready."

That had been foolish. The last thing he wanted was for the Chadra-Fan to think that he was talking to dead men. Asgar was gone. This was his moment now.

The Jedi's eyes burned into the back of his head.

Ro reached for his helmet, slipping it over his face. He needed to be the Eye. He needed to be strong, not like his father, or Loden Greatstorm, or Kisma bloody Uttersond.

The comm buzzed in his ear. "What is it?" he snapped, a little too forcibly.

A frosty voice came over the line. Lourna Dee. "A ship is approaching."

"So?"

STAR WARS: THE RISING STORM

"It is Republic."

They had been found? How? And why was the woman bothering him with it when the course of action should be clear.

"Then make sure they never land, Lourna. Shoot the damn ship down."

Lourna Dee let the channel go dead. This was not going as she'd planned. Reviving Pan had been a risk, but one she had enjoyed, especially seeing the meathead's face when he thought she was going to follow him to Cyclor. Getting most of his Tempest to stay on Grizal—that had been easy enough. After all, he'd left them to face the Togrutas on Valo. But now, now she'd wanted to comm into the *Elegencia,* to gloat, to hear Pan choking on his own blood, if Ro's toxin hadn't stopped his diseased heart. The cypanid hadn't cured him, it had only prolonged his agony.

As for Ro . . . Lourna hadn't decided what to do about Ro yet . . . she'd prepared the lies for when he found that Pan had survived, that he had taken the *Elegencia* to raid Cyclor . . . and that he was now stardust. Depending on how he took the news, Lourna had planned on using it as leverage, or to proceed with her plan of taking the *Gaze* and the Oracle. She didn't need a Dowutin to do that, and if Ro tried to stop her, then she'd rip that hidden syringe from his wrist and take out his eyes one at a time.

The only thing she hadn't prepared for was Grizal being discovered. This was a wrinkle she could do without.

Lourna switched channels on the comm, hailing the Nihil that had alerted her to the incoming craft. "Target the enemy. Bring it down."

"Tempest Runner," the gunner posted at the laser tower responded. "They are signaling. It is Amarant."

Amarant. Another surprise, and one more to her liking. The Lamproid had been one of her most trusted Clouds. She was not what anyone would call a sentimental woman—not if they wanted to keep their skull connected to their spinal column—but leaving Amarant behind had been a particularly bitter pill to swallow. She had plans for the venomous slug, but had thought him dead. And now here he was, returning to base. He would make Storm for this. Unless . . .

She grabbed a disruptor rifle, barking into the comm as she made for the door. "Let him land, but scan the ship."

"For what?"

Wasn't that obvious? Was everyone trying to annoy her today? "For tracking devices, you idiot. Get it done, now."

"Up!"

Amarant grabbed the Kuranu girl, his serrated pincer threatening to break the delicate skin of her arm.

"Don't hurt me. Please."

Pathetic.

The transport's ramp splashed into a puddle of water as it lowered. Amarant sniffed as he dragged the female from the ship. It was raining again. He didn't mind. He liked it. It reminded him of Florn. Amarant could never return home, not after he'd murdered his entire nest, but Grizal was the next best thing. Before the attack on Valo, he'd taken to hunting the rexx-boars in the forest. Maybe he would hunt later today, after he had delivered his prize.

At least the female hadn't been a nuisance as he'd made the long journey to the base. Without a Path, Amarant had been forced to make a series of short jumps, which had taken an age but which the Republic shuttle had handled admirably. It was a good little ship. Perhaps he'd ask Lourna if he could retrofit it with a Path engine and some proper guns?

And there she was, in the middle of the exercise yard, not caring a jot about the rain that hammered against her mask. He'd tried to hate her for leaving him behind, but he knew he would've done the same in her position. She'd said it often enough: Survival was all that mattered.

"I've brought you a present, Dee," he said, shoving the Kuranu forward. The female slipped on the wet rockcrete, landing at Dee's feet.

"*Two* presents," the Tempest Runner said, indicating the Republic ship with her disruptor. "Where'd you steal that?"

Amarant puffed out his thorax proudly. "From the Jedi outpost."

Dee's tone barely changed, but Amarant knew she was impressed. "And who is this?"

The female spoke before he could reply. "My name is Klerin Chekkat."

"She spoke of a great weapon," Amarant added quickly, not wanting the girl to steal his thunder.

"Did she now?" Amarant imagined her eyes flicking up to him. "And you weren't followed?"

Amarant shook his segmented head. "No. I told them I would hurt the female."

"And you checked for homing beacons?"

His long tongue went dry.

"Well?"

"I . . . I didn't think."

Lourna Dee brought up her rifle and fired. Amarant howled as he lost an arm, the flesh dissolving in the disruptor's beam. She shifted, firing again. Another arm vanished.

The barrel didn't drop.

"Have you finished wailing?"

Amarant nodded, the charred stumps burning in the rain.

"You're lucky it's not on full power." Dee didn't shout. She didn't have to. "You could have brought the entire Jedi Order to our door."

Amarant forced himself to speak. "I am sorry, Runner."

"Sorry?" Another squeeze of the trigger. Another limb gone. "Lucky for you, we scanned that junkheap before you landed."

"And did you find anything?"

"You wouldn't be breathing if we did. You were lucky. Now, hiss off. I don't want to see you again today."

Dee turned, slinking back to the main building. "Bring the girl."

A couple of Nihil had been watching from the shelter of the doors.

Now they scuttled over and grabbed Klerin, dragging her after Lourna. The girl didn't struggle.

Amarant watched them go and started to plot his revenge.

The Republic transport was silent save for the constant drum of rain. The ramp was still open, but no one came to investigate. It wouldn't be long. Soon the Nihil would be swarming over the craft to see what they could salvage or adapt to their own nefarious uses.

A panel slid aside in the hold's low ceiling, and Indeera Stokes jumped down, followed by her Padawan and his charhound.

Bell rolled his shoulders, trying to loosen the stiffness caused by hiding in a maintenance shaft for so long. Indeera had only opened the panel once to check on Klerin. The unconscious Kuranu had stirred at the noise of Indeera jumping down and panicked, but Stokes had calmed the young woman, promising they would keep her safe. Klerin's kidnapping had not been part of the plan, and Bell had wanted to spring from their hiding place the moment the Lamproid dragged her from the ship, but Indeera had placed a hand on his chest, indicating for him to wait. He knew she was right. They would have lost the element of surprise, no matter how much it bothered him to place Klerin in even more danger than she already was. He gripped the leather-bound lightsaber Stellan Gios had given him to replace his own, which still languished at the bottom of Lake Lonisa. It had belonged to Stellan's Master, the great Rana Kant, and was an honor to carry. Force willing, he would prove himself worthy of her legacy.

"What now?" he whispered as Indeera peered through the hatch.

"We gather intel."

"And see that Klerin is safe."

"Of course. Do you know how to shield yourself in the Force?"

Bell thought back to the rooftop on Valo. "I've seen Elzar Mann do it. I think I understand the principle."

"Gently encourage those around you to look in the opposite

direction so you can pass unnoticed. I can help at first, but you'll need to take over as we move deeper into the camp."

Bell steadied himself. "I am ready."

"For this and so much more."

Indeera reached into her robes, pulling out a small metal device. "I have to say, the Nihil are smarter than I expected. Scanning for a homing beacon *before* the Lamproid came in to land. That's impressive."

She looked for a good spot and clamped the device behind a bulkhead.

"I mean, it's not like anyone would signal once a ship is safely on the ground . . ."

She flicked a switch, and the tiny unit began to flash. Indeera and Bell exchanged a smile and sneaked from the ship.

Many systems away, Elzar's console beeped. He smiled, feeding the coordinates into his Vector's hyperframe. The frame's navidroid bleeped a response, confirming the route was laid in.

Elzar raised an eyebrow as he read the data scrolling across the Vector's scope. "This is going to be bumpy."

"The way you fly?" Ty muttered from the jump seat. "Why am I not surprised?"

He chuckled, firing the thrusters. "The Force will be with us."

"Good," she replied. "It'll need to be."

Elzar swung the Vector around and shot into hyperspace.

Chapter Sixty-Eight

The *Elegencia*

The *Elegencia*'s navigational console exploded into a blaze of light and fire. Chell was dead before he hit the deck, his blackened corpse rolling to lie beside Pan's lounger. He looked down into Chell's dead eyes and cursed Lourna Dee's name.

His ship . . . his beautiful ship . . . was outnumbered. The few Storms that had made it to the rendezvous were already gone. The Jedi didn't shoot to kill unless they had to, but the rest of the fleet had no such compunction. Lourna had served him up to them on a plate, the little Twi'lek *schutta*!

The ship lurched, nearly throwing him from his seat. The guns were still firing, those loyal to him still at their posts.

More fool them.

Pan hauled himself up, his head spinning. He was sick, he knew that, and he knew what was killing him, but he wasn't going to die here. He tried to make it to the back of the flight deck, his vision blurring. A young Bith ran up to him, one side of his face burned beyond recognition, as he babbled in his native tongue.

"Tempest Runner, what—"

Pan punched the Bith aside, hearing his bulbous skull crack. That's what you got for standing in his way. That's what Lourna Dee would find out for herself.

Had Ro been in on it? If that was the case, she was a bigger fool than he thought. The bastard was dismantling the Tempests one by one, remaking the Nihil in his own image. She would be next, unless he got to her first.

He was out in a corridor now, racing as fast as his bulk would take him. An Emmerian Cloud was blocking his way. Pan pulled the blaster from his leg holster, and the Cloud hit the deck, minus a head.

No one knew about the escape pod. Not Pan's crew, not Lourna, and definitely not Ro. It was fitted with a Path that Ro's father had given him years ago, programmed to return to the one place that no Dowutin ever wanted to go. Sure, launching it would rip the belly out of the *Elegencia,* but the ship was already dead.

He was breathing hard when he reached the secret door, harder still when he had to rip it open, the mechanism having jammed. Once, twice, he almost gave up as he hauled himself through a crawl space that was only just big enough. Gods, he'd never sweated this much. His heart was beating far too fast, and his skin felt like it was too big. Was it too big? Was that even possible?

Finally he found the hatch and swung into the pod. Collapsed into it was probably a better description, but he was in it all the same. The rest of the *Elegencia* had been defined by its luxury. Style over substance? Maybe, but the pod . . . the pod was all about function.

He couldn't relax as he strapped himself into the seat. Struggling to focus, he sealed the hatch and fired up the power cells. Coordinates flashed up on the nav screen. Pan gargled a phlegm-choked laugh. It had been centuries since he'd left Dowut to forge a new life for himself. Who would have thought that he'd be returning after all this time to do so again? He wondered if any of his family were still alive. At least killing them would cheer him up.

The Path control beeped. They were ready to fly.

Pan closed his eyes for a moment, listening to the death throes of his ship, dreaming of the victory that should have been his. He had written his name across the galaxy, and now Ro would take the credit, Lourna at his side. So be it. Pan was dying, he'd accepted that now, but he'd keep going until he had mounted both of their duplicitous heads on a spike.

Pan Eyta slammed his hand down on the Path control, and the rear of the *Elegencia* blew out as the escape pod punched its way into the maelstrom.

High above Cyclor, the battle raged on, Pan's Tempest fighting to the bitter end.

No one even knew he was gone.

Chapter Sixty-Nine

The *Gaze Electric*

"Ro, please. This is intolerable."

Ro silenced Uttersond with a raised finger. Eagerness was one thing, but petulance was very much another. Granted, the Chadra-Fan had no idea what Ro was watching on his helmet's internal display, but that hardly mattered. They were ready when he said and not before.

Ro watched as a Kuranu woman was dragged into Dee's chamber, the images broadcast from Lourna's own mask, positioned strategically nearby. Zeetar was with her, beady eyes peering at the newcomer. At least the Talpini wouldn't go the same way as Pan. Zeetar knew his place. Ro had wondered how Lourna would react to Pan's death, how she would have reacted to the existence of the hidden injector at his wrist. The device of his own devising, constructed after Pan's failed coup before Valo. Filled with a fatal cocktail of Uttersond's deadliest toxins, more potent than anything they had pumped into the Jedi. It had performed admirably, although the element of surprise was now gone, a spur-of-the-moment decision on his part. Ro hadn't expected Pan even to return from Valo. The charge he had planted in the *Elegencia*'s primary bomber bay was supposed to have rid him of the

Dowutin, rigged to detonate when the battle cruiser attempted to jump back to Grizal. The explosion would be blamed on damage caused in the raid and the danger of Path travel. Like Kassav before him, Pan would have become a martyr whose name Ro could invoke to stir loyalty in the Dowutin's retinue. But the device had been destroyed by the Jedi in the battle over Valo—yet another reason to curse their name. When Ro had seen Pan swaggering across the exercise yard . . . Still, the traitorous oaf was dead now, and the remaining two Tempest Runners had fallen in line. No one would challenge Ro ever again.

"Amarant mentioned a weapon." Ro turned his attention back to the interrogation, Lourna Dee's voice tinny over the comlink. The Kuranu's reply, on the other hand, was surprisingly strong.

"Yes. A disruptor field capable of disarming energy weapons."

"What kind of energy weapons?"

The Kuranu was standing tall, despite being flanked by two of Lourna's most imposing guards. "Every kind you can imagine and more besides. Blasters, disruptors, even lightsabers."

Now, that *was* interesting.

On the screen, Zeetar scurried closer, leaving the powersuit he had been tinkering with when the prisoner had been brought in. "And where is this disruptor field?"

"With the Republic."

"Then what good is it to us?" Lourna had asked the very question Ro was thinking.

"Because that is just the prototype, powered by raw recainium."

"Then I hope it poisons them." Zeetar turned back to his suit. "Kill her, Lourna. She's wasting our time."

Ro was inclined to agree. A pity. He killed the vid feed and looked around for Uttersond, but the Chadra-Fan was nowhere to be seen. Ro's stomach churned. Surely the idiot hadn't . . .

He turned to the viewing window as Uttersond's body smashed through it, shattering the glass into a thousand razor-sharp shards.

It's almost time.

Loden had waited long enough, listening to the voice in his head, enduring the affront of the Nihil's experiments. His mind wasn't clear, not by a long shot, but it was more focused than it had been in months. He had known the moment had come before the voice in his head prompted him, when the Chadra-Fan had shuffled into the lab in his grubby white coat, muttering beneath his breath. The lights had gone off, the sounds silenced, and the scientist had limped into the circle of equipment, a hypodermic in his filthy hands.

"Release me."

Loden wasn't even sure if he had said the words out loud. The Chadra-Fan certainly ignored him, priming the hypo.

"You will release me."

He had tried this so many times since his incarceration, trying desperately to influence the minds of Ro and his pet scientist, but it had never worked, not once.

This time felt different.

It is different. They are near. He is near.

He? Who did the voice mean? Surely not Ro. Surely . . .

And then Loden felt it, a presence he hadn't felt since . . .

All at once he was back in the *Nova,* talking to Bell over the comm.

"I look forward to celebrating your elevation, Jedi Knight Zettifar."

"Master . . . thank you."

"I'm not your Master anymore, Bell. You're a Jedi Knight."

Bell. Could it really be him, here of all places? No. Surely not. It was too much to hope for.

Hope is all we have, Loden. You can do this. You have to.

Loden watched a drop of sedative squirt from the hypo as the scientist tested the needle.

"You. Will. Release. Me."

The Chadra-Fan paused, a look of confusion crossing his batlike features as the syringe slipped from his fingers to clatter to the floor.

"I will . . . release you . . ."

Uttersond. That was his name. Loden could remember. He could remember everything they had done to him. All the tests. All the torture. It had to be Bell. Loden was drawing strength from his former Padawan, from their connection. Could Bell feel it, too?

The Chadra-Fan reached over to a nearby console, flicking a switch with a hesitant hand. The binders around Loden's limbs snapped open, and he pitched forward, throwing out weak arms to break his fall.

Uttersond gasped, the spell broken. Loden scrabbled forward, reaching for the hypo. The Chadra-Fan kicked at it, sending the injector scooting out of Loden's reach, turning to shout for his master.

"Ro! The subject!"

Loden pushed out with the Force and Uttersond flew through the observation window, crashing into Ro.

Now. Move.

Loden leapt through the broken window, the Force flowing strength into limbs that had been dormant for too long. He stumbled on the other side, falling forward, his legs unable to support his weight. He fell to his side, trying to push himself up, only to find himself face-to-face with a yellow blade.

"There's no escape," Marchion Ro rasped from the other side of the misappropriated weapon, Loden's vision squirming.

He lies.

But Loden knew the truth. He couldn't escape. Not on his own. He needed help. He needed . . .

"Bell."

Chapter Seventy

The Grizal camp

"Master," Bell whispered.

Indeera looked at her Padawan, warning him to remain quiet. Sneaking into the complex had been trickier than she'd thought. They'd found Klerin being questioned by the woman that Amarant had identified as Dee, but Bell was strangely distracted, struggling to cloud his presence, no matter how many times she tried to show him.

And now there was this, speaking aloud as they hid behind a doorway. Even Ember was keeping quiet. Why couldn't he?

"I'm sorry," Bell muttered, backing away.

Indeera reached out, grabbing his arm. "Where are you going?"

"It's Loden."

"What?"

Bell pulled himself free, Ember going with him. "He's alive, Indeera. I felt him say my name, here . . . now. I have to go."

She let them leave. What else could she do? The moment Bell had said Loden's name, she'd known it to be true. He was right, there was no mistaking the presence she suddenly felt as clear as if the Twi'lek were standing in front of her. It was . . . fractured, yes, but there all the same, amplified by his connection with Bell. Surely that wasn't possible. Surely the Nihil hadn't kept Loden Greatstorm prisoner for the better part of a year?

"Wait."

The word snapped Indeera back to the scene that was unfurling in Lourna Dee's chamber. Klerin had taken a step forward toward the Nihil, her voice filled with a confidence that just hadn't been there before.

"I said it was a prototype," she told Dee. "*My* prototype. My mother took credit for the device, but it was my work. As is this."

She lifted up an arm, her bangle slipping down slightly from her wrist.

"Mother is gone, but this still exists: a portable unit, powered by tolium. I tried to approach one of your . . . associates on Valo, but he tried to take it from me. He's dead now, too."

Was that a threat? This girl was full of surprises.

"Show me," Dee commanded, holding out a hand.

Klerin covered the bangle protectively. "Not until we discuss the price."

"You want to sell it to us?"

It was a shock to Indeera as well.

"Why not? The Republic has no stomach for the device, and they think you already have the plans for the prototype."

"Why?"

"Because I told them."

"I don't trust you," Dee said.

A wise decision, Indeera thought bitterly.

"How do I know you're speaking the truth?" Dee asked.

"You want a guarantee? A sign of good faith?"

"Yes."

"Well, that I can do. There are two Jedi on your base. They smuggled themselves on board the transport. A Master and her apprentice. How's that?"

"Find them," Dee yelled, bringing up her gun as the Talpini clambered into his powersuit. "Find them now!"

Indeera sighed and drew her lightsaber. Elzar needed to arrive now.

The Vector slammed into orbit over Grizal, Elzar immediately jettisoning the hyperframe so they could drop unhampered into the planetoid's atmosphere.

"Do you think they know we're here?" Ty asked.

Laser bolts streaked up at them from the jungle.

"I'll take that as a yes." He used the Force to flick open a comm channel, keeping his hands on the yoke. "Command, this is Laserbird One. We have engaged the Nihil. Location confirmed. Transmitting now."

Elzar's voice crackled over the comm, coordinates scrolling down Stellan's screen.

"Received and understood, Laserbird."

Stellan breathed a sigh of relief. Having Elzar and Ty confirm the location of the Nihil base was his idea. It wasn't that he didn't trust Indeera, but rather that he wanted to be absolutely sure before committing the rest of the drift. Beacons could be scrambled or deceived. Elzar Mann couldn't.

He changed frequency, turning his attention back to the battle. "Porter, we have contact. Can you handle things here?"

"I'm insulted you even have to ask. Go!"

Stellan transferred the coordinates to his hyperframe's navidroid.

"Red Group, you're with me. Follow my lead."

"Are we going far?" Nib asked.

"Farther than expected. Are you ready?"

Burryaga growled a reply, and Stellan's contingent peeled away from the battle.

He just hoped they'd arrive in time.

———

"Ro, we're under attack."

Loden heard the report as clearly as if it had been beamed to his own comlink. He jumped forward, bolstered by his connection to Bell. Ro lunged with the lightsaber, but it was a clumsy move, the hack of a barbarian as opposed to the graceful line of a Jedi who had trained his entire life. Loden feinted back, the tip of the stolen lightsaber burning into the deck. Ro snarled in frustration, but he had already lost the battle. He just didn't know it yet. Loden threw out an emaciated arm and grabbed at Ro's chest plate, not with shaking fingers but with something infinitely powerful. Without pausing he pulled back, the wasted muscles in his chest crying out in agony, but that was nothing compared with the pain Ro felt as he was plucked from his feet. The Nihil leader whizzed past Loden as if caught on a line, the lightsaber tumbling from his grip. The weapon never even hit the floor. Loden caught it as it tumbled, feeling the coolness of the hilt, feeling like he had come home. Ro, on the other hand, flew through the smashed window to slam into the very equipment that had kept the Jedi bound for so long.

Loden turned, fighting to stay on his feet, but still with enough energy to push down with the Force. The lights Ro and Uttersond had used to dazzle him toppled down on the Nihil leader, followed by the table where Loden had hung night and day. Anyone else would have felt satisfaction at the grunt that issued from the masked man, but Loden Greatstorm wasn't anyone. He was a Jedi Master, and he needed to find his former Padawan.

Loden was vaguely aware of Ro pushing himself up from beneath the equipment as he lurched out into the corridor, pounding the pommel of his lightsaber into the controls. The door slammed down, and Loden spun the weapon in his hand, igniting it to burn through the locking mechanism.

A million and one sounds assaulted him at once. The thrum of his blade, the rumble of distant engines, and explosions from outside, as loud and confusing as the cacophony he had endured at Uttersond's hands. He shook them away, only barely aware of where his amputated lekku should have slapped against his shoulders. He had lost so much, but he needed to move. He didn't require a voice in his head to tell him that.

Loden ran, his disrupted balance almost getting the better of him more than once, following the disembodied voice. He found a door, opened it, and stopped in his tracks, wondering if he was still seeing things.

A woman was suspended in a web of tubes and cables, her body withered, the exposed skin parched and colorless, almost like the mummies Loden's ancestors used to bury beneath the grassfields on Ryloth.

"It was you," he whispered, reverentially. "You've been talking to me."

Have I?

He blinked. Had the crone's lips moved? Could those milky eyes see him?

You must go.

"Not without you."

He went to step in through the door, only to be stopped by another wave of vertigo. He sagged against the doorframe, willing the universe to stop spinning.

I am already gone. Here, but there. Far, but near.

"What does that mean?"

He needs you. You need him. I can see it, Loden. Why can't you?

"I am Jedi." It was a statement of fact, a bulwark, to banish the nausea and set him on the right track. The woman was right. She had been right all along. He needed Bell.

My time will come soon enough. Go, Jedi. Be one.

There was a crash from down the corridor. Ro was breaking out.

"Thank you," he breathed.

No. The thanks should be yours, Loden Greatstorm. You brought me back. You showed me the way.

Loden ran.

Chapter Seventy-One

The Grizal camp

Bell ran.

Kant's lightsaber thrummed in his hand, batting back shots from the Nihil as he raced toward the large ship that hung in the skies beyond the Nihil camp. They had spotted him the moment he burst from Dee's building, which was hardly surprising. He was far too distracted to perform a mind trick. It wasn't the rain hissing down or the battle that was unfurling in the air between Elzar's lone Vector and the Nihil gun towers. No, it was the presence that was threatening to overwhelm him, a presence he'd wondered if he would ever feel again.

Loden Greatstorm, his Master, was alive.

Bell had known it on Elphrona. He'd known it at the dedication. He'd known it at Cyclor. It was why Bell hadn't been able to sense him in the Cosmic Force, because Loden wasn't there. He'd been here on that beast of a ship all this time. The craft was vast, easily larger than the *Innovator,* but it didn't matter. He'd search every single deck to find his Master if need be.

The Nihil's laserfire intensified, but Bell barely even noticed. All he cared about was getting up to that ship.

Indeera's comlink crackled, alerting Dee to her position.

Great.

The Nihil opened fire, switching her disruptor to automatic mode, the weapon chewing up the walls of the old prison, including the pillar Indeera had been using as a hiding place.

"Indeera, where are you?" It was Elzar.

"Under fire," she replied, activating her lightsaber as the guards that had flanked Klerin joined the onslaught with overcranked blasters that looked as though they should explode rather than fire. They were actually steaming with every shot.

Indeera swept a hand as if scrolling through data on a screen, plucking the smaller of the two guards from his feet so he slammed into his compatriot. They dropped to the floor in a tangle, but it would only be a short respite before they were back up and trying to murder her, if Dee's disruptor didn't get there first.

"Where's Bell?"

"A good question."

"And Klerin?" That was the Tholothian, Ty Yorrick.

Indeera looked through her whirling blade, seeing the Kuranu being grabbed by the arm by the Talpini in the powersuit.

"She's learning that the Nihil don't negotiate."

"What?"

"She sold us out."

Dee was advancing on her now, the ferocity of the disruptor fire forcing Indeera back.

"Can you get to her?"

"Klerin? Sure. Why, what are you thinking, Elzar?"

"Just do it."

The connection went dead. The man was brilliant, but boy, was he infuriating at times.

Indeera leapt, somersaulting over Dee. The woman tracked the movement, the disruptor fire arcing across the ceiling.

Indeera dropped down in front of the Talpini, slicing through the powersuit's arm before spinning to shield them all from Dee's blasts. Well, maybe not all of them. A stray bolt made it past Indeera's lightsaber, striking the Talpini. He cried out, staggering back in his powersuit as the ceiling blew in above their heads.

"Your friend's in there!"

Elzar Mann ignored Ty's outraged cry as he fired on the building, his bolts ripping through the roof below them.

The Vector streamed through the dust and smoke, coming up to race toward the huge vessel on the other side of the camp.

"It'll take more than a few lasers to take down Indeera Stokes."

"What? Like dropping a building on her?"

The canopy popped over them. Elzar swiveled in his seat. "What are you doing?"

"Checking if they're all right."

Before he could stop her, Ty vaulted out of the aircraft, igniting her lightsaber before she reached the ground. Elzar pulled the canopy back into place, noticing another saber flashing ahead. It was Bell Zettifar, running full pelt toward the colossal ship, deflecting shots from Nihil on the ground.

Where was he going?

Ahead, a hatch opened in the side of the gigantic vessel. A figure appeared in the doorway, Elzar's mouth dropping open as he realized who it was.

Rain lashed against Loden's face, the water getting into his eyes, temporarily blinding him. He reached for the side of the hatch to stop himself from falling over the edge. There was a flash from below, the unmistakable arc of a lightsaber blade.

It was Bell, running toward the *Gaze Electric* with Ember at his heels, while above them a Vector was screaming toward Ro's ship, almost level with where he was standing.

Something moved behind him. Loden whirled around to see Ro. The Nihil leader was staring at him from behind that infernal mask.

Loden raised his lightsaber, trying to ignore how the blade trembled along with his hand. In response, Ro raised his palms. A sign of surrender?

"I am unarmed. I know you, Jedi. You won't harm an unarmed man."

There was a trick coming. Loden wasn't stupid. His head may have been thumping, and he could barely stand on his feet, but he wasn't stupid.

Behind him, the Vector flew ever closer.

"Do you yield?" Loden tried to draw more strength from Bell, from the pilot of the Vector, from every Jedi in the field. It was all he could do to stay upright, his heels against the edge of the hatch, the storm raging at his back.

"Will I get a fair trial?"

"Of course."

The Nihil leader seemed to consider this for a moment, before bringing his hands together, as if expecting Loden to clap him in binders. Loden glanced down at the proffered wrists, momentarily confused. What did Ro think he was? Of course, that was his mistake. This was the trick.

Needle-sharp hypodermics sprang from devices on both of Ro's wrists, the ends glistening with poison. Ro lunged forward, slashing not at Loden's blade but at the hilt in his hand. At any other time, Loden would have been able to react, to bring his lightsaber around, to sever whatever was jutting out from Ro's wrists, but the ravages of recent months and the energy expended in his escape finally proved too much. Loden could only jump back, avoiding the needle points. During his confinement, he'd often thought that Ro was poison; now he knew it as a fact. All it would've taken was a nick. Just one nick. But the Force had shown him the danger, had saved him. It was just a pity it hadn't warned him as he jumped back into thin air.

Loden's eyes went wide as he toppled back, his arms windmilling, the lightsaber he'd only just recovered slipping from his fingers. And then he was falling with the rain. Above, he caught a glimpse of Ro peering over the edge, watching him tumble away. He imagined the hypodermics snapping back into place and then the Nihil was suddenly gone, vanished in a blaze of scarlet light as the approaching Vector unloaded its laser cannons into the open hatch.

Loden called on the Force to slow his descent, but this time the Force didn't answer. He had exhausted what little strength he had. He was finished.

Chapter Seventy-Two

The ruin of the main building, Grizal

"You saved me. After everything I did."

Don't make me regret it, Indeera thought, but contented herself with asking Klerin if she could find a way out.

"Can you find a way out?"

Elzar had brought the roof down but wasn't as good a shot as he thought he was. She would have been crushed by debris, Klerin with her, if it weren't for the Force. Now beams and rockcrete bore down on them as Klerin searched for a gap big enough to wriggle through. Indeera had her back to the Kuranu, a risk she would never have taken if the duplicitous inventor had a weapon in her hands. There were plenty of rocks on the ground, most large enough to brain a Jedi who was struggling to concentrate, but Indeera liked to believe that Klerin's sense of self-preservation would stop her from trying to kill the person who was stopping her from being crushed.

"Well?"

"Give me a moment," Klerin said, grunting as she worked. Indeera glanced over her shoulder to see the Kuranu attempting to pry apart two lumps of reinforced rockcrete.

"You'll never shift them."

"Can't you just wiggle your fingers or something?"

"Not without everything slipping. Can you?"

"Don't be facetious," Klerin snapped. "What was Mann thinking?"

"He was trying to help."

"By burying us alive?"

"Stand back."

The sudden change of tack took the Kuranu by surprise.

"What?"

"Step back from the rubble!"

"Why?"

An amethyst blade burst through the blocks, slicing down and almost catching Klerin who threw herself aside, barging into Indeera.

Dirt streamed down from above their heads.

"Careful!" Klerin screamed.

The block suddenly jerked away, a head appearing in the gap, silver tendrils framed by a silver crown.

"Can you hold it?" Ty Yorrick asked. Her fellow Tholothian was still pretty much an unknown quantity to Indeera, but at this juncture she was happy to accept any help she could get.

"Not for long. Could you—?" The rest of the request was lost as the rubble shifted, Indeera grunting with the effort of holding it all in place.

Yorrick's hand shot up, her own face creasing. "I'll try, but it's never been one of my talents."

"Then what good are you?" Klerin said, trying to shove Yorrick out of the way.

The mercenary showed her by headbutting the girl between her eyes.

"That wasn't very Jedi," Indeera said as the woman dragged the unconscious Kuranu out of the rubble.

"There's a reason for that," Yorrick responded. "Think you can make it through this gap without being trapped?"

"If you can help take the strain. On three?"

"You've got it. One."

"Two."

"Three!"

Indeera jumped forward.

The Vector pulled up, streaming over the huge ship, but Bell could only watch Loden plummet toward him. This was no training exercise and Loden wasn't controlling his descent. The older Jedi was in free fall, but Bell wasn't about to let him die, not now, not after Bell had found him again.

Bell raised his free hand, reaching out with the Force.

Loden slowed.

Behind him, feet were running and a blaster fired. Bell twisted at the waist, his lightsaber coming about. The bolt met plasma and shot harmlessly away, Bell's eyes never leaving his Master. The Nihil kept firing and Bell kept blocking, drawing Loden toward himself all the while. There was no way Bell could keep up this defense, not without letting Loden fall, even with Ember protecting their position with streams of scarlet flame. Soon a bolt would find its target. Soon the Nihil would get lucky.

Maybe not.

Above them, the Vector came about and raked its weapons along the ground.

The Nihil fell silent; no more footfalls, no more blaster bolts, his weapon skidding on the wet rockcrete. Bell sheathed his saber and broke into a run, both hands raised toward Loden. He could do this. He *would* do it.

Bell, a voice echoed in his mind.

Master, he replied.

Bell jumped, catching Loden in midair. He twisted as they slammed into the ground, absorbing the impact, not that Loden seemed to weigh anything anymore. He had been so big, so imposing, and yet now was little more than skin and bones and ... Bell drew a sharp breath as he saw what had happened to Loden's lekku. They were gone, leaving nothing but cauterized stumps.

"Look what they've done to you," Bell said, overcome with emotion. "What they've taken."

"They took nothing," Loden told him. "Nothing that matters. The important thing is what they couldn't touch. What they could never erase. You and me, Bell. The way it's supposed to be."

Loden held out a skeletal hand. Nearby something jerked on the ground. Bell looked up to see Loden's lightsaber skidding toward them from where it had fallen, its hilt finding Loden's waiting palm. The Twi'lek pushed himself up and ignited the weapon, smiling wickedly in the light of the blade. "Now point me in the direction of trouble."

Chapter Seventy-Three

The *Coruscant Dawn*, hyperspace

The *Coruscant Dawn* was on its way back to the Core, Kip's mother sitting up in the medbed she'd had installed in her office.

Kip had only left her side once since arriving at the Temple Outpost, to say goodbye to Jom at the spaceport. Jom had slipped Kip the digits of a private frequency, and Kip had pulled him close, giving the handsome young Valon a long, lingering kiss. The cam droids had recorded the entire embrace, but Kip didn't care. He'd never care about the cams again.

Stellan Gios's face was projected against the wall, as were the rest of his drift: Nib Assek, the Wookiee Burryaga, and two others Kip didn't know, a green-skinned girl and a human boy. Rhil Dairo's cam droid was recording everything, his mom having given the reporter exclusive access for as long as she wanted (subject to senatorial clearance, of course), and Kip wondered how far these images would be seen. He thought of the people who had survived the *Innovator*, Nwo, Leesa, and the rest. Then there was Madam Conserra and the poor Krantian woman who had lost everything but her son. Larep Reza had made sure they were looked after, securing them passage to wherever they wanted. Kip wondered if they were glued to the holonews or whether they wanted to hide away from the news as long as possible? He couldn't blame them if it was the latter, not after everything they'd been through.

But like it or not, history was being made here. The Nihil had struck a terrible blow, but the Jedi were striking right back.

"You're coming up to the Nihil base?" his mother asked.

"Preparing to drop out of hyperspace, ma'am," Stellan reported.

"Discover everything you can about them, Council Member. I'm not going to make the mistake of underestimating them a second time."

Stellan's jaw was set beneath his beard, the bruises along his cheek vivid in the flickering hololight. "None of us are."

"May the Force be with you all, Master Gios. For light and life."

The assembled Jedi repeated the mantra as one—"For light and life"—and the holos flickered out.

Lina Soh leaned back into her pillows and squeezed Kip's hand.

"You okay, Mom?"

She smiled weakly at him, suddenly looking older than she ever had before. Kip glanced up. Rhil had angled T-9 away from the bed.

"I will be, kiddo. I will be. Just stay with me for a while longer, yeah?"

"I'm not going anywhere," Kip told the most powerful woman in the galaxy, meaning every word.

Nihil ships were scrambling into space as Stellan's drift burst out of hyperspace.

"It's about time!" Elzar commed up from the planet below.

"I thought you could handle it."

"I can. I just didn't want you to miss all the fun."

Stellan knew it was the adrenaline talking. At least he hoped it was. Letting Elzar pretend to tap into the dark side with the Lamproid had been dangerous enough, but Stellan wondered if sending him into a potential battle had been the best decision. Still, it was done now. He had already planned a trip to Jedha for the both of them as soon as the time was right, perhaps even gaining special dispensation to visit the Kyber Mirrors beneath the Dome of Deliverance. Usually the Priests of Phirma only opened the mirrors on Reflection Day, but Stellan would pull a few strings, not only for Elzar, but for himself, too. They had a lot to learn together, especially now.

"How are they doing that?" Vern asked as the Nihil ships vanished into hyperspace at altitudes that should've torn them apart.

"We'll find out," Stellan promised his former Padawan, thinking of the data that had been rescued from the sunken *Innovator*. Vam Targes's legacy would be assured, Stellan had no doubt.

He led them down into the clouds, the drift feathering out into a standard V-formation. "Stop as many ships from leaving as possible. We want prisoners to question."

"And their leaders?" Nib asked.

"If the Force wills it." The sight of the Dee woman chasing after the REW played across his memory. "Support the Jedi on the ground and join them if necessary."

Burry mewed his understanding.

"Oh, and Vernestra?" Stellan added, unable to resist.

"Yes, Stellan?"

"Try to keep your Vector in one piece."

"We will!" Imri replied on behalf of his Master.

"I'm glad to hear it, Padawan Cantaros."

He felt a playful nudge in the Force, pleased to know that Vernestra had taken his teasing in the spirit it had been meant. He had complete faith in her, despite her ever-increasing reputation for wrecking ships. Talk about history repeating. As Elzar never failed to remind him, Stellan hadn't been a natural pilot back when they were Padawans. Thankfully some things improved with age.

He dipped down, the drift following to emerge in the middle of a downpour. Smoke was billowing up from a base far below them, a gargantuan battle cruiser hovering above the devastation. Where in Tython's name did the Nihil get their ships?

Lourna glanced behind her as she raced for her shuttle. The Jedi fighters were sweeping in low, skimming the treetops as they prepared to fire. She'd already given the word to abandon the base. There was no way they could win this fight, not now. Most of her Tempest had already scattered, taking to the Paths where they would wait for her word. For all she knew, Zeetar was dead, crushed in the rubble of the main building, not that she was going to go back to check. If he survived, great, if not another Tempest Runner would be found. That was the way of it. Ro probably already had a list of sycophants to choose from.

Not that the Eye seemed to care that his precious base was going up in flames. The *Gaze Electric* hung in the air in front of them, its guns silent. Why wasn't Ro responding? The *Gaze* had weapons capable of targeting an ant from high orbit. A handful of Vectors shouldn't have been a problem, and yet Ro was holding back. Was it another test, to see who survived? Maybe she'd backed the wrong fathier. Maybe she should have sided with Pan. It was academic now. Pan was dead, but she was very much alive and intended to stay that way.

"Treacherous witch."

For a moment, Lourna thought that she'd been wrong, that it was Pan, back from Cyclor to take his revenge. But it wasn't the Dowutin who lunged at her from behind a power generator, but the slithering bulk of Quin Amarant that dropped on her with such speed that she slipped, falling beneath him. "*Believed* in you!"

She twisted, attempting to throw him off, the Lamproid's stinger striking the ground beside her. That was too close. Amarant's remaining pincers cut through her armor, digging deep. Lourna cried out in pain, one hand holding his heavy head back, her arm locked.

Lights flashed to her right. A Vector was coming in from the direction of the *Gaze,* close to the ground, its lasers churning up the ground toward them. Lourna rolled, taking Amarant with her. The Lamproid screamed as his body was ripped apart by the Vector's fire, his thick coils providing just enough defense as the Vector screamed past. Lourna kicked out, pushing Amarant's pulped remains from her, and scrambled up, one thought in her mind—she needed to get on that shuttle.

Marchion Ro came around with a start. The air lock was a mess, sparking cables hanging from the ceiling above his head, the bulkheads twisted and blackened. He had only a vague memory of the Vector firing on him as Loden tumbled from the open hatch. The sudden flare of the laser, followed by blazing heat. He must have thrown himself to the deck at the last minute, his armor saving his life. Not that it mattered. All that mattered was that he'd survived.

He looked up to see his father's ruined face leering down at him. *You think you're so clever. So unstoppable. Indomitable Marchion. Indestructible Marchion. You have no idea how weak you are.*

Ro grabbed one of the cables, pulling himself up. Weak or not, he had no time for ghosts.

He stumbled ahead, grabbing the edge of the hatch to stop himself pitching forward. His breath rasped within his helmet. The heat from the lasers must have scored his lungs. No matter. What he saw was so much worse. The camp lay in ruins, fires burning on the ground. And within the smoke, the accursed flash of plasma blades. One in particular caught his eye, wielded by a dark-skinned Jedi far below, little more than a boy. He was engaged in a fight with two lowly Strikes, batting back their blaster bolts, while beside him stood . . .

No.

No, it could not be.

Loden Greatstorm fought alongside the young Jedi, his lightsaber back in his hands, the lightsaber that by rights belonged to Ro. How could the Twi'lek be alive after everything they'd done to him? Why wouldn't he break?

That is why you should fear them, his father whispered in his ear. *They are indomitable.* They *are unstoppable.*

"We shall see," Ro rasped, his voice loud in his helmet. He reached beneath his cloak, pulling the artifacts he had gathered, the first from his father's treasures, the second from the Kharvashark Ruins. Finally, it was time to put his prize to the test. The Leveler had proved powerful enough while encased in ice. He could only imagine how glorious it would be now that it was free.

No, Asgar said, the old man's voice brimming with fear. *Don't do this. It will be the end of you.*

Ro laughed. "This is why you're dead, Father, and I live. This is not the end. It is only the beginning."

He brought the two halves together, twisting them until they attached, forming a rod that hadn't been seen for generations. His father screamed, but Ro wasn't listening, not anymore. He could almost feel the Leveler baying, deep within the *Gaze*. How hungry it would be, after all those years unable to move, frozen deep beneath Rystan. Now it would feed.

His hands shaking with anticipation, Ro pressed a button on his chest plate. Deep beneath him a trap sprang free with a resounding clang. The artifact glowed brighter than ever, calling the Leveler, guiding its path as it bounded from its cage, claws clattering on the deck plates, breath ragged and guttural.

Ro stepped toward the hatch, the wind catching his cloak. He watched the Jedi cleaning up the camp, Loden and his apprentice, the Vectors twisting in the sky.

"Look at you all," he wheezed. "So noble. So brave. You have no idea what's coming."

Chapter Seventy-Five

Grizal

"That's her, Master. That's the Nihil commander."

Lourna Dee was running for a waiting shuttle, her lekku trailing behind her.

Loden looked confused. "*She's* the Nihil commander? But I thought . . ."

Bell didn't give him time to complete his sentence, breaking into a run to intercept the woman. "We can't let her get away."

Bell felt like laughing, even in the midst of such chaos. This was the way it was meant to be, back with his Master. His *real* Master. He meant no disrespect to Indeera Stokes. She'd taught him well, but now Loden was back. The two of them would stand together now, Bell supporting Loden, helping him recover. The scars would heal; even his lekku could be replaced with cybernetic parts. Bell would nurse Loden back to his full strength, just as the Force had planned all along.

"Bell," Loden wheezed as they ran into the cluster of docked ships. "You go ahead. I . . . I can't keep up."

Ember whimpered as Loden stumbled, his lightsaber spluttering out. Bell spun around, catching him before he could fall.

"No. We can do this together." Bell pressed his forehead against Loden's own. "Do you hear me? The Force is strong."

Loden fought for breath. "The Force is strong. Yes. You're right."

Engines fired behind them. Bell looked up, seeing a shuttle rising from its pad.

"Dee's on that ship. I know it."

"Then we must stop her."

Loden pushed himself, raising a shaking hand in the direction of the shuttle's thrusters. Bell mirrored the movement, reaching out with the Force.

"The Force is strong," he repeated.

Loden nodded. "And so are we."

Marchion Ro watched as Lourna's ship stalled in the air as if it had been caught in a tractor beam, its engine straining. He could imagine her behind the controls, cursing as she realized there was no escape.

The Jedi have her, Marchion. See their power. Fear them.

"Pity them," he wheezed.

He tapped the side of his helmet, opening a vid stream on his heads-up display.

What are you seeing?

"What you never could," Ro told the figment of his imagination. "Uttersond grafted a cam onto its back."

Then he's a fool. You're a fool.

"Tell that to the Leveler."

Ro watched the cam feed, seeing corridors he recognized, not far away. He could hear it now, growling, bestial. Insatiable.

For a second Ro saw himself in the cam as the Leveler tore into the air lock, but the creature didn't want him. He stepped back as it rushed past and, howling, leapt from the ship.

Elzar felt a tremor in the Force and came about. A shuttle was hanging in the air in front of the warship, its engines burning bright. He grinned as he realized what was holding it tight. Bell was on the ground, Loden Greatstorm beside him. They were struggling, the act of stopping the shuttle no mean task, but they were together again.

The universe had been put right.

Something caught his eye, on the edge of the battle cruiser. It was the open hatch he'd blasted, no doubt saving Loden's life in the process. Unbelievably the figure in the armor was still standing, but for a split second Elzar thought he saw something else, something hunkered down on all fours, throwing itself from the air lock.

Elzar's vision flared. Suddenly he wasn't in the Vector anymore, he was back on Starlight writhing on the floor as images of the future tore through his brain. He cried out in confusion, unwittingly pushing down on the flight stick. Why was the Force punishing him like this? The prediction had come true, at least part of it. The Nihil had all but razed Valo to the ground, killing thousands in the process. It was over. It was done.

Wasn't it?

Elzar's Vector plunged nose-first into the ground below.

The explosion, whatever it was, rumbled beneath Bell's feet. It might as well have been a planet away for all he cared. He was focused on the shuttle, staring into the blazing rockets, the glare burning deep into his retinas. He could feel Lourna Dee's frustration as her ship bucked and lurched in the sky, but she wouldn't get away. They would stop her. Loden and Bell tog—

The world shifted.

The ground was gone, the shuttle too, the sky screaming away to a riot of impossible colors. Bell was falling, but there was no one to catch him. He thought he heard a voice, his name screamed in terror.

Bell.

Bell. Help me.

The words bent in on themselves, echoing back and forth, losing all sense of meaning.

He hit something, hard. Pain blazed across his cheek, but he didn't recognize the sensation. He didn't know anything anymore. He didn't know his name or where he was. He barely knew *what* he was.

Mist swirled around him, filling his chest, his skull, his soul. It was thicker than any war-cloud, denser than any fog. And there were teeth inside, teeth and claws and eyes and death. So many eyes. So much death.

The thing in the mist was everywhere at once—running, tearing, chasing him down—and there was nothing he could do, nowhere he could hide. It ripped through him, consuming everything he thought he was and everything he had yet to become. It was uncontrollable, a horror beyond name or understanding, and it was hungry. So very, very hungry.

Bell reached out for the Force, but it had gone the way of the ground and the sky. He was alone and he was powerless. All he could do was scream and scream and scream.

Chapter Seventy-Six

Grizal

Released from the Jedi's grip, Lourna Dee's shuttle shot into the clouds. Ro didn't notice it leave. He was staring at the images from the cam, unable to believe what he was seeing. Unable to breathe.

It had been worth it. All of it. The nights hunched over his father's texts, the days scouring the stars searching for the relics of a forgotten time.

Now the real work began.

Even his father was finally silenced. He knew what his son had achieved. What he couldn't. What he'd been too afraid to try.

Ro twisted the cylinder, calling the Leveler home. That wasn't its name, of course, only what Kufa had called it, the poor deluded hag. She had no idea what she had been guarding all those years, the power she'd squandered.

But Ro did . . . and soon so would everyone else.

The Nihil were gone. The camp was silent. No more blasters, no more battle cries. Above him, four Vectors streaked after the warship, which had turned upon its axis to rise above the clouds. Stellan knew they wouldn't catch it, even as it streaked away into nothing, making an impossible jump, but the Nihil wouldn't be able to run forever, of that he was sure. It was only a matter of time until they discovered the Nihil's secret, how they twisted hyperspace in ways the Republic couldn't fathom. That day was coming, but for now he had other concerns.

Stellan had landed the moment he saw Elzar's Vector go down, a wave of anguish erupting from the cockpit. Now Stellan was racing toward the burning craft, his heart hammering until he realized that Ty Yorrick was pulling a figure from the wreckage, a figure that wasn't moving.

"Elzar!"

Ty looked up at Stellan's shout.

"He's alive," she said as he dropped to his knees beside them. "Just."

Stellan pressed his hand against Elzar's chest. He couldn't feel a heartbeat.

Stellan pulled back a fist, slamming it down above Elzar's heart, over and over.

"Come on," he yelled at his oldest friend. "You're not finished yet. Do you hear me? You're not finished."

Elzar convulsed, coughing painfully.

Stellan sank back on his legs. "Thank the Force. Elzar? Can you hear me? Elzar!"

"Shouting at him won't help," Ty said.

"She's right," Elzar wheezed. "It won't."

Stellan wanted to pull Elzar close to him, but had no idea the full extent of his injuries.

"I thought I'd lost you."

Elzar's eyes flickered open, and he reached up and grabbed Stellan's arm, leaving a bloody mark on his sleeve.

"I thought it was over, Stel. I thought it was finished, but it's not. They're coming, Stellan. They're coming, and we can't stop them."

Elzar's body shook as he was racked by another coughing fit.

"He's inhaled a lot of smoke. I'm surprised he's still with us."

"He's stubborn. Aren't you, Elzar? Hey."

Elzar slumped in Ty's arms, his eyes rolling up into their sockets. Stellan reached for his neck. There was a pulse, weak but there all the same. He would pull through. Stellan would make sure of that.

"Master Gios. Come in please."

Indeera's voice made him start. He pulled his hand away from Elzar, activating his comlink.

"Stellan here. What is it, Indeera?"

"You . . . you need to see for yourself."

Indeera was as pale as a ghost when he found her standing in the middle of a group of abandoned shuttles. Stellan could feel anxiety rolling off her in spades. What in the light's name could've happened to shake a Jedi as experienced as Indeera Stokes?

She looked up before he could ask. "It's Bell."

"What is?"

She nodded to a gap between the shuttles. "See for yourself."

Stellan squeezed past the ships, thinking that nothing could be as bad as what he had seen on Valo.

Once again, the universe proved him wrong.

Bell Zettifar was curled up in a ball, sobbing gently, Ember standing guard. The charhound's hackles rose as Stellan approached. She snarled, flames flashing behind her teeth.

Stellan raised a hand to ward off the animal.

"It's okay, girl. It's me."

Ember's growl turned into a bark.

"What's wrong with her?"

Indeera was behind him now. She pointed beyond the traumatized Padawan to a lump of rock that Stellan hadn't even noticed. The battlefield was strewn with rubble. What was one more rock among the devastation? But this one was different, its shape strangely familiar.

Two legs.

Two arms.

A head, twisted to the side, features frozen into a scream.

Elzar's words echoed through his mind. *They're coming, Stellan. They're coming, and we can't stop them.*

He took an uncertain step forward.

"I think it's Loden."

"Loden? Here?"

"He was on that ship. Bell sensed it. I sensed it, but then . . ."

Stellan bent down beside the petrified body, seeing the line of a noble brow in the rock, the line of ragged Jedi robes. He reached out a trembling finger and brushed what had once been Loden Greatstorm's cheek. The face collapsed in on itself, the entire husk crumbling to dust before his eyes, and for the first time since he was a child, Stellan Gios was afraid.

Acknowledgments

Thirty years ago, two books blew my mind. The first was *Dark Empire* by Tom Veitch and Cam Kennedy, published by Dark Horse Comics, while the second was *Heir to the Empire* by Timothy Zahn, published then by Bantam Spectra. I remember seeing them in the stores and not quite believing my eyes. Here were new stories set in my beloved *Star Wars* galaxy. Both took me on a journey that led me ultimately to write this book, so first and foremost I want to say thank you to those pioneering creators. Without you building so wonderfully on George Lucas's original vision, we wouldn't be here working on The High Republic three decades later.

Which brings me to *The Rising Storm*. There are so many people to thank, primarily Michael Siglain, Lucasfilm Publishing's creative director and Project Luminous's very own Nick Fury. Thank you for inviting me on this adventure of a lifetime and for guiding our ship as we navigated this new corner of the galaxy. Thanks also to my fellow Lumineers—Claudia Gray, Justina Ireland, Daniel José Older, and Charles Soule—and also the creators I've been working with on my other High Republic projects: Ario, Mark, Ariana, Annalisa, Mark P, and Tom over on the Marvel series, and Rachael and Guido on *Monster of Temple Peak*, all of whom coped with me when I was juggling novel, comic series, and graphic novel and who also added their own voices to this period of galactic history.

Then there are my editors at Del Rey, especially Tom for being the best sounding board and helping me find solutions to knotty problems, plus, of course, Elizabeth and Alex, who asked the right questions at the right moments. I can't wait until we're all at a convention again. I miss you, my friends.

Thanks also to Kasim, my editor at Del Rey UK (hey, I needed a shout out for the GB contingent of *Star Wars* publishing), and to our copy editor, Laura, for making sure everything lined up and for making me look good!

Of course, The High Republic has truly been a team effort from the beginning, and I need also to extend my heartfelt thanks and admiration to Lucasfilm's wonderfully supportive Story Group: to Pablo, Emily, Kelsey, Jason, and Matt (see Matt, I *can* write a *Star Wars* without Ewoks or green bunnies!), to James for his constant enthusiasm and to Jen for reminding me on more than one occasion that I wouldn't have an artist to provide character descriptions!

Nearer to home, thanks to my agent, Charlotte; my first readers, Sarah Simpson-Weiss, George Mann, and my darling Clare; and to Chloe and Connie for putting up with me hiding away in my writer's nook to hammer out words.

And finally, thank you, our wonderful, inspiring readers for embracing The High Republic so wholeheartedly. It has been a joy to introduce these new characters to you and to see which you are taking to your hearts. You have made it all worthwhile, and we can never thank you enough.

So, until next time, may the Force be with you . . . for light and life . . .

About the Author

CAVAN SCOTT is a UK number one bestselling author who has written for such popular worlds as *Star Wars, Doctor Who, Star Trek,* Assassin's Creed, *Transformers, Pacific Rim,* and Sherlock Holmes. He is the writer of *Star Wars: Dooku: Jedi Lost, The Patchwork Devil,* and *Shadow Service,* and is one of the story architects for Lucasfilm's epic multimedia initiative, *Star Wars: The High Republic.* He has written comics for Marvel, DC, IDW, Dark Horse, Vertigo, *2000AD,* and *The Beano.* A former magazine editor, Cavan Scott lives in Bristol with his wife and daughters. His lifelong passions include classic scary movies, folklore, audio drama, the music of David Bowie, and walking. He owns far too much LEGO.

cavanscott.com